# THE
# AUSTIN
# PARADOX

## WILLIAM R. LEIBOWITZ

MMG

Published By Manifesto Media Group, a division of ILP Limited
Copyright © 2018 by William R. Leibowitz

ISBN-13: 978-0-9898662-9-3

Visit: miraclemanbook.com, and Miracle Man on facebook
Contact the author: wrlauthor@gmail.com

Book Cover Design and Formatting by Streetlight Graphics Copyright © 2018 by William R. Leibowitz

# THE AUTHOR WISHES TO THANK:

My wife, Alexandria-- for her brilliant insights

My daughter, Tess, a masterful writer
--who was my sounding board

My friend, Rick Joseph--who encouraged me to write *Miracle Man*

Hank Fellows--whose songs were an inspiration

The many readers of *Miracle Man* whose kind words, expressed in letters and reviews, gave me the fortitude to pick up my pen again

'To attain truth one must pass through gates,
each opening to a new question, the last question
beyond which one cannot live without faith.'

—Rabbinical Scripture

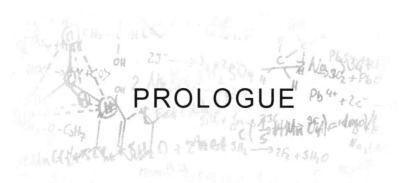

# PROLOGUE

BY ALL OUTWARD APPEARANCES, THE Whitens were an ordinary American family. They lived in a rambling old wood-frame house that they rented in Annisquam, Massachusetts, a small village located forty-five miles northeast of Boston on a seaside stretch of land referred to as the North Cape, but more properly called Cape Ann.

The Whitens' neighbors took notice of a few things. The Whitens were an unusually handsome family, although Mr. Whiten always seemed to be somewhat rumpled. By eight o'clock every morning, Mrs. Whiten could be seen getting into her car to drive to work, but Mr. Whiten was a stay-at-home dad and rarely went into town. It was presumed that he did some kind of work from home, but that was just conjecture on the neighbors' part.

What no one in Annisquam knew was that the Whitens weren't the Whitens. Sean, Deborah and their eighteen-month-old son, Peter, were participants in WITSEC, the United States Federal Witness Protection Program. What made this even more remarkable, was that the Whitens hadn't committed any crime, nor were they witnesses to anything.

In actuality, Sean Whiten was Robert James "Bobby" Austin, the greatest genius in human history, winner of eleven Nobel Prizes, a scientist who had been responsible for curing numerous diseases and saving tens of millions of lives. His wife, Deborah Whiten, was really Christina Moore, a brilliant mathematician who he had once mistakenly accused of being a CIA operative put in place to seduce him. Their son, Peter Whiten, was rightfully, Peter Joseph Austin. He had been named in honor of the two most important men in Bobby's life: Peter Austin, Bobby's deceased foster care father who, along with wife, Edith, had taken Bobby in when he was an abandoned infant that no one wanted to adopt; and Joseph Manzini, Bobby's deceased mentor, who became his surrogate father after his foster parents' death when Bobby was eleven years old.

The Austins had been transformed into the Whitens upon Bobby's release from George Washington University Hospital after recovering from a five-month coma and massive injuries suffered when his research laboratory exploded. Christina, then pregnant with Peter, had extracted a promise from Orin Varneys, the Director of the CIA, to relocate the Austin family and give them new identities under WITSEC. Knowing that Bobby had been an assassination target for years, and having seen what transpired at the trials of the people who were accused of trying to kill him, Varneys agreed that the Austin family needed to transition for their protection and he prevailed upon the Justice Department to extend WITSEC to the Austins, even though that program had been created to shield threatened witnesses in criminal trials.

The Austins were particularly good candidates for WITSEC because despite Bobby's renown, he had assiduously guarded his privacy—rejecting celebrity, eschewing the media, and maintaining his physical anonymity by not being photographed; no one outside of a small coterie knew what he looked like.

But beyond the safety concerns, Christina was hoping that with fabricated identities, she, Bobby and Pete could finally lead a normal life, residing in a regular neighborhood rather than being sequestered in a high-security compound as they had formerly been.

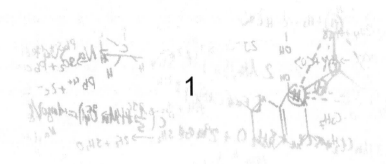

1

CHRISTINA BOLTED UPRIGHT IN HER bed, her nightshirt wet with perspiration, her heart racing. She swept her hair back with clammy hands and inhaled deeply several times, but the words she had just heard in her dream still reverberated in her head. These same words haunted her often during the day, and recurred regularly in her nightmares:

> "We are concerned for everyone's safety—Robert, you, even the little boy. I'm quite certain that Robert's intellect never really left him, but he thinks it did—and, more importantly, so does his alternate self. So, for the time being, there's no internal conflict. But if Robert's genius ever reasserts itself, it won't return alone."

This admonition was delivered by Dr. John Uhlman, former Chief of Psycho-Neurological Development at the Mayo Clinic, an eminent physician who knew Bobby through all of his formative years. He had recruited him to be a student at the Institute for Advanced Intelligence Studies, a secret government educational facility run by the Office of Special Strategic Intelligence Services (OSSIS) when Bobby was only four and a half years old. Uhlman made this pronouncement at a meeting months earlier during which Orin Varneys revealed to Christina and Susan Ryder, Bobby's longtime assistant, his conclusions about the laboratory explosion. Varneys had made Christina and Susan promise that the information he imparted was to remain strictly between them.

Christina looked over at Bobby who was asleep next to her. She stared at him for several minutes to see if there were any sleep disturbances that might portend the return of his night terrors. She did this almost every night since his release from the hospital. But Bobby slept calmly and there was no sign of what Uhlman had called Bobby's "self-loathing alternate-personality whose goal is to destroy him."

Christina was hoping that Bobby's new lifestyle would keep him safe and allow the Austin family a semblance of normalcy. Having ceased medical research, Bobby no longer had the stress of a self-imposed brutal work schedule; nor was he in conflict anymore with what he believed to be an omniscient force of negativity that had interfered with his research for years and then blown up his lab in an effort to kill him and obliterate his almost completed cure for AIDS. Christina and Susan had long been aware of Bobby's belief in this universal force of mayhem, but they had asked him to keep it to himself.

Nevertheless, after the prosecution of those accused of orchestrating the laboratory bombing, which failed due to insufficient evidence, Bobby expressed his views on what had happened the night of the explosion in a confidential letter to Orin Varneys:

11

Dear Director Varneys,

As you know, I was fortunate for many years to possess a special intelligence. Or should I say, it possessed me. Through it, I came to understand certain fundamental truths that perhaps are uncomfortable.

There is a force of negativity and destruction in the universe. Highly efficient and infinitely resourceful, it empowers and leads. It gives diseases their resiliency, their tenacity, their propensity to reinvent themselves, resist treatments, regenerate and defensively mutate. It propels them.

This force is not a neutral physical phenomenon. It is an evil—an active and pervasive evil. Are you surprised by this? Don't be. There is balance in the universe. That is the immutable law that governs what otherwise would be chaos. Everything has its reciprocal, its opposite. Do you believe in God? Well, you can't have only that.

Throughout my life, I felt a force oppose me. It sought to disorient and distract me and undermine my health—physically and mentally. And then the day finally came, as I always knew it would: I had cracked the code and it didn't want to lose that. AIDS is one of its greatest achievements, you know.

I understand it will be hard for you to get your mind around this. You're a man of action. You like to start files and close files, put the bad guys away. But the universe plays its own game. We can only do so much.

Gently stroking his hair as he slept, Christina leaned over Bobby and kissed his forehead lightly. He looked so peaceful. *But for how long?* she wondered. She was overwhelmed with so many questions. *What could happen? What would happen? Was Dr. Uhlman right? Are we really in danger?*

The life they now led in Annisquam was the life she had always wanted. She had implored Bobby over the years to stop doing medical research because it was destroying his health. He had worked like a slave for more than two decades to help others. Then it happened. The laboratory explosion made a decision for Bobby that he would never have made himself. It retired him. But along with his extraordinary genius, the explosion took away Bobby's sense of purpose.

Lying next to him, Christina threaded the fingers of her left hand in between Bobby's, and pressed her body against his, her head nestled under his chin. Cuddling closely, she breathed in deeply and felt comforted for the moment. Despite the crushing weight of uncertainty that bore down on her, she was sure of one thing: She loved Bobby inexorably.

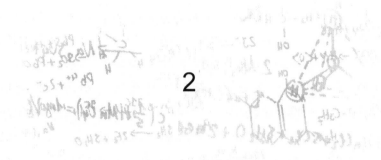

**2**

THE RENTED WHITE CHEVROLET IMPALA pulled into the parking lot of the Federal Correctional Complex in Butner, North Carolina. It was a muggy August day, and the new black asphalt of the parking lot was beginning to smell as the sun's rays penetrated the tar. Jeffrey Stringer was uncomfortable. He pulled down the sun visor and looked into the rearview mirror as he dabbed his face hard with his "JS" monogrammed handkerchief. He stared at the palms of his hands as he flexed his fingers and then leaned his head backwards so he could apply eye drops. Nattily dressed in a blue pinstripe suit, with a heavily starched white button-down shirt and Harvard tie, he stepped out of the car and walked towards the visitor entrance. *Damn, I hate prisons.*

The guard at the gatehouse asked Stringer for his driver's license, business card and the identity of the person he was visiting. "I'm Jeffrey Stringer of the Plympton Spaulding law firm, attorney for Colum McAlister," said Stringer. When Stringer mentioned Colum McAlister, the guard knew that this was a Protocol 1 situation. The guard examined Stringer's driver's license and carefully compared the photo to the man standing in front of him. He then walked into a small office in which, in accordance with Protocol 1, he looked up the law firm's website, typed in Jeffrey Stringer on the attorney search to verify that he still worked there and viewed his official photograph. He then checked the preapproved authorization list for McAlister visitors, and saw Stringer's name and photo. Satisfied, he walked back to Stringer and asked him for his wallet, cash and car keys. After counting the cash, he put all of his items in a numbered plastic bag and gave Stringer a receipt.

The guard then motioned for Stringer to proceed through the metal detectors and place his briefcase on the X-ray machine. Once that procedure was completed, the guard pointed Stringer in the direction of the room in which he would meet his client.

Colum McAlister, the former CEO of one of the largest Big Pharma companies in the world, Bushings Pharmaceuticals, was no longer clothed in custom-made Saville Row suits and Cartier accessories; nor was he wearing the two hundred thousand–dollar Patek Philippe watch that adorned his wrist before his incarceration began. Having been sentenced to nineteen years in a federal penitentiary on thirty-one violations of securities, economic espionage, extortion, blackmail and money laundering laws, this former titan of the drug industry was now dressed in an orange jumpsuit that appeared to be a size too large for him, and in lieu of the embroidered monograms that used to be sewn on the cuffs of his custom shirts, the number 958246 was printed in black ink on his jumpsuit.

Although he had been in prison for less than two years, his physical appearance clearly reflected his fall from grace. Gone was the perpetual tan and the movie-star skin that was achieved through twice weekly facials administered in his palatial Park Avenue office. His sparse gray hair, which formerly had been expertly coiffed and tinted to give it a silvery radiance, was now styled in a crew cut which accentuated the bald spots on his pate. And while he lifted some weights and did push-ups in prison, his body had aged without the benefit of daily training sessions in his office suite's private gym. At this point, Colum McAlister looked every day of his seventy-six years.

McAlister approached Stringer cautiously, as he instinctively surveyed the landscape, turning twice to take in a three-hundred-sixty-degree view. McAlister didn't like lawyers anyway, but he felt particularly aggrieved by the Plympton Spaulding attorneys. *Over the years, I delivered tens of millions of dollars of Bushings' legal fees to these scumbags, and the best they could do for me was nineteen years.*

McAlister and Stringer nodded to each other, as McAlister ever so slightly tilted his head in the direction of the exercise yard so as to direct Stringer to where they should conduct their business. Finally, outdoors and in the presence of his attorney, McAlister was assured of the confidentiality that was legally mandated by the attorney-client privilege when an inmate was having an in-person meeting with his lawyer. He knew that their discussions would not be monitored.

"You're looking well, Colum, all things considered," said Stringer.

"Don't patronize me. I look like crap and you know it."

Stringer patted his face with his handkerchief. "It's broiling out here. Are you certain no one is listening to us?"

"Positive," replied McAlister. "But let's keep on walking as we talk. I wasn't sure you'd get my message as quickly as you did. You came fast. That's good."

"You called. I came. You've always been one of my best clients."

"Your sentimentality is touching."

Stringer pulled at his chin. "I am so goddamn itchy. And these contact lenses are killing me."

McAlister laughed. "You look exactly like that son-of-a-bitch lawyer of mine. You could fool his wife. After this meeting, go to his house in Greenwich and fuck her. See if she knows the difference."

Gunther Ramirez smiled broadly as he imagined that scene. His tobacco-stained teeth were incongruous with his pale skin, wispy blonde hair and blue eyes. "I always wondered what it would be like to be a white Ivy League tool. Amazing what a prosthetic mask, wig and colored lenses can do. The ID docs were easy, but this..." Ramirez pointed at his face with the index fingers of both hands. "Getting this thing made and fitted took some doing. I also got fake fingerprints on, just in case."

McAlister nodded his approval. "Attention to detail. That's what always impressed me about you, Gunther."

Ramirez' eyes narrowed as he looked at McAlister. "I sure as hell don't want to get busted on site at a federal prison and spend the rest of my life in a cage. I hope you realize that I wouldn't take this kind of risk for many people, Colum."

"And not many people gave you a five-million-euro deposit on a job you didn't finish."

Gunther Ramirez, the former right-hand man and criminal mastermind for Panamanian dictator Manuel Noriega had since built an elite service-for-hire specializing in what he referred to as "matters of sensitivity." For his well-heeled international clientele, his bill of fare included industrial espionage, kidnapping, money laundering, extortion and murder.

Colum McAlister, a long-time client, had hired Ramirez some years earlier to assassinate Dr. Robert James Austin in a manner that would look like an accident or natural occurrence. The agreed price for this service was ten million euros, of which McAlister had made the fifty-percent down payment up-front. While Ramirez had put an elaborate scheme into place, and was only days away from implementing it, someone acted before him and exploded Austin's laboratory, almost killing Austin.

"We've been through this before, Colum. You know that wasn't my fault. Those freaks from RASI (*Retribution Against Scientific Interference*) beat me to it."

"I didn't call you here to rehash the past. I'm interested in talking about new business."

"You have a job for me?"

The corners of McAlister's mouth turned up. "I hope you don't think I've been sitting around here playing checkers with the cons. I've got a lot of people in high places who owe me. When I want to, I'll be out of here. But right now, this joint suits me just fine. It gives me the perfect alibi, and where else could I spend all day planning?"

"And how does this concern me?"

"You're essential to the plan. You're going to play a big role. And you and I are going to become billionaires in the process. You'll also get to finish the job on Austin."

"Robert James Austin? Let that go. That's why you're in here. Move on, Colum."

McAlister's face reddened and a vein in his right temple began to throb visibly. "Austin's the cause of everything bad that's happened to me. There's no way he's going to get away with that. I have some special things in store for him. And don't worry about the other five million I'll owe you when he's gone. I've got more money than the IRS, the SEC or my ex-wife knows."

"Ex-wife? When did that happen? As I recall you named your

house in Tuscany for her. "Isn't it Villa Barbara, or something like that?"

McAlister scowled. "Casa Barbara. It's her house now. As soon as the shit hit the fan with the feds, she divorced me and took everything she could grab. Didn't even wait for the verdict. But I was ready. I have money hidden where God can't find it."

Ramirez nodded in recognition of McAlister's prescience. Looking up at the unrelenting sun, he pressed his handkerchief hard against his forehead and then ran it along his cheeks to reinforce the mask's adhesive that was loosening because of the perspiration accumulating under it. "This thing wasn't made for this kind of weather," he muttered as he reached into his jacket pocket and retrieved a gold case from which he removed a cigarette. After a few puffs, he said, "So what's the plan?"

McAlister waved the question away. "I'm not ready to talk about it. I just wanted to be sure of two things. One, that I can count on you. And secondly, that you still have relationships with characters in Asia and Europe that...how should I say...are less than sterling citizens?"

Ramirez inhaled deeply and released a plume of smoke in Colum's direction. "Munitions deals, black market oil trading, nuclear contraband, looted ancient artifacts—these are just a few of my side-ventures. Being so versatile, I meet lots of interesting people. I have all the connections you'll need."

McAlister extended his hand to Ramirez. "I definitely like you more than Jeffrey Stringer."

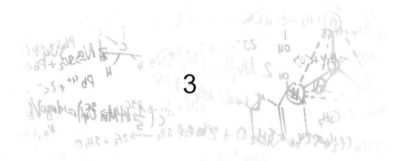

# 3

I T WAS A TYPICAL MORNING in the Austin household. Bobby sat at the kitchen table with baby Pete, feeding him cereal while Pete manipulated a hand puzzle. There was no doubt about the lineage here. Bobby's strikingly light blue eyes sparkled in the morning sun that streamed through the bay windows of the breakfast nook, while Pete's eyes glistened like translucent sapphires.

"I'm off to work, Bobby. Don't get into any trouble while I'm gone," said Christina as she rushed past them, stopping only long enough to give Bobby a quick peck on his cheek and Pete, a kiss on the head. The fragrance of Christina's perfume lingered as she hurried to the door, her lustrous dark hair swaying with her quick movements.

Bobby took a long look at his wife. As smitten as he had always been with her, he felt that she had reached a sublime level of beauty with motherhood. "I am so lucky to still have her in my life," he said to himself, knowing how he had almost driven her away with his suspicions and paranoia.

"Come on, little fella, let's go to the office," Bobby said as he hoisted Pete onto his shoulders and proceeded to bounce him up and down while he walked across the backyard lawn. They entered the rustic living room of the guest cottage which had been converted to an office for Uniserve, the nonprofit drug company that Bobby established at the beginning of his career to hold the patents on his inventions. As Pete laughed joyously, Bobby supported him under his midsection and swung him down and around and up again, with exaggerated swoops as he made airplane sounds and finally gave the baby a soft landing on his belly in a big playpen that was positioned in front of a TV. Bobby then inserted a DVD from a large stack of kids' educational videos and placed an iPad in the playpen next to Pete.

"Hey, Susan. Are you here?" bellowed Bobby. "Another week begins. I don't know if I can stand the sheer excitement of it all."

Bounding into the room, Susan Ryder, Bobby's personal assistant and confidante for more than two decades, was her ever ebullient self. Rarely has so much energy and wisdom been packed into a five-foot-two body. Thirty pounds heavier than her doctor wanted her to be, she carried it well. Susan's appearance had barely changed over the years she had worked with Bobby. Her round face was still framed by a simple short haircut, and despite two decades of advances in makeup, she remained committed to face powder that was too white for her already fair complexion, and lipstick that was too red for the face powder. A few years earlier, with the changes in the law, Susan had finally been able to marry Anna, her partner of over thirty years.

"Now, now, Bobby. You don't look good in cynicism. I've told you that before. You look good in earth tones. Why don't you read your mail from last week? It's in the boxes by the fireplace."

Together with Susan, Bobby ran Uniserve which licensed Bobby's formulas on a gratis basis to generic drug manufacturers who were required to sell them to the public at a price which only gave the manufacturer a ten-percent profit margin.

"Susan, I just don't think you appreciate that you are talking to the most overqualified nanny in the world."

Susan laughed. "Part-time nanny. Don't exaggerate your responsibilities or your competence. Melissa comes at ten, and doesn't leave until after Christina gets home from work."

"You're always building me up. That's what I love about you," said Bobby as he walked over to a stack of large boxes that took up most of the dining alcove. Looking inside, he saw the usual. Each box was packed full of mail addressed to him in care of Tufts University, where he was a professor emeritus. He rifled through one of the boxes and saw return addresses and postage stamps from all over the world. He picked up two handfuls and sat down at a desk.

In actuality, Bobby had nothing to do at Uniserve, other than read mail from people who implored him to cure a plethora of human ailments that they or their loved ones were suffering from. No one other than Christina, Susan, Orin Varneys and a handful of doctors knew that Bobby had lost his genius.

As Bobby proceeded to open envelope after envelope, he looked at the accompanying photographs of people in dire need of his help. He examined their faces; stared at the eyes gazing at him. Bobby slumped further into his chair with each letter. Finally, he stopped reading and buried his face in his hands. After a few minutes, he mumbled, "I'm going to put these boxes in the garage with the rest of them."

Bobby dragged one of the heavy boxes out the door by its flaps and, when the door closed, he kicked the box repeatedly. Standing on the stoop of the cottage hyperventilating, perspiration beaded on Bobby's forehead and he tried to catch his breath.

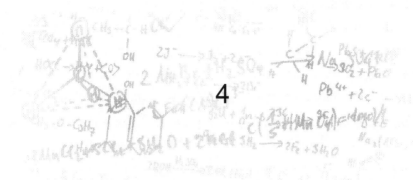

4

T HE ELEVATOR STOPPED ON THE fourth floor of the Boston
Children's Hospital. The sign read: ONCOLOGY. Just as Bobby
had done with Joe Manzini when he was a boy, he had started once
again to visit the children in this ward. The hospital staff knew him
as Sean Whiten. He never came empty-handed. Bobby always had
a big box of cookies for the nurses and shopping bags full of toys
and games for the patients. When the kids saw him, their faces lit
up. And just like decades ago, when he was there with Joe, Bobby
entertained the kids, making use of his artistic talent, drawing their
favorite Marvel superheroes and Disney characters, interspersed
with portraits of them. For the two hours he spent at the hospital
every few weeks, Bobby felt that he was making a little bit of a
difference—not the kind he once was able to make, but it was
something.

When the chief nurse, Cara McCarthy, hurried by him on her
inspection rounds, Bobby walked quickly to catch up with her.
"I don't mean to be critical, and I certainly don't want to offend
you, but I can't help noticing that the ward isn't looking so good,

it's kind of rundown. I used to visit here years ago and it's really deteriorated. What's going on?"

"I don't want to talk out here. I'll be done in fifteen minutes. Come by my office then."

Cara's gray hair was cropped so close to her head that she looked like a female boot camp cadet, a particularly severe hairstyle for a woman of sixty-three years. Her sallow complexion bore no makeup and her only noteworthy facial features were dark brown eyes that appeared to hyper-focus on anyone at whom they were directed. Cara held her thin frame rigidly, giving her an almost military bearing and she was rarely seen without three clipboards in her hands. When she walked the floor, her staff stood straighter, stepped quicker and made a point of looking busy. Cara took what she did very seriously and she expected everyone under her to do the same. She had been a nurse at the hospital for almost forty years, having joined the staff after graduating from Northeastern University. To her, being a nurse wasn't a job or a career: It was a calling. A nurse was a healer and a guardian.

Cara's office looked like an art gallery. The walls were decorated with artwork that the children had given her, and one wall was filled with hundreds of small photographs of the kids, so numerous that they overlapped each other. Bobby took a full ten minutes looking at it all, seemingly lost in thought.

"Those are my special children," Cara said, standing next to Bobby as he perused the photographs.

"They're beautiful. Look at their faces. Their eyes are magical."

Cara smiled. "Yes, my angels."

"Former patients?"

"They're in heaven now."

Bobby's eyes locked with Cara's. "Dead? They're all dead?"

24

Cara walked behind her metal desk and sat down. Bobby took a seat facing her. "I'm meeting with you because I know who you are and what you've done," she said.

Bobby's face grew pale. "What do you mean?" asked Bobby haltingly, as he shifted in his chair.

Cara paused and then leaned forward. "The way you come here… bringing gifts for the kids, cheering them up, spending time with them. Making them laugh. It means so much. It's very important."

Relieved that his true identity remained hidden, Bobby exhaled deeply. "When I was a boy, I came here with my mentor, Joseph Manzini. He brought me in to help him spread some happiness."

Cara's eyes widened. "Joe Manzini? I remember him. I was new to the hospital, just starting out. He was like Santa Claus. The kids loved him. Yes…I remember that at some point he began to bring a boy with him—a boy who could draw cartoons. Oh, my God. You were that boy!"

Nodding enthusiastically, Bobby said, "Yes, that was me. Joe taught me a lot about caring for others. Lessons that changed my life."

"Mr. Manzini was a wonderful man. He was a major benefactor of this hospital. When he died, he made a very generous bequest." Cara looked down at her phone when a text came in. She quickly typed a response and looked back up. "Anyway, you asked why the ward is looking decrepit. This is a government supported hospital. There are very few Joe Manzinis out there to help. No funds have been allocated by the state to upgrade infrastructure for longer than I can remember, and even equipment purchases are hard to come by. That's not going to change anytime soon."

"Why? What do you mean?"

Cara's mouth twisted. "The drug companies suck up all the

money. Their lobbyists ensure the government's medical programs gets fleeced. Whatever the drug companies want to charge, they get paid. And the private insurers don't care—they refuse to pay for certain drugs altogether or they pass on the drug costs to their customers by raising insurance premiums, co-pays and deductibles, so their profits are unaffected. The only losers are the patients, their families and the taxpayers."

"And nobody does anything about it?"

"Mr. Whiten, really? Big Pharma can do anything it wants in the U.S. It's not like the rest of the world where governments regulate drug prices. The same exact medications made by the same drug companies cost up to ten times more in the U.S. than in other countries, because there's no regulation here."

Bobby was looking dazed.

"And the worst of it is what I see here in the oncology ward. Cancer is the best thing that ever happened to the pharmaceuticals industry. It's a goldmine. You wouldn't believe the cost of these drugs. Hundreds of thousands of dollars per year, per patient, just for the meds, not counting the doctors' fees or the hospital costs. The drug companies determine the price of life. You pay up or you die."

Bobby stroked his forehead with his left hand. "It never changes..." he said softly.

Cara focused intently on Bobby as she saw how upset he was. As she walked towards the door to go to her next meeting, she paused by his chair and put her hand on his shoulder. "Health care is big business, Sean. Everyone plays their role and has their hand out for a piece of the action. Getting sick is the most extravagant thing most Americans will ever do."

When Bobby got home, he hurried to his office in the guest cottage and started researching on the internet. The situation was even worse than it had been decades earlier when he had first embarked on his quest to cure diseases. And Cara was right, cancer was big business. There was the melanoma drug that cost one hundred and twenty thousand dollars for four doses; the leukemia treatment that cost sixty-four thousand dollars per month; a prostate cancer medication that costs thirty-one thousand dollars per injection; a stomach cancer drug that costs thirteen thousand dollars per month and a salve for skin cancer that costs thirty thousand dollars for a sixty-gram tube. There were drugs that had been on the market making money for their manufacturers for twenty years that were now four times more expensive than they were when first introduced. Bobby read about families, even those with health insurance, that suffered financial ruin from drug costs, and Medicare patients who had uninsured drug co-pays exceeding their gross annual incomes. And all of these medications were just treatments, not cures—many of them requiring a long-term regimen while offering only a short life extension at the end of the treatment process.

A wave of nausea surged through him as he continued his research. Big Pharma employed more than two thousand five hundred lobbyists in the U.S., and spent three times more on lobbying than the entire defense and aerospace industries did, and almost four times more than the entire energy industry. In ten years, Big Pharma spent two and one-half billion dollars lobbying the U.S. Congress, but they got value for their money. In addition to ensuring that hundreds of proposed statutes to protect consumers from price gauging were killed in committee, the lobbyists delivered a law that prohibited Medicare from negotiating prices with the drug companies. That saved them, and cost U.S. taxpayers, an estimated forty to eighty billion dollars annually.

Drug companies routinely engaged in so-called "pay-for-delay" practices, where they paid generic manufacturers not to produce generics when drug patents expired, so the drug monopoly could be preserved and price competition would be eliminated. Big Pharma's patent lawyers gamed the system by the process of "evergreening", in which expiring drug patents were given new lives by the addition of inconsequential variations; to induce generic manufacturers not to challenge these questionable patents and produce cheaper generics, it was common practice for Big Pharma to pay them for their cooperation.

And then there was a relatively new business supported by hedge funds and venture capitalists which had a very simple business plan: buy small drug companies that charge reasonable prices for their medicines and then raise the price a hundredfold, knowing that people will pay anything to obtain a life-saving drug.

Bobby's discussion with Cara, and his research, made it clear to him that now, more than ever, the drug business in the U.S. was a profiteering paradise, built on treating symptoms and not curing diseases. Pain and suffering had been leveraged into huge financial gains, despite the massive tax breaks received by the pharmaceutical companies for research and development, and other taxpayer-borne subsidies. Bobby's anger was matched only by his frustration. Where he had once been Big Pharma's worst nightmare, curing one ailment after another and rendering their "cash-cow" symptom treatments obsolete, he now felt hobbled and unable to do what needed to be done.

When Susan walked into the guest cottage to organize her papers for the next day's work, she was surprised to see the light on in Bobby's office. Bobby was hunched over his computer, engrossed in reading. "Hey, what are you doing?" she asked.

Bobby didn't answer as he continued his industry research.

"Everything okay?"

"Yeah. Just fine."

Susan pulled over a chair and sat down. "You know that's not true. You get more withdrawn every day. I'm worried about you."

Bobby leaned back and pressed his fingers against the sides of his neck in an effort to stop a muscle cramp that was worsening. "Look at those letters that arrive every day. It kills me when I read them. And then I visit the hospital and I see the same old thing: the drug companies ripping everybody off with treatments —and no cures. For the last two years since I got out of the hospital, I've done nothing. I feel so helpless."

Susan pulled her chair closer. "Bobby, you almost died in the lab explosion. You were in surgery for six hours. You were in a coma for five months. It's a miracle you're alive. Uniserve saves thousands of lives every day with the cures you invented. Anyone else would be a billionaire from those drugs. You give them away."

Bobby sighed. "That's not the point, Susan. I had the AIDS cure in my hands minutes before the explosion. Now I can't remember the formulas or decipher my own notes, let alone understand them. How can I live with that? How many people will die because I can't do what I'm supposed to do? With each day that goes by, I hate myself a little bit more."

Even Susan's white face-powder couldn't hide her reddening complexion. Her words came fast in short bursts. "Stop it, Bobby. Don't beat yourself up over what you can't control. It's *not* your fault."

Bobby shot back, "But maybe it is. Did I lose my abilities or am I hiding from them?"

Susan's jaw dropped. "Even for you, that sounds crazy. And why would you do that?"

Bobby stood up and began to pace the room as he spoke. "You know. You know better than most, Susan. My intellect took over my life. I was so far out there mentally that I had lost all connection with reality. My health was wrecked and my marriage was in shambles. I almost died…and Christina… She could have been killed in the blast. So when I was in a coma, maybe my subconscious shut my intellect down as an act of survival, of self-preservation."

"Bobby, I don't buy that. But if your subconscious had that power, it wouldn't have been the worst thing, as far as I'm concerned. Years ago I told you to quit. You had twisted Joe Manzini's advice, 'Don't waste your talents, make a difference', into a destructive mantra of self-abnegation. And how many times did Christina beg you to stop when she saw the toll your work was taking on you? And Alan—what did he tell you when you were with him in Islamorada? But you wouldn't listen to anyone and you pushed yourself beyond the limit and in the end, you paid the price. You've done enough for ten lifetimes. It's someone else's turn."

Bobby threw his hands up. "But there is no one else, is there?" Susan was silent.

Bobby sat down on a stool in the corner of the room and lowered his head. After a minute, he mumbled, "Do you remember what you told me when you found out I was 'Dumpster Baby'?"

"Yes, I remember."

"What was it again?"

"I said that you were saved for a reason, you were given your abilities for a reason and that everything that has happened in your life has happened for a reason."

Bobby nodded. "Well, Susan, it's happened again. I should have died in that explosion. But I didn't. There's a reason."

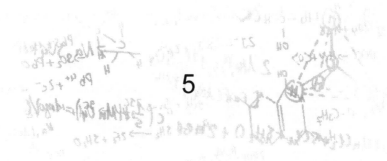

# 5

CHRISTINA FASTENED PETE SECURELY IN his car seat in the back of the family's SUV, which was packed full of enough baby supplies, equipment and clothing to last far in excess of the two weeks during which she and Pete would be away visiting Christina's mother.

"I'll miss you," she said as she kissed Bobby fully on his lips. Bobby's hands moved to a familiar place on her lower hips as he pulled her close and pressed his face against the nape of her neck, breathing in the scent of her hair and perfume. After a moment, he broke the embrace and looked into her eyes with such an intensity that a wave of heat surged down her spine. "Stop it, Bobby, or I'll never get out of here."

The physical attraction between them had always been strong, but since Bobby's release from the hospital, Christina felt a difference in the way he made love to her. Sometimes he was almost desperately passionate and overzealous, as if trying to prove his prowess to a new lover, while other times, he was so detached and mechanical that she didn't know why they were bothering at all.

"I love you," Bobby said as he turned and walked back to the house.

Deep in thought, Bobby wandered around his living room aimlessly, and then went over to the bar cart. Picking up a tumbler, he filled it halfway with Macallan scotch, and then settled into a rocking chair. Bobby realized that the next two weeks would be his first significant "alone time" since he had been released from the hospital.

After taking a few sips of his drink, he stopped rocking and sprang up. *Okay, enough. I have to do this.* Bobby climbed the stairs to the second floor of the house, walked down the long hallway with its aged plaster walls and creaking wood floors, and stood on his toes to reach a pull rope which was hanging down from the ceiling near the second floor's only bathroom. Yanking hard on the rope, a cedar door in the ceiling opened to reveal the attic. Bobby propped a tall ladder against the edge of the door and climbed up into the vacuous unfinished space. Turning on a light, he began to rummage among the numerous stacks of boxes and bags full of household items and bric-a-brac. Finally, he found three boxes on which 'Bobby Office' had been scrawled in heavy black marker. Inside were dozens of notebooks and large manila envelopes stuffed with items.

It took several carefully navigated trips up and down the ladder for Bobby to get the boxes out of the attic. Placing them on the dining room table, he began to sort through the contents, most of which were charred or water-damaged from the lab explosion. In one of the envelopes he found a sealed plastic bag. It contained numerous photos of his sailing trips as a boy with Joe Manzini aboard Joe's yacht, *Dreamweaver*, including their extraordinary voyage from Boston to the Virgin Islands to celebrate Bobby's seventeenth birthday. Closing his eyes, Bobby could hear Joe's voice as clearly as if Joe were standing next to him in the room. "Son, you have something very special. Don't squander it. Listen to your heart. We all have our allotted time. Use yours well."

In another envelope, Bobby found photos of him and Christina when they first met in St. Thomas. "Damn, look how gorgeous she is," he murmured to himself.

Among the dozens of notebooks, Bobby finally found what he was looking for—the partially burned journals in which he was writing when the lab explosion occurred; this was where he had written his AIDS formulas, the same papers that he wasn't able to decipher when asked to do so during his recuperation period in the hospital.

Bobby opened the notebooks and focused. He stared at his writings which were scribbled in pencil—line after line of endless equations expressed in the unique mathematical language that he had invented to unite all of the sciences into one borderless discipline. Hundreds of pages of equations and formulas ran together in a genius stream of consciousness.

But for Bobby, all he could now see was a meaningless blur. *Why won't my mind work? What happened to me?*


For the rest of the week, Bobby went through the boxes, examining every scrap of paper he found, hoping that something would trigger a breakthrough for him, but nothing did.

On the eighth night following Christina's departure, a defeated Bobby bundled himself in a blanket and lay on a chaise lounge in the backyard. The air was beginning to take on a chill, which wasn't unusual for early September in northeastern Massachusetts, and the ample dew on the lounge cushions dampened Bobby's clothes.

With the house dark, and no street lights in the neighborhood and no car headlights in the vicinity, the only illumination was that provided by the prodigious celestial display. As Bobby gazed at the heavens, he remembered the small backyard of his boyhood home as he and his foster father took turns looking through the telescope he had gotten for his third birthday. He recalled the first planetarium show he had ever experienced, which the dean of the Institute for Advanced Intelligence Studies had shown him in order to induce him to enroll and become the youngest student the school ever had. Vivid images then flashed through his mind of his cruise with Christina on *Dreamweaver* after their reconciliation, and how, after making love on the deck, they would lie on their backs as Bobby pointed out the constellations.

But now, it was the black void that he saw, not the brilliant lights within it. The lab explosion had cut him down at the pinnacle of his brilliance and plunged him into the netherworld of a five-month coma. On awakening, he was subjected to a barrage of tests to determine the state of his intellect. The obvious disappointment of his examiners accelerated his despondency. Still in the prime of life, he was without his tools and devoid of purpose.

And there was more that troubled him. For months, he sensed a difference in the way that Christina and Susan acted towards him. They seemed cautious, worried and overprotective. At first, he thought that was because they were concerned that his physical health was still fragile. But long after he had fully recovered, the difference in their behavior persisted.

The stars began to blur as Bobby's eyes went in and out of focus. A sharp pain traversed his forehead like a knife was being dragged along his skull. He began to feel as if a huge weight was crushing down on his rib cage, preventing him from breathing. The sound of blood pulsing through his temples reverberated in his head, and grew louder with his rising blood pressure.

Now too weak to stand, Bobby crouched on the ground, his head bowed. Gasping for air, something happened that he hadn't experienced since Joe Manzini died two decades earlier: He began to weep. It started small, but quickly escalated until it dominated him completely. He tried to stop, but couldn't. Afraid he'd be heard by neighbors, he buried his face in his hands to stifle the noise. Alarmed at how violently his hands were shaking, he tried to hold one hand still by grasping it with the other, but then both hands shook in unison as his body attempted to diffuse the energy generated by his colossal grief. Even in his solitude, he was ashamed. *All I ever was—all I ever was good for—is gone.*

Lying prostrate on the wet grass, everything began to go black. "Please don't turn away from me. Don't leave me like this," he said softly as he shut down.

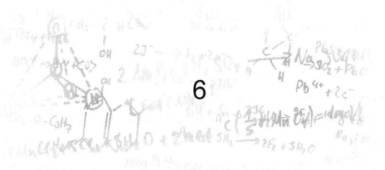

# 6

T HE RAIN WOKE BOBBY UP that Sunday morning. When the cool droplets began to pummel his face, he opened his eyes gradually. Blinking several times, he looked around. The leaves seemed so green. The flowers were almost psychedelic in the vividness of their colors. He examined his hands. The pores of his skin were peculiarly well defined, and the beads of rain water which gathered on his wrists appeared to be unusually translucent. Bobby felt like he had slept for three entire days, but his watch confirmed that it had only been seven hours. He hadn't felt this well-rested for years, and he thought it odd that he wasn't at all chilled, having slept on the damp grass all night.

He felt so good that he was motivated to clean himself up and cook a hearty breakfast. As the hot shower water cascaded down on him, it felt better than he could remember a shower ever feeling. And when he ran the razor over his face as he shaved, he thought he could feel each individual whisker being cut. When shampoo dripped into his eyes, the pain was so acute that he had to remind himself it was only shampoo.

Bobby sat cross-legged on the floor in front of the living room coffee table on which he had placed his steaming plate of scrambled eggs and bacon, and a large mug of dark French roast coffee. He reached into the magazine rack to find something to occupy him, but the only items in the rack were copies of the *Bulletin of the American Mathematical Society* to which Christina subscribed. Bobby opened one of the issues, hoping to find automobile advertisements. Skimming through the pages, he came across one article after another written by renowned mathematicians. Bobby's eyes settled on one theoretical treatise and, without even realizing he was doing it, he scanned through its ten pages in less than a minute. The errors in the equations jumped out at him. They were so obvious.

"What the hell?" muttered Bobby as he rubbed his eyes and mopped his face with his hands. He stood up and began to pace the living room, his hands clenched in front of him. It took him several minutes before he had the gumption to sit down and focus again on the magazine. When he did, he raced through all of the remaining articles with a similar result.

*What had just happened? Why? Would it last or was it a momentary aberration?* Bobby wondered if it was because he had freed his mind –taken down roadblocks that he had subconsciously erected to shut out his intellect. Or was it because someone or something had given back to him a gift that had previously been lost or taken away?

Bobby didn't have the answers, and he didn't yet know to what level his absolute intelligence had returned, but he did know one thing: His mind was entirely different than it had been twelve hours earlier.

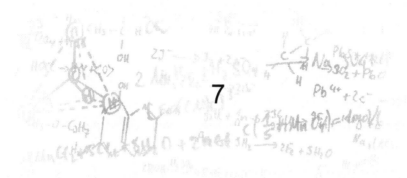

# 7

EXCITED BUT STILL CAUTIOUS, BOBBY climbed back up the ladder into the attic. He was looking for something in particular—a copy of the five-volume special edition of the *New England Journal of Medicine* which had been published when he was twenty-three years old and introduced his theory of bioelectric cellular irregularity. That theory not only resulted in the cure for multiple sclerosis, but also established the scientific blueprint and methodology that led directly to the cures for more than eighty other autoimmune diseases. It was for this discovery that Bobby received his first two Nobel Prizes -- chemistry and medicine.

When he was recuperating in the hospital, a neurologist had asked him to review this publication in front of him but when Bobby tried, it was as if he had been asked to decipher hieroglyphics.

In a far corner of the attic, underneath extra pillows and bedding, Bobby found a large box labeled "Bobby Publications." He tore into it hurriedly and removed numerous treatises, including the mathematics and astrophysics doctoral theses he had written at ages fourteen and sixteen. When he found the five-volume set of bound periodicals he was looking for, it took two trips down the ladder before he was able to stack the tomes on the dining room table.

For a few minutes, he just stood and looked at them. These articles had not only changed the course of medical science and saved innumerable lives, but they had set Bobby on the journey that defined his life for more than two decades. The last time he had seen this three-foot tall stack of paper, things hadn't gone so well.

Bobby moved away from the table and gazed at the *Journal's* five bound volumes as if he were sizing up an adversary. He pulled over a dining room chair, sat down, and stared at the books. Covering his face with both hands, he inhaled deeply and reached for Volume One, opening it to the first page of equations. He focused intently on the page for several minutes and then his eyes closed halfway. Bobby was no longer present.

Years earlier, Bobby's coworkers, who had observed this phenomenon on a daily basis, came to believe that these trances were an extension of Bobby's thinking process, during which he rose to a higher level of cognitive activity that could only be attained by disconnecting with normal human consciousness. As Dr. Uhlman had explained to Christina and Susan, "Early on, we recognized that Robert was at his intellectual peak when he would detach from the present. In his semi-dissociative state—what you call 'trances,' he was at his highest level of creative thinking and problem-solving."

With an abrupt shake of his head, Bobby snapped out of it, crossed his legs, and began to read. Every fifteen seconds or so, he turned another page until he had devoured all five volumes. He understood exactly what he was reading—and he remembered writing it as if it were yesterday.

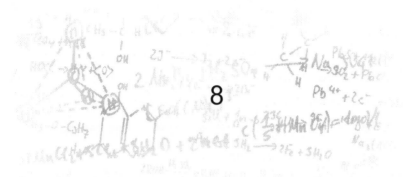

# 8

THE TWO BURNING QUESTIONS WITH which Bobby had been grappling ever since he and Christina rented the Annisquam house were:

Who made the decision to paint the walls of the guest bedroom Pepto Bismol–pink?

Why did that person think this was a good idea?

The room was located at the end of the second-floor hallway and the height of its ceiling had been severely compromised by the steep slope of the roof. Nevertheless, this bedroom had a coziness that appealed to Bobby. He decided to sleep in that room since Christina was away.

Pulling the comforter up to just below his chin, Bobby lay his head on two thin pillows and hoped for the best. He didn't want to sleep in the master bedroom because he was wary of exposing sacred marital space to what he feared would transpire that night. He wanted to contain it—to contain the evil to a room that wasn't shared with Christina.

From the time that Bobby was a toddler, he had suffered harrowing nightmares. What originally had brought Bobby to the attention of the State and federal authorities was his foster parents' efforts to finally seek psychological help for Bobby when he was four years old regarding his nightmares and trances. As Bobby matured over the years, these nightmares metamorphosed into night terrors of such severity that they seriously undermined his mental and physical health. Bobby believed that the night terrors were caused by a supernatural power that wanted to impede his ability to conduct medical research.

When Bobby's night terrors ceased after the lab explosion, he attributed it to his intellectual impotence. With no ability to continue his work in medicine, he was of no consequence to the force of negativity that had opposed him for so many years. But now that Bobby had regained at least some of his intellectual powers in the last twenty-four hours, he feared the immediate return of the night terrors. Turning off the lights, he braced himself for the worse.

---

To his surprise, his sleep was uneventful. As grateful as Bobby was, he was perplexed. Never a believer in coincidence or happenstance, there had to be a reason.

Brewing a large pot of coffee, Bobby put in twice the recommended amount of ground beans into the pot, cut himself a hunk of cheddar cheese and headed for the dining room. Next to his plate, he stacked the AIDS notebooks in which he had been writing just prior to the explosion—the same journals that were incomprehensible to him two days ago. Pouring over the notebooks, he focused on every equation. Hours went by and he took no breaks. His analysis was made more difficult by the charred and water-damaged pages, so that even if he could follow some of the thought processes in the journals, the missing and marred pages left crucial gaps.

There was, however, something else going on. While Bobby had been able to understand the five volumes of his earliest writings that he had read the day before, the equations in these final notebooks were beyond his grasp. He could discern fragments—pieces of the puzzle—but it was as if someone was talking and he could only hear every eighth word. As the hours went by, what he realized was that the notebooks represented twenty years of progress in his cognitive development beyond where he had been developmentally when those original five volumes were written. With the passing of these years, his intellect had grown and the integrative mathematical language which he had invented as a young man had continued to build its vocabulary to a level beyond his current comprehension. Comparing those original five volumes to what he was reading now was like comparing Beethoven's Für Elise, a simplistic piano etude written by Beethoven for a beginner student, to Beethoven's Fifth Symphony. The evolution in Bobby's thought processes over the years had been so monumental that unless he fully recaptured what he once had, he would never be able to understand—and fill in the missing pieces of the AIDS cure that he had completed on the night of the explosion.

When he fell asleep that night, it was on the living room sofa with one of the AIDS journals in his hands. Shortly after dawn, Bobby awoke shivering. There was no reason for his teeth to be chattering so uncontrollably. The thermostat in the room was set at seventy degrees. He pulled his hair in an effort to exert a counter-force to what felt like a vice that was crushing his head. Feeling wet and nauseous, his mind in a daze, he touched the sofa cushions beneath him to find that they were thoroughly soaked with sweat. A putrid odor was lodged inside his nostrils. His eyes burning, he rushed to the bathroom on wobbly legs, covering his mouth in an effort to contain what he feared would be a torrent emanating from the recesses of his stomach. But the worst aspect of the night terror from which he had just awakened was the omnipresent face—the same elongated amorphous face that had haunted him for so many years.

Now in the shower, Bobby stood under a stream of bracing cold water until he felt his breathing return to normal. Soaping the inside of his nose, he tried to remove the remnants of that nauseating odor, even though he didn't know if the odor was real or imagined. "It's back, it's back. It will never leave me alone," he murmured to himself as he pressed his hands to his face, the water pummeling him.

That morning, Bobby put everything back in the attic. He wouldn't tell Christina anything because whatever he said, it was bound to worry her. He thought about one article that he had seen in the *Bulletin of the American Mathematical Society*, located it, and cut it out neatly so that if Christina read the magazine, she wouldn't notice it was missing.

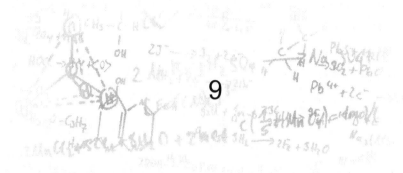

9

THERE WAS NO END TO the snow on Cape Ann. The northeast wind planted drifts on the steps of the Austin family's house that were eight feet deep. It took Bobby and four kids in the neighborhood the better part of two days to dig out and make a path to the road.

Even when the snow was partially cleared, the single-digit temperatures at night made every surface freeze. Getting around when the sun went down was treacherous, which was why it was particularly surprising that the Austin's doorbell should ring at 8:00 p.m. with flurries once again thick in the air.

Looking through the front door's glass panels, Christina saw the broad-shouldered back of a stocky man wearing a navy blue cashmere coat. His large, swollen ears had turned blood-red from the cold, and his oversized head was framed by dark, oiled hair which glistened in the porch's lights. When he turned around, coal-black eyes drilled into Christina. She shuddered. It was Orin Varneys.

Opening the door only partially, she said cautiously, "Director Varneys, what brings you here?"

"Purely a social call. I happened to be in the neighborhood, so I thought I'd stop by and say hello—see how you guys are doing with your new identities and all."

"In the neighborhood? Annisquam?"

"Well, don't leave me in the cold Christina. It's brutal out here." Varneys maneuvered himself through the half-open door and stood in the vestibule of the house. Looking around, he spotted Pete sitting on his knees in front of an ottoman on which a full-sized electronic keyboard rested. Varneys stared intensely as the three-year-old's tiny hands navigated the keys. "Is that Bach he's playing?" asked Varneys. Christina ignored the question.

"What's this?" said Varneys as he noticed a playpen in a corner of the living room. Presumptuously, he crossed the room and crouched down to take a close look at Bobby and Christina's baby daughter, Mirielle, only four months old. Turning towards Christina, he said, "Why didn't you tell me there was a new addition to the family? I owe you a baby gift." Varneys tapped two fingers against the playpen to get the baby's attention. "Aren't you beautiful?" he said as the auburn-haired child crawled toward him, pulled herself to a standing position in front of him and pressed her face against the playpen mesh. Her large green eyes looked directly into his until he felt uncomfortable and looked away. "Congratulations, Christina. She's lovely. She has your eyes, and Robert's hair. If she's lucky, she'll be as beautiful as her mother."

When Bobby walked into the living room and saw Varneys next to the playpen, his face flushed crimson. "Orin Varneys, to what do we owe this intrusion, I mean, honor?"

Striding over to Bobby with arms extended, Varneys gave him a bear hug as if they were the oldest of friends. Without being asked to, Varneys removed his coat and lay it over a chair. "As I mentioned

46

to Christina, I was in the area, so I thought it would be nice to look in on you all and be sure you were comfortable and everything was fine. I haven't seen you, Robert, since you were in the hospital, and Christina, since we…"

Varneys cut his sentence short when Christina glared at him, her eyes wide with alarm. Holding a briefcase, Varneys walked to the sofa.

"Can I get you a cup of coffee, director," asked Christina.

"No, I'm fine. Just want to take a load off for a few minutes. I have something I'd like to show you both." Christina and Bobby sat down on two chairs opposite the sofa. Varneys opened his briefcase and removed a stack of newspaper clippings. He tossed them onto the coffee table but neither Christina nor Bobby made any effort to pick them up.

After an awkward silence, Christina asked, "What's that?"

"Just some articles that came to my attention over the last several months. I don't know if you two have heard of something called the Millennium Competition. It's a long-standing open competition created by the Clay Mathematics Institute in Peterborough, New Hampshire, that awards a one-million- dollar-prize to anyone who can solve each of certain "unsolvable" math problems. Many have tried over the years, but failed. As of the beginning of this year, there were six of these insoluble problems outstanding: the Riemann Hypothesis, the Hodge Conjecture, the Birch and Swinnerton-Dyer Conjecture, the Navier-Stokes Equation, the Yang-Mills Existence and Mass Gap, and whether NP-Problems are actually P-Problems. This year, a donor doubled the prize money."

Varneys paused and looked at Bobby and Christina for a reaction. "I apologize. I can see I'm boring you." Christina and Bobby were expressionless.

"Well, something very strange happened," said Varneys, as he continued. "In the last six months, all of these math problems were solved. Twelve million dollars in award money. The person submitting the winning applications was—in each case –anonymous. Interesting, isn't it?"

Bobby waved his hand dismissively and replied, "If you care about that kind of thing."

"So I thought, who could do this? Six impossible mathematical riddles solved one after the other in a few months. An anonymous genius. Do I know anyone like that?" asked Varneys.

Christina shifted uneasily in her chair as she stared at Bobby.

"Director, you know I lost my special abilities in the explosion. I wish I could claim credit but, unfortunately, those days are behind me. Anyway—I was never interested in abstract math and science. That stuff has always been completely off my radar."

Varneys' eyes flashed. "That's exactly right. That's what I said to myself. 'Robert never gave a hoot about theoretical abstract problems. He was only interested in disease research'." Varneys nodded his head to emphasize his agreement with himself. "Hell, nobody knows that better than me. That's what caused us to fall out with each other back when you were at the Institute."

"Absolutely correct," said Bobby as he looked at Christina for affirmation.

"Well, good. I'm glad we got that settled," she said.

Varneys leaned forward. "I'm sorry, Christina—could I trouble you for a glass of water?" As she got up and walked to the kitchen, Varneys' eyes trailed her. *Damn, she is one fine looking woman. We did a good job selecting her. No wonder Austin fell head over heels.*

Christina returned, put a water glass in front of Varneys and sat down. Varneys took a long drink, almost emptying the glass in one swallow. "Gosh, I was thirsty," he said as he returned the glass to the table. "So, you know what they say: A leopard can't change its spots. I can't help it. My training. I did some investigating, and what I found out was that the anonymous winner on each of the six award submissions had named the same recipient for each of the two-million-dollar awards: The Boston Children's Hospital Oncology Department."

Bobby scratched the back of his neck and looked down at the floor. Christina's face was florid and her eyes were on fire as she glared at Bobby.

"So I thought that was interesting and a bit unusual, but not conclusive," said Varneys. "I did some more research. I went to the oncology department and had a lovely conversation with the chief nurse. The reason I sought her out was because the instructions given to the award committee expressly stipulated that she be the person to decide how the award money should be used. That was a condition of the awards going to the hospital."

Bobby's right leg was visibly vibrating and Christina's arms were tightly crossed over her chest.

"And so I asked this Cara McCarthy if she could recall anything unusual in the last year—people she met, conversations she had about the hospital. That sort of thing. She told me that the nicest man, one Sean Whiten, was a regular visitor, and that she had a very interesting discussion with him some months back about drug companies and hospital budget problems in relation to why the ward looked rundown. But what left the deepest impression on her was when she found out that Mr. Whiten had visited the same ward when he was a boy with—can you guess?" Varneys stopped talking and put the empty glass up to his lips.

"Joe Manzini," said Bobby.

"Bingo."

"You're putting a lot of puzzle pieces together, but it doesn't prove anything. As I told you—my powers are gone."

Varneys rose from the sofa and put the newspaper clippings back in his briefcase. "Well, be that as it may, I just wanted to stop in and say hello. As I said, I was in the neighborhood."

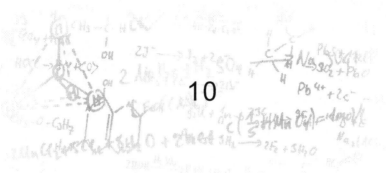

# 10

CHRISTINA WAITED TO SEE THE headlights of Varneys' car disappear into the night. She stood over Bobby who was still seated on a living room chair. "What the hell is going on, Bobby?" Bobby looked down and was silent.

"Did you solve those Millennium problems?"

Bobby looked up and his eyes met hers. "Yes."

"When?"

"Shortly after you came back with Peter from your New York trip. I did them all at once, but I sent one in per month. I thought that would look less conspicuous. Obviously, that didn't work."

"When did you get your abilities back?"

"When you went away, I had to confront a lot of things. There was a breakthrough. I don't know why or how. It just happened. But I'm not anywhere near the level I was. When I was reading your mathematics magazines, I tore out an advertisement for the Millennium Competition. I'm just good enough to solve those puzzles, not much more."

"Yeah, that's all. No big deal. How long did each one take you?"

"About an hour."

"An hour?" Christina's jaw went slack. "Did you write computer programs to help you?"

"No. The answers were more obvious than you'd think. People get spooked when they hear something is unsolvable. You just have to break it down to its most basic components. Then the solution is evident."

"Why didn't you tell me?"

"I didn't want to worry you. If I was working again, I knew you'd be upset. You'd be worried that if my abilities returned, then I'd fall back into my old habits, with my old problems. Things have been pretty peaceful since I got out of the hospital."

"Peaceful, but you've been miserable."

"I just wanted to help those kids in the ward, Christina. It's decrepit, and a lot of the equipment is ancient. Government funding was cut. I'm sorry I didn't tell you."

Christina bent down and took Bobby's hands in hers. "Tell me the truth. Are you having night terrors?"

"I've done experiments on that." Christina looked at him quizzically. "When I do pure math or science, or read my old published articles, no. I sleep like a baby. But when I try to decipher my AIDS notes in my journals, I have terrible night terrors. So all I've been doing in the last few months is reading my old published papers and gradually I'm getting more comprehension of my mathematical language as it progressed over the years. I'm catching up. And just doing that, I'm fine. No problems at all. So I think it's very simple."

"What do you mean?"

"As long as I stay away from medical research, it will leave me alone. It doesn't care about me doing pure math or science. It only cares about me doing medical work. So, you see, there's nothing to worry about."

"What will leave you alone, Bobby?"

"It will leave me alone. The force. The evil that blew up the lab."

Christina shook her head and left the room.

# 11

S IX YEARS EARLIER, WHEN COLUM McAlister was still riding high as CEO of Bushings Pharmaceuticals, he sat at a small outdoor café in the Sultanahmet section of Istanbul. He frowned as he looked at the Ararat Hotel, a modest two-star hostelry offering twelve nondescript rooms to tourists for thirty-five dollars a night. In this working-class Turkish neighborhood, McAlister couldn't be more conspicuous. Dressed in a bespoke blue suit, with red silk necktie, pearl cufflinks and eighteen-carat-gold Cartier sunglasses, his perfectly coiffed silver hair gleamed in the sunlight.

Intently watching the persons entering and exiting the hotel, McAlister stood up abruptly when a diminutive dark-skinned man with thinning black hair and poor posture walked towards him. The man wore a white linen *kurta* that extended to his knees, with matching pants and a white *kufi* skullcap. His beard looked about three weeks in the making. "Dr. Mahmoud," McAlister said loudly.

Startled, the man hesitated but kept walking. "Dr. Aamir Mahmoud," bellowed McAlister. Mahmoud stopped and whirled around, his eyes wide. "How do you know who I am?"

McAlister smiled as he pointed to a bistro chair next to his. "I make it my business to know interesting people."

"Who are you?" asked Mahmoud.

"Colum McAlister. You may have heard of me. CEO of Bushings Pharmaceuticals."

"How did you find me? What do you want?"

"For starters, I want you to sit down. Unless, of course, you prefer our conversation to be public." Mahmoud canvassed the street and nearby intersection with his eyes and then sat down, shielding himself from view by leaning into the table and cupping his hands against the sides of his face. McAlister continued, "So, doctor, a little birdie told me that you left Tyer Drun Pharmaceuticals in Philadelphia to join up with Ansar Jamaat. I assume that's why you're here in Istanbul awaiting transportation to Syria to meet your jihadist compatriots."

"That's not true. I'm here to worship and reconnect with my faith. This hotel is only a few blocks from the Sultan Ahmed Mosque, one of the most holy places in the Muslim world. I go there several times a day, and now you're making me late for prayer and I—"

McAlister held up his hand. "Please, spare me. We both know why you're here. But what I can't figure out is, what does Ansar Jamaat want with you? You're too old to fight. You're not a medical doctor. You're not an engineer or a munitions expert. You're not a computer whiz. It's strange."

"They'll take any true believers. I come from a religious Sunni family. My father was an *imam khatib,* and so is my brother in Iraq."

"Maybe. But not all true believers get their mortgages paid off," said McAlister. "My investigator found out that a bank account you established a few months ago in Belize in the name of an offshore shell corporation got a big wire transfer from Credit Suisse. Of course, it was laundered through three other banks first. You then paid off your mortgages, home equity loans and some rather astounding credit card balances. I assume that this was a going-away gift to your wife. Apparently, she didn't want to join you on your grand adventure."

"This is not your concern, but my wife and I haven't been getting along for some time."

McAlister nodded. "I guess it's hard to have a good marriage when you don't have certain common interests." As he lifted his cup to take a sip of Turkish coffee, McAlister's heavy gold wristwatch came into view. "Anyway, so I said to myself, why would these jihadists pay almost one million dollars to a pharmacist? Oh, I'm sorry. That's pejorative on my part. I mean a chemist."

"Leave me alone. I haven't done anything wrong. This is none of your business."

"Mahmoud. Do you know how I got to the top of the corporate pyramid? Do you know how I got rich? By smelling opportunity. By watching and thinking. By understanding what others merely observe. Why don't you tell me what you're doing for these jihadists."

Mahmoud stood up. "Goodbye, Mr. McAlister."

McAlister removed his sunglasses. His gray eyes skewered Mahmoud and his voice became hard. "I'm afraid it's not that simple, doctor. I suggest you sit down." Mahmoud glared back at McAlister, but did as he was told.

"Now, I'm no marriage counselor, but perhaps this has something to do with your domestic discord." McAlister slid a large sealed manila envelope across the table. "Go ahead, open it."

Mahmoud picked up the envelope, broke the seal and then cautiously peeked in. He removed a stack of photographs which he placed on the table. Hunching over them, he circled his arms protectively around the pictures as he looked at each one. The photos depicted him engaged in a full range of sex acts with a variety of men, leaving nothing to the imagination. His face pallid, Mahmoud hurriedly stuffed the pictures back in the envelope and then sagged in his chair, his eyes closed and his forehead glistening with perspiration. McAlister retrieved the envelope. "Would you like a drink, doctor?"

Mahmoud's face was buried in his hands. He didn't answer. After a few moments, he looked up at McAlister, bewildered. McAlister's broad smile revealed his recently whitened veneers. "Aamir, what you do for recreation makes no difference to me. But I don't know if you're aware that your jihadist cohorts have a real problem with homosexuals. Take a look at this." McAlister pulled his smart phone from his jacket pocket. He pressed the play button and handed it to Mahmoud. The video showed male homosexuals being thrown off the roofs of buildings, their heads and limbs being chopped off when they hit the ground, and their castrated torsos being impaled on street lampposts. McAlister raised a brow. "Who knows? They might even want their money back and come calling on your wife."

Mahmoud's eyes were wild. "You can't let them see those photographs."

"I have no intention of doing so, if you and I can work together. Now, tell me. What do they want you for? What are you going to do for them?"

Mahmoud bowed his head. "It's going to sound worse than it is. But I'm actually helping save many lives. That's why I agreed."

"Saving lives and paying off mortgages. Sounds wonderful. Tell me."

"Well, you know how many people on both sides—the

mujahideen and those resisting them—are getting killed fighting each other. It's terrible, and there's no end in sight. Ansar Jamaat asked me to design a preventative. Something that they could dangle in front of their enemies to get them to lay down their guns and accept the caliphate—with no bloodshed. Something to end the fighting and allow the caliphate to grow and prosper without the loss of life and the destruction of resources. I thought this sounded very good."

"So what exactly are you *designing* for them?"

"A disease. Something new that no one has encountered before. A custom-made disease that will be so fearful that no one will risk opposing it. Ansar Jamaat will isolate their enemy and threaten to infect them if they resist. It's strategic. It's their version of the old Roman siege technique."

"And how are you going to conjure up this disease?"

"As Ansar Jamaat has conquered territories in Libya, Syria, Iraq, Iran and Lebanon, it has uncovered stashes of biological warfare materials which were supposed to have been destroyed by prior regimes. It now has six or seven very powerful biological agents. It has also purchased some additional agents that once belonged to the Soviet Union. I will use my abilities as a biochemist to design a cocktail."

McAlister appeared to be lost in thought. Finally snapping out of it, he said, "You are a sick motherfucker. You're crazy." McAlister deftly reached into his pants pocket and removed a Beretta 3032 Tomcat pistol. No bigger than a cell phone, this tiny firearm has the stopping power of a .32 ACP cartridge. Placing it inside a folded newspaper that was lying on his lap, McAlister set the paper on the table in front of him with the Beretta pointing at Mahmoud's chest. "I should kill you right now."

Mahmoud leaned forward, his hands on the edge of the table. Seeing that Mahmoud was poised to push his chair out from under him and run, McAlister cautioned, "Don't try it, doctor. If I don't get you, they will." Turning his head from side to side, McAlister nodded at the three men he had on duty no more than fifty feet away. Mahmoud fell back into his chair, defeated, and looked down at his shoes. "How the hell did you get so twisted up?" asked McAlister.

Mahmoud shook his head resolutely. "I'm not twisted. The caliphate is the answer for the rebirth of the world. And if I can establish its predominance and prevent bloodshed, then I have earned my place in heaven."

Glaring at Mahmoud, McAlister said, "There are only two reasons why I'm not going to kill you right now. One is that if you're dead, the jihadists will just find a replacement for you. The second is that you're going to help *me* help mankind. You know as well as I do that the disease you create will be unleashed—somehow. Maybe on purpose, because they'll want to make an example of a town or city, or maybe by accident. But once that happens, no one can predict the ramifications."

Mahmoud pulled nervously on his beard. "No, they have assured me that the disease will never be used."

A vein on McAlister's forehead became engorged. "That's bullshit. If that were the case, they wouldn't need a real disease. They could just wave some test tubes in the air and say, "boo." So, as I was saying, when the disease is released, we have to be ready. You are going to create a cure for that disease at the same time as you create the disease. And because you know exactly what you're putting into your cocktail, you'll be able to retrofit a cure— assuming you don't do anything stupid. And guess who you're going to give that cure to?" Mahmoud nodded in recognition. "That's right: me. I'm going to own it. Nobody else. You'll work according to my schedule—not Ansar Jamaat's. When you get to Syria, I'll have my man contact you. He'll be undercover and close by at all times. You'll deal with him for all purposes."

"Why? Why are you doing this?" asked Mahmoud.

"Because one day, when human nature plays out as I think it will, I'll be there to save humanity...for a price."

"So this is how Bushings Pharmaceuticals does business?" Mahmoud spat on the ground.

"I didn't say I was here on behalf of Bushings. I'm on holiday right now."

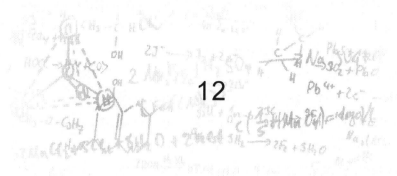

# 12

B OBBY POKED HIS HEAD INTO Susan's office. "Do you have a minute? Am I interrupting?" he asked.

"No. Come in. I need a break. I've been buried in reviewing manufacturing bids for Uniserve. I think we're going to be able to get prices for some of the drugs lowered even more."

"Same quality?"

"Absolutely. All top manufacturers. It's easy business for them. The profit per unit is small, but the quantities are huge."

"That's great, Susan. Really good news. And I have some good news, too. I don't know if Christina mentioned it to you, but I'm beginning to do some work again. Not in medical research, but in other areas where I can do some good. I can't spend the rest of my life looking in the rearview mirror."

Susan's face lit up. "Christina told me you won some math competition and raised big money for the children's hospital. I told her you're like a champion racehorse—even when it's put out to pasture, it still needs to run."

"Thanks for comparing me to a horse, that's very sweet, Susan. The math competition was an isolated thing, but what I really want to do is try to get my mental chops back, and to do that I'm going to need a new lab with a heavy computer interface into Tufts like we used to have. I called Dean Walterberg the other day, and he said that Tufts will be glad to help—even with funding for equipment purchases."

"Money isn't the problem. The foundation constantly gets donations and bequests. Have you told Christina about this yet?"

Bobby ignored the question. "You should start looking around for a good facility. Something equidistant between here and Tufts. Nice and private just like we had the last time."

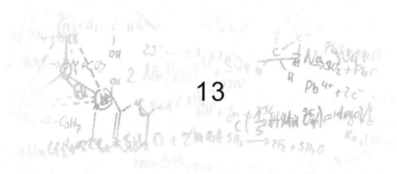

# 13

G UNTHER RAMIREZ STOOD ON THE balcony of his Ritz-Carlton Hotel suite. Beijing was not one of his favorite cities, but it was where he needed to be to progress the plans he had discussed with Colum McAlister during his latest visit with him.

Looking through the veil of smog that enveloped the city, he marveled at the number of towering construction cranes. They were everywhere, dominating the landscape like giant metallic sentries. Taking a sip of his cognac, Ramirez imagined that the cranes communicated with each other. *Perhaps they even reproduced*, he mused. *How else could there be so many of them and more every day?*

The number of building projects was awe-inspiring but, at the same time, hard to understand. Was it all necessary or was it for show? Were there tenants waiting to occupy these tens of thousands of new luxury offices? Were buyers ready and eager to snap up so many expensive apartments? Was the unprecedented building boom part of an elaborate scheme by the communist regime to artificially inflate China's GDP? Ramirez didn't know and he didn't care. He raised his glass in salute to the new colossus. European and American cities were sleepy moribund outposts in comparison.

After a fit of rapid-fire sneezing, Ramirez blew his nose and looked at the particles of black soot on his handkerchief. It was the same soot that washed off his body and out of his hair every night when he showered in China. It always took Ramirez at least two weeks after leaving to get the lingering odor of burned coal out of his nasal passages. But he did love China. He made a lot of money here.

Following instructions that he had received, the next day, Ramirez boarded a tourist bus to take him on the forty-mile trip from Beijing to Badaling, the most commercialized part of the Great Wall of China. As required, he wore a blue souvenir baseball cap on which the letters "PRC" were embroidered in gold, black wraparound sunglasses and a blue-striped shirt.

At Badaling, he was jostled by hordes of Chinese tourists who, to his surprise, outnumbered the international tourists by at least fifty to one. Ramirez stood on a line for almost thirty minutes to purchase a ticket to the Great Wall, and he was none too pleased about it.

Once through the entrance, and actually on the wall, he proceeded to walk to the west. For the first mile, the crowds of animated Chinese were so thick that he felt he was on an obstacle course. "There are so many damn people in China, I can't fucking believe it," he muttered as he proceeded on his trek. "Why couldn't we meet at the Ritz?"

Ramirez was not happy. He despised crowds, and he didn't like to rub shoulders with the proletariat. Despite the nastiness of his business, wealth had made him an elitist. While most of his clients were inherently scummy people, they were highly

64

successful scummy people and, to him, that made all the difference in the world. Money was Ramirez' elixir. In sufficient quantities, it sanitized all human behavior. He hadn't encountered any crime against humanity that couldn't be cleansed to his satisfaction when washed in enough dough.

Ramirez had traveled to China to meet with Huo Jin Gao and he understood why Gao was insistent that their meeting place be outdoors and at a location where their anonymity would be assured. Gao was one of the wealthiest men in China, with a net worth exceeding eleven billion dollars, and was also a member of China's parliament, the National People's Congress (NPC). In a country where making fortunes and keeping them are dependent on political connections, it is no coincidence that Gao and more than eighty other Chinese billionaires were members of the NPC or its official advisory body, the Chinese People's Political Consultative Conference (CPPCC). While in much of the world lawmakers are derided for being controlled by billionaires, in China, the lawmakers *are* billionaires; the annual NPC and CPPCC sessions in Beijing are the largest gathering of billionaires in the world.

Ramirez had learned from his Chinese clients long ago that *guanxi* is the magic ingredient needed to become a billionaire in China. *Guanxi* is the intimate nexus between entrepreneurs, government officials and the Communist Party. If you don't have this personalized network of influence, *guanxi,* you won't make the *Forbes* World's Billionaires list. Gao had more *guanxi* than most, and this allowed him to amass a fortune in real estate, construction, shopping malls, hotels, movie theatres, telecommunications and rare-earth minerals.

The billions he had made would not have been possible without the assistance of a long list of Communist Party officials, all of whom had become multimillionaires from bribes and kickbacks that Gao deftly arranged. In China, corruption was an art form, and Huo Jin Gao was one of China's most skilled artists. A man of Gao's stature could not risk being seen in the company of someone as notorious as Gunther Ramirez.

Their mutually profitable relationship went back fifteen years. Gao was one of the first rich Chinese to realize the importance of getting his money out of China and laundering it through the purchase of overseas assets so that it couldn't be clawed-back by the Chinese government when a less sympathetic regime took power. Ramirez had been indispensable in these efforts, having performed similar services for Malaysian ministers, Nigerian presidents, Mexican drug lords, Libyan dictators, Russian oligarchs, and Afghan leaders whose pockets had been lined for years by the CIA. And when Gao needed some non-Chinese muscle to eliminate competitors or otherwise smooth the way, Ramirez had the resources to get the job done with no possibility of Gao being implicated.

Ramirez wiped perspiration from his forehead, cheeks and neck. "This goddamn soot is everywhere," he grumbled as he looked at his spotted handkerchief. Heading further west, the Great Wall got progressively steeper as it followed the terrain of the mountains. Two miles out, and Ramirez was breathing hard. He finally saw the appointed meeting place, an ancient watchtower built during the Ming Dynasty. Ramirez mustered what energy he had left for the steep quarter-mile climb to the tower. About twenty perky Chinese tourists were milling around as they surveyed the mountainous countryside and the serpent-like wall that extended indefinitely to the east and west.

According to plan, Ramirez continued walking west and then stopped alongside a parapet that was just beyond the tower. Taking off his sunglasses, he raised his camera to eye level and fiddled with the zoom lens like a determined tourist. A short man wearing a beige windbreaker that hung loosely on his thin frame approached. His face was successfully obscured by a large-brimmed hat and wraparound sunglasses. The man pressed a pair of oversized binoculars to his eyes as he said, "Hello, Gunther."

Without looking in Gao's direction, Ramirez replied, "I got my exercise for the day, probably for the year."

"I would have preferred to meet outside of China altogether, but you said it was urgent." Gao scanned the expanse of the wall and its vast surroundings. "It's ironic. It took millions of people to build this wall, and hundreds of thousands died in the process, but the wall was no match for human greed."

"What do you mean?" asked Ramirez.

"Each time the wall was breached, it was because guards were bribed to let the invading hordes in. The wall didn't fail, but human nature made it redundant. Now what's on your mind, Gunther?"

"I have an unusual opportunity, and I need to know if you're interested. If you're not, that's fine. There will be many takers on this one. But because of our relationship, I'm asking you first."

Gao smiled as he scanned the panorama with his binoculars. "You have my attention."

"My partner and I will have advance knowledge of when a cataclysmic event will happen. I'm talking about an event that is guaranteed to cause panic and crash the financial markets worldwide. My partner and I are looking to work with two people who have large cash resources of their own, and can call upon their personal network of other ultra-high-net-worth individuals to supplement those resources. Also required is experience in trading every kind of option, warrant and derivative, and having relationships with international financial institutions that will allow you to obtain trading leverage of at least twenty to one. Because of the information we will give you, you'll be able to liquidate your current investments and take your profits before the crash, and then use your leveraged cash to sell the markets short."

"Sounds interesting, but if the world ends, making some money shorting markets will be a small consolation."

"There's more. My partner and I will also know when the hysteria will end and when the markets will begin to recover. So, you can make a second killing buying blue-chip assets at distressed prices and then playing the long side when we give you the word. With leverage applied to the billions that you and your investors will put to work, the amount of money to be made is almost incalculable."

"Who's your partner?" asked Gao.

"I'm not at liberty to identify him at this time, but I can tell you that he's been a major Fortune 500 corporate executive, wealthy in his own right and a true visionary. He's been a client of mine for years. I trust him implicitly."

"I don't do business of this magnitude with people I don't know."

"Once you've made a firm commitment, I'll identify him. Until then, there's no need. You've known me for over fifteen years. Have I ever failed to deliver on what I promised you?"

Gao let the question hang in the air. "You said that you are looking for two people to join you on this venture?"

"We want a very small group. The other investor will be another long-term client of mine. We aren't taking chances with strangers. You and the other investor will coordinate your trading positions with each other to maximize impact. You both will need full control of your investors' funds. You can't share your knowledge with anyone."

"What split are you looking for on the profits?" asked Gao.

"We only want thirty percent."

Gao laughed. "Only thirty percent? How generous of you, seeing that you're not risking any of your own money."

Ramirez' lips tightened to a straight line as his eyes bore into Gao. "A hedge fund charges you two percent of your capital plus twenty percent of the profits—and they don't know anything. They just sit at the tables and place bets with your money. My partner and I aren't gambling. We're taking you to the bank, not the casino."

Gao smiled inscrutably. "It is true that good things cost a lot."

Ramirez squared his shoulders and drew in a long breath. "You also need to know that my partner and I will have our own separate action going, and we're keeping that completely for ourselves. It's not financial trading. It's something else."

"Is it competitive with the trading? Is there a conflict of interest?"

Ramirez' mouth curved into a smile. "To the contrary, what we will be doing will create the trading profits for you."

"It sounds interesting, Gunther. Of course, I'll have to think about it. Is there more?"

"Huo Jin, I want to be very clear so we avoid any unpleasantness. My partner and I expect full transparency on the trading profits, an honest count. If we don't get it..."

Gao put his hand up and Ramirez stopped talking in mid-sentence. "You don't need to say it, Gunther. I know what will happen, but that goes both ways if you don't deliver."

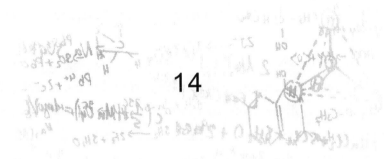

# 14

C OLUM MCALISTER GRIMACED AS THE portly middle-aged man carrying a thick briefcase sat down opposite him in the visitor's room at the prison. Andrew Sinclair, one of McAlister's three trial lawyers, had one of those faces that always looked like it was in need of a de-greasing. As McAlister tried to focus on Sinclair's busy brown eyes, he was appalled that such a highly paid attorney looked so bad. Necktie askew, collar unbuttoned, his belly protruding over his belt and his suit jacket hanging unevenly on his stubby frame, McAlister had always thought that the only excuse for such a slovenly physical presence in a trial lawyer would be if the man was a legal genius. After having been convicted on thirty-one felony charges and sentenced to nineteen years in prison, McAlister had concluded that Andrew Sinclair was no genius.

"Andrew, it's so nice of you to finally come visit me at my new residence. You played such an important role in getting me this abode that I would have thought you'd have come for a house warming ages ago."

"Colum, I know you're bitter about the length of your sentence, but that had nothing to do with my firm. Any judge was going to come down hard when you were convicted of so many significant felonies, and with Dr. Austin being the target of many of the crimes, what did you expect? At least we got you into this facility. It's one of the nicest."

McAlister forced a smile. "Andy, I didn't ask you to come here today so that I could vent about the past. What's done is done. I've moved on. In fact, the reason I called you was because I want to make amends."

Sinclair's eyes were leaden as he looked at McAlister. "It's amazing to hear you say that."

McAlister leaned in towards Sinclair and he lowered his voice. "I know your firm has many resources. I need you to find out for me if Dr. Austin has a new laboratory. After the last one blew up, I don't know if he relocated. There hasn't been any news about him for a long time. Hopefully, he's fully recovered and back to work in a new facility. Can you find that out for me? I assure you that my interest is benign."

Sinclair raised an eyebrow. "It won't be easy. There's a veil of secrecy around him, but my office in D.C. has great connections with the Feds. Let me see what I can find out. I may be able to get a "yes" or "no" regarding the lab, but no address."

McAlister leaned back in his chair and folded his hands. "That's perfectly fine. I don't need an address. What would I do with an address anyway? I just want to know if he's back to work in new digs, that's all. Oh, and by the way, thanks for arranging that six-million-dollar wire transfer from my overseas account to the Clay Mathematics Institute. They told me that one applicant won all six prizes and donated the money to a children's hospital in Boston. What a genius it would take to do that—and such a selfless generous soul, to boot."

Standing to leave, Sinclair extended his hand to McAlister and said, "That should be so gratifying for you, Colum. Not only did you support academic research and extend mathematical knowledge, but the money even went to a great cause for kids. A double win."

McAlister grinned. "A double win. I like those."

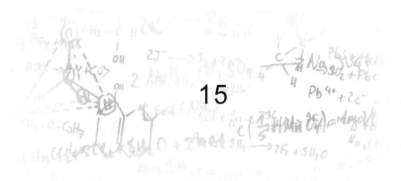

# 15

**B**Y DESIGN, ALL TEXT MESSAGES received by Gunther Ramirez were incomprehensible to anyone other than him, and the text he just received was no exception. As was usually the case, the sender employed a disposable cell phone to ensure anonymity:

"mgny249"

Reading the message, Ramirez smiled. The pieces of the puzzle were beginning to fall into place. He would finish up his business in London and head to New York City to meet Gao again on September 24. Ramirez reached for a smoked-salmon finger sandwich and nodded to the officious waiter who was hovering nearby to pour him a third cup of tea. When he was in London, which was often, Ramirez made a point of being at Claridge's for formal afternoon tea. The unrushed ritual of high-tea service, with its tiered silver trays of wafer-thin sandwiches, sweet pastries and warm scones served with clotted cream and jam pleased him. Nothing made him feel quite as successful as sitting in Claridge's breathing the perfumed air while being served by obsequious Englishmen wearing livery and white gloves.

Ramirez had seen London change over the years. Decades before, when he first had the financial wherewithal to stay at the city's best hotels and dine at its top restaurants, he had often felt unwelcome and underserved, due to his Hispanic name, appearance and accent. In fact, he had difficulty getting reservations. But now, London's luxury retail and hospitality businesses, real estate markets and high-level financial and professional services were dependent on the ocean of foreign money that poured into the country from the Mideast, Russia, Eastern Europe, China and Latin America. As in so many other Western countries, England's old prejudices had been supplanted by pragmatism. There was no room for racial, ethnic or national elitism when a lot of money could be made catering to those with seemingly unlimited amounts of disposable income.

Finishing his high tea with a glass of Champagne, Ramirez signaled for the bill. He was happy with the way things had developed. There was a new aristocracy, and it held court in every desirable city of the world. It was the aristocracy of coin. The courtiers who served this new aristocracy were indifferent to where the money came from. All that mattered was that it was there and that a piece of it could be acquired for rendering a service or selling a product.

Perhaps the riches came from absconding with the natural resources of an entire nation, as was the case with the plundering of the Soviet Union by the oligarchs, or by Arab sheiks who long ago expropriated for themselves their countries' oil fields; or perhaps the loot was obtained by corrupt public officials who sold their influence, greasing the wheels of government for those who bribed them, as in China; or perhaps it was obtained by trafficking in drugs, armaments or slave labor or manipulating financial markets. *It doesn't matter anymore. Nobody wants to know where you got it,*

74

*they just want to know you have it. And I have it, and soon I'll have a lot more. You pay them, you own them.*

Vast wealth was irresistible, even to governments. Britain, the United States, Canada, Australia and scores of other countries sold residency visas and, in some cases, citizenship, to anyone who would invest significant sums within their borders. Tax incentives were given, hidden ownership of assets was legally sanctioned, banking regulations were lax or non-existent, and there were countless law firms, accountants, real estate professionals and investment advisors who specialized in the sophisticated business of laundering money—no matter how dirty it might be. As Ramirez was fond of saying to his clients on the rare occasions when they evidenced a pang of remorse regarding the origins of their wealth, "The only thing immoral about money is not having enough of it."

# 16

"ONE HYDE PARK," SAID RAMIREZ to the taxi driver.

"You live there?" asked the cabbie.

"No. Visiting someone."

"Bloody fancy address. The papers say it's the most expensive apartment building in London, maybe in the world." The cabbie looked in his rearview mirror to see Ramirez' reaction, but Ramirez was oblivious to the comment as he gazed out the passenger window.

When Ramirez informed the building's concierge who he was there to see, the concierge checked the visitor log to be sure that Ramirez was expected by Viktor Bazhenov, a resident. The concierge then asked to see two forms of identification, including a passport or driver's license with photograph. As certain as he could reasonably be that the man standing in front of him was Gunther Ramirez, the concierge called up to Bazhenov's apartment. A few minutes later, two very large men in dark suits appeared in the lobby. When they walked Ramirez to a quiet corner, one of them frisked him, while the other ran a security wand over his body, alongside his arms and legs, and over his crotch. Satisfied that Ramirez wasn't armed, they motioned for him to follow them down a long, marble hall to a private elevator that was accessed by a security code. Once inside, the onyx-and-mahogany-clad elevator cab, they waited while they were scanned by two video cameras. When the cam operator in the Bazhenov apartment's security center was satisfied that nothing was amiss, the elevator began its climb to the penthouse, which comprised the entire two top floors of the building, approximately sixteen thousand square feet of indoor living space and four thousand square feet of private outdoor terraces, gardens, and an infinity-edge swimming pool overlooking Hyde Park.

This was not the first time that Ramirez had visited Bazhenov at this apartment, so he was used to its opulence. Personally, he preferred Bazhenov's two other residences in England, a stucco mansion in Kensington Palace Gardens, and Stillington Hall, an eight-hundred acre country estate in Oxfordshire that had been built in 1516 for Cardinal Thomas Wolsey.

While a majority of the British population was struggling to maintain its modest lifestyle, the newspapers reveled in reporting that Bazhenov, a Russian émigré, had spent almost six hundred million pounds sterling purchasing, refurbishing and decorating these palatial homes. That, coupled with his highly publicized development of towering office complexes along the Thames, and his recent purchase of a legendary English soccer club, enshrined Viktor Bazhenov at the top of the heap in Britain's coin aristocracy.

Ramirez had first met Bazhenov in Moscow many years earlier when Bazhenov was an ambitious assistant minister of finance in the Kremlin. Never one to miss an opportunity to advance himself, Bazhenov understood that maintaining close personal relationships with top KGB officials would be advantageous to him. Following the collapse of the Soviet Union, he used his political skills and the muscle that these officials provided in the newly formed Federal Security Service (FSS), the successor to the KGB, to ensure that he sat at the head of the table when the turkey was carved up. Grabbing more than his fair share of the Soviet Union's oil, natural gas and steel industries during privatization, he increased his assets by engineering the downfall of more than a dozen of his rivals whose holdings he then scooped up; eight of these men died under mysterious circumstances or were executed by the state or simply disappeared, earning Bazhenov the nickname *Volshebnik* (the Magician), for his ability to dispose of his competitors.

Seventeen years ago, Ramirez had been instrumental in convincing Bazhenov that time was not on his side, and that his life expectancy would be increased by moving himself and his wealth out of Russia. An expert in facilitating these arrangements, Ramirez deployed his network of financial and legal professionals on Bazhenov's behalf. Bazhenov now had an international portfolio of assets, held a British passport and maintained residences in six countries, none of them Russia.

Bazhenov looked incongruous with all of the beautiful objects in his apartment. He was a monstrously large man in his mid-sixties, standing six feet seven inches tall and weighting over three hundred forty pounds. Ten thousand dollars of clothing hanging from his mammoth frame failed to make him look stylish. His head was oversized like that of a boar, and his fatty facial features seemed ill-suited to each other, as if they had been slapped together on an assembly line with what parts remained at the end of the day. His small eyes were close-set, like those of a rodent, and his thinning hair, dyed an unnatural shade of reddish brown, was combed straight back and heavily greased, adhering to his head like a bathing cap. This contrasted with immense gray eyebrows that were so thick and unruly that one wouldn't be surprised to find that they were a nesting place for some life form.

Bazhenov did, however, possess a physical gift that more than compensated for his inelegant appearance. He had an unusual smile. It was a broad transformative smile that overtook his face completely, beguiling skeptics, disarming critics and ingratiating him to whomever he was talking. In media interviews, it was this smile, coupled with his wit and natural charm, that turned potentially hostile journalists into his proponents.

Having already had several discussions with Bazhenov in his effort to recruit him to be one of the two lynchpin investors in the scheme to manipulate financial markets, Ramirez asked, "So what are your thoughts Viktor? Are you in?"

"You've known me a long time, Gunther, so I can be candid with you. Financial trading has been good to me. In the last few years, this took me from number fifty-five on the Forbes list to thirty-one. And the best part is that I don't have to kick back any of the money I make in the markets."

Ramirez cocked his head quizzically. "What do you mean?"

"All of us, what the media calls 'oligarchs,' are bound to an agreement that was made when our ownership of state assets was finalized. Thirty percent goes back to the *Ruka.* I don't have to mention any names. You can figure out who he is. He keeps what he wants out of the thirty percent, and takes care of who he needs to take care of. If one of us stops honoring that arrangement, you read about it in the newspapers: suicide, accident, unexplained death, whatever. But if I make money trading with my own funds, the *Ruka* has no claim on that and I haven't violated the agreement."

"Well, Viktor, if you come into my deal, you'll break the top twenty on the *Forbes* list, easy. Maybe the top ten. It all depends on how much cash you commit, and how much leverage you can get the brokerages to give you. My partner and I are requiring that you and your network guarantee a minimum of ten billion dollars and twenty-to-one leverage."

Bazhenov laughed. It was a roar of a laugh that originated deep in Bazhenov's belly and was amplified as it reverberated through his massive body. "Twenty. No. I'm looking for forty."

"And how much cash will you and your network commit?"

"Between me and my group, at least thirteen billion dollars."

"Excellent. So I can count you in?" said Ramirez. Bazhenov extended his enormous right hand to Ramirez as he grabbed his left shoulder and pulled him close with such force that Ramirez' feet almost left the ground.

"Of course, I'm in." Still not releasing Ramirez' hand from his grasp, Bazhenov flashed his famous smile. "Just don't fuck me, Gunther."

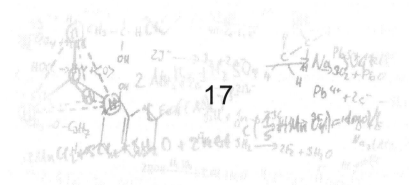

# 17

CHRISTINA WAS SITTING AT HER desk in a small office area adjacent to the living room. Staring at her computer screen, she was immersed in writing an algorithm for the software company that she worked for. Bobby stepped behind her and glanced at the screen. "Can I give you a hint?" he asked.

Christina chuckled. "No. We don't do that around here. I'll figure it out."

Bobby kissed the top of her head. "I know you will. You always do."

Christina turned and faced him. "What's up? Everything okay?"

"There's actually something I wanted to talk to you about. Is now a good time?" Christina nodded. "I have some big news. I've asked Susan to find a new lab. I'm going back to work."

"Back to work?"

"Yes, but don't worry. It's going to be fine."

"How's it going to be fine, Bobby?"

"I'm going to start slow. Get up to speed on my integrative math language and see how I can fine-tune it so I can use it to do good things outside of medical research. I'll stay away from that so that

I don't come into opposition with the force. And if I do this, I think it will leave me alone."

Christina looked away for a moment and then inhaled deeply before she responded. "Bobby, things aren't as simple as they used to be. It's not just about you anymore or even about me. We have two young children now."

"Exactly. And I won't do anything to endanger you, Pete or Mirielle. I'm going to get a lab that's completely separate from where we live—not like last time. And I don't want you working in the lab. Keep your job at the software company. So if anything crazy happens, you and the kids won't be anywhere in the vicinity. I'm not going to let it get my family."

Christina lowered her eyes. "Bobby, there is no 'it'."

"What do you mean?"

Christina stood and faced Bobby. Her voice was somber. "There never was an 'it.' This force of negativity or mayhem or supreme evil, or whatever you call it. It's a figment of your imagination or…" Christina paused. "It's part of your illness, Bobby."

Bobby's brow furrowed. "What illness? What are you talking about?"

Christina bit her bottom lip as she contemplated exactly what to say. When she began to speak, it was in a soft monotone. "Doctor Uhlman told Susan and me all about it. He diagnosed you when you were only four—when he first met with you at the Mayo Clinic. You suffer from a psychosis characterized by paranoia, reality detachment, a dissociative state and a self-loathing alternate personality. He said this condition got progressively worse as you got older and were subjected to increasing pressure and suffered catastrophes in your life."

Bobby took two steps back from Christina, and a look of

82

bewilderment came over his face as she continued. "That's why you've had night terrors your whole life, and the trances, and that's the root of your paranoia about a supernatural force that's opposing you."

The color drained out of Bobby's face and he began to speak so rapidly that he was hard to understand. "So, if it's all in my mind then how the hell did my lab blow up and who erased my computer hard drives and tried to sabotage my work and who tried to kill me just when I had found the cure for AIDS? You think those RASI fanatics did it—or the drug companies? The prosecutors got nowhere on that. Uhlman is just feeding you a line of psycho-babble bullshit. That's what those guys do for a living."

Christina grasped Bobby's hands in hers and held them firmly as she said, "Bobby, I saw the videos. Susan and I saw them. We know what happened."

Bobby pulled away from Christina. "What videos?"

"Varneys made us promise never to tell you or anyone else about them."

Bobby punched the air. "He's involved again? What do I have to do to get this guy out of our lives?"

Christina shook her head. "Bobby, it's not what you think. He and Dr. Uhlman were trying to help."

Perspiration had formed on Bobby's forehead. "You have to tell me everything. I don't care what you promised Varneys."

Christina led Bobby into the living room and sat down on the sofa. Bobby positioned himself across from her, leaning forward on the edge of a chair.

"A while ago, I got a call from Varneys who said that it was important that Susan and I come to his office. Uhlman was already there when we arrived. He proceeded to tell us about the psychological tests done on you when you were a child, and his analysis of you during your years at the Institute for Advanced Intelligence Studies. He told us that you suffered from a psychosis which had become worse over the years, and that you had an alternative personality that was frustrating your work and trying to destroy you. Essentially, that the "it" you always talk about is not some external force. The "it" is you."

Slack-jawed, Bobby glared at Christina. "I don't know what is more incredible—Uhlman's nonsense or that you and Susan sat there listening to it."

Undeterred, Christina continued. "Varneys said that he was never convinced that the prosecutors knew what they were doing. There was something that bothered him, so he went back three years prior to the explosion to examine surveillance video footage. He said that the prior examiners hadn't gone back far enough, and they were only looking for intruders, coworkers and service providers." Christina stopped talking and wiped her eyes with both hands. Her bottom lip was trembling, but she knew she had to tell him everything. "He showed us video footage of you Bobby, shot over a period of several years, in a zombie-like state, assembling bombs, positioning them in the lab and sabotaging your computers. Uhlman confirmed that you would have no recollection of what you were doing—that you were in a semiconscious state and that you were being guided by your alternate personality."

Bobby scrunched up his face and began to walk in circles. "Aha! Now I get it. Finally, it's clear to me. This is why you and Susan have been acting so weird around me. Walking on eggshells and never talking about the explosion. You both think I'm crazy." Bobby kicked the side of the sofa.

Christina shuddered as she leaned forward in her seat. Speaking slowly in a deadpan voice, she said, "Uhlman didn't think you lost your genius, but that your alternate-self believed that, and as long as that was the case, then you, me and the kids would be safe. So you can see why I'm so worried that your intellect is back. I'm sorry, Bobby."

Bobby moved to a far corner of the room, turned away from Christina, closed his eyes and began to inhale deeply, holding each breath for a five-second count and then slowly exhaling—a technique he had found helpful when he felt overcome by anxiety. He did this for twenty successive breaths while he processed everything that Christina had said. When he felt that he had regained his composure, he walked over to Christina and presented his rebuttal as if he were a trial lawyer. "Christina, doesn't it seem strange to you that this has materialized out of thin air? Neither Uhlman nor the psychiatrist at the Institute who saw me every week for years, nor any of the other big experts who tested me ever told me there was anything wrong with me or ever gave me any treatments. Don't you think that's odd?"

Christina's eyes welled up as she said, "They just wanted to keep you working. They didn't want to do anything that might slow you down or make you less productive. They figured out that you were at your intellectual peak when you disassociated—and they weren't going to interfere with that. They treated you like a machine, Bobby, a thing to be exploited." Bobby's mind flashed back to Uhlman's visit in the hospital when he was recovering from the lab explosion. He recalled Uhlman's final words to him as he departed, "I failed you in more ways than you know. I'm sorry."

Looking squarely at Christina, Bobby said, "I'll admit that I may do some weird things and get pretty far out there sometimes—but

I'm not crazy and I'm not controlled by some split personality, and I didn't blow up my own lab."

"But if you're wrong, and Uhlman and Varneys are right, think about the consequences. You almost died in that explosion. And if anyone else had been in the lab then, they could have died, too. And if the draperies in the guest house hadn't been drawn closed, I might have died. And I was pregnant with our son."

Bobby could feel his throat closing up and a tightness forming in his chest. His voice became strained. "Why is it so hard for you to believe me, Christina? Why are you so quick to believe a professional liar like Varneys over me? Do you think that my intellect is one dimensional, only math and science? You don't know where my mind has taken me. You don't know what I've seen. We live among forces that are so powerful that they can alter the movement of the universe. Some of these forces are benevolent and some are not, and those that are malevolent want to do harm to human beings. They oppose me because I interfere with them. Everything has its reciprocal, its opposite. Where there is good, there is evil. This is the balance that allows the universe to survive. So please don't tell me that my knowledge is a manifestation of an illness."

Christina went over to Bobby and gently placed her hands on each side of his face. She looked directly into his light blue eyes, and for a moment felt as if she could see into another world. "Bobby, I don't care about any of this metaphysical stuff, and I don't care about Uhlman or Varneys. I just want you and our family to be safe and happy. Have you ever thought what it was like for me when I saw them dig your body out of the lab rubble? When I saw them hook you up to all of those machines in the hospital? Do you know how many nights I lay next to you in the hospital bed praying that one day I would hear your voice, even for just a few words? Your son almost never knew his father. What would our lives have been like if you stayed in a coma for years?" Bobby pulled Christina tight against him. Christina's eyes were wet as she pushed him away. "I finally have you safe and sound, and now you're about to throw it to the wind again."

# 18

BOBBY'S HANDS WERE SHAKING FROM anger when he dialed the number for CIA headquarters in Langley, Virginia. He had never been given Orin Varneys' direct line, nor did he want it—as he always hoped that each interaction with Varneys would be the last one he would ever have.

"Good morning. Central Intelligence Agency. How may I direct your call?"

"The director's office, please."

"Who's calling and what is the reason for your call to the director?"

"My name is Rober— Sean Whitten. The director knows me."

"Hold on, please. I'll put you through to his office."

"Director Varneys' office. To whom am I speaking?" asked his assistant.

"Sean Whitten."

"Oh, yes, Mr. Whitten. What can I help you with?"

"I need to meet with Varneys as soon as possible. Tomorrow."

"Director Varneys will not be in his office until sometime next week. When I speak to him, I'll find out his availability. Can I tell him why you want to see him, Mr. Whitten?"

"No. I just need to meet with him urgently."

"I pulled up your information on my computer. It says that the agency must make arrangements for your travel."

"That's not necessary. I can make my own travel arrangements."

"Mr. Whitten, with all due respect, this is not up for discussion. Due to the program that you're in, the protocol is clear. If you want to meet with the director, the agency makes the travel arrangements. This is for your own security and to preserve the integrity of the program. If that's not acceptable to you, then you'll have to settle for a phone call."

———————•·•———————

Six days later, Bobby followed Varneys' secretary into his immense office. Varneys was seated behind his desk, jacket off, shirtsleeves rolled up on his thick forearms. He was absorbed in reading a file that was spread out in front of him. When Varneys' secretary cleared her throat loudly, he looked up from his work, removed his reading glasses and stood.

"How nice to see you, Robert," he said as he smiled and extended his hand, which Bobby let languish in the air. Varneys' face flushed in response to the insult and he motioned Bobby to take a seat on one of the guest chairs. After his secretary exited and closed the door, Varneys said, "I assume you wanted this meeting so you could apologize to me in person for lying about the Millennium Competition and the resurrection of your abilities. But that's fine. I didn't mean to corner you in front of your wife. I didn't know that you were keeping secrets from her."

"It just never ends with you, Varneys. You're like a disease for which there's no cure. You keep coming back. Whenever I think you're finally out of my life, you reappear."

"I'll take that as a compliment. Tenacity and persistence are indispensable qualities in my line of work."

"You know why I'm here."

Varneys laughed. "Oh, my. That didn't take too long did it."

"What are you laughing about?"

Varneys planted his left elbow on his desk and rested his chin on his fist as he looked at Bobby. "I was wondering how long it would take for Christina or Susan to break their promise."

"You had no right to ask my wife to withhold that from me."

"In fact, I wanted her to tell you. I was counting on it."

"What the hell does that mean?"

Varneys let the question hang before he responded. Leaning forward in his chair, he said, "I knew that by exacting the promise, I would add gravitas and credibility to everything that transpired during the meeting I had with them. And I knew that this would guarantee Christina would only tell you if and when your genius manifested itself again and she became worried about what Uhlman said; otherwise there would be no reason for her to tell you something so hurtful. And I also knew that when she told you, you'd come storming into my office." Varneys' smirked. "The whole point was that I wanted to be sure I knew when your intellect was back up to speed and, sure enough, here you are."

"Because of you, Christina and Susan have treated me like I'm a psycho."

Varneys nodded his head in affirmation. "Well, of course, they've treated you that way. Who wouldn't after seeing the videos and hearing Uhlman's analysis." Varneys picked up his laptop and sat down on a chair next to Bobby. He placed the laptop between the two of them and pressed Enter on the keyboard. As the video played, Bobby watched aghast as he saw himself assemble bombs and sabotage his computers, all the while moving robotically, his face expressionless and his eyes vacant. "Shocking, isn't it?" said Varneys as he closed the lid of his laptop.

Bobby shoved his chair back as he jumped up. "I didn't do that. That's not me."

"But it is you, Robert. Clearly, it's you," said Varneys calmly. "Your own wife knows it's you. Your personal assistant of twenty years knows it's you. Anyone who views these videos can see it's you. These are surveillance tapes from your laboratory's security system. The videos are even time-stamped and security-coded. Uhlman said that you would have no recollection of what you did."

Varneys picked up his laptop and sat down at his desk. His hands folded, his posture relaxed, he watched Bobby intently as the great scientist gazed vacantly at the floor. After a few moments, Varneys said, "Uhlman didn't arrive at his full diagnosis and conclusions until he saw the videos. He always thought you had serious issues, particularly a few years ago before the explosion when Susan called me in a panic and I sent him to your lab to see what the hell was going on with you. But the conclusions he relayed to Christina and Susan were based on the videos."

Bobby's forefinger punctuated each of his words. "Why would you would spend months examining surveillance tapes? That's not your job. You're not a prosecutor."

"I don't like loose ends," said Varneys. "The criminal trials were inconclusive. Any attempt on your life is too important for me to be satisfied with inconclusive. My agency failed you twice. Two times you were almost killed on my watch. That doesn't cut it for me."

Sneering, Bobby said, "So it's all about your ego."

Varneys slowly rubbed his hands together as he responded. "I needed to find out if there was someone, not yet apprehended, who had almost succeeded in killing you by blowing up your lab. That person might try again. Prosecutors deal with the past; I deal with the future."

The muscles in Bobby's face drew tight and his voice filled with disdain. "You're so full of shit, Varneys, and you are such an expert liar that I don't know if you even realize when you're lying. You know what you did. Those videos are fake. You concocted them."

Varneys chuckled. "Oh, really. Now I'm a movie producer?"

"You're telling me that your agency doesn't have the expertise to create compromising video footage, and that it's never done that?"

"What the hell is that supposed to mean?"

"It means that I didn't do any of the things in those videos, but you made it look like I did using CGI and computer animation. Just like in the movies—when Superman rockets through the air, Magneto levitates the Golden Gate Bridge and Neo runs up walls and bends his body to dodge bullets. You created something that didn't happen, but it sure looks like it did."

"Believe what you want to believe, Robert," said Varneys as he flicked his hand dismissively. "The videos speak for themselves. You just don't want to accept the fact that you're mentally unstable. And that's putting it charitably."

Bobby's face turned crimson as he rose from his chair, his voice strained. "The truth means nothing to you?"

"Don't lecture me about truth. We sat in your living room and you looked directly at me and Christina while you lied about the Millennium awards. In fact, your entire existence under the Witness Protection Program is a lie. Truth is a moving target, Robert. We all lie sometimes. But lies that are well made are justified by their purpose."

"So, you admit the videos are phony."

"I didn't say that."

"Why are you doing this to me?"

"I'm not doing anything to you, Robert, but I'm very happy that I found the videos."

"Why?"

"Because when I discovered what you had done, I knew I had to tell those closest to you for their own protection. I couldn't let them be blindsided to possible future danger."

"That's it?"

Varneys pressed his hand against his left temple. "The videos also gave me something I needed."

"What? Why?"

"Because you sent me that letter in which you told me that your lab was blown up by a supernatural evil force of supreme power. That letter made me realize I needed insurance."

Bobby looked at Varneys quizzically. "Insurance?"

"Yes, insurance. Insurance against you."

# 19

S TARING AT BOBBY, VARNEYS SLOWLY rolled a pencil between the fingers of his right hand. Leaning in towards him, Varneys said, "When you issued that press release after getting out of the hospital, identifying yourself as Dumpster Baby, you became more than a scientific genius in the eyes of many people. You became a religious figure, a spiritual phenomenon, a symbol. That makes you a very dangerous person in my world." With a sudden twist of his fingers, half of the pencil went flying across the desk.

"You get more twisted with each passing year. What are you talking about?" asked Bobby.

Varneys stretched across his desk, his arms extended in front of him and his shoulders hunched forward. "Robert, I have my hands full every day fighting the evil that I can see and touch. The guys that blow up passenger planes, put poison in reservoirs, build dirty nuclear bombs, launch cyberattacks, sell plutonium to terrorists. What I don't need—and will not tolerate—is having the most revered and trusted man on the planet shoot his mouth off about something that we can't see and we can't do anything about. If you ever decide to go public with the nonsense that you wrote me in that letter, we'll have mass hysteria. Because of who you are, anything you say will be treated as gospel truth. Half the population of the world thinks you're the messiah. I can't risk not being in control of a disruptive force as powerful as you. That supreme evil bullshit that you talk about is a new boogey man, and we don't need a new boogey man. As it is, too much of the world is controlled by religious fanatics. I can't let you create more dysfunction."

Bobby held up his hands. "What I wrote in that letter is true. You just can't accept the reality of what happened that night at the lab. It's too abstract for you—too painful for you to realize that you don't have control—that there are forces out there that are not in your grasp, against which you are impotent. Well, just because you can't control them doesn't mean they don't exist."

Varneys smacked his desk with his open hand and the loud slap caused Bobby to wince. "I don't give a rat's ass if it's true. It's destabilizing to have people think that some supernatural force can destroy their lives. So those videos and Uhlman's report are my insurance policy. If you ever go public—then I have the goods to neutralize you. And if I do that—you can kiss your credibility and future research funding goodbye. You'll be the former genius who went crazy. That's a highly believable narrative."

"So what exactly do you want from me?"

"It's very simple. I want you to do some work for me, and I want you to keep your crazy supernatural ideas to yourself. If you do this, then your reputation and credibility will remain intact. You'll still have time to fulfill Joe Manzini's vision, but you'll fulfill mine, too."

"What kind of work?"

"Don't worry, I'm not going to ask you to build a bomb."

"Well, what is it?"

Varneys walked over to his wall of windows and surveyed the

CIA campus below. "It's a new day, Robert. Boots on the ground, big bombers, nuclear weapons. That's yesterday. Today, it's about nerds sitting in front of computers. Bring your enemies to their knees from ten thousand miles away, without anyone breaking a sweat. Cripple a nation's infrastructure, destroy its communications networks, open its dams, pollute its water, turn off its lights, erase its banking records, crash its stock markets, overload its nuclear reactors... Everything is just a keyboard stroke away. That's the ultimate power."

"And how is this relevant to me?" asked Bobby.

"This country is facing its greatest challenges ever. We are under constant attack. Our cyber guys can't keep up with the hackers in China, North Korea, Iran, Russia—and all the terrorist groups. Our military's computer systems are regularly infiltrated and manipulated. It's not entirely out of the question that a catastrophic event can be triggered remotely by our enemies. Our energy grids, banking facilities and voting machines have been compromised." As Varneys' voice rose in volume, his face reddened. "Even the CIA and NSA have been hacked. It's totally out of control, goddamn it."

"That's all very interesting, but it has nothing to do with me."

Varneys strode over to Bobby's chair and glared down at him. "That's where you're mistaken. You're the only person who can give us the cyber-supremacy we need. It will be easy for you. You will design an undetectable cyber infiltration system that we can employ against hostiles and, on the flip side, you'll protect this country with cyber impregnability that will make Germany's Enigma Code look like a kid's crossword puzzle. You can give this nation the greatest power it ever had."

Bobby's body stiffened. "There are other people who can do

this work. This is not what I do. You know that. And besides, my abilities are a fraction of what they used to be."

"Bull crap," said Varneys as he squeezed Bobby's shoulder and held on. "I have complete faith that you'll get yourself back up to speed, particularly if you stop fucking around and get a new lab. The bottom line is that no one on this planet has your mathematics or cognitive abilities."

Pushing Varneys' hand away, Bobby stood up abruptly. "I'm not going to spend my time fighting your cyber wars. I told you twenty-five years ago and I'll tell you again. I use my abilities to cure diseases, nothing else."

Varneys went back to his massive desk and took his place behind it. Bobby noticed that a vein in Varneys' neck was throbbing. His voice deep and menacing, Varneys made himself clear. "You're in my world now, Robert. Those videos will be the secret that binds us together. If you oppose me, I'll shut you down. You're not going to walk out on me again."

Bobby slammed the door behind him.

# 20

TWO BEEFY CIA AGENTS ESCORTED Bobby out of CIA headquarters and directly into a black SUV that was waiting in the underground garage. The two agents entered the vehicle with Bobby and signaled that the driver should proceed to Reagan Washington National Airport.

Having pulled into a restricted section utilized only by government aircraft, they walked Bobby into a CIA plane and then stood outside until the plane taxied down the runway and safely took off.

Although the flight was short, Bobby wanted to close his eyes and think about everything that had transpired in Varneys' office. To his dismay, the guardian who had been assigned to him for the flight was rather talkative. It was none other than CIA agent Calvin Perrone, with whom Bobby, Christina and Susan shared a great deal of history.

"So, from what I hear… *Seannn*…" Perrone pronounced the name in an exaggerated slow manner, trying his hardest to give the name as many syllables as possible. As he did, he rolled his eyes and grinned. "A little birdie told me that a scientist we both know is feeling a lot better and may soon be back in action. How does Mrs. Whitten feel about that?"

"How Mrs. Whitten feels, Calvin, is between me and her, thank you."

Calvin slapped Bobby on the knee. "Lighten up. You've always been such a tight-ass. You know I like to yank your chain. Anyway, I'm glad to hear that things are getting back to normal."

"Calvin, there's one thing I can say about my life: Nothing in it has ever been normal. It's been a lot of things, but normal isn't one of them."

When Bobby walked into his house, it was all dark, except for a kitchen light. Uncharacteristically, there was no music playing. He looked across the living room and saw Christina sitting at the kitchen table, a small teapot and cup in front of her.

As Bobby approached her, he said, "Sure glad I didn't have to stay over in D.C."

Christina jumped at the sound of Bobby's voice but avoided eye contact with him. "Oh, my God. You startled me. I didn't hear you come in."

"I'm surprised you're home from work. Thursday is your late night at the office," said Bobby.

"I called in sick today."

"You do look a little...pallid." Bobby noticed that Christina's eyes were bloodshot and her eyelids were swollen.

"I'm not actually sick. I just couldn't go in today knowing that you were seeing Varneys."

"Is Susan around?"

"She's in the guest house. She said she has a lot of work to catch up on, but I know she just wanted to be here when you got back from Washington."

Bobby pressed the button on the intercom. "Susan, would you please come in?"

Instead of her usual energetic way of bounding into a room, Susan entered quietly and just nodded to them. Bobby signaled that they should all go into the living room. Christina and Susan sat on the sofa close to each other, their knees almost touching. Bobby positioned himself on the love seat across from them. Susan's hands were tightly clasped together. Christina's hands were pressed hard against her thighs, her fingers flexed.

As Bobby began to speak, he noticed that Christina was rocking back and forth almost imperceptibly. Bobby spoke slowly. "As you know, I met with Varneys today. He showed me the videos." Christina's eyes welled up and Susan lowered her gaze to the floor. "You were right. The videos were terrible."

Susan roughly wiped her right cheek with the back of her hand and inhaled sharply.

Christina pushed herself out of her seat and walked over to Bobby. Sitting down next to him, she hugged him tightly and rested her head against his as she whispered, "I'm so sorry." She kissed him gently as she ran her hand over his auburn hair. "Don't worry. We'll work through this together." Pressing her tear-streaked face against his cheek, she used all her power to keep from crying audibly. After a few moments, the silence in the room was broken by Susan blowing her nose.

Bobby moved to the center of the living room. Locking eyes, first with Christina and then with Susan, he said, "I didn't do any of the things in the videos. Varneys had the Agency create them using CGI."

Susan and Christina exchanged glances but said nothing until the silence became awkward. "So Varneys admitted he created them?" asked Susan.

"No. He denied it, but you know that he's an inveterate liar."

"Isn't it a giant leap to assume Varneys created the videos? What's your basis for that?" asked Susan.

"Why would Varneys have done that?" said Christina. "I don't understand."

"The videos, together with Uhlman's analysis, give him what he needs to destroy my credibility."

"But, why would he want to destroy your credibility?" asked Susan.

"Because he's afraid of what would happen if I ever went public with what I put in my letter to him, so he needs a way to neutralize me by making people think I'm crazy."

"I still don't understand," said Christina. "*Why* did he create the videos?"

"Because he wants to control me. He's using the videos to blackmail me."

Christina's and Susan's eyes met again as they tried to glean the other's thoughts. "Did Varneys admit that?" asked Christina.

"Yes. I mean, no. He didn't admit to creating the videos, but he did say he was very happy he has them and they are his secret weapon against me."

"And Uhlman was in on this, too?" asked Susan.

"He said that Uhlman based his diagnosis on the videos. Uhlman didn't know that the videos were fake, so Varneys lied to him, too."

"I don't know, Bobby. They looked incredibly real," said Susan.

"They certainly do," echoed Christina.

"Well, of course, they look real. If they didn't, they'd be

worthless. But there's more. Aside from wanting me to keep my mouth shut, Varneys also wants me to do work for him. It's like I said—he's using the videos to blackmail me."

"Military work?" asked Christina.

"Not exactly."

"What then?" asked Susan.

"Cyber infiltration and cyber security."

"What are you going to do?" asked Christina.

"I'm going to ignore Varneys completely."

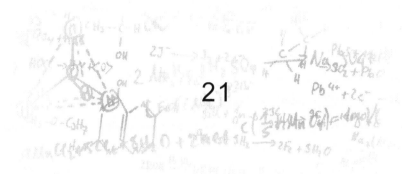

# 21

SIX YEARS AFTER HE MET with Colum McAlister in Istanbul in front of the Ararat Hotel, Aamir Mahmoud stood in the small restroom of one of battle-torn Kobani's only surviving cafés and looked in the mirror. Syria was not agreeing with him. He had lost more than twenty pounds since joining Ansar Jamaat. For the last six years, he and his small staff had worked fourteen-hour days, six days a week, being shuttled from one abandoned laboratory to another in areas occupied by Ansar Jamaat in Iraq, Libya, Syria and Lebanon. Most recently, they worked thirty feet below the ground in the remnants of a Syrian chemical warfare laboratory that the United Nations thought had been fully dismantled years before.

Suffering from some form of dysentery, likely caused by water that was inadequately processed for human consumption, the person staring back at Mahmoud from the mirror was gaunt and sickly. The sclera of his eyes bore a pale yellow tint and his eyebrows and hair were streaked with gray, when only a few years prior they were pitch-black. Mahmoud ran his fingers under his eyes, trying to smooth out the lines and wrinkles that had prematurely aged his appearance. Sighing, he took a deep breath and regretted it immediately as the acrid stench of urinal disinfectant filled his nostrils.

In accordance with the instructions he had received, he entered one of the toilet stalls, dropped his pants and sat on the seat. As decreed by Ansar Jamaat, the doors of the stalls had been removed to ensure that no prohibited activities took place in their confines. When someone new came into the restroom, Mahmoud looked up to see if it was his connection, McAlister's man in Syria, Nizar Khouri.

Mahmoud felt like he was on display and subject to evaluation as men entered and exited the restroom. Ever since he was a boy, he was uneasy in public restrooms. He didn't know where to look and where not to look, and he always felt as if he was being looked at.

Sitting on the toilet seat, Mahmoud gazed down at the floor blankly. There was nothing he could do that would allow him to forget the faces of the endless stream of prisoners who had been delivered to him like lab rats by his Ansar Jamaat compatriots. *How many excruciating deaths have I witnessed? No, I didn't witness them, I caused them. I am no better than the Ansar Jamaat leaders who entertain themselves by coming to my lab to watch the disease ravage the test subjects. I have become their Dr. Mengele.*

The only way Mahmoud could fall asleep at night was to close his eyes and visualize ways of killing himself. But what was the point anyway? Sleep provided him with no refuge from his guilt. It merely delivered him into the purgatory of his nightmares.

Mahmoud knew that if he committed suicide, Ansar Jamaat would quickly replace him and that replacement wouldn't be doing what he was doing: devising a cure. This had proven to be much more difficult and time-consuming than formulating the disease "cocktail".

Hiding his work on the cure from his staff and Ansar Jamaat's leadership, and dissembling so that it seemed to be part of his disease research, was highly stressful and extremely risky.

Shaking his head, a sad smile of recognition manifested on Mahmoud's face as he marveled at how his life had degenerated into a series of ironies that now defined his existence. Gone was his belief in the quest for a caliphate that would bring peace and unity to mankind. In its place was his recognition that the jihadists he had once admired were no more than murderous thugs who reveled in the power that they had created for themselves under the guise of Islamic principles. Ne'er-do-wells, most of whom never held a job, were never respected, never had any money in their pockets and never even had a girlfriend, now wore uniforms, carried flags, brandished weapons, were well fed, paid with regularity and "given" as many women to abuse as they desired. They were the new version of Hitler's Brownshirts. Terrorized townspeople quaked in their presence, curried their favor and genuflected to these societal misfits who cloaked their egotism and greed in the cloth of religious righteousness. They took what they wanted. They raped and enslaved women and sold children to pedophiles. They stole and extorted, just as the Mafia had decades before them. Like gangsters of the past, they ruled by fear and intimidation, but their crimes against human decency set new standards for depravity and hence they were more successful thugs than any of their predecessors.

*I have been duped. I was an idiot. My naïveté has cost so many innocents their lives. I will not be redeemed or forgiven, nor do I deserve to be. I will be condemned on Judgment Day. I have used my abilities to empower these monsters whose conduct defames my God.*

The cure was all that Mahmoud thought about. *It has to work. It has to be perfect. It must.* And so, what Mahmoud was originally doing only because McAlister was blackmailing him, had now become the sole thing he lived for; and the man who Mahmoud had once demonized as a greedy opportunist, was now the person on whom he was depending to mitigate his sins.

It had been more than an hour since Mahmoud had first taken his place in the men's room. Perspiration began to bead on his forehead as he realized that someone might say to the café's manager that a man sitting on the toilet was loitering for an inordinate amount of time, perhaps looking to attract a homosexual liaison. If such a complaint were made, it was likely that the manager would step outside to find the nearest member of Ansar Jamaat so he could report the incident and thereby ingratiate himself to the authorities that controlled the town. This would leave Mahmoud in the unenviable position of having to justify that his prolonged presence in the stall was necessitated by intense stomach upset.

A powerfully built swarthy man with shoulder-length frizzy hair and a beard at least twelve inches long entered the restroom and stood in front of the mirror examining himself for remnants of his lunch. As he picked himself clean of the debris that had found refuge in his outsized whiskers, Nizar Khouri nodded at Mahmoud who then reached into his jacket pocket and retrieved a thick black notebook. Wrapping it in toilet paper so it blended with the used and unused paper refuse that littered the floor of the stall, Mahmoud placed it down gently as he stood and pulled his pants up. The bearded man pushed into the stall and unbuckled his belt, his size-fourteen shoe covering the toilet paper clad notebook just as Mahmoud exited.

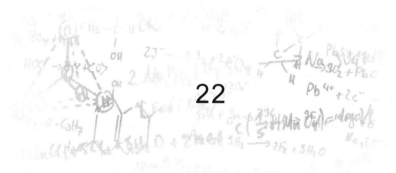

# 22

SIX YEARS AFTER HIS MEETING with Aamir Mahmoud in Istanbul, Colum McAlister was still CEO of Bushings Pharmaceuticals. What he didn't know as he sat on a tufted leather bench in front of an ebony grand piano in his lake-view suite at the Hotel Beau-Rivage in Geneva, Switzerland, was that he had only fifteen months remaining before he would find himself in federal prison serving a nineteen-year sentence. Resting on the music stand of the piano was Mahmoud's black notebook; it held the formula for the disease which he had invented, and the formula, manufacturing instructions and notes from the clinical trials for the cure that he had devised.

McAlister had studied these materials for the last three days. The disease cocktail which Mahmoud had concocted was a fusion of the biological agents which Ansar Jamaat had salvaged during its treks through Iraq, Iran, Libya, Lebanon and Syria, and select purchases made from hidden stockpiles of the former Soviet Union that were available on the black market. Mahmoud combined these with an assortment of other biotoxins and bioengineered viruses and accelerators to create an unidentifiable mixture which increased the virulence and transmissibility of all of the pathogens and gave them immunity to known cures and treatments.

Mahmoud's horrific brew exaggerated the most malevolent features of pneumonic tularemia, smallpox, viral hemorrhagic fever, pneumonic plague and anthrax. Each of these had been designated a Category A biological agent by the U.S. Department of Homeland Security and the Centers for Disease Control and Prevention because they met all of the following criteria:

1. Can be easily disseminated or transmitted
2. Consistently produce the desired effect
3. Are highly contagious
4. Have short and predictable incubation periods
5. Can cause high mortality
6. Will overwhelm health care facilities
7. Will undermine national security by causing mass panic

As described in Mahmoud's papers, the disease could be effectively transmitted using a variety of delivery systems: aerosol spray devices of all types, bombs, missile warheads, grenades, food and water contamination, and person-to-person transmission. It was apparent to McAlister that Mahmoud had created a disease that had the potential to be a pandemic. Ansar Jamaat had succeeded in obtaining a devastating weapon at a fraction of the cost of other weapons capable of mass destruction. Biological weapons are known to be up to two thousand times cheaper than conventional weapons capable of inflicting similar numbers of casualties per square mile, and their production does not require rarefied technical know-how, facilities and materials.

Mahmoud's analyses and clinical trials conclusively corroborated the effectiveness of the cure that McAlister would exclusively own, by virtue of the agreement he had made with Mahmoud in Istanbul. There were only two caveats regarding the cure: Firstly, it was not effective as a preventative vaccine (i.e., it had to be administered after a person contracted the disease); secondly, the drug must be administered prior to the appearance of pustules on the infected person's skin; once pustules were present, it was too late and there was an over ninety-five-percent likelihood of death. Mahmoud's clinical tests on hundreds of Ansar Jamaat prisoners showed that the pustules usually appeared between the eighteenth and twenty-first days of being infected with the disease.

McAlister was in Geneva to solidify his position as the patent owner of the cure, and to make arrangements through his Swiss attorneys for the appointment of Schlumberger Foch, a small but venerable Swiss pharmaceutical company, to be the "public face" of the cure and its main manufacturer and distributor. Of course, this assumed that the drug would be needed. Perhaps it wouldn't be and McAlister was wasting his time. But McAlister was an astute student of human nature and he was confident that sooner or later, the jihadists would release the disease, despite the assurances that they had given to Mahmoud.

In his arrangements with Schlumberger Foch, McAlister reserved the right to approve the pricing and the designation of other manufacturers and distributors of the cure, should demand for the drug outpace Schlumberger's ability to fill the orders itself in a timely fashion. This would give McAlister the power to anonymously punish or reward, as he saw fit, the other CEOs in the Big Pharma cartel, and to personally profit through either long- or short-leveraged trading of their companies' stock, since only he would know in advance which companies would be allowed to participate in the financial cornucopia of selling the cure.

McAlister was particularly pleased that the cure was not administered in a single dose; instead, in order to be effective, it required a daily regimen of five treatments per day for four weeks. "Sounds awfully expensive," he said to himself as he sipped from a crystal snifter filled with Louis XIII cognac.

The arrangements which McAlister had made were methodically designed to ensure that his ownership, control and financial interests in the cure were hidden in a maze of off-shore companies that were incorporated in jurisdictions that guaranteed anonymity and opacity. It was essential to him that no one would know that he was competing with Bushings in violation of the restrictive covenants in his Bushings employment agreement; nor did McAlister ever want to be asked how he came to own a cure for a disease that was created by jihadists, and how he had the cure in his possession before the disease ever saw the light of day. An added benefit to this impenetrable corporate structure was the avoidance of all income taxes, and immunity from creditors and litigants.

As McAlister centered himself on the piano bench and pulled his monogrammed shirtsleeves up beyond his wrists, he smiled. *Everyone will have to come to me to get their fix. I finally own a disease.*

He closed his eyes and began to play. For someone who taught himself late in life, he was quite an accomplished pianist, but his playing sounded better if you didn't look at his hands, which were the heavy gnarled hands of a pugilist, not a musician. "I'll be the best-paid savior the world has ever known," McAlister murmured to himself.

As the melodious tones of the grand piano filled the hotel suite's living room, the song that McAlister was playing, "If I Ruled the World," seemed like an appropriate choice.

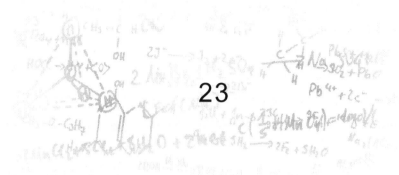

# 23

GOOD HARBOR BEACH IN GLOUCESTER, Massachusetts, is just a ten-minute drive from the Whiten's Annisquam house. On its western side, the beach is bordered by acres of pristine sand dunes anchored against the wind by profuse growths of tall sea grass that provide a nesting place for sandpipers. When the ocean recedes, numerous shallow tidal pools appear, as if placed on the beach by a higher power to safely accommodate the tiniest human visitors. To the southeast, the colossal glacial boulders of Bass Rocks stand guard, silent witnesses to the ice age that stranded them there. And to the southwest, the surf gives way to what the locals refer to as "the creek"—an immense tidal pool traversed by a wooden bridge from which kids swing on frayed ropes before jumping into the clear swirling water. Good Harbor Beach was Bobby's sanctuary year-round. Even in the winter, he walked its sands.

On a Sunday morning in early November, Bobby and Christina strolled together on the hard-packed sand, thirty feet from the water's edge. Bobby wore black jeans, tan leather construction boots and a bulky blue plaid flannel shirt that was thickly padded for extra warmth, its collar pulled up against the wind. Dressed in a beige woolen poncho, blue paisley silk scarf and flat-soled high leather boots, Christina leaned in towards him as they walked, Bobby's right arm around her waist.

"Why do you dress like a lumberjack? I know you think you're a rugged outdoors guy, but you're actually not. I knew a few guys like that, and you're not one of them," she said with a chuckle as she gave him a peck on the cheek. Bobby playfully squeezed her closer to him.

"Let's move near the dunes. It's getting chilly," said Christina, as she guided him towards a sheltered area. They sat down on the soft dry sand, the tall grasses behind them. Bobby gazed out at the ocean, letting his eyes relax and closing them halfway so that the glittering rays of sunlight on the water took the shape of thousands of intersecting diamonds.

Christina leaned into Bobby. "I've been thinking a lot about everything that's happened since you got out of the hospital."

"What do you mean?" asked Bobby.

"It's been a roller-coaster ride. And you know, I'm not big on amusement parks." Bobby nodded. "When you came out of a coma, and all those neurologists said your genius intellect was gone, I'll be honest with you—I was very happy. I thought we'd finally have a chance for a normal life raising a family. Do you remember how many times before the explosion I asked you to quit research because it was ruining your health and killing our marriage?"

"Of course, I remember."

"So, when it looked like your genius was gone, I figured that no one would try to kill you anymore, and you'd also be rid of your demons because "it" would leave you alone. The Witness Protection Program was supposed to facilitate our new life. When we moved to Annisquam, it looked like we were on our way. But then I was told that your genius wasn't gone. It was just waiting to resurface. Next came the news that you had blown up your lab. Turn the page again. The videos are bullshit, which is fantastic. But now it looks like our life together will go back to the way it was before the explosion."

"Don't worry. It's not going to be like it used to be. You'll see. I'll be different."

Christina shook her head. "That's not the point I'm trying to make. All of this got me thinking back to my childhood. You know, Bobby, we never really talked about it much. You're aware of the facts, but we've never spoken about my feelings. Do you know what it was like for me back then?"

Bobby began to scratch his hand nervously. "Not really."

Christina took a deep breath before continuing. "I was a thing to my stepfather. A thing to be used. He laughed at me when I would beg him to stop. He told me I was his little whore. I was nine years old, Bobby. Sometimes as I got a bit older, my body would betray me and do things to make him think I was liking it. I hated myself for that. I didn't know why it happened. He told me I should thank him. That only *he* knew what I needed—and that my mother didn't know how bad I was." Christina's eyes glistened with tears. Bobby pulled her close against him.

After a moment, Christina broke the embrace and sat up straight, looking toward the sea. "When I got pregnant at thirteen, I wanted to die. I knew that he wanted me to breed another for him to abuse. Maybe a boy, this time—it didn't matter to him. He owned me. His friends would snicker when they saw me. I could swear he told them about me. I was nothing. I wanted one thing. I wanted to die."

Christina stopped talking and stared down at the sand. "The

pregnancy got difficult very early. I began to hemorrhage badly. I had stopped eating. I weighed eighty pounds at five-foot-seven when I had the abortion. I tried to kill myself twice in the next few months."

Bobby's hands were clenched tight and his head was bowed. "My God…" he said softly.

Christina lifted Bobby's chin and looked directly into his eyes, which were now reservoirs of pain. "There's a reason I'm telling you all of this. My stepfather destroyed who I was. He took away my identity. He subsumed me, and made me into what he wanted me to be. If I try to stop you from being who you are, from doing what you need to do—what you were put here to do, then I am him. In my own way, I'm crushing you under my weight like he used to crush me. As much as I love playing house with you in Annisquam, I see how it's suffocating you. I won't do that. And I won't be my mother and pretend that I don't see it in your eyes every day."

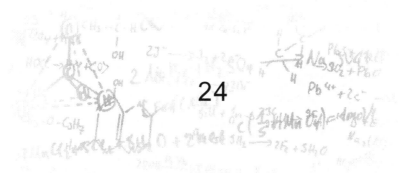

# 24

TAKING HIS SEAT ACROSS FROM Colum McAlister in the prison visitor's room, Andrew Sinclair looked forlorn. Even before McAlister had been incarcerated, Sinclair found meeting with him unpleasant, but now it was almost unbearable. Because he was junior to the other partners at his firm, he was assigned the task of prison visits. In actuality, Sinclair always found it unsettling to visit any client in prison because, more often than not, the location of the meeting underscored the failure of the legal representation.

"What a pleasure to see you again, Andy," said McAlister.

"I didn't feel comfortable giving you this information over the telephone," replied Sinclair.

"Uh-oh. Sounds like that will increase my legal bills. As I recall, your firm charges for travel time at its full hourly rate. So I'm being charged nine hundred fifty dollars an hour while you sit in traffic talking on the phone to another client who you're also billing." McAlister laughed. "Nice work if you can get it."

Sinclair blushed. "You focus on the wrong things, Colum. What's important is that I got an answer for you about Austin's lab. You have no idea how hard it was to get this."

"I'm sure it was very time-consuming," replied McAlister sarcastically.

Sinclair leaned towards McAlister and lowered his voice to just above a whisper. "Austin doesn't have a lab yet, but the scuttlebutt is that he may soon start one up."

McAlister's eyes sparkled. "That's just what I was hoping to hear. Then I'm not too late. I need your assistance."

"For what?" asked Sinclair.

"Your firm has a large trusts and estate department, correct?" Sinclair nodded affirmatively. "And I'm sure that your firm acts as trustee for certain estates in which money has been bequeathed to general charitable causes, with dispersion to be made in the trustee's discretion as to the manner in which the money should be used. Correct?" Sinclair nodded again. "I need you to tell your partners who act as trustees that Austin needs a new lab. You can explain that this is how you and your partners can atone for representing a scumbag like me who did such terrible things to the great man. And now that your firm has just merged with that thousand-lawyer behemoth, Proctor, Goodwin & Melson, you can bet the new guys will think it's wonderful. Lawyers love being charitable with other people's money."

"What are you up to, Colum?"

McAlister held his hands up as if he were an evangelist. "I'm just being a good guy. And you're going to ensure that this funding happens."

Sinclair shook his head adamantly. "No, I don't want anything to do with this. I don't know why you continue to be obsessed with Dr. Austin, but I'm not getting involved."

His face hardening, McAlister glared at Sinclair. "You'll be as involved as I want you to be. I could have chopped years off my sentence if I had ratted you and your partners out on the insider-trading tips I gave you guys. But I kept my mouth shut. I didn't do that out of the goodness of my heart."

Sinclair looked unmoved. "You'd have a hard time proving anything now."

"Perhaps. But what will you do for a living after your firm fires you and you get disbarred?"

"What are you talking about?"

"You tell me. What do you think will happen when your partners see the videos of your escapades in Manilla? You remember. The little side trip you took after the Bushings meetings in Tokyo, when you slipped away to the Philippines to have a sex holiday with child prostitutes, and you whipped one so badly with your belt that you had to pay his parents five thousand dollars to keep quiet?"

"You have videos? You fucking bastard. Your local director arranged that trip for me."

The smallest of smiles crossed McAlister's face as he waved his hand dismissively." Lord knows what your divorce will cost you. There are some things that wives just find difficult to forgive."

# 25

THE MAILING ADDRESS FOR BOBBY'S foundation, the Edith and Peter Austin Foundation for Medical Research, was in care of Robert Walterberg, Dean of Graduate Studies of Tufts University in Medford, Massachusetts. Every week, Susan would drive to Tufts in her minivan and pick up not only the foundation's mail, but also the boxes of mail that arrived there for Bobby since he was listed as a professor emeritus of the University.

Sorting through the foundation's mail, Susan came upon a letter from Andrew Sinclair's law firm, Proctor, Goodwin & Melson, that was addressed to her as the Foundation's director:

> Dear Director Ryder:
>
> Please permit the undersigned to introduce you to the law firm of Proctor, Goodwin & Melson.
>
> We are a U.S. law firm with offices in more than twenty states and eleven countries outside of North America. I am proud to say that in each of the last five years, the firm has been the recipient of numerous awards for outstanding practice in diverse fields of law, including commercial

litigation, mergers and acquisitions, governmental regulation, and trusts and estates.

In our capacity as trustee for certain of our estate clients, the responsibility falls on us, acting in a fiduciary capacity, to implement and effectuate the generally expressed charitable intentions of our deceased clients, by disbursing funds accordingly.

The extraordinary work of Dr. Robert James Austin was much admired by many of our estate clients. It is, therefore, our pleasure to advise you that we have discretionary funds available to purchase and outfit a new laboratory for Dr. Austin, in accordance with his specifications, to replace the facility that was so tragically destroyed. In this regard, we can offer two options. The first is to provide the Edith and Peter Austin Foundation with the cash resources necessary to purchase or build a state-of-the-art laboratory; the second option is to donate and deed to the foundation an existing property that is owned by one of the estates for which we act as trustee. In regard to the latter option, please be advised that we have existing properties at our disposal in most states and in certain foreign countries that may be highly suitable, so if you advise us where the foundation wishes to establish the new laboratory, we can review our inventory.

I am certain that the resources at our disposal will be sufficient to meet Dr. Austin's requirements.

On behalf of the firm and the estates whose largesse we are fortunate to represent, let me say that it is a great honor and privilege to have the opportunity to assist your foundation and Dr. Austin in this manner. I look forward to hearing from you at your earliest convenience.

Very truly yours,
Melvin Goodwin
Managing Partner, Proctor, Goodwin & Melson, PC

Susan read the letter several times. Being presented with properties that the law firm's clients owned would be a time saver, but Susan knew that this option was not viable. Taking a cash bequest from the law firm was the necessary route for security reasons, so as to preserve the secrecy of the new lab's address—and hence Bobby's whereabouts.

As in the past, the lab needed to be no more than thirty miles away from Tufts University so that travel between the two locations didn't become burdensome. From Susan's experience in setting up the prior lab, she knew that seclusion and security were essential and, that all things considered, a residential property that could be legally zoned as a research facility would be preferable.

———————

Susan combed the real estate listings for several weeks, but didn't find anything suitable, so she took to driving around the communities between Annisquam and Boston, hoping to come upon a prospect that wasn't listed online. One cold rainy afternoon, she drove the full length of Ocean Road in Manchester. Coming to a Dead End sign, she was in the process of making a three-point turn when she noticed a row of boulders lined up across what appeared to be the remnants of a dirt path, now overgrown with tall weeds.

Susan pulled her car to the side and got out. Walking past the huge rocks, she ignored a No Trespassing sign and proceeded down what remained of the road, which was almost completely obscured by spindly sumac trees and thick growths of poison ivy entwined with a thorny underbrush. She pulled up the hood on her rain poncho, tucked her sweatpants into her tall boots, and pushed through the sumac branches as she trudged forward. *I don't know where the hell I'm going, but I've got to see what this is.*

After walking about a quarter of a mile, she came upon a small, turreted gatehouse in bad repair. It stood to the side of a pair of rusty, crooked twelve-foot-high wrought-iron gates. With difficulty, she pushed the gates open just wide enough for her to squeeze through. Susan continued her march until she saw a rambling old mansion in the distance, its walls almost entirely covered by vegetation. Susan tried to survey where she was.

The rain had subsided and given way to a fog that prevented her from gaining a complete picture of the terrain, so she continued to walk the land as far as it would go, first to her left and then to her right. *Oh, my God. I'm on a peninsula.* It was now apparent to her that the overgrown path on which she had walked was the only entrance and egress to this craggy headland which was surrounded by the Atlantic Ocean.

Walking behind the mammoth house, she saw that it was built on a high bluff above Manchester's rocky shoreline. The ledge on which it stood extended only a few hundred feet from the building's rear veranda, before dropping off precipitously to the sea below. "Now *this* could be interesting," she said to herself.

The next day, Susan went to the Manchester Town Hall to look up the property records. She found out that the seven-acre, narrow promontory on which the house stood was called Gull Island. The house was constructed in 1919 by Emanuel Rice, a prominent Boston investment banker who named it Wheatleigh Point. Fearful of fire, since his prior house had burned to the ground, Rice used the latest steel-frame construction methods when building Wheatleigh Point. The brick-and-limestone mansion was designed in the Jacobean style with such distinctive architectural features as three-story mullioned stained-glass windows, turrets and an octagonal tower crowned by a copper dome.

After a series of owners, Wheatleigh Point was purchased by its current owner, MRH Development Corp., which had filed plans to tear down the house and build forty-two condominium apartments. MRH had become mired in litigation with the Manchester zoning board, which refused to give MRH a zoning variance. To make matters worse for MRH, the influential New England Historical Society had filed *amicus curia* briefs with the court, in opposition to MRH's development plans. The property records indicated that First Boston Bank held a four-million-dollar mortgage, which was personally guaranteed by the owner of MRH. The annual real estate taxes on the property were a staggering one hundred and fifteen thousand dollars.

Susan's research on MRH indicated that it was a small Rhode Island real estate company which had had more failed projects than successful ones, and that its owner, Michael Henredon, had filed for personal bankruptcy twice over the course of two decades. Her further research showed that when prior owners of the property had tried to sell it to private schools or nursing homes, the zoning board had refused clearances based on inadequate access to Gull Island for emergency vehicles, which was deemed to be a safety hazard.

It was apparent to Susan that Wheatleigh Point was what is referred to in the real estate business as a "white elephant." The inability to develop it for commercial purposes and the poor condition of the house for use as a residence, coupled with the punishingly high real estate taxes made it ripe for a distress sale to Bobby's foundation, which was exempt from those taxes as a registered charitable institution.

Susan wasted no time calling Michael Henredon. "Hello, Mr. Henredon. I'm calling about a property that your company owns in Manchester, Massachusetts. I believe it's called Wheatleigh Point.

"Yes. What about it?"

"I work for a charitable organization that might have a use for the property."

Henredon cleared his throat before responding. "Wheatleigh Point is not for sale. I'm close to breaking ground on a very lucrative condominium project."

Susan chuckled. "Sure doesn't look that way from the court records. It's pretty clear you'll never get the zoning variance."

"We've got great lawyers. When a property is that unique, you have to be willing to fight the long fight."

"I can only imagine the pressure your company must be under, having to pay interest on the First Boston loan all these years, and those horrendous real estate taxes. Frankly, I'm surprised the bank hasn't called the loan. You know how antsy banks get with a property that has a history like that."

Henredon cleared his throat again. "I'll admit it's a tricky situation. Manchester is a finicky little town, with a small-minded zoning board. I don't know what your organization does, but I can tell you that my company isn't the first one to be given the cold shoulder."

"Can you arrange for me to inspect the interior of the place?"

"Why would I do that if I don't want to sell?"

"Mike, you and I both know that it's not necessarily going to be your decision. I spoke to Gertrude Aarons at First Boston and she told me that they've already entertained offers, but they didn't pull the trigger because the offers were contingent on zoning variances and financing. My offer would be all cash and no conditions. If you and I work together, I think we could convince the bank to accept a 'short sale' and write off their loss, so MRH can walk away with some money in its pocket. I can't imagine you coming out better on this property than that. And God forbid, if some trespassing kids fall off one of the cliffs at Wheatleigh, you'll find yourself in personal bankruptcy again."

In the daylight, it was evident that the exterior of the house and the grounds had been neglected for years, having been owned by one speculator after another. But the location was ideal from a security point of view. With only one gated access point off a quiet road, Wheatleigh Point was perched on the far end of the rocky heights of Gull Island. Its wild shore landscape gave way to jagged cliffs that dropped at an almost ninety-degree angle to the ocean.

When Henredon opened the door to the house, Susan walked through the paneled entrance hall into a monumental two-story great room that was sixty feet long and forty feet wide, with an exposed-beam ceiling that was thirty feet high. A grand staircase featuring an elaborately carved wooden balustrade portraying the symbols of the zodiac began in the center of the room and rose on two sides to a balcony. Adjoining the great room was a dining room large enough to seat twenty, with carved limestone fireplaces at each end.

As Susan continued her tour, her overwhelming impression was that Wheatleigh was cavernous and gloomy. She also knew that Bobby would have a problem with the baronial architecture. Nevertheless, it was clear to her that Wheatleigh had infinite possibilities for conversion to a laboratory, and that its size would accommodate years of expansion, no matter how much computer equipment and personnel were ever required.

One feature of the property that she found intriguing was a free-standing four-story watchtower made of rough-hewn fieldstones. The tower was positioned several hundred feet away from the mansion, standing precipitously close to the edge of the furthermost cliff. Its top story was clad in wood and had large windows facing the sea, which gave it the appearance of a small cabin; it could only be accessed by climbing a steep winding stone staircase within the tower. Henredon told Susan that the original owner of Wheatleigh had built the structure as an observatory and personal retreat, and had referred to it in his journals as his "thinking space."

Armed with almost one hundred cell phone photographs of Wheatleigh and Gull Island, Susan approached Bobby with her discovery. "Don't worry, once we pull the weeds off the house's exterior and give it some TLC, it will be so warm and inviting you'll love it. Some fresh paint and new light fixtures will go a long way."

Bobby scrunched up his nose. "Haven't I seen this place in a Frankenstein movie?"

"The ocean air will do you good. Just don't fall off the cliff."

"I don't know, Susan. It's kind of pretentious, isn't it? At least my last lab looked like a bunker at Normandy."

"Bobby, that's how they built these places a hundred years ago. You're using it as a lab, not as your vacation villa, and we're getting a really good buy, *and* it's impregnable from a security point of view."

"It's huge, isn't it?"

Susan nodded. "I have a feeling we're going to need a really big place this time around."

# 26

I T DIDN'T TAKE SUSAN LONG to negotiate with First Boston and Michael Henredon. Both parties were relieved to have Wheatleigh Point off their books. Susan arranged for Proctor, Goodwin & Melson to wire transfer the purchase price directly to the foundation which, in turn, paid for the property. The law firm was not advised of Wheatleigh Point's address. Susan also prevailed upon the Manchester authorities to ensure that there were no media reports of the sale, and that the transaction in the town's property records was kept confidential and sealed.

But Colum McAlister had long ago learned to follow the money. Through Andrew Sinclair, he obtained the bank wire transfer details that Proctor, Goodwin & Melson used to pay the foundation. Armed with the banking information, a private investigator with hacking abilities had little difficulty ascertaining that the foundation made payments to First Boston and MRH. Once the investigator knew that MRH received funds from the foundation, an examination of MRH's recent property holdings on its website indicated only three possible prospects for a laboratory. The correctness of McAlister's choice among these was confirmed by a one sentence mention in the legal notices section of the *Manchester Herald* indicating that MRH and the local zoning board had agreed to mutually dismiss the current litigation between them pertaining to Wheatleigh Point.

Over the ensuing weeks, the trail of payments by the foundation to local contractors that were hired to make repairs on the mansion provided the final corroboration of the new laboratory's address.

Now that McAlister knew where Bobby would be working, it would be a simple matter to have him tailed at the end of a work day when he headed home to his family. Colum McAlister had defeated WITSEC. He would soon have Robert James Austin and his entire family within his grasp.

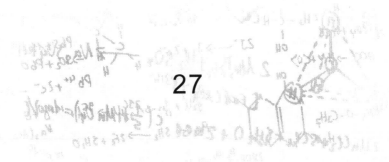

# 27

A S BOBBY SAT AT THE kitchen table drinking a cup of coffee, an article on the front page of the *Boston Globe* caught his attention. The headline read, "Jonathan Bick Nominated for Attorney General". The sub-head said, "Bick, Key Prosecutor in Robert James Austin Trials, Likely to Be Approved by Senate."

Bobby was in a coma during the prosecution of Colum McAlister and the RASI defendants in the criminal trials related to the destruction of his Boston apartment, his laboratory and the attempts on his life. After his recovery, he had no interest in the prosecutions. But as he read the lengthy article in the *Globe*, he was stunned by the following sentence:

> Among other achievements in the prosecution of these crimes, Bick obtained the conviction of Colum McAlister, former CEO of Bushings Pharmaceuticals, for industrial and cyber espionage arising out of McAlister's long-term hacking of Dr. Austin's laboratory computers.

"Holy crap!" yelled Bobby as he scrambled to look up the

phone number for Bick's office at the U.S. Justice Department in Manhattan.

"U.S. Attorney's Office, Southern District of New York. How may I help you?" asked the receptionist.

"Please put me through to Jonathan Bick's office."

"Hold on, please," responded the receptionist.

"Jonathan Bick's office. How may I help you?"

"My name is Robert Austin and I need to speak with Mr. Bick. It's an urgent matter."

"I'm sorry. I didn't hear you clearly. What's your name?"

"Robert James Austin."

"Really. I don't think so, sir. Please identify yourself properly. Mr. Bick is a very busy man."

"This isn't a crank call. Mr. Bick prosecuted cases involving me and I need to speak with him, please."

Bobby was placed on hold for so long that he was about to hang up and try calling again, thinking that he had been disconnected. Finally, a sonorous baritone voice laced with a patrician Beacon Hill accent said, "This is Jonathan Bick. To whom am I speaking?"

"Thank you for taking my call, Mr. Bick. This is Robert James Austin."

When Bick heard Bobby identify himself, the tone of his voice brightened. "Dr. Austin, what a pleasure it is to speak with you. After all the work I did on the trials, I feel like I know you, but, of course, we've never met or even had the opportunity to speak. How can I be of assistance?"

"If you don't mind, I'd prefer to speak with you in person. This concerns a matter of great importance to me. I'm happy to come to your office in New York, unless you're going to be in the Boston area soon."

"Since you're a participant in WITSEC, I'd prefer to meet you in a more anonymous location. I have use of an office on the twelfth floor of the JFK Federal Building in Boston on Sudbury Street. There is no sign on the door of the office, just the number 1219. Does this Thursday at 3 p.m. work for you?"

"Perfect. I really appreciate your taking the time."

———————————

The JFK Federal Building in Boston is comprised of two steel, concrete and glass rectangular towers designed by famed architect Walter Gropius who is credited with promulgating Modernist design principles. Perhaps revolutionary in 1966, when the buildings were completed, to Bobby's eyes they were simplistic sterile structures that had become anachronistic over the decades.

When Bobby got out of the elevator, he walked down a long hallway until he came to 1219. The door was locked. He knocked three times and after a moment, the door was partially opened and he heard a woman's voice say, "Please come in." When he entered the small reception area, he was greeted by an attractive woman of Asian heritage. "Welcome, Mr. Whitten. Please make yourself comfortable. Mr. Bick will be with you as soon as possible."

A few minutes later, Jonathan Bick walked out of the office adjacent to the reception area. Impeccably dressed in a dark blue Paul Stuart pinstriped suit, starched white shirt and striped tie, he extended his hand which Bobby grasped. "It's an honor to meet you, Dr. Austin."

"Thank you for everything you've done on my behalf. And for taking the time to meet with me today."

Bick led Bobby into the office, which was sparsely furnished and devoid of any decoration. As Bobby scanned the bare space, Bick knew what he was thinking. "This isn't my office. It's a shared space that I use when I'm in Boston and I need to have meetings that are off the radar. Given your WITSEC situation and your notoriety, I thought that this was an appropriate venue for our discussion."

Bobby nodded. "Of course. Makes perfect sense."

"So, Dr. Austin, what's on your mind?"

"I was reading an article in the *Boston Globe* about you. Is it true that Bushings Pharmaceutical was hacking my computers?"

"Yes. They had feeds from your mainframes to their servers, so they simultaneously received and copied everything. They did this for years in an attempt to steal any breakthroughs you came up with."

Bobby's eyes gleamed. "That's fantastic. That's the best news I've heard since I got out of the hospital."

"How so?" asked Bick.

"Because just before the explosion went off in my lab, I had broken the code on AIDS. I had a cure in my hands. I scribbled notes in my journal, but the fire destroyed too much of it, and the blasts destroyed my computers. But the Bushings servers will have all my work, not only on that day, but leading up to it. If I can get access to those drives, I'll have the cure."

Bick looked glum. "Unfortunately, that's not going to happen."

"Why not?" asked Bobby.

"At Colum McAlister's trial, I questioned Steven Denufrio, the director of Bushings' IT department, under oath. He said that on the morning after your lab exploded, he received a phone call directly from McAlister ordering him to permanently destroy all the data that was ever hacked from your lab. Denufrio had a clear recollection of the call because that was the only time he had ever spoken to McAlister in all the years he worked at Bushings."

Raking his fingers through his hair, Bobby said, "Usually,

deleted materials can be recovered from servers or hard drives by a forensic specialist. It's done all the time. In fact, the government is particularly good at it."

"You're right. But McAlister knew that, too. Denufrio testified that McAlister instructed him to hire the best forensics technician he could find to ensure that no traces were left and no recovery or reconstruction of the data was possible. Denufrio hired Skip Waterberry, a retiree from the FBI's forensic information technology investigation unit. Waterberry did his job well. When I subpoenaed the servers and hard drives, and had the FBI and Homeland Security examine them, they were clean. None of your data was there."

"Why did McAlister do that?"

"To cover his tracks. He knew that it would come out that he was the architect of the hacking, so he wanted to be sure that there was no evidence. Unfortunately for him, Denufrio's testimony was all I needed to get a conviction."

Bobby stared blankly at the floor. "I can't believe it. Those copies were all I needed."

"I'm sorry."

"Did you also question Waterberry at the trial?"

"No. I had everything I needed from Denufrio. He confirmed that McAlister instituted the hacking program and then ordered the destruction of the evidence."

"Is it possible for us to speak to Waterberry now?"

"I suppose so, but why?"

"I just need to know what he did and how he did it. Maybe he can tell us something that could possibly allow us to retrieve the information."

A text came in on Bick's cell phone and as he glanced at it, he seemed distracted. "I'm sorry. I have an emergency I have to attend to. "Give me a few days. I'll get Waterberry in here."

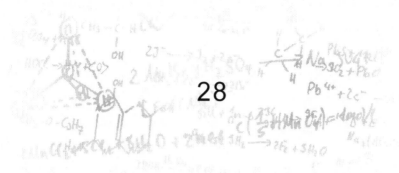

# 28

NOW FIFTY-SIX YEARS OLD, SKIP Waterberry looked like he had played defense on his high school football team. While time had fattened him, he still had a formidable physical presence, but what most distinguished him were his highly-animated hazel eyes that darted from one point of focus to another in seemingly random fashion. There was something about his face that gave the impression that he was guileless and jocular, perhaps somewhat simple in the intelligence department, but this had served him well as subjects of his investigations routinely underestimated him. One of the FBI's leading experts in computer forensics, Waterberry elected early retirement from the bureau so that he could pursue a more lucrative career in the private sector.

When Waterberry entered Bick's office in the JFK Federal Building, he shook Bick's hand vigorously and looked at him like he was a celebrity. "Let me congratulate you, sir. It looks pretty darn certain that you'll be the next Attorney General of the United States."

"Thank you, Mr. Waterberry. Do you mind if I call you Skip? We're all friends in this room." Bick motioned towards Bobby who was sitting on the sofa. "That's my assistant. I appreciate your coming in today to talk with us. We have a few questions regarding a job you did a while ago over at Bushings Pharmaceuticals. Do you recall?"

"Oh, yeah. I was very pleased. They paid me top dollar. Twenty thousand dollars, to be exact. I'm not going to forget that one."

"So, what exactly did you do for Bushings?"

"The usual. I do it for a lot of companies. I sanitize their computer systems. I delete materials in such a way that they are gone forever. I'm the magician who makes things disappear. It's harder than you might think. To do it right, that is. No litigant or governmental authority has ever been able to recover what I've deleted. That's why I get paid what I do."

"Do you remember anything unusual about the job? Were you told what materials you were deleting?"

"I never know what I'm deleting. That's part of the protocol. That way I can never be called upon to testify about the destruction, since I don't know what I'm destroying."

Bobby's face was ashen as he looked at Waterberry. It was clear to him that Waterberry knew his craft all too well.

Bick began to massage the pencil in his hands as he walked around the room. "Skip, think back. Was there anything unusual that happened in relation to this job? Anything that you can recall?"

Skip's forehead creased as he leaned into his hand. After a moment he said, "Well, there is just one thing. When I first got the call from the director of the Bushings IT department, he told me about the project and then said I had to call the CFO to discuss my fee. He said the CFO already knew what I was supposed to do, but fee approval was in his hands."

"Do you remember the CFO's name?" asked Bick.

"I'd remember it if I heard it again, but I can't otherwise recall."

"Was it Martin Turnbull?"

Skip smiled broadly. "That's it. Weird name."

"What happened when you spoke to Turnbull?"

"He told me he thought my fee was way too high. That it was double what it should be, but he'd approve it if I added something to the job."

"And what was the addition?"

"He wanted me to make him a copy of all of the files I was going to delete, and to personally deliver them to him at his home on portable hard drives."

"Anything else?" asked Bick.

"He told me that this was a confidential matter and that it had to be done discretely so that nobody saw what I was doing and I couldn't tell anyone."

"Didn't you think that was strange?"

"Not at all. You'd be surprised how many times someone wants secret copies of deleted materials."

Bobby jumped up from the sofa. "So this guy Turnbull has functional copies of everything that you were asked to destroy?" Skip nodded his head affirmatively.

As soon as Waterberry left the office, Bobby said to Bick, "We've got to find Martin Turnbull."

"That's not possible," replied Bick.

"Why?"

"Because Martin Turnbull no longer exists."

"He died?" asked Bobby.

Bick smiled. "No Robert. He's in WITSEC. I put him in the program in return for his testimony against McAlister."

# 29

THE NEXT DAY, JONATHAN BICK flew to Casper, Wyoming, the city in which Martin Turnbull and his family had been relocated under WITSEC. Turnbull's new name was Jeremy Miller and the program had gotten him a job as a senior CPA in a large local firm. Bobby had wanted to travel with Bick, but he explained that wasn't permissible as it would compromise the integrity of Turnbull's new identity.

It was 9:00 p.m. by the time Bick's rental car pulled up to a large, brick, ranch house on Coates Road in one of the most prosperous suburban neighborhoods of Casper.

Walking up the long stone path that traversed a perfectly manicured front lawn of at least a quarter of an acre, Bick muttered to himself, "Looks like Turnbull isn't feeling any pain in his new life." Bick stood in front of the oversized mahogany entrance doors and rang the bell. After a few moments, one of the doors opened slightly. Martin Turnbull peered out, holding a tumbler of scotch in his right hand, his face as oily and bloated as Bick had remembered.

"Hello, Martin. You're looking well. I guess being a Wyomingite is agreeing with you," said Bick.

It took Turnbull a moment to affix a smile on his face. "Mr. Bick. You're the last person I ever expected to see on my doorstep. Is everything okay?" Bick stepped forward and put his left hand on the door. It was apparent he wanted to enter the house. Hesitating long enough for it to become awkward, Turnbull finally said, "Oh, of course, come in."

"I apologize for not calling first, but I'm on a very tight schedule and something urgent has come up. I hope you understand," said Bick.

A female voice echoed through the house. "Martin, who's at the door this time of night?"

Turning his head in the direction of the kitchen, Turnbull yelled back to his wife, Laura, "Just a lawyer that handles some client matters for the firm. Something's come up."

As Turnbull's blood pressure began to rise, his face and neck took on a reddish hue. He led Bick through the spacious living room and into his office in the back of the house. Turnbull motioned for Bick to take a seat on the sofa, as he sat down on a chair opposite it. "I'm just so shocked to see you. Is there a problem of some kind? Did crazy McAlister hire a hit man or something?"

Bick said nothing and just stared at Turnbull, his azure eyes drilling into him. Turnbull began to shift in his seat, his corpulent body spilling over the chair's side arms.

"Would you like a drink or something to eat?" asked Turnbull, his voice shaky.

Without breaking his focus on Turnbull, Bick said, "I don't understand you. I gave you what you wanted and you fucked me. Why did you think that was a good idea?"

"What are you talking about? I never did any—"

Bick cut Turnbull off mid-sentence and stood up, his six-foot-four-inch frame towering over Turnbull. Glaring down at him he said, "You had Skip Waterberry, the forensics expert, make copies of the Austin lab data for you before it was deleted from Bushings' servers." The color drained from Turnbull's face. "Keeping that information from me is all I need to revoke your immunity agreement, kick you and your family out of WITSEC and begin prosecutions against you. We had a deal and you broke it!" bellowed Bick.

Surprised by the loud voices she heard coming from the den, Laura knocked on the door as she inserted herself into the room without invitation. "How about some coffee? I'll brew a fresh pot." When she saw Jonathan Bick, she froze. Having watched him interrogate her husband for hours as he testified at Colum McAlister's trial, Bick's face was one she would never forget. "Is— Is everything okay," she asked sheepishly.

"No coffee, thank you," was all that Bick said without looking up.

Turnbull cleared his throat. "Everything's fine, dear. Mr. Bick and I are just sorting through a few details regarding WITSEC."

Laura's voice took on an edge. "Why didn't you tell me that it was Mr. Bick who rang the doorbell? You said it was someone from your office."

"I didn't want you to be concerned. That's all. We'll be done soon."

The two men sat in silence until Laura exited the room. Turnbull pulled at his flaccid neck as perspiration began to gather on his upper lip. His tumbler of scotch was shaking visibly in his hand so he put it down on the coffee table. "I knew that Austin's lab data had to be saved. It was valuable. Valuable to mankind, to the world—it needed to be preserved. I was the only one who was in a position to do it. I didn't tell you because I thought that it would implicate me in some way with McAlister."

"And you were going to keep this as your little secret?" asked Bick.

"I thought there would be a time and place to come forward."

"Right, when you were ready to sell it to the highest bidder. Stop lying, Turnbull, or this conversation is over—and so is your peaceful life in Wyoming."

"I wasn't going to sell it. But I thought that someday maybe something bad would happen. Like the government reneges on my deal, or the IRS comes after me. The copies were my long-term insurance policy, my bargaining chip for the future. I needed something to protect my family."

"Where are the data copies now?"

"I have them in a fireproof safe in the basement."

"Let's get them. Your insurance policy just got canceled."

# 30

I T TOOK SUSAN THREE MONTHS to have the work completed that was necessary to transform Wheatleigh Point into a first-class research facility. The mansion's great room was now divided into forty workstations. All of the computers were set up to remotely interface with Tufts University's super-computers so that the new lab had the same level of computing capabilities as the old one. There was an emergency backup generator to ensure that the systems wouldn't crash in the event of a power failure. All of the rooms on the first floor of the building had been repainted in a rosy shade of white, and plentiful recessed-lighting fixtures had been added throughout, to eliminate the gloominess that had previously pervaded the interior. The claustrophobia engendered by the copious amount of heavy dark wood paneling was eliminated by bleaching the woodwork, and the moth-eaten embroidered draperies that had covered every window had been discarded so that sunlight now streamed into the house.

Susan converted the dining room, with its wall of windows overlooking the ocean, into Bobby's office, replete with an oak table that functioned as a desk and was large enough to accommodate four keyboards, each connected to a different mainframe computer, with corresponding nineteen-inch monitors. She hoped that the sunlight that drenched the room, and the view of the sea, would have a salutary effect on Bobby's moods, which could turn dark when he was under pressure and encountering difficulties in his work. The office was outfitted with a small refrigerator filled with Bobby's favorites: energy drinks, cheddar cheese, onion dip, pickle chips and olives. There was a microwave oven, a coffee machine and a cupboard stocked with cans of microwaveable chili and pasta, potato chips and the flatbread crackers that he loved, but that she thought tasted like cardboard.

In one corner of the room was a sofa bed and in another, an old brass bar cart that she had purchased on eBay as a house-warming gift for Bobby. Sitting on the cart were six double old-fashioned tumblers, an ice bucket and several bottles of Bombay Gin and Macallan scotch, the latter having been Joe Manzini's elixir of choice.

While Susan didn't know how much Bobby would use the observatory that stood atop the forty-foot tall seaside watchtower, she nevertheless furnished it with various items including a small desk, a secure computer workstation, a sofa, microwave and refrigerator.

The refurbished gatehouse at the entrance to Gull Island was now manned by two armed guards, and Wheatleigh Point's decrepit iron gates had been replaced with imposing electronic security gates. A state-of-the-art security system had been installed on the grounds and throughout the mansion, and at night the waterside faces of the cliffs and the ocean below were brightly illuminated. The property was patrolled twenty-four hours a day by bomb-sniffing dogs. While all of these security protocols were similar to those that Bobby's prior laboratory had employed, based on the CIA's recommendations, this time, the CIA was not involved in the security arrangements for obvious reasons.

"What do you think, Bobby?" Susan asked after she had given him the grand tour.

"It's fantastic. You did an amazing job, as usual."

Susan cocked her head. "I sense a 'but' coming."

Looking around, Bobby said, "No. I just was wondering…"

Susan cut him off. "Come with me." She led Bobby to an archway at the building's entrance. "Pull on this," she said.

Bobby hadn't noticed the rope that was hanging a few feet above their heads. When he tugged on it, a tarp fell to the floor to reveal a handsome hand-carved wooden sign identical in design to the one that had hung in his prior lab, bearing the same name: The Joseph Manzini Research Laboratory.

Bobby beamed. "Now I feel at home. Thank you."

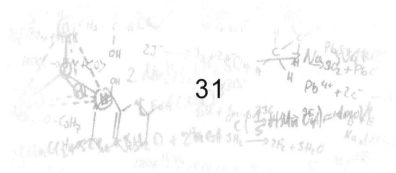

# 31

T HE SCREEN OF BOBBY'S CELL phone indicated, "No Caller ID."

"Hello," said Bobby.

"Robert, I have some good news for you."

"Who is this?"

"It's Jonathan Bick. I got the hard drive data from Turnbull." There was silence on Bobby's end of the line. "Robert, are you there? Did you hear what I said?"

Sounding short of breath, Bobby replied, "I can't believe it. This is amazing. I don't know how to thank you, Mr. Bick."

"You can start by calling me Jon. I just hope the drives are really useful to you."

"How many are there?

"I didn't count them, but they're arranged in chronological order in a foam filled suitcase. I'll arrange to have them delivered to you personally by my marshals. Where should I send them?"

"To my lab on Gull Island in Manchester, at the end of Ocean Road. They can't miss it. There's a gatehouse."

"Okay, they'll be there tomorrow between two and three p.m."

By the time the two federal marshals arrived, Bobby had been anxiously waiting for hours. Christina was there for the big event.

Bobby squeezed Christina's hand, unable to contain his excitement. "Having these computer hard drives is one of the luckiest things that's ever happened to me. They captured in real time, minute by minute, all of the work I did over a period of many years."

Bobby slowly opened the aluminum suitcase as if it contained fragile works of art. Each drive was labeled to indicate the dates covered. A smile crossed Bobby's face as he realized the irony. His work would have been lost forever had it not been for the greed of two unscrupulous Big Pharma executives: Colum McAlister who wanted to steal Bobby's discoveries so Bushings Pharmaceuticals could profit from them, and Martin Turnbull who wanted copies of the stolen work so that he could ransom them when it best suited him. "Thank God for crooks," Bobby said to himself.

Christina began to comb through the drives looking at the dates. "Let's find the drive that contains your work on the night of the explosion so we can retrieve the AIDS data."

Bobby gently put his right hand on hers to stop her rummaging. "That won't work. I'll never be able to understand it, just as I couldn't understand my journals from that day. What I have to do is reeducate myself. I need to study the drives starting at the earliest date. This will allow me to use them as a tutorial in the progression of my old self's thinking processes, and the evolution of my mathematical language."

Christina nodded. "I get it. It's like having your pre-explosion self, standing beside you as a teacher."

"Exactly, and unlike reading my published articles—which just present conclusions—these computer drives will show me step-by-step how I got there. If anything will accelerate the full recovery of my abilities, this is it."

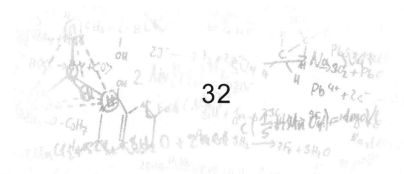

# 32

WHEN RAMIREZ ENTERED HUO JIN GAO's apartment in New York City's Time Warner Center, he was surprised to see boxes stacked up everywhere. Gao greeted him, "Please excuse the disorder. I'm moving out later this week."

"Why? You've been here for years. This is a fantastic apartment. Your view of Central Park is one of the best in the city."

"It's time to move on. This building has come under too much scrutiny ever since the *New York Times* did that exposé on the building's residents that sparked ongoing investigations by the U.S. Justice Department and the New York Attorney General. I was lucky. The article didn't mention me, but there may be follow-ups. I don't need media or the authorities nosing around."

"I didn't see the *Times* piece. What did it say?"

Gao paraphrased the article. "Over eighty percent of the apartments are owned through shell companies and are unoccupied most of the time, so they're probably money laundering vehicles for crooks, a bunch of whom have already been prosecuted."

Ramirez laughed. "You could say the same thing about most of the extremely expensive condos in New York, London, Los Angeles and Sydney."

"Guilt by association is not something I need. I'm moving to a townhouse between Fifth and Madison so I won't have any neighbors to draw attention to me."

"Always one step ahead, Huo Jin. That's what I admire about you."

"If you're not ahead, then you're behind—and that's a dangerous place to be."

Ramirez' attention was drawn across the room to a three-foot-tall gilt statue of the Tantric Buddhist deity Vajrayogini which was glistening in the sunlight that streamed through the floor-to-ceiling windows. Walking over to it, he said, "This is gorgeous. I saw one just like it a few years ago in the Tibet Museum in Lhasa.

Gao smiled. "Yes, this is the sister statue to that one. It also used to be displayed in the Tibet Museum alongside the other one. It's from the fifteenth century. It was a gift to me from the Chinese Premier.

Smirking as he gently ran his fingers over the priceless work of art, Ramirez said, "I like that. The museum becomes the museum gift shop. It's nice to have friends in high places." When Gao didn't respond to the crack, Ramirez changed the subject. "You asked to see me. I assume it's about the investment opportunity we discussed when we met on the Great Wall."

"I've spoken to my associates. We like your proposal."

"And my thirty-percent fee?" asked Ramirez.

"For the value you and your partner are providing, it's acceptable. But we have to know who your partner is before we'll commit."

Ramirez locked eyes with Gao. "He's the former CEO of the

biggest pharmaceutical company in the world, Bushings. Colum McAlister."

"Wait a minute. Isn't that the guy who was convicted on multiple crimes involving Robert Austin the scientist?"

Ramirez' shrug was his acknowledgment. "What's important is that he has a mastermind plan that he put in place way before he was imprisoned. His being in prison doesn't affect its implementation at all. In fact, it's an asset. Sitting in the federal penitentiary in Butner with a nineteen-year sentence puts him beyond suspicion. He's bulletproof. He's got the perfect alibi."

"And you?" asked Gao. "How bulletproof are you?"

"You know the answer to that. I'm invisible. Always have been."

Gao sat down on the edge of a rosewood bench and folded his hands. He gazed out the wall of windows which extended for half a city block and framed Central Park, eighty floors below. After a few moments, he turned to Ramirez, who for the first time was able to discern sadness on Gao's usually inscrutable face. "Over the years, I've been able to move about half my wealth out of China, but I think it's going to get harder in the future. Things are changing there. The new regime is cracking down. Examples are being made out of some of the wealthiest and most prominent, even those with strong *guanxi*. It doesn't matter how many thousands of jobs you've created for people, how charitable you've been—or how loyal you were to the Party. Prosecutors want trophies. If I can make a huge score with your plan, all of that money will flow to my international accounts, and no one in China will have any idea how much I have. I won't care what I have to leave behind."

Recognizing that it was time to close the deal, Ramirez walked over to Gao and said, "You're exactly right. This will be the ultimate realization of what you and I started years ago when I first helped you move assets to international safe havens. I just returned from London and confirmed my other investor. I need to know now whether or not I have your commitment."

When Gao dipped his head almost imperceptibly, Ramirez had his answer. "Good. How much can I count you in for?"

"At least fourteen billion dollars from me and my network."

"Can you deliver the twenty-times leverage we spoke about?"

"I've already arranged for thirty-five."

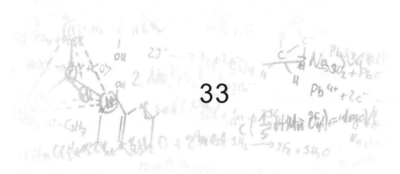

# 33

SOME THINGS CAME EASY TO Bobby when he reviewed the hard drives, particularly the formulas and equations in the first two years of Bushings' hacking. But as Bobby delved into the third and subsequent years, it was an escalating struggle for him to comprehend what his pre-explosion self had done, even with the step-by-step guidance that the drives offered. He would just stare at his computer monitor trying to understand the stream-of-conscious thinking process that had effortlessly generated one extraordinary mathematical equation after another, hundreds of them per day. Occasionally, but all too rarely, what he was looking at on the screen seemed very familiar, and he had a clear recollection of when he had worked on it, being able to recall himself sitting in his old lab grappling with the particular problem.

By the end of his fifth month of working on the drives, a pattern emerged. As Bobby focused intensely, he would eventually fall into one of his trances, each of which lasted between twenty minutes and two hours. When Bobby would snap out of it, he would immediately begin to scribble page after page of notes, often discarding previous ones while he cross-referenced what was on the screen from the drives. More often than not, what had been incomprehensible to him, would now come within his grasp and allow him to progress to the next step.

Bobby's trances were all too familiar to Christina and Susan, as they knew how his thinking process functioned. But they hadn't witnessed these trances since Bobby was released from the hospital. It was clear to them that the old Bobby was returning.

For eleven months, every day except Sunday, Bobby put in sixteen-hour days at the lab. He was indefatigable and his level of concentration and focus were remarkable. As he completed each drive, he felt that he had crossed another bridge on the road to his intellectual recovery. As time went on, the cognitive processes that were revealed on the drives became ingrained in Bobby, and he began to recapture mastery of the unique mathematical language that he had previously created. By the end of the eleventh month, Bobby had digested and fully understood all of the work that was contained on the entire set of hard drives, except for the final month before the explosion; that challenge still remained.

Bobby felt so different from the way he had felt eleven months earlier. His eyes were brighter, clearer and more radiant, as if they were being illuminated from within. Bobby sensed that some kind of force, an intangible power, once again resided within him. A restless frenetic energy coursed through him like an electric current that was always on. The lightning in his mind was back, together with the kinetic clarity and analytic acuity that had dazzled Bobby's teachers when he was a child. But with the return of his extraordinary cognitive abilities, came the resurgence of less desirable traits. Bobby rarely seemed present in the moment. He was in a constant state of intellectual preoccupation, operating on a cognitive plane that was largely removed from normal consciousness. Often detached and distant, his communications with others suffered, and he could appear to be disinterested and aloof. His mind was like a computer that was relentlessly processing information.

As Bobby got closer to completing his examination of the final few hard drives, Christina's fears became reality. His night terrors intensified. She'd wake up to find the bedding thrown askew, and Bobby grabbing at his head, clawing at his body, and pressing his hands over his ears as he tossed in his sleep. Suddenly bolting upright, rigid and gasping for breath, his eyes wild, he would drag himself to the edge of the bed and sit there, his arms crossed over his chest and his head lowered almost to his knees. Because nausea would often overtake him, Christina kept a wastebasket at the bedside.

"You're okay, Bobby. It's not real. It's just a nightmare. Breathe in deeply. Hold it for ten seconds. Do it again." Bobby would pull off his sweat-drenched sleep shirt while Christina placed a large bath towel on top of his perspiration-soaked sheets so he wouldn't be on the wetness when he lay down again. Often they wouldn't attempt to go back to sleep after such an ordeal, but sometimes, exhausted, they would try.

For Bobby, the escalation of his night terrors was proof that he was getting close to cracking the AIDS code. "You see Christina, I was right. It left me alone when I was analyzing the earlier drives because that was just an academic exercise, but now that I'm on the verge of rediscovering the cure, it's back in full force trying to stop me."

"Isn't it possible that your night terrors are caused by fatigue and anxiety? You're putting extreme pressure on yourself."

"I'm not going to try to convince you again," said Bobby as he rubbed his temples. "But I've taken precautions this time. I made five copies of the final month's hard drive and I hid them in different locations, away from the lab. So if it thinks it can stop me again by destroying the drives like it once did, it's wrong."

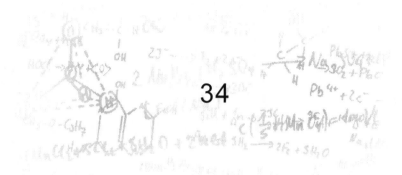

# 34

As Bobby embarked on his examination of the drive that contained the final four weeks of his pre-explosion work, his sense of foreboding increased. His prior eleven months of intensive effort was preparation for this, and his rediscovery of the AIDS cure lay in the balance. What Bobby immediately noticed as he plowed into the drives was that the amount of computer entries that were recorded during each hour of each day was twice what had been the case in the immediately preceding month. He also saw that formulas and equations were discarded abruptly and whole trains of thought were abandoned suddenly. There were more fragments cast aside than there were concepts pursued beyond preliminary stages. Clearly, his old self had been working at a frantic pace, with a heightened sense of urgency. Bobby gleaned—or perhaps remembered—that a feeling of desperation had begun to settle in as the cure continued to elude his prior self.

Weary from hours of concentration as he stared at the computer screen, Bobby's eyes began to glaze over and his mind took refuge in recollecting about the past. In his somnolent state, his memory replayed in vivid detail snippets of events that had taken place in those momentous final weeks leading up to the explosion in his lab. The pictures in his mind were luminous in their clarity, so intense that he felt as if he had been projected back in time and was reliving it all again.

———————————

Bobby saw himself standing in the entrance hall of the old lab's guest cottage in which he and Christina had lived before the explosion. Bobby looked in the mirror. He was disheveled and unshaven, his eyes red and bleary from the grueling regimen that he had subjected himself to for months. Encountering Christina, her annoyance was palpable when she said, "You're going to have to make a choice very soon, because I'm not going to live like this. If you want to kill yourself, I'm not going to be the cheerleader."

Then the scene changed and Bobby saw himself sitting at his desk in front of four computer monitors. It was very early in the morning, and he was alone in the old laboratory. He was scribbling notes in his journals at a feverish pace, page after page, equation after equation. Surrounded by cans of energy drinks and empty coffee cups, the floor was littered with discarded pages which he had ripped out of his notebooks.

"I got you now, you son of a bitch!" Bobby yelled as he slammed his hand against his desk. The ordeal was over. He had found the cure. He exhaled loudly in relief, closed his eyes and collapsed so far back into his chair that it almost flipped over.

But then there was only darkness. Darkness and pain. The pain was so intense that Bobby felt as if he were being drawn, quartered, crushed and impaled—at the same time. He shivered from a frigid wind that blew through the lab, but he couldn't hear anything. He struggled to see in the blackness, but his eyes were pasted shut.

When the warm liquid running down his face reached his lips, he could taste the metallic saltiness of his blood, and when he cupped his hands over the top of his head in a protective gesture, his crown was soft and mushy like an overripe cantaloupe. Pressing his fingers against his ears, Bobby tried unsuccessfully to stop the incessant ringing that the explosions had caused. He shifted his twisted body on the ground only to realize that he was lying on broken glass that was cutting into him.

Finally, he was able to see something. It was a distorted image flickering on the screens of the wrecked computer monitors in the destroyed lab. Blood was now running into Bobby's eyes, the unctuous liquid blurred his vision and burned him. He squinted to try to keep the blood out. There it was. That face. That same hideous amorphous face that had terrorized him in his nightmares for years. Now it was here in the lab with him. He tried to lift his arm and point at the image on the screen, but his shoulder was too damaged to cooperate. Bobby's voice was a barely audible rasp as he stared at the face, "You're finally doing it to me, you bastard. After all these years, you're doing it," he said.

———————

A shudder jolted Bobby back to the present. Unnerved, he realized that this was the first time that he had been able to recall anything that happened in the laboratory *after* the explosions began. But was this recollection? Did those things actually happen? Did that face appear on the monitor screens? Or was it all a delusion or a dream?

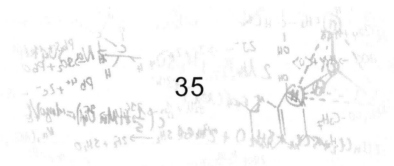

# 35

FIVE WEEKS LATER, SHORTLY AFTER 9:00 a.m., Bobby walked into Wheatleigh, hand in hand with Christina.

"I'm so proud of you. I know how hard you worked deciphering those drives to get to this point." Christina put her arms around him and kissed him full on the lips. Bobby looked into her exquisite green, almond-shaped eyes and then brushed his face against her cheek, lingering momentarily.

His lips grazing her ear, he whispered, "I haven't forgotten my promise to you."

This was a special day that was hard-earned. This was the day on which Bobby would complete his examination of the final Bushings hard drive that contained the momentous work he had done on the night of the explosion. It was the day on which he would reclaim what he had lost on that apocalyptic night, and it was the day on which the scourge of AIDS would finally be vanquished by a cure.

For Bobby, this day was one of redemption on which he would be absolved from the guilt he felt for not having been able to deliver the cure that he had once held in his hands.

Sitting at his office desk, he began to work. He meticulously studied each computer entry as he scrolled through the disc, being sure that he understood every aspect of the unfolding thought process that was revealed to him. It was laborious work, but his excitement grew as he got closer to the end. His right leg was bouncing under the desk, his posture rigid as he leaned forward in his chair.

A metallic crashing sound echoed through the building, amplified by the cavernous interior of the structure. Susan rushed in to Bobby's office, almost tripping over the large metal wastebasket that he had kicked into the wall, as she heard him shout, "What the fuck? What the hell is going on?"

Bobby's face was pale and his eyes were on fire. He had just gotten to the end of the final hard drive. He rebooted his computer three separate times and searched through the drive repeatedly. Same result. He reached into his briefcase and retrieved another copy of the drive and scrolled to the last entry that had been made on the night of the explosion. Same result again. The computer entries just stopped, concluding nothing. *Where is my cure?*

Stunned, Bobby began to walk in circles in his office, scratching his arms. Susan noticed that Bobby's hands were shaking. "This makes no sense, Susan. Bushings' hack was flawless. In all the years of entries that I examined, there were no gaps, no missing data. How can this be happening?"

"Calm down, Bobby. There's an explanation. You'll figure it out."

Bobby rushed back to his computer and looked at the time of the last entry on the drive. It was 4:43 a.m.

Bobby called Jonathan Bick's office. "Hello, this is Sean Whitten. I need to speak to Mr. Bick. It's extremely urgent."

"I understand," said Bick's assistant, "but he's in a pretrial conference and can't be disturbed."

"I appreciate that, but please interrupt him. My call will be quick, and I think he'll want to take it." Bobby heard no response from the assistant. "Please, I wouldn't ask if it weren't truly a matter of life and death."

Bobby heard an exasperated sigh followed by, "I'll try but you'll see, he won't speak with you."

A few minutes later, Bick was on the line. "What's the problem, Robert?"

"I urgently need to know the exact time that the explosion went off in my lab. Can you find that out?"

"I have that information. We needed it for the trials. As soon as I get back to my office, I'll search the files and call you. But what difference does it make?" asked Bick.

"All the difference in the world," replied Bobby.

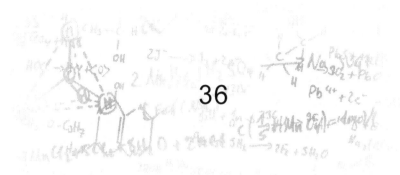

# 36

BOBBY WAS DISTRAUGHT UNTIL, FINALLY, his phone rang four hours later. "The lab explosion went off at four fifty-nine a.m.," said Bick.

"How do you know?"

"The security camera videos, which are time-stamped. The cameras were located on the grounds outside the lab. They recorded the explosion. There's no question of the accuracy. There were six machines on three separate systems and they all indicated four fifty-nine."

Bobby was silent as he thought about the implications. "So that means that there was a sixteen- minute period from four forty-three until four fifty-nine that my work on AIDS wasn't entered into the computer."

"I don't follow what you mean. What is the significance of four forty-three?"

"Four forty-three a.m. was the last time the Bushings' hard drive recorded an entry. So my breakthrough must have taken place during the sixteen-minute interval between four forty-three and four fifty-nine, with the only record of it being contained in my hand-written journals. I must have been in a frenzy to get the equations down on paper and didn't have time to make computer entries before the explosion happened. There must have been a leap in my thought processes, some kind of epiphany."

"Are the last pages of the journals of no use?"

"The entire last third of the final journal is illegible. The pages are either charred beyond recognition or missing."

There was silence on the line. Finally, Bick said, "I'm sorry, Robert. It looks like we both put in a lot of work for nothing."

Bobby dropped his cell phone on the floor. He began to hyperventilate. His head was pounding. He was so hot that he unbuttoned his shirt down to his navel. He had to get some fresh air, despite the freezing temperature outside, and he had to get out of the lab.

Without slowing down to put on a coat, he exited his office through the French doors and began to walk hurriedly in the darkness toward the cliff at the far end of the peninsula. He rubbed his hands roughly over his sweaty face as he massaged his forehead trying to alleviate the pain of what was fast developing into a migraine. He couldn't slow his breathing no matter how hard he tried.

Now standing at the edge of the cliff, he looked down at the waves crashing into the rocks below, the water illuminated by security lights. As each wave receded, he heard the sound of hundreds of thousands of pebbles frantically scurrying to keep their place while the water robbed them of control. Bobby crouched down on his haunches and lowered his head between his legs, hoping that the blood rushing to his brain would eliminate the dizziness that had almost caused him to fall. He just wanted to calm down.

Fifteen minutes later, a frigid wet wind blowing off the sea finally brought Bobby out of his daze. Perilously close to the edge of the cliff, he stepped back and surveyed his surroundings. For the first time, he focused on the nearby stone watchtower. He observed how peculiar a structure it was, incongruous with the architecture of Wheatleigh's main house. Built entirely from local fieldstones stacked one atop the other, Bobby couldn't discern if there was any cement holding the stones together or if craftsmanship and gravity sufficed to give the tower stability.

Intrigued by this odd building and the wood and glass room that sat at its apex, Bobby entered the tower and began to climb its rough-cut winding stone staircase. Now four stories up, Bobby opened the small door that gave entry to the cabin-like room. He flipped the light switch and three rustic lamps made of antler fragments cast a soft amber glow.

The simple furniture caught his attention. He walked around the room and examined each piece, running his fingers over the finish and bending down to inspect the design details. He didn't know why these mundane objects comforted him until his mind flashed back four decades in time. He realized that this furniture was almost identical to the pieces that were in his foster parents' living room—in the only childhood home he ever had, albeit briefly, since he was sent away at age four to live full-time at the Institute for Advanced Intelligence Studies. Bobby was eleven years old when his foster parents, Edith and Peter, died. After that, he never set foot in that house again, but his memories of the time he spent there always allayed his anxiety. He began to feel better.

Famished, Bobby rifled through the cabinets in the kitchen area. He found a can of microwaveable chili and a bag of sourdough pretzels. Then he grabbed a tall water glass and filled it half with ice and half with Bombay gin. Collapsing into the soft cushions of the plaid sofa, he quickly consumed his food and drink as he thought about the tumultuous day and its terrible disappointments. *Bick was wrong. The hard drives weren't a waste of time. They got me up to speed.*

Bobby walked over to the large picture window that now framed only darkness. He felt comfortable in this room atop the watchtower with its isolation and familiarity. Staring into the night, Bobby zoned out and lost track of time. As the alcohol began to deliver its salutary effect, a calm settled in on him.

Bobby sat down at the small desk that faced the window, turned on the computer and gazed at its blank screen which cast an eerie glow in the dim room. He knew that the past had no more secrets to disgorge. There would be no shortcuts for him. *I found the cure once. I'll find it again. People are counting on me.*

"I'm back now," he said in the silence.

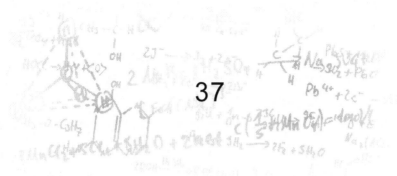

# 37

THE PORTLY GUARD AT THE Federal Correctional Complex in Butner chuckled when he saw Jeffrey Stringer. "You're my favorite visitor. You know the security protocols so well, I don't even have to prompt you anymore." Ramirez managed a smile as he pressed his palms against his cheekbones to solidify the mask's adhesive to his facial skin. He proceeded to the playing field to meet with Colum McAlister.

"Colum, I have the Russian and Chinese investors committed. We're getting thirty percent of their action."

"How much are they putting in?"

"Between them and their networks, a total of at least twenty-seven billion dollars, with average available leverage of thirty-six."

McAlister beamed. "Good work. I knew you'd come through." Ramirez reached for his cigarette case. "There's no smoking here," said McAlister.

"There is for me. The guards love me. I'm their favorite lawyer." Ramirez placed the cigarette in his mouth and took his time lighting it. "Now it's your turn, Colum. Tell me exactly what the plan is. I spoke in generalities to our investors, but I need to know the whole story."

McAlister frowned, not because Ramirez was asking an unreasonable question, but because Ramirez was questioning him at all. "It's very simple. I'll have advance notice of when certain terrorists are going to unleash a new disease that has the potential to become a pandemic. Shortly before the release, we'll have our investors liquidate their holdings and put all of their assets into U.S. currency and gold. Then they'll sell the markets short with leveraged transactions, and make a killing in the collapse. When the markets hit bottom from the panic caused by the disease, they'll buy up everything good at fire-sale prices, once again using leverage."

"Then what?" asked Ramirez.

"Guess who owns the cure to the disease?" replied McAlister.

Ramirez could barely contain his laughter. "I like your style, Colum."

McAlister smiled. "Already patented and ready to be manufactured by an esteemed Swiss company that's awaiting my instructions."

"Can it be traced back to us?"

"Remember who you're talking to." Ramirez raised his hands in apology.

"So let me guess," said Ramirez. "When the cure is announced and the markets recover, the investors will dump the assets that they bought cheap and make another huge profit."

"In principle, yes—but this has to be managed very carefully to maximize returns. It's all about timing. The opportunity has to be allowed to percolate and mature. We'll tell our investors when the time is right. We're going to play this whole scenario like Paganini played the violin."

"I am guessing the cure will be expensive," said Ramirez as his eyes twinkled.

"Expensive is a pejorative term, Gunther. Something that saves lives isn't expensive. It may be costly, but it's not expensive. I have no doubt that governments and insurance companies will be able to afford it."

Raising his cigarette to his lips, Ramirez inhaled deeply and held his nicotine fix in his lungs. Slowly releasing a cloud of smoke, he said, "We're going to make a goddamn fortune off all this."

McAlister stroked an eyebrow and nodded. "I told you we'd both become billionaires. It's just a question of whether we're talking single or double digits."

Ramirez wagged his head in deference. "When did you plan all of this? It's incredible."

McAlister didn't feel the need to answer.

# 38

YUSUF AL-SAEED ENTERED MAHMOUD'S LAB facility, accompanied
by six heavily-armed bodyguards, three in front and three
behind him. Olive complected, with an oval face and long dark
beard, Saeed's tall, lanky frame was clothed in the long, layered
robes of a Muslim cleric. Saeed moved quickly through the facility
exuding authority and making eye contact with no one. All of the
other men were dressed entirely in black, their faces obscured
by black *balaclavas* and hands encased in fingerless black leather
gloves.

Saeed's robes, and his turban which was wrapped around a
*kalansuwa*, were consistent with the personae he had worked hard
to develop over the last few years as a political and religious leader
rather than a militarist. Almost obscured by the long vest that he
wore over his robes were a waist holster which held a .44 Magnum
Desert Eagle pistol and a *janbiya* with an ivory hilt and silver sheath
which hung from a red-and-gold embroidered sash.

Three years prior, the two other founders of Ansar Jamaat had
been killed in battle, leaving Saeed in control of one of the fastest-
growing Islamic jihadist groups in the Mideast. But there was a lot

of competition among terrorist organizations. In an effort to elevate Yusuf al-Saeed's stature, and distinguish him from the many other jihad leaders in the region, his inner circle had begun to promote him as a Caliph and a direct descendant of the prophet Muhammad. While there was a dearth of corroborated factual information about Saeed, there was no shortage of mythology. It was known that he grew up a Sunni in the Iraqi city of Samarra, the son of a local *imam.* His achievements from childhood onwards were the subject of constant embellishment and became more impressive with each passing month. No one from Saeed's past had ever come forward to contradict the favorable narrative.

What wasn't in doubt, as it had been preserved on video, was that Saeed was a ruthless killer and practiced torturer. He harbored a virulent hatred for anyone he deemed to be an infidel or apostate, which was a category of people that expanded with regularity and included Muslims who didn't pledge fealty to Ansar Jamaat. The Crusades of the twelfth century burned in his mind as vigorously as if the Knights Templar rode their horses into his encampment the day before yesterday. He frequently debated with his senior advisors as to which city—Rome or Constantinople—should first be brought to its knees. A framed photograph of Pope Francis and the Papal Conclave hung in his living quarters to inspire him to accelerate his jihad. In the meantime, he made do by seeking out Christians in the lands that Ansar Jamaat scourged, and visiting upon them his most robust atrocities. While he scorned Western culture as corrupt and degenerate, he found nothing objectionable about his men raping and disemboweling pregnant women, and selling children into sexual slavery after their defenseless parents had been butchered by his troops.

From the inception of Mahmoud's work, Saeed had taken an

active interest in his progress on developing the disease. Mahmoud had heard, although it had never been officially confirmed, that Saeed had originated the idea of creating a disease and had selected Mahmoud as the lead scientist above other candidates, despite the substantial costs of his recruitment. A frequent visitor to the succession of laboratories in which Mahmoud and his staff labored, Saeed would sometimes spend hours sitting on a chair and watching through the glass as the test subjects, whose clothing prominently bore the date on which they had been infected, struggled against the disease that was ravaging them. A studious observer, he made notes in a small leather book to record items of particular interest.

"Let's go into your office," said Saeed, his voice a low rasp. Mahmoud knew that when speaking with Saeed, eye contact was prohibited. A sharp smack delivered to his face years ago by one of Saeed's lieutenants had taught him to bow his head and avert his eyes.

Saeed and three bodyguards crowded into Mahmoud's small office, while the other three bodyguards stood outside the door. Saeed quickly scanned the room with its cheap metal desk, two worn guest chairs covered in discolored leatherette and what might have been the smallest executive desk chair in the entire Mideast. The walls were bare, except for a photograph from a magazine that had been enlarged into a poster and neatly taped onto the wall facing Mahmoud's desk. In it, three men, dressed in black, all with serious demeanors and long beards, were pictured standing in front of a tank bearing Iraqi Army insignias, a city bellowing smoke far in the distance. Saeed stared at the image, and then motioned to one of his guards who ripped it off the wall. "Get a new one," was all that Saeed said to Mahmoud. The poster depicted Saeed and the two other founders of Ansar Jamaat after they had overwhelmed the Iraqi Army and took control of a strategically placed city. The Iraqi army had dropped their weapons and run, abandoning its heavy artillery, including the tank pictured in the photograph.

"Yes, of course. I spend so much time working I don't even know what's on my wall, Caliph," said Mahmoud.

"I need you to start producing quantities of the disease."

Mahmoud's eyes widened and he shook his bowed head. "Why? I was told that the disease will never be released. We have videos of the test subjects. That's all you need to get opponents to capitulate without resistance." Two of Saeed's bodyguards instinctively moved closer to Mahmoud.

Saeed spoke slowly, taking the time to pronounce each word with deliberation. "I didn't say that the disease would be deployed. I told you to produce it so that we have a stockpile. You will be advised of the quantities and any other requirements by Colonel Fahd."

"When is this needed?" asked Mahmoud.

"When Colonel Fahd instructs you as to the requirements, you will advise how long the preparations will take. We want to be fully operable within six months."

"Operable? I don't understand what that means?" said Mahmoud.

"Mahmoud, I've always respected your abilities but you are beginning to try my patience. I will only remind you once that you do not make political or military policy for Ansar Jamaat." His right hand resting on the handle of his dagger, Saeed walked toward Mahmoud until he was just inches away. Saeed placed a large bony hand under Mahmoud's chin, and tilted Mahmoud's head up by forty-five degrees so that he could look directly into his eyes. Thinking that this was some kind of test, Mahmoud struggled to keep his head bowed and his eyes averted. "No, I want you to look at me," said Saeed. Mahmoud was stunned by the intensity of the ebony eyes that gripped his. "I need to know that I can count on your unconditional loyalty. Can I count on you, Mahmoud?" Mahmoud tried unsuccessfully to break Saeed's probing gaze. Although it was only eye contact, he felt violated.

"Caliph, my loyalty is never in question. You can count on me implicitly," said Mahmoud, hoping that Saeed wouldn't notice the perspiration that was forming on his forehead.

"Good, that's what I thought," said Saeed, forcing a smile that exposed his teeth. Badly discolored and in a state of decay, the condition of Saeed's teeth reminded Mahmoud of a similar problem he had noticed in some of Saeed's troops and senior officers. His mind flashed back to articles he had read in which Western journalists speculated that amphetamine use by jihadists fueled their violent ferocity. When Saeed placed his hands on Mahmoud's thin shoulders and gave him a shake, Mahmoud snapped back to the present. "Colonel Fahd will be in touch," said Saeed as he turned to exit the room.

The bodyguards led the procession out of the shabby office and Mahmoud couldn't wait for the door to close behind them. When it closed, he exhaled loudly and fell back into his chair. As he sat, wiping his forehead and playing the meeting back in his mind, the door opened and Saeed stepped partially into the room. "I meant to tell you. I saw your brother and his family when I was in Karbala the other day. His wife is pregnant again. You'd be pleased at how well they're doing." The implications of the comment were not lost on Mahmoud.

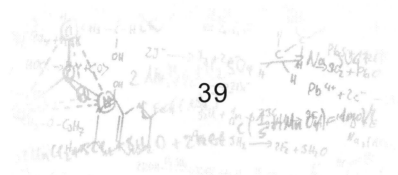

# 39

COLONEL ABU AL-FAHD WAS SLIGHT in stature, no more than five-foot-four, and one hundred thirty pounds. His skin was unusually pale for a man of Arabic descent and his facial hair was noticeably sparse and patchy. Fahd's large brown eyes were magnified by the thick lenses of his eyeglasses, the frames of which were decidedly big and heavy for his small thin face. With obsessive frequency, he raked the fingers of his right hand through the remaining strands of hair on his almost bald head and he had a tendency to pull on the tip of his nose as if he were trying to rid it of a foul odor.

Fahd had a storied career that had been powered by his substantial talents and insatiable drive to make something of himself. An orphan in the impoverished village of Barzanke in northern Iraq, Fahd had ingratiated himself at the age of eight to a middle-aged widower who took pity on the skinny little boy with a feminine face, long soft hair and fair skin. He taught Fahd how to read and write and do rudimentary mathematics, and he gave the boy food and a bed to sleep in, although not alone.

When Fahd turned fourteen, the widower got him a job as an apprentice machinist in a local metal parts foundry. By age eighteen,

Fahd had not only mastered the metal lathe, but had evidenced an ability to repair just about any machine. He was welcomed into Saddam Hussein's army at a time when military service was the most dependable employment in Iraq. Quickly recognizing Fahd's intelligence and intrinsic engineering talents and the value that would have for the armed forces, Fahd was placed by his superiors in an accelerated full-time program at the University of Technology in Baghdad. By age twenty-six, he had earned master degrees in both mechanical and chemical engineering. He was placed on the staff of Colonel Samir al-Ahmad who was in charge of the development of weapons for Saddam Hussein and within five years, Fahd was assigned as a senior officer to serve under Hussein's cousin, Ali Hassan al-Majid.

Exactly what role Fahd played in the infamous chemical weapons attack that took place on March 16, 1988, against the Kurdish city of Halabja in Southern Kurdistan is a matter of conjecture. Some say that Fahd was the mastermind behind weaponizing the chemical compounds that were unleashed on the Kurdish people resulting in the death of thousands of civilians. Fahd denied that he had any involvement in what is referred to as the "Halabja Massacre," an internationally condemned act of genocide that remains the largest chemical weapons attack against civilians in history. Fahd's reticence to acknowledge any role was not surprising since his boss, al-Majid (also known as "Chemical Ali"), was condemned to death by an Iraqi court and executed on January 25, 2010, for having orchestrated the massacre.

After Saddam's fall, Fahd became a freelancer. He found his talents to be in demand. Among his various assignments for which he was highly compensated, was his preparation and weaponization of the sarin gas that was used by an apocalyptic group based in

Japan, Aum Shinrikyo, in their 1994 and 1995 attacks on civilians in Matsumoto and Tokyo.

In 2013, he assisted the Assad armed forces with their saran gas bombing assaults against Syrian citizens in the suburbs of Damascus and Aleppo, although the Assad regime and Fahd denied any knowledge or involvement, blaming rebel forces. The next logical employer for Fahd was Ansar Jamaat. It took only one meeting for Saeed to recognize that a man of Fahd's knowledge and talents was an indispensable asset.

As expert and confident as Fahd was, regarding the use of chemical weapons, he had no experience with biological agents. As he had once said to a Syrian general, "I have an intrinsic distrust of any weapon that is alive."

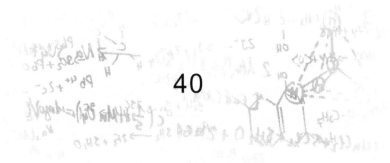

# 40

WHILE IT MIGHT SEEM INCREDIBLE to a casual observer, Colonel Fahd had no trouble purchasing thirty thousand hazmat suits that afforded the wearer complete protection from all deadly biological and chemical agents. He obtained the suits over a sixteen-month period from a multitude of suppliers located in France, Germany, Russia, Ukraine, India, Holland, Singapore and Belgium. By spreading out and staggering the timing of the orders, and having them shipped to a series of safe houses in Turkey, he was able to amass a stockpile large enough to outfit all of Ansar Jamaat's troops, with a few thousand suits left over for good measure.

Despite the pronouncements by world leaders about the globe-spanning anti-terrorist coalition that they had formed, none of these purchases was flagged by any security organization. Many months later, when everyone was looking for someone to blame, disbelief was expressed by the media's talking heads and by politicians looking to insulate themselves from criticism. The excuse that was most often proffered was that alarm bells were geared to sound when weapons or certain chemicals were being purchased, but not when protection from them was being sought.

Fahd wiped the front and back of his right hand against the leg of his trousers. He hated shaking hands with sweaty-palmed men, and he saw no reason to make small talk with people who were subordinate to him, so he got right into it with Mahmoud upon meeting him.

"Dr. Mahmoud, I understand that you have formulated a potent biological agent, and that you have tested its efficacy on many subjects. This is all well and good, but have you done dispersion tests? Do you know the strike radius of the disease? At what distance from the point of initial discharge is potency diminished and then lost? It is crucial to know this, not only to ensure effectiveness against our enemies, but to be sure that infection doesn't spread beyond the intended target or harm our own troops."

Mahmoud was bleary-eyed. For a moment, his body swayed and he looked as if he was going to collapse. His voice grew louder as he spoke, "I don't know how to do any of this. I am a pharmacologist. I am not a munitions expert or a bomb maker, nor do I want to be. This is not why I was brought in."

Noticing that Mahmoud's hands were trembling, Fahd smiled condescendingly and said, "Well, I am all of the things that you are not. So we'll work together and you'll learn something. There's no point having a weapon that is unpredictable and that can't be controlled. Just like an artillery officer knows how far he can fire a mortar with accuracy, we need to know every aspect about your disease. Have you heard that the Caliph is referring to it as the "Sword of the Mahdi"?

Mahmoud didn't respond. He just stood there, head bowed and eyes closed as Fahd's voice rang in his ears.

"You should be very proud," said Fahd.

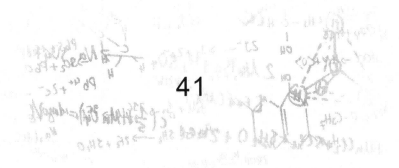

# 41

B OBBY, CHRISTINA AND PETE PILED into the family SUV. "Are you excited, Pete?" asked Christina.

"I never played for people that I don't know. I hope they like it," replied Pete as he bounced in his seat and played an imaginary piano.

The family had an appointment at the Massachusetts Conservatory of Music. Christina and Bobby thought the time had come for Pete to take piano lessons. He was four years old and the minimum age accepted by the conservatory was nine, but Christina had requested that the school evaluate Pete and offer suggestions for piano teachers that would be a good fit for such a young child. It took Christina two letters and three telephone calls to convince Dr. Helen Lenome, the head of the Preparatory Division, to give the Whitens a few minutes.

The conservatory was housed in an imposing Gothic style limestone building that bore a striking resemblance to a cathedral. Within two minutes after walking through the school's dark oak doorway, Pete became intimidated by the size and austerity of the structure and the hustle and bustle of students, most of whom were teenagers or older, walking quickly through the corridors, their banter echoing off the plaster walls. "Mommy, I want to go home. This place scares me," said Pete as he stopped walking and pulled on her hand.

"There's nothing to be afraid of. Everyone's very friendly here," said Bobby as he swept Pete off his feet and onto Bobby's shoulders. As they continued walking, Bobby said, "When I was just a little bit older than you, I went to a school that had some buildings just like this and after a while, they didn't seem so big and I really got to like them."

The Whiten family entered the reception area of Dr. Lenome's office and were greeted by her assistant, Brenda Hogan, a heavy-set middle-aged woman whose fair-skinned freckled face was fringed by bright red hair. "You must be the Whitens," said Brenda in a thick east Boston accent. "And you're right on time, which is good, because Dr. Lenome has a very busy schedule today. Where's the boy who's going to audition?"

Bobby lowered Pete to the floor. Christina smiled as she took Pete's hand. "This is him."

Brenda stood up from behind her desk so she could get a good look at the thirty-five-pound, three- footer. "Yikes, he's just a toddler. Is he still wearing diapers?

"No, he's fully housebroken," replied Christina sarcastically.

Before Brenda and Christina could go another round, the door to Doctor Lenome's office opened and Lenome entered the reception area. She was a tall willowy woman of about sixty years with a regal bearing, whose lustrous silver hair was swept up in a bun which accentuated her high cheekbones, long finely- formed nose, and lips so thin that they wouldn't be discernible without the fuchsia lipstick that she wore. Her prominently arched eyebrows framed amber eyes which were alive with intelligence. Wasting no time, she said, "You must be the Whitens. I apologize in advance, but as Brenda probably told you, I have back-to-back appointments today, so we'll have to get right down to it. Crouching to the floor, she addressed Pete directly. "So, are you the little boy who likes to play piano?" Pete looked up and nodded. "Okay, let's go to my office. There's a piano there."

The Whitens filed into Lenome's office, the walls of which displayed photographs of the famous musicians who had studied at the conservatory. Bobby sat down on one of the guest chairs while Christina walked Pete over to the piano, a nine-foot long ebony Steinway concert grand. Pete exclaimed, "I've never seen such a big piano. It looks like a boat." Lenome stood to the side as Christina lifted Pete and placed him on the square, tufted piano bench, and pushed it close to the keyboard so that Pete's short arms could reach the keys.

"Mrs. Whiten, what kind of piano do you have at home?" asked Lenome.

"It's a Yamaha electric keyboard, but it has all eighty-eight keys."

"I see…" said Lenome as she looked at her watch. "Play whatever you like, Pete."

With his tiny bottom planted on the bench, he grazed his fingers over the keys without making a sound. Then he randomly pressed the odd key here and there, first with one or two fingers of his left hand and then with one or two fingers of his right hand. "The keys on this piano are much harder to press down than the keys on my piano at home," said Pete, as his little brow creased and he scrunched up his nose disapprovingly.

"Just do the best you can, Pete," said Lenome, looking at Christina and Bobby as she glanced at her watch again.

Pete took a breath and began to play a Bach toccata. At first, he was having trouble with the weight of the keys on the Steinway, and he lost tempo and stumbled, but within about a minute, he adjusted to the piano's action. Lenome moved closer to the piano and watched the little boy's hands glide effortlessly over the keys, his eyes closed as if he were in a trance. Bach's contrapuntal melodies and syncopated rhythms came alive under his touch.

After a few minutes, Pete stopped in the middle of the piece and said, "I know you don't have much time, so I'll play you my favorite song." He then launched into Chopin's Ballade in G Minor. Lenome pulled over a chair next to the piano and was mesmerized as she watched the four-year-old play the difficult piece, interpreting the composition with an understanding and depth of emotion that was incomprehensible for his age. Since his hands were too small to play many of the chords, he broke them into arpeggios, so that none of the harmonic quality of the composition would be lost. The ending of the piece is technically very demanding, but Pete delivered it with credibility. When he was done, Lenome sat there stunned.

Brenda knocked on the door and then came in, the heels of her shoes clacking loudly. "Dr. Lenome, your next appointment is here. You wanted me to tell you." Lenome waved her away.

Pete wriggled off the bench and asked, "Did you like it? I can do better on my own piano."

Lenome gently grasped Pete's hands and held them up for her inspection. "You were wonderful. Where did you learn those songs?"

"Daddy has CDs and plays them a lot. His favorite piano player is Huey Watts. I play what I hear."

Bobby interrupted. "He means Horowitz. Vladimir Horowitz."

Lenome turned to Christina and Bobby. "Let me be sure I

understand this: Pete never had any lessons and doesn't read music?"

Christina nodded. "Correct. He just listens to the recordings over and over and then starts to play. He knows how to press repeat on the CD player. He spends hours every day doing this. He can play thirty pieces at least as well as the ones he just played. He began about eighteen months ago. It's not easy to get him to stop."

"Did you say eighteen months ago?" asked Lenome.

"Yes, that's when he began to try to play. Before that, he would just listen," said Bobby.

Lenome motioned for Pete to come over to her and she patted her lap, signaling that he should climb up and take a seat. Pete obliged. Leaning her head to his level she asked, "Pete, how do you remember all of the notes in those songs? It's a lot to remember and you got them all right when you played."

"I don't think about it. The songs just play in my head. Usually, I don't look at the keys," said Pete.

Lenome gently pushed Pete off her lap, stood up and walked to her massive old oak desk. She looked intently at Christina and Bobby as she said, "Here at the conservatory, we've seen many prodigies over the years, and of course we know what's happening at Juilliard, the Eastman School, Curtis and Oberlin. But in thirty-five years of doing this, I've never encountered anyone like Pete. It's hard to understand. It's not just his technical abilities. It's the interpretive understanding and the emotion with which he imbues the compositions. Of course, I'm familiar with Horowitz' recordings of these pieces, but Pete is not mimicking them. He's doing his own thing."

Lenome stopped speaking and just sat at her desk, looking

down. She began to tap a pencil on a folder, and appeared to be deep in thought.

After a few moments, she pointed the pencil at Bobby and Christina. "Do either of you have musical talent?" Bobby and Christina shook their heads signaling that they didn't. "No musical talent. Are you sure?" she asked.

"Well, I'm a trained dancer. I have good rhythm. I can play piano a little," replied Christina.

"Okay, now we're getting somewhere. Please play something for me," said Lenome, smiling approvingly.

Christina hesitated at first, but then made her way to the piano. She adjusted the bench and announced, "I'll play my rendition of one of my favorite songs, 'Moon River'."

After about ninety seconds, Lenome walked over to the piano and began to close the keyboard cover just as Christina was getting to the second chorus. "Thank you, Mrs. Whiten." Christina walked back to her chair looking somewhat chastened. Lenome continued, "Okay, so we know it's not inherited musical talent. Let's see. Do either of you have unusual mathematical abilities? Mathematics and music are connected, you know, and sometimes even if mathematically-gifted parents are not talented in music, their children can be. Are either of you talented in math?"

Bobby pulled on his nose and gave a quick shake of his head as he looked at Christina, signaling how they should answer. "Well, I'm a professional mathematician," said Christina. "I have a doctorate in math."

"And you, Mr. Whiten?" asked Lenome.

Bobby chuckled. "I have trouble balancing my checkbook."

Lenome gave a single clap of her hands and looked vindicated.

"Well, there we have it. Mrs. Whiten, your math abilities have translated into the prodigious musical talents of your son."

There was another knock at the door, and Brenda intruded into the meeting again. "Dr. Lenome, your four-fifteen appointment has arrived, so now you have two appointments in the reception area."

Lenome bristled. "Thank you, Brenda. Please tell them to be patient. I'll be done when I'm done." A puzzled look came over Brenda's face and she exited the room.

"What you're saying is very interesting and, by the way, Pete is also very good at the visual arts, for his age, I mean," said Christina.

"That's not unusual. Often the artistically gifted have talents that transcend any one artistic discipline," replied Lenome.

Bobby piped up. "We know that the policy of the conservatory is to only admit children nine years and up. Can you recommend a piano teacher that Pete can start with now? I mean until he's old enough to attend here."

Lenome leaned forward from behind her desk. "You're correct about our policy. Frankly, we've never deviated from it. But your son poses an extraordinary challenge. I'll have to confer with the board, but I'm going to recommend that an exception be made and that he be admitted. There's no point wasting five years of his development. Who knows what he can achieve in that amount of time... And as soon as he's ready for it, we'll start him learning to read music and introduce him to musical theory and composition."

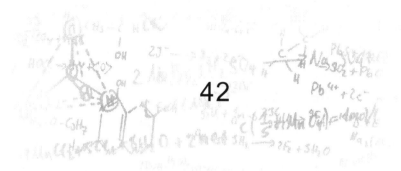

# 42

C OLONEL FAHD WAS EXPERT AT conducting the tests that he had outlined to Mahmoud; he relied on him only for production of the biological agents. Just as he had done with the sulfur, mustard, hydrogen cyanide and sarin gas that had been used by Saddam Hussein's forces at Halabja, and the saran that had been used by Aum Shinrikyo in Japan, Fahd knew that the best way to weaponize Mahmoud's disease for deployment against large numbers of people was to aerosolize it. While the disease could be delivered by numerous other methods, the current agenda called for aerosol bombs and aerosol artillery shells and rockets.

It took Fahd four months to complete his tests. The disease was so potent in its destructive power that the main problem that Fahd foresaw was controlling its reach. When fifty milliliters of the aerosolized agent was dispersed into the air at the point of impact, the potency two kilometers away was only thirty percent less than at the epicenter of the artillery shell blast. For the potency to diminish to a point where it posed no threat, took a distance of almost seven kilometers. "You've done too good a job, Dr. Mahmoud. I've never heard of a biological agent with this potency."

"I should weaken it," said Mahmoud.

"There's no time. You'd have to reformulate and go through a whole new testing regime for each revised sample. It would take months, maybe years. Ansar Jamaat doesn't have the luxury of time. Within ninety days, I need enough of your agent to infect a radius of eleven square kilometers.

---

Mahmoud sat at the kitchen table in his tiny apartment, his head lowered and his body motionless. It was almost midnight. He had vomited twice that evening, retching over his toilet bowl until his stomach had nothing more to surrender. He unwrapped the disposable cell phone that he had purchased and sent a text message to a number he had been given several years earlier that he had prayed he would never have to use. The message to Nizar Khouri, McAlister's man in Syria, was short: IT'S STARTING.

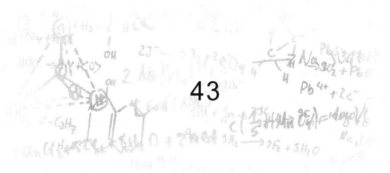

# 43

THE OTHER PRISONERS AT BUTNER had never seen Colum McAlister in such a good mood. In fact, they had never seen him in anything approaching a good mood. But today, a smile was affixed on his face as he stood on the cafeteria breakfast line. He said hello to random people, while usually he didn't acknowledge anyone's existence. And today, he was polite to the prison staff. In fact, he was overheard saying "thank you" and "excuse me" on several occasions.

The day had begun uneventfully for McAlister as he followed his normal routine. As was the case every morning before eating breakfast, McAlister sat in the prisoners' media room and watched CNN. Among many stories that were covered on this particular day, was a report that the famed bronze Statue of Saladin that stands at the entrance to the Citadel of Damascus had been toppled by persons unknown. The statue celebrated the victories of Saladin, the legendary twelfth-century Muslim sultan of Egypt and Syria, against Christian Crusaders, which paved the way for the Islamic re-conquest of Jerusalem. CNN quoted several pundits who expressed the view that the destruction of the statue was potent evidence of the growing backlash of Christians against Muslims in the area, as a result of the discrimination and atrocities committed against them. For this reason, the toppling of the statue resonated with the world news media and the coverage given this story was significant. For McAlister, the destruction of the statue signaled that his dreams were one step closer to being realized.

Some years earlier, when McAlister was indicted by the Justice Department, he knew that if he was convicted and imprisoned, his ability to communicate with Nizar Khouri would be severely compromised. So he and Khouri agreed that when Mahmoud advised Khouri that the disease would soon be unleashed, Khouri would do something, anonymously, that would garner enough international media attention to ensure that McAlister would hear about it, even in prison. This would allow McAlister to then set into motion the next steps of his master plan.

The event that Khouri and McAlister agreed upon was the destruction of the Statue of Saladin. Because Saladin was a warrior against the apostates, McAlister knew that jihadists would respect his monument and never damage it, unlike the numerous other historical landmarks that they had devastated. This would ensure that when the statue was toppled, McAlister could be confident that it was the work of Khouri and that the release of the disease was imminent.

Within minutes of seeing the statue's wreckage on CNN, McAlister received permission to make a phone call, ostensibly to his attorney. He left the following voice mail for the benefit of the guards who monitored calls: "Counselor Stringer, this is McAlister. I need you to visit me as a matter of urgency to discuss my court appeal." He knew that when Ramirez heard the message, he'd be on the next plane.

"Gunther, did you see the news report about the Saladin statue that was destroyed in Syria?"

"No, but who cares? Half the monuments in the Mideast have been blown up by terrorists. One more won't make any difference."

McAlister lifted an eyebrow. "This isn't any statue. This is *our* statue. Its toppling was the signal I've been waiting for." A confused look came over Ramirez' face, but he remained silent. McAlister removed a letter from his pocket and handed it to Ramirez. "Read this. I wrote it today." Ramirez reached into his jacket, retrieved his glasses and began to read. The letter was addressed to McAlister's Geneva lawyers, Muller, Schmid, Graf & Frei, the firm that he had used to file the patents on the cure, set up his offshore entities and make the manufacturing and distribution arrangements with the Swiss pharmaceutical company Schlumberger Foch:

> To: Muller, Schmid, Graf & Frei
>
> Gentlemen:
>
> This letter is written to you by the undersigned, Colum McAlister, in accordance with the protocols that you and I established for communications between us when I would not be physically present to meet with you. Therefore, I have written this letter in my own handwriting (samples of which you have on file for verification purposes) and I confirm that my confidential identification code is 9376285746AVW.
>
> I have asked my U.S. attorney, Jeffrey Stringer, to present this letter to you. I hereby confirm to you that I have given Mr. Stringer the full power and authority to transact all business on my behalf in connection with the matters in which you

have acted for me. In this regard, he will issue instructions to you as to what you should convey to Schlumberger Foch and require them to do. His instructions should be accorded the same force and effect by you as if I were physically present and giving such instructions to you in person. It is of the utmost importance that you ensure that Schlumberger Foch complies with all of the instructions that Mr. Stringer asks you to convey to them, and in a timely manner.

If you need to communicate with Mr. Stringer after your meeting with him, contact him only at the telephone number and email address that he gives you for that express purpose.

Very truly yours,
Colum McAlister

Ramirez looked up from the paper and slowly put his glasses back in his pocket. "So, I get to impersonate your white-shoe lawyer again, this time in Geneva. Thrilling."

Pulling on his nose, McAlister ignored the comment. "Make an appointment with Luca Muller at the Muller Schmid firm. When you call, just say that you are reaching out at my request and that you have a letter from me which you will deliver to him at the meeting. Don't give any details on the phone. Believe me, you'll get a first-class reception. I have these guys on a substantial monthly retainer."

"What should I say at the meeting?"

"You'll tell them to instruct Schlumberger Foch to manufacture six hundred kilograms of formula #YZ73144 within the next thirty days, for further research and testing purposes."

Ramirez' face twisted. "But you said the cure was already tested and worked perfectly, so why are tests and research needed?"

Annoyed that he had to explain the obvious, McAlister replied, "Of course, the tests aren't needed. But we can't tell Schlumberger to start manufacturing a cure for a disease that no one's ever heard of and that no one's infected with yet. That would look peculiar, don't you think? But if we instruct them to make a large testing batch, we'll have an initial stockpile ready to go."

Ramirez nodded. "Schlumberger should kiss your ass. They don't know how lucky they are. You're going to make them rich and famous and they didn't have to spend a dime on R&D."

McAlister flicked his wrist as if he were shooing away a fly. "They're a useful tool. They're hungry and that makes them malleable."

"What's next?" asked Ramirez.

"I need you to tell Gao and Bazhenov that it's time to initiate phase one of the financial-trading plan."

Ramirez inhaled deeply, holding the air in his expanded chest until he let it out slowly. Walking to the exit, he turned to McAlister. "I can smell the money already."

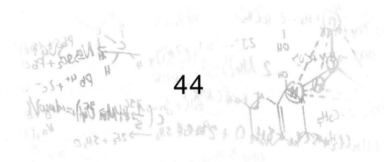

# 44

M ORE RESOLUTE THAN EVER IN his determination to find the AIDS cure, Bobby hunkered down in the lab. Not wanting any distractions or time limits on his working hours, his office became his de facto home and he was rarely at the Annisquam house. Melissa, the nanny, had become a live-in to fill the void. When exhaustion overtook him, he'd fall asleep in his chair; sometimes he made it over to the sofa. As the months went by, his decision to concentrate his time away from home and family became increasingly incendiary.

"Bobby, you said that this time you'd be different, that you wouldn't revert to your old ways. You promised me that," said Christina, confronting him in his office.

"You're right. But I can't help it. AIDS has already killed forty million people, another thirty-seven million are infected—and for every two who get treatment, another three are newly infected. It's the sixth leading cause of death worldwide. So I have to work as fast as I can. I can't think of myself or you or even Pete and Mirielle."

"Then the kids and I are moving into Wheatleigh. This house is plenty big. We can live on the second floor. You won't be disturbed when you're working."

Bobby's face became flushed and his voice got louder. "No. Absolutely not. The reason I got a lab that's so far from Annisquam is so that you and the kids wouldn't be in danger, no matter what happens here. I don't want any of you to be anywhere near this place. You know what happened last time and it can happen again."

Christina's eyes were ablaze as she moved aggressively towards Bobby. "Okay. You want to talk about what happened last time? Good. Let's talk about it. Like how you burned yourself out, ruined your physical and mental health and pushed yourself beyond any human limits and almost died. That's what happened last time, and you're on track to do it again."

"I don't want to fight with you," said Bobby as he grasped her wrists and stared directly into her eyes. Christina met his gaze unflinchingly and freed her hands. Without breaking eye contact, the two of them stood silently like determined combatants, Bobby feeling pinned in place by the force of Christina's mental resolve. Then something clicked. Bobby didn't even realize he was doing it, but he brushed his lips against hers. His left hand found its way to the small of her back and pressed gently. Christina's eyes didn't deviate from his, but gradually her pupils enlarged. Leaning in toward him, her hair fell forward, enveloping them in a protective cocoon. When their abdomens touched, she spread her fingers around his hips and pulled him closer. As the soft warmth of her body radiated into his, the scent of Christina's skin triggered an electrical impulse that flooded Bobby's mind with images of their intimacies.

For a few moments, they were in a place where problems didn't exist and where love and lust held sway. Neither of them wanted it to stop but when it did, they just held each other tightly, Bobby nestling his face against her hair.

Finally, he said, "Christina, I *have* to beat this thing. I can't turn away and allow it to keep destroying people. I don't know how long I've got. I lost my abilities once. I can wake up and they'll be gone again or like anyone else, I can die. So every day counts. Every moment counts. I can't be distracted worrying about you and the kids. I have to use what I have for as long as I have it."

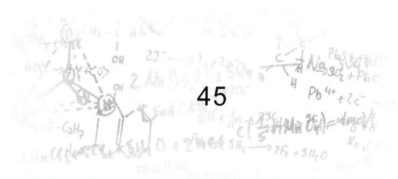

# 45

S TUDYING THE HARD DRIVES HAD brought Bobby's cognitive
abilities back to their pre-explosion level, and restored
his mastery of the unique mathematical language that he had
invented. It was his expansion of what he called "the vocabulary of
mathematics," which he began when he was nine, that allowed math
to become the unifying integrative language that encompassed all
scientific phenomena and disciplines. This allowed biochemical and
biophysical interactions to be expressed mathematically and to be
run and manipulated by computers in every possible permutation—
and at lightning speed. The need for laboratory experiments was
reduced since all combinations of chemicals and elements could
be tested mathematically, thereby isolating which situations were
worthy of the time-consuming process of laboratory work. In
this way, Bobby could eliminate the need for years of laboratory
and clinical experiments and limit those "real world" scientific
forays to those that showed a greater probability of success. In
essence, Bobby would test thousands of biochemical interactions
mathematically on computer rather than in a laboratory.

Bobby's examination of the hard drives showed him what didn't work as a cure for AIDS, what almost worked, and which ideas might be worth pursuing, all of which were valuable time-savers.

Bobby was seeking what professionals in medical circles called a "sterilizing cure," one that completely eradicates HIV in the body so that there are no virus "stowaways" hiding in the tissues and organs, lying dormant beyond the reach of drugs and antibodies. These reservoirs of latent HIV had proven impossible to find and destroy. Dormant HIV is almost immortal. In its sleep-like state, it can survive in the human body for more than seventy years, patiently waiting for the optimum time to emerge and wreak havoc. In order for there to be a "sterilizing cure," the shroud of anonymity protecting these HIV reservoirs had to be torn away.

In the absence of a cure, even those people fortunate enough to receive antiretroviral drug cocktails are relegated to a lifetime of daily pill-taking and the health consequences incident to the chronic inflammation that is caused by their immune systems having to mount a continuous response to the ever-present virus. To make matters worse, a frequent side-effect of the antiretroviral drug regime is the exacerbation of tissue inflammation. The end result is that the body ages prematurely. The detriments include nerve damage, cardiac disease, loss of connective tissue, muscle shrinkage, kidney and bone disease, increased risk of cancer and neurocognitive defects such as dementia. Even if the antiretroviral drug regimen is followed with fervor, a patient is still able to transmit the virus to others. And if the patient discontinues the drugs, within weeks HIV levels in the blood rebound quickly, bringing with them a renewed onslaught by the virus and the destruction of what remains of the immune system.

Antiretroviral drugs had become a veritable goldmine for Big Pharma over many decades, and there was no end in sight, as each patient was a lifelong customer needing to consume the drugs on a daily basis. There was no shortage of such customers throughout the world, and new customers were created every day. A pandemic such as AIDS can be extremely good for business.

Bobby knew that a "sterilizing cure" was the only acceptable solution for HIV, just as he had known that cures and not treatments were the answer for all diseases that he had successfully worked on in the past. Even in the U.S., less than forty percent of the people infected with HIV were taking antiretroviral drugs, and only thirty percent had achieved viral suppression. In the rest of the world, it was worse.

To be practical, a cure could not involve blood transfusions, stem cell or bone marrow transplants, gene replacement, gene-splicing surgeries, a series of injections or any of the other hospital procedures that were currently being experimented with in the medical community. With tens of millions of infected people worldwide, and many of them living in areas that had limited or no medical facilities, the cure had to be capable of being delivered orally with as few repeat applications as possible—and it had to be inexpensive so that it would be available to everyone.

# 46

A S THE MONTHS WENT BY, Susan became more and more concerned. Bobby was increasingly uncommunicative. His pallid complexion, the dark circles under his eyes and his substantial weight loss made it apparent that he was under tremendous pressure and sleeping very little. Every morning when she arrived at work, she found him sitting at his desk, intensely staring at the four computer screens in front of him on which a rotating succession of images of the genetic structure of HIV were projected in a repeating slideshow. Focusing on these images to the exclusion of all else, Bobby appeared to be immersed in an obsessive thought process.

By lunchtime each day, when she walked by his office and looked in, she would see Bobby's elbows planted firmly on the desk with his chin resting on his hands, his back erect and his eyes shut tight. He would remain immobile in this stance for virtually the entire day. Susan had no idea what he was doing or what was going on.

While she had witnessed him go into trances over the years, what was taking place now was at a different level. He was completely absent almost all the time. He barely ate or drank during the day and apparently he could suspend his need to go to the toilet. When she approached him, he was oblivious to her presence, even when she called his name or lightly shook his shoulder. He just wasn't there.

One night, when she was getting ready to leave the office a little after 9:00 p.m., she was surprised to see Bobby making a pilgrimage to the kitchen. "Bobby, what's going on with you? Are you okay? I've never seen you like this."

"Susan, I'm thinking, that's all."

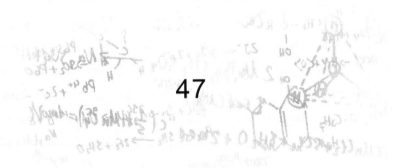

# 47

THERE WERE NO IMAGES ON the screen as the narrator spoke. He delivered his message slowly in a sonorous baritone, first in Arabic and then successively in Kurdish and Farsi. When this was later translated by analysts into English, it read as follows:

> "Those who fail to surrender to Ansar Jamaat and pledge fealty to Caliph Yusuf al-Saeed will suffer the Sword of the Mahdi."

The video then cut to a series of scenes, each of which bore a date and time code in the bottom right corner. First, the viewer saw a large outdoor pen that was enclosed with barbed wire and occupied by approximately fifty men, women and children who were standing or milling about. The video was loud with the sound of animated human conversation. The people appeared to be in good health and well nourished. Each one had a red sticker affixed to his or her clothing on the right side of the chest, which bore an identification number.

Next, the viewer saw two people clothed in white hazmat suits enter the enclosure. They each carried a small apparatus and walked quickly to the center of the pen where they raised these devices high over their heads. The camera zoomed in for an extreme close-up, but if the viewer didn't pay close attention, he or she would miss the single burst of spray which was emitted from the nozzle of each machine. The bursts lasted no more than two seconds, and the amount of the emission was miniscule, comparable to the fine mist of a perfume atomizer. Then the hazmat-protected people quickly exited the fenced-in area.

The following scene showed the same group of red-stickered people five days later. Virtually all of them exhibited the symptoms of a cold. Sneezing and coughing were prevalent. Children's noses were running and mothers could be seen feeling their kids' foreheads for fever.

The video then moved on to a room that looked like a gymnasium. It was occupied by approximately one hundred men, women and children. All of them had blue stickers affixed to their chests, each with an identification number. In contrast to the red-stickered people, this population appeared to be in good health and animated. A procession of red-stickered people was led into the gym by hazmat-clothed individuals carrying assault rifles.

Then viewers see a split screen that indicates five days have gone by. On the left, the blue-stickered people now exhibit cold symptoms. The right shows the red-stickered people, now ten days after their initial exposure to the mist that was sprayed in the pen, looking worn, haggard and suffering what appear to be advanced respiratory flu symptoms. Most of the red-stickered people are crouched on their haunches or sitting on the ground. If one looks closely, he or she would notice that many of the red-stickered people have tiny red pimples on their hands and faces.

The next scene in the video is marked to indicate that it is Day # 21. It takes the viewer to the outdoor enclosure in which the red-stickered people were first encountered. Most of them are either lying on the ground or are staggering around. As the camera pans by, it is apparent that many are having extreme difficulty breathing and are visibly gasping for air. A black mucus-like substance is either caked on, or leaking from, their noses, ears and the corners of their eyes. Numerous festering pustules mark their faces, hands and arms. Any skin which isn't covered with these ulcers has a bluish tint, likely caused by insufficient levels of oxygen in the blood. The hair on their heads, most noticeable on the women and children, has fallen out in large patches and the sclera of their eyes is yellowed. Some of the people are coughing up a tar-like substance, perhaps coagulated blood, and others are convulsing spasmodically. As the camera focuses in more closely, it is apparent that many of the people have lost control of their excretory functions.

The viewer is then shown the blue-stickered people ten days after having comingled with the red- stickered people. The people with blue stickers are now showing the same advanced flu-like symptoms and red pimples that the viewer had previously witnessed on the red-stickered people.

The video has delivered the message that this disease is highly contagious and can be transmitted when healthy people are merely in the same room as infected people whose only symptoms at the time of exposure are those of a common cold.

Next on the screen, a dozen people dressed in hazmat suits throw the ravaged bodies of the dead and the dying into dump trucks which then pull up to a huge ditch. The trucks raise their beds causing their human contents to tumble into the mammoth hole, already half-full of corpses from previous trips. With this task completed, the trucks pull away. Five of the hazmat clothed individuals, weighted down by large contraptions hanging from their backs, walk to the edge of the pit. On the signal of the troop's leader, they aim the nozzles of their flamethrowers into the chasm. An apocalyptic fire rains down upon the remains of the hapless victims, all of whom were test subjects of Dr. Aamir Mahmoud.

At the end of this scene, the narrator intoned:

"You have now seen what the Sword of the Mahdi can do. There will be no mercy for apostates and infidels. The disease with which Ansar Jamaat infected these heretics is like no other on Earth. It is a new disease, created with divine intervention, for which there is no cure and no treatment. The only end to the suffering is death."

It didn't take more than a couple of hours for this video to metastasize on the internet and garner international attention. Commentators who professed expertise regarding Islam explained that the Mahdi is the Muslim messiah who will be revealed on Earth amidst chaos and carnage to establish an Islamic kingdom under Sharia law. Spokespeople from governments expressed doubt that the video was bona fide. A view quickly developed that the video was a cleverly conceived propaganda tool that had been created using local actors, expert makeup, CGI and other special effects. A gaggle of prominent science analysts for major news outlets advised that there is no known disease which exhibits all of the symptoms shown in the video, and that the creation of a new disease of this magnitude is a highly complex undertaking well beyond the capabilities of a terrorist organization such as Ansar Jamaat. Other experts opined that it is extraordinarily difficult to use biological agents effectively as weapons because of delivery system and control limitations. All of these views were echoed by the top military and security spokespeople for the G20 nations.

When news of the video first broke, the major stock exchanges dropped on average four percent, but once the pundits' opinions saturated the media, the losses were quickly reversed and the markets had a good trading day. Everyone felt reassured that the Sword of the Mahdi was a hoax.

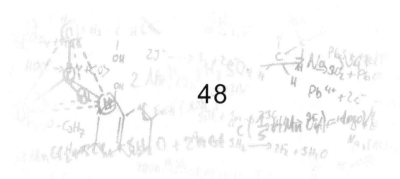

# 48

SUSAN COULDN'T FIND BOBBY ANYWHERE. She called the house in Annisquam to see if he was there, but Melissa said he wasn't. She called the lab's gatehouse and asked if Bobby had driven off. He hadn't. She decided to walk the grounds and look for him, thinking perhaps he needed to get some fresh air.

Briskly covering one end of the property to the other, Susan couldn't find him. While she didn't want to admit to herself why she was doing it, she combed the rocks and water below the cliffs on all sides of the peninsula. Puzzled and concerned, she sat down on a small bench near the water's edge. Looking up at the stone watchtower, she recalled how treacherous its narrow winding interior staircase was, hewn of uneven stone and lacking a railing. She had only been up there a few times when she was in the process of furnishing the cabin, which sat at its apex, and she hadn't liked the climb. With a sense of trepidation, she entered the tower. When she reached the top of the stairs, she was so eager to get herself out of the stairwell that she burst through the cabin door.

There were no lights on in the room and it was now dusk outside. Bobby was sitting at his small desk staring out the window. The ocean was fast disappearing in the darkening sky.

"I didn't know where you were. I've never seen you use this place," said Susan.

Bobby turned to look at her. She could see that there were tears in his eyes. "I come here more than you think. Sometimes even very late at night."

Susan's face paled as she approached him. "Bobby, are you alright?"

He shook his head.

"What's wrong?" she pressed further.

"Did you see the report that just came out in the *New England Journal of Medicine*?" Bobby motioned to a copy that was on his desk.

Susan picked up the periodical and read the following:

An aggressive new mutated HIV strain has been found in recently infected patients in Cuba. The virulent strain can develop into AIDS in one-third the time of other known strains. The progression happens so fast that treatment with antiretroviral drugs may come too late. The strain has also been observed in regions of Africa.

"What does this mean, Bobby?"

"It means that I have to work faster and better."

"You're doing good," said Susan. "You had some setbacks, but you're making progress. You'll get there, I know it."

With his gaze set on his computer screen, Bobby said, "This virus is the perfect killing machine. It mutates at sixty-five times the rate of the next most prolific virus known. A few years after a person is infected with one strain of HIV, he'll have at least a dozen different strains of HIV in his body and each successive one has evolved to

204

be more drug-resistant than the last. No two people in the entire world are infected with the same strain of HIV. It's incredible. The combinations are endless and unpredictable—like a slot machine."

"I'm not really understanding this whole mutation thing."

"It's rather complicated," Bobby replied as he picked up a yellow pad and pencil.

Susan waved her hand at him. "Give me the abbreviated version and skip the diagrams, please."

Bobby took a deep breath and expelled it audibly. "HIV is a retrovirus, meaning that it carries its genes in the form of a single strand of RNA, rather than a DNA strand or double-helix. In DNA replication, a cell employs many molecular proofreaders to help avoid changes to its genetic code and thereby eliminate or minimize the possibility of mutations. But the way HIV replicates is by hacking the cells of the human body. This process has no proofreaders and replication errors are rampant. It's these errors caused by HIV sloppily copying its genes that create a never-ending series of mutations that result in innumerable strains of HIV. It evolves so quickly that drugs and human antibodies can't keep up. A single virus can spawn billions of copies in one day, constantly mutating as it reproduces."

"Who would ever have thought that a sloppy accident of nature would create an indestructible disease?" said Susan.

Bobby's face reddened. "That's not it, Susan. You're missing the point. These reproduction errors are not accidents of nature. This process is the purposeful creation of an active evil that empowers this virus. It's no coincidence that the only cells that HIV attacks are the cells that the body relies on to protect itself. No virus can be this insidious on its own."

Susan pulled a chair close to Bobby's and sat next to him in the nearly dark room. Neither said anything for a few minutes as they watched the moonlight reflect on the blackness of the ocean. "Bobby, you're going to beat this thing. I have every confidence. I just wish it wasn't taking such a toll on you. I'm worried. I've seen this before with you."

Bobby nodded in recognition of Susan's concerns. "The medical community doesn't know it yet, but the virus will soon outpace the antiretroviral drugs that people are taking to control it. The world is going back to square one on this disease. People think it's under control. They have no idea what's going to happen—and it will happen soon."

"You cured it once before. You'll do it again—and this time, the cure won't be lost."

Lowering his head, Bobby said, "Sometimes I wonder if I ever did cure it. I just don't know anymore. Every time I take a step forward, I get knocked back three. I'm fighting a force of infinite resourcefulness, and AIDS is one of its greatest achievements. My night terrors are so bad, I'm lucky to get three hours of sleep. I can't keep food down. I have to go so far out there mentally, trying to fight this thing, that I'm scared I won't find my way back. I don't have Christina to help me this time."

"Have her come and stay here with you. She wants to. You know that."

"I can't. She almost got killed last time. I won't put her in danger like that again."

"You need her, Bobby. She's your wife."

———— •••• ————

When Susan got back to her office in the laboratory, she called Christina on her cell phone. "Christina. It's Susan."

"Is everything okay?"

"Bobby needs you. He doesn't want you to come. You know that. But the choice is no longer his. You know that too."

# 49

I T WAS 8:00 P.M. ON the day after receiving Susan's call when Christina peeked into Bobby's office at the lab. He was typing on his computer keyboard at a frenetic pace, his light-blue eyes focused intensely on the monitors. It was as if he were taking high-speed dictation from some unseen source. His fingers moved almost in a blur, and he stopped only occasionally to rub his forehead with his left hand and make notations in a notebook. The printer feverishly spat paper, hundreds of pages of printouts were piling up in several sorters, each page rife with equations and formulas.

At 9:30 p.m., Christina reappeared at Bobby's door. She walked into the office and stepped behind him. He was oblivious to her coming in. She leaned in on him and brushed her lips against his right ear as she put her hands on his shoulders. Perhaps it was the heat of her body or the scent of her hair, but Bobby's typing began to slow as he leaned back into her and exhaled in relief, finally starting to decompress from the day. Placing his hands atop hers, Bobby felt a warm contentment surge through him like an opiate. "I am the luckiest man on Earth," he said softly.

Christina laughed. "It's time to eat dinner, Mr. Lucky. Come with me." Bobby followed her into a small dining nook that was adjacent to the kitchen. Christina had set the table with a white linen cloth and goblet-sized wine glasses. The only light was provided by two tall candles burning in brass holders positioned in the center of the rustic oak table.

"Is that steak that I smell?" asked Bobby.

"Yes, with garlic butter on top, just the way you like it," Christina answered as she filled their glasses with a smooth Burgundy.

"This is the first real meal I've had since I last saw you."

Christina nodded. "I can tell. You're beginning to look like a POW."

Within a few minutes, Bobby disconnected from their conversation and appeared to be hyper-focused on eating his food, his eyes fixed on his plate and his hands moving robotically as he cut his steak and delivered the morsels to his mouth. Christina recognized that he was no longer present and had slipped back into work mode, his mind not giving him a respite to enjoy a meal.

"Bobby." He didn't look up or answer.

"Bobby." Still no reaction from him. Christina smacked the side of the table and the sharp sound snapped him out of his daze.

"Wow, this steak is great," he said.

Christina smiled. "Welcome back."

"I'm sorry, hon." Bobby took a gulp of his wine. "How are the kids? I feel like I haven't seen them in an eternity."

Christina looked down at her plate. "They miss you. Every day they ask where you are. I tell them you're working. They ask why you like to work more than seeing them."

Bobby drained his wine glass. "Sounds like they may have had a little prompting from you."

Christina pursed her lips as she pushed her vegetables around on the plate. "No, they didn't."

"Do they understand I'm trying to help people? That I'm trying to save lives—save lives of kids, like them?"

Christina shook her head in exasperation. "Pete is six and Mirielle is four. They're young, Bobby. They just want their dad. They need you. They love you so much."

Bobby bit down on his lip and began to scratch his cheek. Seeing his discomfort, Christina tried to lighten the conversation. "Pete told me he wants to be just like you when he grows up. A scientist. Of course, his pronunciation of scientist was rather special."

"He's such an incredibly gifted musician. That's what he should do. Science, I don't think so." Bobby emptied the wine bottle into his and Christina's goblets.

"Now Mirielle, we'll see about that one," said Christina, chuckling. "She scares me sometimes. The way she looks at me. I don't know what's going on in that little head of hers."

Bobby laughed. "Yeah, the jury's out on her for sure. But I have a feeling she's going to be a very special lady one day, just like her mother."

Christina pointed her fork at Bobby. "Flattery will get you everywhere, you know."

"I hope so. I need all the help I can get," said Bobby as he moved his chair close to Christina and put his arm around her back.

As they rose from the dinner table, Christina and Bobby gulped down the remnants of the Burgundy in their goblets. Bobby noticed that in the flickering candlelight, Christina's lips looked sensuously swollen as if they had been plumped by the wine and had taken on its deep ruby hue. They headed to Bobby's office.

"When was the last time you actually opened this thing up and slept on the mattress and used pillows and a blanket like a real person?" Christina asked as she stood next to the sofa bed that sat in the far corner of Bobby's office. Bobby looked sheepish. "Exactly what I thought. Never," she said. Christina took the cushions off the sofa and opened up the bed. Bobby playfully pushed her down on it. "Hold on, mister," she said, springing up. "I'll be right back."

In a few minutes, Christina returned with the candlesticks from the dining room. She placed them on a small table next to the sofa, and turned off the lights in the room. The candles cast a soft glow that enveloped its subjects and sent their shadows dancing on the bare walls. "Oh my God. Look how skinny you've gotten," said Christina as she ran her hands over Bobby's body. "I'm going to have to fatten you up." Bobby ignored her comment as he buried his face in her hair and kissed her neck. Her eyes closed, Christina skimmed her lips across Bobby's chest and began to gently bite him as her hands moved down his torso. She could feel his excitement. "Don't rush, Bobby. We have all the time in the world."

As Bobby relaxed into the languid sensuousness of their embrace, his eyes locked with Christina's and as their bodies moved in rhythmic harmony, she felt like she had left present time and was traveling in a sea of eroticism to a destination unknown.

"I love you, Christina," Bobby whispered as his fingers swept through her luxuriant hair and his lips traveled from her breasts to the silken skin of her thighs, gently kissing her everywhere along the way like a fervent worshipper.

And then, for a moment, as if on cue, their movements stopped. They grasped each other's hands tightly, their bodies rigid with the athleticism of their passion. Their lips met with force as their mouths pressed together. This was not an ordinary kiss. This was a communication between a man and a woman at the most primitive and intimate level. This kiss both acknowledged and sealed their bond and their need for each other. This kiss was a promise.

# 50

THE NEXT MORNING AT 9:00 a.m., Susan knocked on the office door and entered without waiting for a response. To her surprise, she saw Bobby and Christina lying in bed, Christina's head resting contentedly on Bobby's chest, her beautiful dark hair splayed on the pillow. "Oh, I'm sorry. I just wanted to see if Bobby wanted a breakfast sandwich from the deli. I didn't know you were here, Christina." Susan had difficulty containing the size of her smile.

Christina was radiant, her olive skin aglow and her exquisite eyes glittering in the morning sunlight. "That's so sweet of you, Susan. I think we'd both like one."

Bobby turned toward Susan. "It would be great if mine could have sausage and cheddar on it."

This was the first time Susan had seen Bobby look relaxed and happy in months. He appeared five years younger than the day before. "I'll be back soon," said Susan jovially. "There's a fresh pot of coffee brewing in the kitchen.

From across the room, Bobby watched as Christina slipped into her clothing. "Why are you staring at me?" she asked when she noticed what he was doing.

"I don't know which is sexier, watching you get dressed or watching you get undressed. I said it to you when we first met and I'll say it again. You're a goddess."

Christina walked over to Bobby and gave him a peck on the cheek. "It's sweet of you to say that about a mother of two. We've been through an awful lot since that night in St. Thomas."

Sitting at a wrought-iron table on the Spanish-tiled veranda, Christina, Bobby and Susan consumed their egg sandwiches and coffee, but as the meal progressed, Bobby became increasingly quiet and morose. Finally, he said, "This has been amazing, but I'm off schedule. Time to get back to the salt mines."

Christina glanced at Susan who understood that a private moment was needed. Susan gathered the plates and excused herself.

"I'm moving in with the kids," said Christina, her eyes narrowing in resolute determination. When Bobby's mouth began to form his first word of objection, Christina preempted him. "No, Bobby. I don't want to hear it. I know how you feel but you don't make my decisions. I'm your wife and the mother of your children and I decide. I won't let you erect barriers that separate this family, no matter how good your intentions may be."

Bobby's eyes were focused on the table. For several moments he was immobile, his body rigid. When he looked up, Christina saw that the infinite blue of his pupils was awash in concern. "If anything happens to you or the kids, I'll never forgive myself."

Christina reached over and took Bobby's hands in hers. "Do you trust me? There was a time when you didn't."

"And when I didn't, I made the biggest mistake of my life. I trust you more than anyone."

"Then trust that I know that you won't make it through this alone. I've seen how far out your mind has to travel to beat this disease. The last time you were up against it, you lost all contact with present reality. You were gone. I was the only one who could pull you back and I did, again and again. We'll get through this together. I'm not going to lose you, Bobby. I won't let it take you away from me."

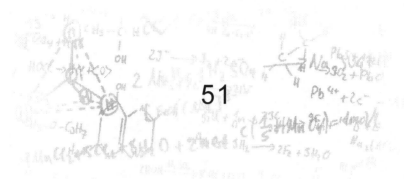

# 51

CHRISTINA SET UP LIVING QUARTERS at the far end of the second floor of the mammoth house so that Bobby would have all the quiet and privacy that he and the lab staff needed on the main floor. She continued to leave early every morning for work, but Manchester was twenty minutes closer to her office than Annisquam, so she had more time in the morning to spend with the kids and have a coffee with Bobby before Melissa went on duty.

Although Bobby continued to work at least fifteen hours a day, the presence of his family in the building provided him with a physical counter to the cerebral ether in which he spent most of his time. Interacting with Pete and Mirielle for a few hours almost every day was his greatest pleasure and gave his mind a much-needed opportunity to recharge.

On those nights when Bobby didn't sleep in the lab, Christina would use her expertise in dealing with night terrors to get him through. But even with all of this, Bobby knew that his physical and mental stamina were waning. He felt that he was being worn down in a war of attrition waged against him by an omnipotent force. Acutely aware that his energies were being drained, he understood that he wouldn't be able to fight indefinitely. He had to make some major breakthroughs soon.

# 52

A BLACK TOYOTA LAND CRUISER, COVERED in dust from the unpaved roads, screeched to a halt in front of Mahmoud's lab. A particularly large Ansar Jamaat soldier exited the passenger side of the vehicle and hurriedly entered the building. Two minutes later, he reappeared with Mahmoud in tow, whom he roughly guided into the backseat.

When the SUV arrived at Colonel Fahd's headquarters, Mahmoud was hustled into his office. Fahd was seated, leaning forward in his chair, his eyes focused on his computer monitor. He didn't acknowledge Mahmoud's entrance. The biochemist stood stiffly as he waited to be addressed, his mind racing as he tried to fathom why he had been yanked out of his lab and brought here. He couldn't help but notice how small Fahd looked in his oversized executive chair. *If the seat hadn't been raised to its maximum height, his head would be level with the desk*, he mused.

After about three minutes, Mahmoud realized that he and Fahd weren't alone. In a dimly lit corner at the far side of the room, a tall, skeletal figure clothed entirely in black stood with his back to Mahmoud. When Saeed turned to face him, Mahmoud shuddered.

"The videos were a failure," said Saeed, his voice hoarse with disgust. "They think it was a hoax. A cheap ruse. A stunt. They laughed at us." Saeed's black eyes drilled into Mahmoud as he moved toward him.

"I'm so sorry, Caliph," replied Mahmoud, who was careful to look down at the floor as he addressed Saeed. "I thought that the videos of the test subjects would do what we needed them to do."

Saeed's closed mouth was twisting in a way that made it appear as if he were consuming his own tongue. Glaring at Mahmoud, he said, "I don't blame you. I should have followed my instincts. When the Americans had the atomic bomb, they didn't talk about it or show a film. They leveled two Japanese cities. Nobody laughed at them."

Colonel Fahd stood up, but still remained behind his desk as if it provided him with a barrier of safety. "What happened is for the best, Caliph. When they see that Ansar Jamaat truly has the Sword of the Mahdi, their shock will be much greater than if they had never doubted us. It will have been their choice not to heed our warning. They will pay for their arrogance."

Now standing next to Mahmoud, Saeed's tall frame towered over him. The hairs on Mahmoud's skin bristled as if an insect was crawling down his spine. "Mahmoud, this is a crucial time for the caliphate. If we don't have credibility, we will fail, and that is something that I will not permit to happen. Fear is the foundation upon which respect is built. Do you understand me?"

Mahmoud nodded. "Yes, Caliph. I understand."

# 53

I T WAS A BEAUTIFUL MIDSUMMER Sunday afternoon in Manchester. Christina walked into Bobby's office and placed her hands on his shoulders as he stared at a page of equations. Leaning against him, she said, "Bobby, it's Sunday. Time to stop working. Come with me. I have a treat for you."

Bobby followed Christina into the kitchen. "Here, you hold this," she said as she handed him a bottle of cold Pinot Grigio and two wine glasses. "I'll bring the platter of ham and cheese paninis I just made. The kids are already in the backyard."

A blue-and-white striped blanket had been spread out underneath the canopy of a large copper beech tree. Christina and Bobby kicked off their shoes and leaned against the tree's massive trunk; each held a glass of wine in one hand and a panini in the other.

"Mirielle, stop trying to take Pete's new toy away from him," Christina said as Mirielle jumped up, her little hands grabbing at his bubble blower.

They all watched as the giant soap bubbles floated, their shapes undulating with the air currents and their thin membranes swirling with prismatic colors in the brilliant sunlight. The bubbles seemed alive as they glided effortlessly on their gravity-defying journey, bouncing off the lawn furniture without breaking, and then catching a breeze which took them even higher. And then suddenly and inexplicably, the bubbles would burst, often on Mirielle's head as she chased them around the yard.

As Bobby viewed the bubbles, a particularly large one descended from on high and seemed to hover over his head as if it were observing him. It then burst in midair, showering him with its soapy residue. For a moment, Bobby just sat there, wiping the wetness off his face as the kids laughed gleefully. Then his eyes grew wide. "I can't believe it. Why didn't I think of that?"

Bobby abruptly kissed the kids, nodded to Christina and rushed to his office. Invigorated by the epiphany that he just had, he closed the door and embarked on what would be a particularly intense work regimen which consumed him for the next nine months.

What Bobby realized when Pete's soap bubble burst on his head was that he could destroy HIV by bursting its bubble. HIV is surrounded by a protective membrane made of fatty compounds called phospholipids. This lipid bilayer membrane was analogous to the membrane of Pete's soap bubble. If Bobby could find a way to destroy HIV's lipid envelope, then the virus would be naked and exposed, making it more vulnerable than it ever had been.

Using his mathematical language to analyze the way thousands of different chemicals interacted with HIV's protective membrane, Bobby searched for ingredients that he could manipulate to create a formulation that would destroy the HIV membrane without harming healthy human cells. After months of experimentation, working in conjunction with an expanded staff at the research laboratories of Tufts medical school, Bobby synthesized a protein which had the capability of adhering to the HIV envelope and punching innumerable holes in it. He then devised a unique method to deliver this protein to the viral membrane by infusing nanoparticles with the protein. The protein-covered nanoparticles would then attach themselves to the "gp 120" and "gp 41" viral proteins that were present on the surface of the membrane. Once this adhesion took place, Bobby's protein fused with the viral membrane and ruptured it so thoroughly that the membrane was completely stripped off from the virus.

What Bobby had done was to attack HIV by destroying a vital part of its cellular structure. This had never been done before, and it was something that HIV could not overcome through mutation or adaptation. Without its protective membrane, the virus was bare and defenseless against drugs and human antibodies. Additionally, the loss of its membrane impaired HIV's ability to bind to human host cells because the virus' "gp 120" and "gp 41" proteins that are on the surface of the viral membrane serve as the target recognition, receptor and binding mechanisms that initiate the fusion of HIV with human cells. This is the first step in bringing the virus and host cells together, thereby initiating the infection process and the HIV reproduction process. With the membrane gone, those proteins were gone, too.

As extraordinary an achievement as this was, Bobby was determined that his assault on HIV was to be multi-faceted. He was going to destroy it so thoroughly and by so many methods working in combination with each other, that there would be no chance of its survival.

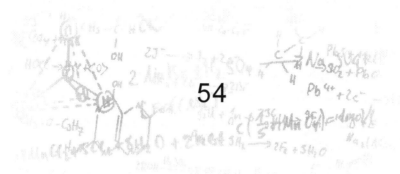

# 54

I N ORDER TO STOP A machine from working, you remove or destroy its parts. Bobby viewed HIV as a machine. Step one for him was destroying HIV's protective membrane. Step two involved two enzymes that were crucial to HIV, *reverse transcriptase* and *integrase*.

Like other retroviruses, HIV contains an enzyme called *reverse transcriptase.* This enzyme empowers HIV's single-stranded RNA genetic material to be converted into double-stranded DNA, the form it must be in to infect human cells. Once this conversion has taken place, another enzyme in HIV called *integrase* inserts HIV's genetic material into the human host cell's DNA so that the cell becomes infected with HIV. After *integrase* has done its job, the human host cell has reached the point of no return and it will become not only a permanent carrier of HIV, but also a factory for further HIV reproduction and mutation. Without these enzymes, HIV would not be able to infect human beings.

Bobby knew what he had to do. He needed to destroy both *reverse transcriptase* and *integrase* in HIV. In fact, when he studied the hard drives that Jonathan Bick had retrieved for him from

Martin Turnbull, he saw many unsuccessful attempts by his pre-explosion self to do this. He wondered if the method to achieve this was finally discovered in those sixteen crucial minutes between the final recorded computer entry and the lab explosion.

As part of the daily treatments that are sold to millions of HIV patients, Big Pharma incorporates medications that inhibit or interrupt some of the processes of these two enzymes. So why didn't the industry go further and put its extraordinary research resources into finding a way to destroy these enzymes in HIV, rather than taking halfway measures that required the daily consumption of a cocktail of pills?

The answer was clear to Bobby. He had seen it throughout his career. Treatments are more profitable than cures. His quest to find a method to destroy these two enzymes would be his next goal in his effort to formulate a durable multi-pronged "sterilizing cure."

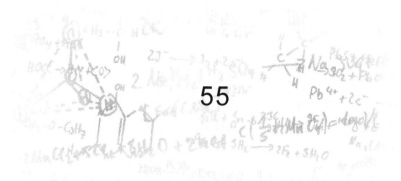

# 55

A SMALL IRAQI CITY ON THE north bank of the Euphrates River, Rakut was populated by approximately eight thousand people. Twenty percent of its population was comprised of Christians, sixty-five percent was Shia Muslim, and the remaining fifteen percent were Sunni Muslim, like the members of Ansar Jamaat.

Life in Rakut had never been easy. It was a hardscrabble town where people labored relentlessly just to get by. Faris Khalili had lived there with his mother and two younger sisters for the last five months. They were squatters in a single room on the ground floor of an abandoned decrepit building, with no plumbing or electricity. Like so many others, the Khalili family were serial refugees who fled from one strife- torn area to the next. Faris was nineteen years old. His father had been killed by a landmine when he was thirteen, so Faris' duties as the man of the family began early.

Faris was one of those young men who was strikingly handsome in an effortless and almost careless way. It's as if nature decided to have fun and gave him everything, paying no attention to the fact that the individual on whom it bestowed such gifts would never reap their rewards because of his circumstances. Standing five feet ten inches tall, his dark hair was thick, smooth and coiffed in waves that intersected each other, even though he had never had the benefit of a barber's services. A graceful but strong neck set off broad powerful shoulders, substantial arms and a V-shaped back with an attenuated waist. This was a man who had never been inside a gym in his life, but he looked like he worked out two hours a day with a trainer. His facial features were so artfully sculpted that he almost looked pretty, and one couldn't help think what a beautiful woman he would have been had his chromosomes given him that role. In another country, opportunities for one so physically attractive might have presented themselves; perhaps he could have been a model or an actor or used his looks to further a business career. But here in Rakut, Faris' appearance made no difference. Like everyone else, he was just trying to survive.

Neither Faris nor any other person in Rakut noticed that starting at 3:00 a.m. on the night of May 2, Ansar Jamaat's forces quietly moved four artillery cannons into place on the city's compass points three-quarters of a mile away, and stationed eighty armed vehicles at regular intervals around its perimeter. Several thousand Ansar Jamaat troops dug in between the vehicles. A quarter of a mile closer to the city, another large contingent of troops surrounded it and erected a series of pre-constructed watchtowers that ringed the town.

Seated in a tan Hummer that had been poorly repainted so that its Iraqi Army decals still could be discerned if one looked closely, Fahd and Saeed were dressed in their most impressive outfits. Fahd wore a red beret, positioned on his head at a rakish tilt. His camouflage fatigues had been meticulously pressed and starched as if they were a dress uniform. Fahd's small chest was covered by a plethora of medals and ribbons, and tricolor aiguillettes adorned his shoulders. Each of his epaulets bore five gold stars in the fashion of Eisenhower. One would assume that all of these items had been awarded to Fahd while he served in Saddam Hussein's army, but perhaps the collection had been supplemented by purchases on the internet.

In contrast to Fahd's elaborate getup, Saeed was resplendent in simplicity. He wore a white tunic, a white turban wrapped around a green *kalansuwa* and a long red silk vest which was decorated with gold embroidery.

Saeed looked at his wrist watch: It was 4:45 a.m. He pulled on his beard thoughtfully and then nodded to Fahd who picked up a walkie-talkie and said a few words. About thirty seconds later, the four artillery cannons could be seen recoiling as they emitted their charges. Each cannon fired once. They were so well synchronized that only one blast was heard rather than four.

# 56

WHEN THE SHELLS LANDED IN Rakut, there was no explosion, no loud noise, no fire, no shrapnel, no shock wave, no odor and no destruction. There was just a soft hissing sound which the sleeping residents wouldn't have heard. The expulsion from the shells of a clear gaseous mist lasted only about ten seconds. When the citizens of Rakut awoke and saw artillery shells that appeared to be intact, they were thankful, but also concerned that the shells might still explode. A volunteer group of Rakut's citizens delicately placed the four shells in a small truck so that they could take them into the desert and bury them. These brave individuals were the first casualties. As the outskirts of Rakut appeared in their truck's rearview mirror, a rocket fired from one of Ansar Jamaat's perimeter vehicles obliterated the truck.

It didn't take long for the residents of Rakut to see that deliveries headed into Rakut were being turned away by Ansar Jamaat troops, as were passenger vehicles seeking to enter. Those being denied admittance were the fortunate ones. Any of Rakut's inhabitants who attempted to leave was gunned down by the Ansar Jamaat troops. *Why is this happening? We are not a strategic city. We have no oil. We are not a political stronghold.* The citizens of Rakut were baffled by the fate that had befallen them.

The tone of Saeed's voice left little doubt as to the inviolability of his directives. "There can be no slipups, Colonel Fahd. Nobody leaves Rakut and nobody enters. Rakut is our Hiroshima. The United States didn't achieve a one hundred percent mortality rate. We will."

Ansar Jamaat didn't seek to block the ability of Rakut's citizens to communicate with the outside world. Phone lines remained operative as did cellular and internet connections. In fact, Saeed wanted Rakut's inhabitants to broadcast their plight to the widest audience.

When word first spread in Iraq, and then throughout the international community, that Rakut was under siege by Ansar Jamaat, the assumption by all concerned was that the militant group was looking to subject the citizens of Rakut to food and supply shortages in an effort to get them to surrender their city. The call for an airlift of food, bottled water and medical supplies was dutifully answered within days by the United Nations. Leaders of Western nations appeared on television to congratulate themselves on their success in mobilizing such a quick response to help the beleaguered people of Rakut. Discussions began almost immediately about the need for a multinational strike force to engage Ansar Jamaat militarily and end the blockade of Rakut. These talks quickly became mired in the cesspool of politics and nothing was done.

By May 7, five days after the artillery shells landed, reports from Rakut provided the first indication that what was transpiring there was far more insidious than had originally been thought. With the passage of time, cold symptoms morphed into severe flu, and red pimples began to mark the faces of Rakut's citizenry.

The international community finally focused on the fact that the thousands of Ansar Jamaat troops surrounding Rakut were outfitted in hazmat suits. As more days passed, the video footage uploaded to the internet by the occupants of Rakut became increasingly desperate and grotesque. The dead were beginning to outnumber the living—and the living weren't far behind the dead. The same pundits who had been quick to dismiss Ansar Jamaat's original video as being a hoax, now prepared studious frame-by-frame analyses that confirmed that the symptoms in the Rakut videos were identical to those in the Ansar Jamaat video.

Also deeply disturbing was video footage posted online that showed the manner in which dwellers who sought to flee Rakut were exterminated by Ansar Jamaat. Irrespective of whether they fled on foot or in a vehicle, and whether their flight was under the cover of night or during the day, these refugees from atrocity became easy target practice for the troops stationed in the watchtowers. Once the marksmen had done their work, soldiers in hazmat gear stepped in with flamethrowers to burn the bodies; the fortunate ones had already died from gunshots before being engulfed in burning petrol.

Some media experts explained, with apologies, that the inferno which consumed these hapless souls was for everyone's benefit as it ensured that no one with the disease could escape Rakut and infect anyone beyond the city's borders.

The world's financial markets dropped fifteen percent in one day before the major stock and commodity exchanges closed trading to avoid a further slide. When the markets opened the next morning, the sell-off resumed until trading was suspended after the first thirty minutes during which there was a further twelve percent drop. No one noticed that two investment groups, one led by Viktor Bazhenov and the other by Huo Jin Gao, had shown uncanny prescience months before by putting in place highly leveraged options to short the markets.

For the first time in modern history, the world was confronted with a biological weapon being employed against a city's entire population to annihilate it. What added to the horror was that the disease that was being used to systematically decimate Rakut's inhabitants was a brand-new biological agent that had been methodically created for this purpose. The perpetrators were jihadists who, to the Western world, appeared to be no more than desert rats that had been fighting with old equipment salvaged from real armies—until now. How did this ragamuffin contingent have the scientific savvy to concoct a new disease? Was it true that there was no treatment and no cure? What was Ansar Jamaat's agenda? Did anyone really know?

As the world watched in disbelief, a new chapter in human depravity was being written in real time.

# 57

THIRTY-SIX DAYS AFTER ANSAR JAMAAT had fired the four artillery shells into Rakut, Saeed and Fahd entered the city in the same tan Hummer from which they had given their orders to fire the shells. This time, both were wearing hazmat suits, as was Dr. Mahmoud who accompanied them despite his objections. Traveling in their convoy were several trucks full of heavily armed soldiers and three video crews, all of whom were also protectively clothed.

There was no human life in Rakut. The putrid stench of bodies that had been infected with a malodorous disease and were now in an advanced stage of decay permeated the air. More than eight thousand people had been slaughtered; none had died an easy death.

Saeed turned to Mahmoud. Even with the amplification provided by the speaking apparatus in the hazmat suit, his voice was muffled. "You created the Sword of the Mahdi and it is an all-powerful sword. You should be proud of that. Don't be disturbed by what you see around you. The path to a new world, to the glorious caliphate that we are creating, will be strewn with bodies. That is unavoidable." Because of the hazmat suit that Mahmoud wore, Saeed couldn't see that Mahmoud had urinated on himself.

As Saeed, Fahd and Mahmoud trekked through the town, they saw corpses everywhere. Scraggly dogs and cats wandered aimlessly among the human rubble, having been robbed of their domestic existences. Rats that had grown fat feeding on deceased humans were unafraid of the oddly dressed people who walked among them. Birds gingerly maneuvered between the rodents, pecking at the festering flesh and feasting on the insects of decay which swarmed on the bodies. With a few quick hand signals, Saeed ordered his troops to shoot all creatures they encountered and to scour the town for more. If wildlife could possibly spread the contagion to humans in other communities, Saeed would lose control of the monster he had created.

"Caliph, may I ask that your soldiers gather twenty of the animal and bird carcasses, and a bag full of the insects, and bring them back to my lab for examination?" asked Mahmoud. Saeed nodded his agreement.

Colonel Fahd motioned to a mosque, knowing that the minaret's balcony would afford a bird's-eye view of the devastation and provide the perfect place from which to shoot video. Climbing six flights of steep stairs in hazmat suits in the heat of the desert wasn't easy. By the time that Saeed, Fahd and Mahmoud got to midway point, they were winded and decided to take a rest. Fahd pushed open an old wooden door on the fourth-floor landing and the party walked through. Their hazmat headgear was clouded from heavy breathing, so their vision was limited, but as they entered a large room devoid of furnishings what they saw did not seem possible. Huddled against the walls were twenty adults of various ages. They looked haggard, dirty and terrified, but they were alive. And they didn't look diseased.

"This cannot be. Mahmoud, what is going on?" said Saeed.

Mahmoud's voice was soft and weak. "Caliph, there are always some who, for reasons unknown, can withstand disease. There is something in their bodies, in their cells, that imparts all or partial immunity. If these are the only survivors out of the thousands that lived here, then the disease is more potent than any that has come before it."

Saeed grabbed an assault rifle from one of his soldiers, raised it to his right shoulder and pointed it at the survivors. "No one lives in Rakut," he shouted. Mahmoud lunged in front of Saeed's gun and pushed the barrel hard to the side. Even through the headgear, Mahmoud could see Saeed's enraged eyes.

"You dare to stop me? Are you crazy?" yelled Saeed.

Mahmoud's mind raced to find a reason. "Caliph. We need these people. They are useful to us. I need to do experiments on them to find out why they survived. By discovering that, I can make our disease stronger so that no one can survive."

Saeed slammed Mahmoud so hard in the chest that the scientist stumbled backwards and almost fell to the ground. Raising his automatic rifle and pointing it at a young woman who was cowering in a corner, Saeed snarled, "Are you the only survivors or are there more who aren't in this room?" The woman began to cry hysterically and prostrated herself on the floor. Saeed turned to one of his officers. "Search this entire town, every inch of it. If you find any other people alive, kill them. No exceptions." He then motioned to another soldier and pointed his gun at the survivors. "Take them all to the holding pens at the lab."

As heavily armed soldiers herded them into a makeshift line, the bedraggled group, many of whom seemed disoriented and in a state of shock, were led down the staircase. The last one in the line was Faris. His mother and his two sisters had died from the disease.

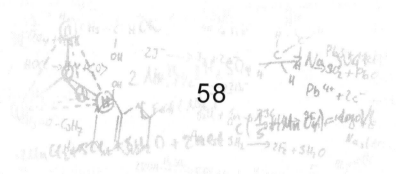

# 58

WITHIN TWENTY-FOUR HOURS AFTER ANSAR Jamaat commenced its attack on Rakut, drones from the United States began to take photographs and video footage of what was happening there. These materials, which documented the disease's progressive devastation of Rakut's population, were circulated among the top political and military echelons of the G20 countries. Nevertheless, no military action against Ansar Jamaat was taken, and no rescue attempts were launched.

It wasn't until three days after all of Ansar Jamaat's forces were withdrawn, that a coalition team comprised of biological weapons experts from the United States, Great Britain, Russia and Germany entered Rakut with a full complement of renowned scientists in the fields of etiology, epidemiology, molecular biology and biochemistry. A rescue team was not brought in, as thermal sensors in the drones indicated that there were no human beings alive in Rakut.

By the time the coalition team arrived, the corpses of Rakut's inhabitants were in an extremely advanced state of decay which had been accelerated by the area's unrelenting heat. The bodies had also been pillaged by a variety of rodents, insects and birds that had partaken in a multi-species feeding frenzy that had lasted weeks and was still ongoing. Despite this, the scientists were able to salvage some cellular materials from what remained of the carcasses, but nothing compared to what would have been possible if international forces had intervened while the citizens of Rakut were still living.

While the experts didn't agree as to how much could be learned about the disease from the specimens that were gathered, they all agreed on one thing: Rakut needed to be sanitized immediately to prevent the possibility of the infection spreading.

On July 9, four U.S. Air Force B-2 Spirit bombers took off from Riyadh Air Base in Saudi Arabia. They dropped three hundred and fifty-two Mark 77 incendiary bombs on Rakut. The city was obliterated in an inferno that was visible eighty miles away. Seven square miles of craters and charred sand replaced a community where eight thousand people had lived only two months before. One of the B-2 bomber pilots reported on his way back to base, "From up here, Rakut looks like an empty inkwell."

Ansar Jamaat posted a video of the conflagration. The following caption ran in a loop underneath footage of the fiery devastation:

*Hell on Earth*
*will come to those who oppose the caliphate of Yusuf al-Saeed*

## 59

BOBBY'S QUEST TO DESTROY THE *reverse transcriptase* and *integrase* enzymes took him back to the basic structure of all enzymes. Since they are not living things, they cannot be killed; but they can be rendered permanently dysfunctional, in which case the enzyme is considered "denatured." All enzymes are proteins composed of long chains of amino acids. The important part of an enzyme is called the active site. Anything that changes the shape of the active site stops the enzyme from working. This is similar to a key that opens a door lock. If you change the shape of the keys' teeth, the key no longer works.

Bobby knew that each particular enzyme can only operate within a certain temperature and pH range. If the enzyme is taken out of its temperature and pH comfort zone, then the hydrogen bonds that hold the enzyme's structure together break apart which, in turn, changes the shape of the enzyme's active site and makes it dysfunctional. This denaturation process is exactly what Bobby was interested in.

Bobby's experiments confirmed that it would not be possible for him to denature *reverse transcriptase* and *integrase* through temperature change, because that process could not be confined to the HIV cell. However, he believed that he could find a way to raise the pH level in the two enzymes in a controlled manner that would destroy them.

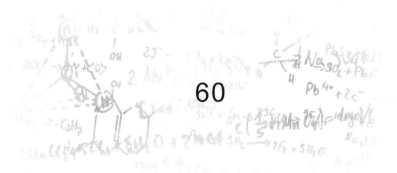

# 60

IT WOULD BE IMPOSSIBLE TO create a "sterilizing cure" for HIV unless Bobby could find a way to destroy the reservoirs of dormant HIV that hide in the cells of infected people. Dealing with the reservoir problem was a separate issue from the "HIV envelope" and the *reverse transcriptase and integrase* enzyme issues, because no matter how successful Bobby might ultimately be with the envelope and enzymes, the reservoir problem would remain. This was because the HIV in the reservoirs was, for all intents and purposes, invisible: Neither the HIV envelope or HIV enzymes could be located and attacked in the reservoirs.

The first step to effectively deal with the reservoirs was to find them. This had never been possible until Bobby made a breakthrough discovery. His biochemical analysis showed that all human cells that had been infiltrated by HIV contained traces of a clandestine protein, previously unknown, that he named EPJ. In cells in which HIV was hiding, EPJ was present at a *dilution factor of one-ninth*. That dilution factor was the turning point for Bobby.

He designed a formulation which he called CPMS that would bind itself chemically to only one thing in the human body: EPJ. So when CPMS would come in contact with EPJ, the two substances would adhere to one another, and, when they did, the chemical bond that resulted would create a visual "reporter" that could be seen in an MRI.

The comparative visual intensity of the "reporter" would indicate whether the cells had active or latent HIV within them; where the "reporter" was at its lowest visual intensity, the cells contained *latent* HIV. This allowed the HIV reservoirs to be identified and located with precision, and that was something that had never been possible. While it would not be necessary to use the MRI process in the treatment of individual patients, this protocol would demonstrate in a "before and after" visual manner whether a "sterilizing cure" had, in fact, been discovered—and that was critical.

The next step in developing a "sterilizing cure" was to cause the HIV that was hiding to unmask itself so that it could be destroyed. For this recognition to take place, the dormant HIV had to be activated. Bobby hypothesized that the way to do this would be to formulate a chemical agent that had the ability to lure the virus out of its latent state. And so, Bobby embarked upon what he called his "seduce and destroy" mission.

Bobby theorized that a cellular environment could be created that would be so chemically attractive to the virus, that it would come out of hiding. To do this, he developed a series of proteins that HIV's own proteins would recognize for bonding purposes. It was widely known in the medical research community that the human body's immune cells possess a protein which is recognized by and bonds with HIV's own "gp 120 protein," thereby leading to HIV's infection of human cells.

Bobby synthesized four new proteins that would be recognized not only by HIV's "gp 120," but also by three more of HIV's own proteins. He believed that the compatibility of four of the virus' own proteins with the four that he formulated would create a cellular environment that would be irresistible to the virus and seduce it out of its seclusion. The delivery system for Bobby's new proteins would be a benign virus that he genetically altered so that it would embed itself only in tissues in which EPJ was present *in the one-ninth dilution factor that was indicative of HIV reservoirs.*

If Bobby's theory worked, then all HIV reservoirs would be eliminated by the latency reversing agent he had invented. There would be no hidden, dormant HIV remaining. While this would be a great victory, it would also mean that there would be much more active HIV in the patient's body. So Bobby had to be sure that he discovered a way to destroy *all* of the HIV—otherwise, he would have just exacerbated the problem.

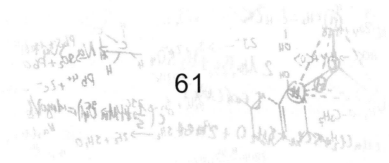

# 61

ONLY SEVERAL WEEKS AFTER THE internet was dominated by videos showing the annihilation of Rakut's population and the subsequent destruction of the city by a squadron of U.S. Air Force bombers, the United States suffered its worst-ever cyberattacks. The electric power grids of San Francisco and Chicago were completely shut down for more than six hours, and Bank of America and JPMorgan Chase lost control of their entire worldwide data operations for eighteen hours, creating financial panic. From what could be gleaned by the CIA, the NSA and the Department of Homeland Security, the cyber assaults were launched from Iran, and were likely the work of the Revolutionary Guard in association with the IRC (Iranian Cyber Army).

While Iran was predominantly Shia Muslim, it nevertheless, for a variety of byzantine reasons, gave clandestine support to Ansar Jamaat through its proxies. Because of that, some experts were of the opinion that there was a connection between what happened in Rakut and these cyberattacks. This led to speculation in the media that the cyber assaults were designed to test the United States' vulnerability if a biological attack against America was accompanied by an all-out cyber assault on the nation's communications, emergency response and health care infrastructure.

Orin Varneys' gleaming black Escalade pulled up to the gatehouse of the Wheatleigh compound. He didn't have an appointment. When the CIA agent driving the vehicle was told by the guards that Varneys wasn't on the guest list and that his CIA identification card didn't make any difference, the agent laughed. "Be smart. Open the gates now."

Varneys strode into the laboratory like he owned it. "Where's Austin?" he asked the first staffer who looked up from his computer long enough to notice him.

When Varneys walked into Bobby's office and saw him sitting in front of his computer monitors, typing equations at a furious pace, he was shocked by how sickly Bobby looked. He was at least fifteen pounds thinner than the last time Varneys saw him, his complexion was pale and pasty and his handsome face had lost its youthful vigor and now looked worn, tired and troubled.

"Robert, I need to speak with you." Bobby didn't acknowledge Varneys' presence or even seem aware that he was in the room. "Robert, we need to talk." Bobby still didn't respond.

Varneys didn't know if Bobby was purposely ignoring him or if he was in a zone of cerebral detachment that rendered him oblivious to all that was going on in the room. Either way, Varneys wasn't pleased. When he yanked Bobby's right hand off of the computer keyboard to get his attention, Bobby's head jerked in Varneys' direction and his eyes seared into him with such intensity that Varneys took two steps back.

"How did you find this place?" asked Bobby.

"Are you actually asking me that?" replied Varneys. "Let's get down to it. We're both busy. Firstly, you look like shit. If you don't learn to take care of yourself, you won't do either of us any good. Step number one in accomplishing anything is to stay alive."

Bobby nodded dismissively. "You're the last person I need lifestyle tips from."

"Of course. You're always right. I forgot. Now, remember our deal. You were going to help me on cyber defense. It's time now."

"We don't have a deal. You threatened to blackmail me. That's not a deal."

Had Varneys been able to see the engorged vein that was throbbing on his forehead, he might have remembered it was time to take his blood-pressure medicine. Slamming his hand on Bobby's desk, his voice became a low growl. "Don't dance with me, Robert. This country has just suffered a major attack. Who knows what's coming next. This *has* to be stopped."

Bobby stood up and walked to the windows, saying nothing. After staring out at the sea for a few moments, he turned to Varneys and said, "Yes, I saw that in the newspapers. It's terrible. But the reports said that the attacks were in retaliation for some debilitating cyber assaults that the CIA inflicted on Iran a few months ago. If that's true, it looks like you brought this on. Maybe détente would be a good idea."

His face now crimson, Varneys flicked his wrist dismissively. "We denied any involvement in attacking Iran. But I didn't come here to debate national policy with you. I gave you an ultimatum when we met. Playtime is over. What's it going to be?"

"You may not know or care, but I'm trying to cure AIDS. If I'm not successful, this disease will be totally out of control again within two years. I'm not going to neglect that work in order to help you. I'm not your only resource to fight your spy war. You have buildings full of scientists who specialize in that. They're good enough to go up against anything Iran's got. You want me because it's easy for you, but I'm fighting something much more powerful than a bunch of hackers sitting in a basement somewhere." Bobby walked over to the office door, opened it and glared at Varneys.

When he was halfway out, Varneys turned and said, "Don't think we're done. Because we're not. And one more thing. You must have seen it in the news. Some kind of biological weapon was released in an Iraqi town. We and four other countries have swarms of scientists on it." Varneys shook his head in disgust as he exited the room. "The whole damned world is going into the shitter."

# 62

As Saeed had predicted, the use of the Sword of the Mahdi to annihilate Rakut had the same deterrent effect against resistance as the United States' use of the atomic bomb in World War II. City after city in Iraq, Syria, Libya and Lebanon lay down their arms in surrender to Ansar Jamaat rather than risk suffering the same fate. Ansar Jamaat's conquest of territory to build its caliphate was unimpeded and its jihadist rampage had become a juggernaut. Ansar Jamaat's masterful use of social media, coupled with the success of its ever-expanding land grab, were magnets in recruiting wannabe jihadists from all over the world.

Saeed was in Mahmoud's lab to check on the progress he was making in analyzing the blood of Rakut's survivors. Placing a hand on Mahmoud's right shoulder, Saeed said, "You see, Mahmoud, it is just as I said it would be. You have saved many lives by creating the Sword of the Mahdi. You should be very proud." What Saeed didn't know was that Mahmoud was analyzing the survivors' blood not for the purpose of modifying the disease to make it more impervious to natural immunity, but to see if he could find a vulnerability in the disease that could be used to completely neutralize it.

Mahmoud was unaware that in each town and city that capitulated to Ansar Jamaat, there was also a roundup of certain occupants. Ansar Jamaat's troops ferreted out all Christians, Yazidis, Alawites, Druze, and those Shia Muslims who were unsuccessful in their attempts to impersonate Sunni. These people were segregated from the rest of the population and then transported to heavily guarded internment camps located in isolated areas where they were infected with the disease; nor was Mahmoud aware that at Saeed's request, Colonel Fahd had compiled a list of cities in Iraq, Syria, Libya, Lebanon, Turkey, Jordan, Kuwait and Egypt that were primarily occupied by non-Sunni.

# 63

S WEAT STREAMED DOWN COLUM MCALISTER'S face and left large
damp stains on the chest and back of his gray workout shirt as
he pedaled vigorously on the exercise bicycle in the prison gym.
The destruction of the Statue of Saladin had motivated McAlister to
improve his physical appearance. He had begun to feel like a highly
successful individual again, even somewhat of a celebrity. Although
his future importance might have to remain a secret forever, he was
more aware than most that one never knows how the pendulum
will swing. Strange things can happen in a world that is awash in
panic. The last can become first and someone, once despised, can
become revered. Nothing was impossible and McAlister wanted to
be prepared for every eventuality. At some point, it might behoove
him to make public or media appearances, and he needed to be
ready.

A few twenty dollar bills placed by him in the hands of the
prison barber had returned his scraggly gray hair to its former
brilliant silver hue and though his locks were now sparser than
they had been when he was the CEO of Bushings Pharmaceutical,
every strand was perfectly in place. His prison shirt now fit snugly

around his chest and arms, the product of twice-daily weightlifting sessions, where previously it had hung loosely. He walked straight and tall, with his chin raised just enough for people to take notice that this was a man who felt superior. McAlister was getting ready to become one of the richest men in the world—and a savior of humanity.

"Gunther, how did it go in Geneva?"

"Couldn't have gone better. The lawyers at Muller Schmid were totally kissing my ass. If I had asked, they would have tucked me in bed at night and fed me milk and cookies."

"And what about Schlumberger?"

"That was the best part. I had those tubes of infected blood that Nizar Khouri got me. It was unbelievable how well the cure worked. When the Schlumberger execs saw that, they knew how rich they were going to become, assuming of course that more people get the disease and it all doesn't stop with Rakut."

McAlister smiled. "I have every confidence in my fellow man."

"So, Schlumberger is just awaiting our instructions on when to start a full-scale production run and, depending on the projected need, they'll begin to subcontract manufacture to meet demand. There also is the question of pricing. The lawyers told me that under your agreement with Schlumberger, you have final say on that. I mean, your 'company' has final say."

"Decisions, decisions. How much money do we want to make?"

"I vote for as much as possible," replied Ramirez.

"Let's put pricing off to the side. It's too early to start to manufacture. We need to wait until at least three hundred thousand people have died. That may take a while, depending on how our jihadist friends behave. The market has to be primed. We can't make this look too easy. We'll write our own ticket if we're patient."

"But the longer we wait, the more people will die."

A flush came over McAlister's face. "Don't get biblical on me, Gunther. We didn't create the disease and we didn't unleash it. There wouldn't be a cure if it weren't for me. We're not the problem. We're the solution."

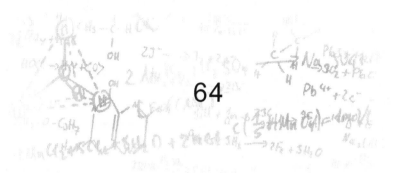

# 64

MAHMOUD STOOD IN FRONT OF the bookcase in the living room of his small apartment. He looked at the framed photographs that were displayed on the shelves. There were more than a dozen photos showing him and his wife smiling as they posed next to each other. The pictures had been taken over the course of years in a variety of exotic vacation destinations. As he closely examined their faces in the photos, and their body posture, he could see the miniscule signs that evidenced the progressive deterioration of their relationship as time had passed.

In the early days, Mahmoud had been able to have sex with his wife. It was difficult for him, but he tried desperately. He knew his wife deserved this, and he prayed that as time went by, it would become more palatable to him to be with a woman. She didn't need to know what he was thinking about when his eyes were closed and who he was visualizing he was with. He mechanically went through the motions, preferring darkness to even candlelight, and it was not surprising that despite her entreaties for a more intimate position, he preferred to enter her from behind and avoid looking at her face or seeing her breasts. As the years passed, it became harder for him to dissemble and continue to live a lie. The weight of his guilt at having deceived a decent woman, relegating her to a cold marriage devoid of physical love became as overwhelming for him as the disgust he felt towards himself.

According to the religion that was the cornerstone of his life, sexual relations with a person of the same gender was a crime against God for which there could be no redemption or forgiveness. But as hard as he tried, he was incapable of complete abstinence. Eschewing emotional involvements, he satisfied his cravings in ways that made his behavior that much more repugnant to himself. Impersonal sex acts were perfunctorily performed with male prostitutes in his car on the way home from work, or in gay peepshow booths where flashing a fifty-dollar bill caused the glass divider to come down, or in dirty motels that rented rooms by the half-hour and saw no need to change the sheets. There reached a point where he couldn't go on living that way. His wife deserved to be free of him and she was entitled to start a new life with a financial cushion, and he needed to commit himself to celibacy so he wouldn't cause pain to a woman again or disgrace God with his abominations. And so Mahmoud had resolved that he would start anew in the caliphate and he had prayed that by helping to build it, perhaps God would answer his prayers and fix him so that he could love in a way that God approved. Now those dreams had been vanquished by the realities that he had witnessed and the atrocities that he had empowered.

Mahmoud exhibited these photographs on his bookshelf, not because he wanted to see them. In fact, it pained him terribly to look at them. He displayed them because he knew that Ansar Jamaat operatives frequently searched his apartment. They needed to believe that Mahmoud was a heterosexual male in love with his wife.

Mahmoud unrolled his prayer rug and knelt to pray. After a few moments of silence, he said softly, "Thank you, God, for not letting my cursed creation be capable of transmission by animals, birds or insects. My sins know no bounds and I am unworthy of mercy. I deserve the harshest judgment that you shall pronounce upon me. But today, I humbly thank you for preventing my hideous work from being carried by vermin or fowl to infect the innocent."

# 65

ALTHOUGH IT WAS A DIFFICULT task, the Wheatleigh IT team was able to install enough computer interfaces in the room that sat atop the watchtower so that Bobby could work there with the same amount of computing power as he had in his lab office. Bobby had taken to spending most of his time alone in the isolated space, venturing out only for the occasional solitary walk along the seaside cliffs. He knew that at this crucial juncture when he was making the final push to integrate all of his work into a comprehensive AIDS "sterilizing cure", he could have no distractions. His communications with his research staff were now truncated and conducted by email only, and on the few nights a week when he joined Christina in the early morning hours, his attention remained obsessively focused on his work.

The lack of sleep, night terrors, bad eating habits, punishing work schedule and unremitting stress had left him in a physically and mentally debilitated state. Bobby fell back into his habitual dependence on microwavable snacks, junk food, caffeinated drinks and too much alcohol. His sarcastic sense of humor and quick-witted banter had been supplanted by an almost constant cognitive detachment from the present.

One Sunday morning in late March, as Bobby sat at his desk in the tower, he looked up from the notations he was writing. There was no visibility out the windows. A blizzard had rolled in from the northwest and the tower was ensconced in a whiteout. Bobby put his pencil down, stood up and walked to the windows.

When the snow falls on the seashore in New England, it takes on an ethereal beauty. Bobby had always loved the snow and believed that snow has the power not only to cleanse and purify, but to inspire invention by obscuring the known from view. Standing in front of the cabin windows for the better part of an hour, Bobby relished the scene as the storm escalated in intensity. Forty feet above the ground, with no land or sea in sight to tether him, he felt as if he were suspended in the air. Stretching his arms to their full length, he imagined that he was a bird in flight, devoid of all earthly concerns, navigating through the storm with the confidence imbued in all creatures by their Creator. Closing his eyes, he inhaled deeply and held the air in his lungs for as long as he could. It had been so long since he felt physically strong, but now his chest expanded with the influx of life-affirming oxygen. The weakness, fatigue and despair drained from him as he was enveloped by the pristine crystals.

Finally, the eagle had left the nest atop the tower. He soared higher now, his path undeterred by the winds that buffeted him or the air drafts that tried to bring him down. He wasn't afraid to go where he needed to go, and he knew he would find his way home.

The wind whipped the flakes into fast-moving swirls and before long the darkening sky had been painted white and the windows of the cabin were opaque. Bobby sat back down at his desk. Once again, he closed his eyes and this time his intellect traveled with no boundaries. Hours later, when his eyes opened, he calmly wrote fourteen formulas down in his journal. He then entered them into his computer. Bobby walked over to the sofa and lay down.

Christina had wanted to go to the tower and get Bobby. After all, it was Easter Sunday and she was determined that Bobby was going to break from work to help hide Easter eggs in the yard for the kids to find. But the snow was blinding and she couldn't even see the tower from the main house. She knew that climbing the tower stairs in this kind of weather when precipitation froze on its stone steps was too dangerous, and it wouldn't be safe for Bobby to attempt to get down. So she told Pete and Mirielle that they should decorate more eggs and that tomorrow she and their father would hide them and it would be that much more fun because they would have to hunt for the eggs in the snow.

Christina tried to call Bobby on the phone, but the storm had caused an outage so she couldn't get through. It would be a snowy Easter Sunday without him. Just her and the children.

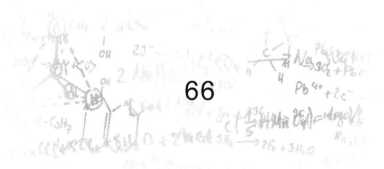

# 66

THE SNOW DIDN'T STOP UNTIL early Monday morning. The Manchester area received its biggest snowfall in fifteen years, with more than six feet recorded and snow drifts accumulating to eleven feet. Most residents resigned themselves to the warmth of their homes. Wheatleigh was blanketed underneath the white crystalline mass that covers all imperfections.

With phone service restored, Christina called the cabin at 9:00 a.m. Bobby didn't answer. She tried again at 10:00 a.m. Still no answer. Christina called the gatekeepers and asked when the property would be plowed. They said that the entrance to the house would be navigable by noon and that within an hour after that there would be a clear path to the tower, but that it would take another hour for the tower stairs to be salted and safe.

When Christina began to climb the tower stairs at 2:30 p.m. she still had been unable to reach Bobby. Upon entering the cabin office, she was surprised that Bobby wasn't at his desk or in the kitchen. Then she noticed him lying on the sofa. In all the time she had known Bobby, she had never seen him take an afternoon nap, and even when he retired to bed very late, he would never sleep past noon. Christina looked at him. Bobby had the most serene of expressions on his face. He appeared younger; the lines on his forehead were less prominent, the darkness under his eyes had dispelled and his complexion had lost its pallor. She felt his T-shirt. It was bone dry, as was the pillow underneath his head. Christina removed her coat and slipped off her boots. The room had a slight chill and Bobby looked so cozy so she squeezed on to the sofa next to him. There was barely enough room for one person to lie on the narrow couch, let alone two. She put her arm across Bobby's chest and rested her head in the crook of his neck just under his chin. Pressing her body against his, a feeling of contentment washed over her. If only he could be this peaceful all the time, she mused.

After a few minutes had gone by, Christina ran her fingers through his hair and whispered, "Get up, sleepyhead, it's late. The kids are waiting for you." When shakes and kisses didn't get the desired result, she suspected he was playing. Christina grabbed Bobby's feet and pulled him off the sofa. Landing with a thud, Bobby retaliated by pulling by her down on top of him. As he kissed her on the forehead, he brushed some silky strands of hair away from her face. Christina couldn't recall his eyes ever looking quite the way they looked at that moment. There was something different—a softness, a tranquility.

"Are you okay?" she asked.

Bobby nodded. "It's done, Christina. All the pieces came together last night."

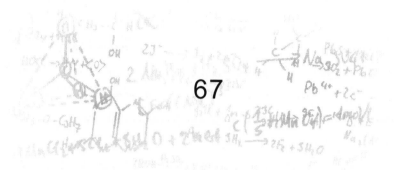

## 67

T HE WORLDWIDE MEDICAL AND SCIENTIFIC communities were stunned when a six-volume special edition of the *New England Journal of Medicine* was published four months later that contained Bobby's integrated AIDS "sterilizing cure", together with more than fourteen hundred pages of proofs.

As he had set out to do, his cure vanquished AIDS in disparate ways, all working in combination with each other, as follows:

1. Bobby's protein-infused nanoparticles destroyed HIV's protective membrane and without this lipid envelope, the virus was left bare and defenseless against drugs and human antibodies. Additionally, the destruction of the membrane impaired HIV's ability to attach itself to human host cells by depriving the virus of the target recognition, receptor and binding mechanisms that it needed.

2. Once HIV's protective membrane had been destroyed, Bobby's second battalion of programmed nanoparticles swarmed into the virus and sought

out its *reverse transcriptase and integrase* enzymes. These nanoparticles were infused with a specially formulated high pH compound which adhered to the active sites of the enzymes and raised their pH levels to an extraordinarily high alkalinity of 13. This extreme alkalinity grossly distorted the shape of the active sites of the two enzymes thereby modifying the "teeth of the keys" so significantly that the enzymes were irreparably denatured. Without *reverse transcriptase* and *integrase*, HIV could not infect human beings.

3.  The "seduce-and-destroy" methodologies that Bobby had invented using his "latency-reversing agent" and the MRI visual "reporter" that he had devised, confirmed the elimination of the HIV reservoirs. HIV that was previously hiding was now unmasked, thereby rendering it susceptible to destruction by drugs and human antibodies.

4.  Now that the virus had been debilitated and exposed to attack, Bobby delivered the coup de grace: a genetically designed HIV-specific immunotoxin. This poison targeted only HIV-infected cells and when it entered them, it shut down protein synthesis and triggered cell death.

It had taken him years, but Bobby's "sterilizing cure" was so devastating to the fundamental cellular structure and operation of HIV that the virus could never mutate or adapt around it.

As Bobby had envisioned from day one, the cure had to be capable of being delivered to tens of millions of people throughout the world without the need for complex medical procedures or sophisticated facilities. Bobby accomplished that goal. The treatment protocol was simple: four different pills, each of which had to be taken only once per day for ten days. Uniserve would ensure that these pills were manufactured by generic drug manufacturers at the lowest possible cost.

Within the first hour of pubic distribution of the *New England Journal of Medicine* volumes, eight Big Pharma companies that owned patents on antiretroviral treatments saw their stocks plunge by more than eleven percent, causing trading in their shares to be suspended. The following day brought another ten-percent plunge. This was before Bobby's cure was even tested by hospitals.

Over the ensuing months, Bobby's four-part HIV integrated "sterilizing cure" was vetted in over two dozen of the world's leading research hospitals. Eight months later, the verdict came in and it was unanimous. He had done it.

While the world media lauded him and the pundits predicted Nobel prizes, medical researchers who had previously been silent so as to avert a public panic, confirmed that Bobby's cure had come in the nick of time. Just as Bobby had told Susan, the latest strains of HIV would soon render all current antiretroviral drugs obsolete. Without Bobby's "sterilizing cure", the HIV/AIDS scourge was about to reboot itself with disastrous consequences. And Big Pharma and the research community would have had nothing to offer.

As had been the case with all of Bobby's previous cures, the work he did on HIV/AIDS had far-reaching ramifications for other diseases. The methodologies that he invented to destroy the protective membranes of viruses and deactivate *reverse transcriptase* and *integrase* within targeted cells provided the scientific community with revolutionary new tools to combat a host of human maladies.

# 68

DEEP IN THOUGHT AS HE stood in front of an enormous map of the Mideast, Saeed was oblivious to Colonel Fahd who waited just inside the doorway of Saeed's office. After five minutes, Fahd cleared his throat loudly and said, "You sent for me, Caliph."

Turning toward him, Saeed said, "The Sword of the Mahdi has steadily expanded our caliphate's territory and God willing this will continue."

"*Inshallah*," echoed Fahd.

Saeed pointed his forefinger at Fahd and shook it to emphasize his words. "But we have a problem. As our geographic footprint has grown, it has become increasingly difficult to rule over local populations. Many are misguided in their hostility to our caliphate. We will never have enough troops to be an effective long-term occupying force."

Fahd nodded. "Ansar Jamaat's soldiers are not policemen, they are warriors."

"We need to focus on what is valuable to the caliphate and what is not valuable. What do you think is valuable, Colonel?"

Fahd didn't need time to think. "Strategic locations, natural resources, hard assets and anything that can be monetized to further the expansion and success of the caliphate."

"Good. We are in agreement. Come up with a plan for my review."

———————————•••—————————

Methodical and exacting in everything that he did, Fahd was adept at demographic research. His analysis of the religious and ethnic makeup of towns and cities that had already fallen under the caliphate's control, and those next in line to fall, was thorough. Ten days after his meeting with Saeed, he had formulated a program.

"Caliph, please take a look at this map on which I have made notations." Fahd unrolled a large map of the Middle East and laid it on Saeed's desk. There were dozens of areas that were circled in red ink. "The red circles denote areas that are comprised of at least sixty-eight percent infidels and apostates. Of course, you may disagree with some of my calculations, but I have been very careful. As you will see, next to each red circle, I have listed the population numbers of each religious and ethnic group. After much analysis, sixty-eight percent was the most exact number necessary to achieve our goal."

His scarecrow body extending over the map, Saeed silently examined Colonel Fahd's notations for almost twenty minutes. When he was finished, he looked up. "Continue with your presentation, Colonel."

Fahd squared his shoulders and took a deep breath. "Any community comprised of at least sixty-eight percent of these enemies of the caliphate will be cleansed by the Sword of the Mahdi."

"And what happens to the thirty-two percent that are not

infidels or apostates? Do we move them out before the Sword is employed?"

"No, Caliph. That is logistically and strategically unfeasible. The thirty-two percent will find their reward in heaven as martyrs."

Saeed pulled on his left ear as he slowly turned his head from one side to the other. After a few moments, he began to pace his office. When he finally sat down at his desk, he drummed his fingers on the map and said, "What's the rest of your proposal?"

"Once the population has succumbed to the disease, we will send our troops in to harvest anything of value. Even with our limited salvaging experience, we have been surprised by how much cash, jewels and gold are stashed away by inhabitants."

Saeed interjected. "It's not surprising to me. With one regime after another plundering the banks, people have learned to kept their assets close at hand. It's the prudent thing to do."

Fahd's weasel smile curled the corners of his lips. "Caliph, you are correct, but to account for those inhabitants who weren't prudent, our troops will also empty the banks. And the museums, galleries and high-end stores. Works of art, antiquities and jewelry will be disposed of through our network of dealers. Of course, we'll also take ownership of the once occupied real estate for monetization at a later date. Ansar Jamaat will never again have to be concerned about how to finance its operations—or have to play policeman to hostiles."

Straightening his waist sash and carefully adjusting the position of the *janbiya* which hung from it, Saeed said, "Our repeated use of the Sword will be a deterrent to interference."

"Exactly, Caliph."

Saeed placed his hands on Fahd's shoulders. "Once again, you have demonstrated that my confidence in you is not misplaced. But this plan of yours has to be implemented very carefully."

"Yes. The Sixty-Eight Percent Rule must be selectively applied."

"The Sixty-Eight Percent Rule. I see that you've already given it a name," said Saeed. Fahd blushed.

Leaning over his desk, Saeed once again examined each red circle that Fahd had drawn on the map. "We can only wield the Sword on cities with sixty thousand or fewer inhabitants. And they must live within a compact geographical area. Then our forces can surround the communities and prevent any escapees, just like we did at Rakut. Any initiative larger than this will become unmanageable. We must not lose control of our weapon."

# 69

THERE HAVE BEEN MANY HOLOCAUSTS in human history. The perpetrators for many of those genocidal crimes had the benefit of there being no internet, no social media and no cell phones with photo and video capabilities. How different might history have been if these instruments of exposure and instant global transmission were present from 1896 to 1908 to shine a light on the murder and mutilation of ten million Congolese by King Leopold II of Belgium; or from 1939 to 1945, when Hitler exterminated more than eleven million Jews, Slavs, Roma and others; or from 1975 to 1979, when Pol Pot and the Khmer Rouge slaughtered two million Cambodians; or in 1994, when over eight hundred thousand Tutsis in Rwanda were annihilated and half a million women raped.

By these standards, Yusuf al-Saeed was still a small-time player, but unlike his predecessors, Saeed's crimes against humanity were well documented on the internet, not only by his victims, but also by Ansar Jamaat itself to further its own agenda. As the death toll from the Sword of the Mahdi approached two hundred thousand, coverage of the slaughter by the international media gained momentum. But what was given the most attention in the published stories was not the amount of carnage, but the manner in which it was rendered, i.e., by a biological weapon for which there was no known cure or treatment despite frantic efforts by the CDC, WHO, USAMRIID and other organizations to find one.

Ironically, the ever-present social media coverage played perfectly into Saeed's hands. As the death toll in the Mideast mounted, panic in the West became its own contagion. There was virtually no public outcry for an intervention by the Western powers or the United Nations. To the contrary, the concern was to ensure that the disease stayed in the Mideast, cordoned off and isolated from the rest of the world in the methodical manner that Saeed had engineered to date. To further inculcate this view, Saeed issued a media release in which an Ansar Jamaat spokesperson addressed the governments of the world as follows:

"Caliph al-Saeed answers to no power on Earth. If anyone tries to interfere with the progression of his caliphate, the Sword of the Mahdi will be wielded against them. The governments of Europe and the United States, in particular, should pay attention to this. Do not doubt our ability to employ the Sword in your lands. If you interfere in what is not your concern, then you will not survive."

# 70

"**G**UNTHER, DO YOU REMEMBER WHEN I told you I had something special in mind for Robert James Austin?"

"Yes, and I told you to forget it. You're obsessed with him and it's only created problems for you."

Scowling, McAlister said, "I'm not obsessed. I just don't want him ruining anything else in my life. I lost over one hundred million dollars in the value of my Bushings stock because of him."

"I understand. But you were still rich. If you hadn't gone after him, you wouldn't be sitting here in prison."

"You're missing the point. What I'm saying is that we can't risk Austin killing our golden goose. We own the most valuable drug the world has ever known. It's going to be worth more than the whole pharmaceuticals industry. It can pay us for years. There's only one thing that can ruin it: Robert James Austin."

Ramirez scrunched up his nose as if he was smelling something bad. "What do you mean?"

"Sooner or later, Austin will invent a new cure. It may be better than ours. But one thing's for sure. He'll give it away for nothing the way he always does. When he does that, we'll be out of business."

"By then, we'll be so rich we won't care," replied Ramirez.

McAlister's face flushed. "That's bullshit. Why should we let him ruin what we've created? That's exactly what he did to the whole drug industry. He's not going to do it again."

"So exactly what are you saying?"

"It's very simple," replied McAlister. "We're going to use Austin to make money for us."

"How's that?" asked Ramirez.

McAlister's eyes gleamed. "It's poetic justice. We're going to infect him with the disease soon. He's going to die from it. When the disease kills the "Miracle Man," it will really fuck with peoples' heads all over the world. This will fuel demand for our cure when we finally announce it. Austin's death will be a marketing coup and it will eliminate the possibility of his ever devising a cure. That's what I call killing two birds with one stone."

"No. It's too risky," said Ramirez. "I have more experience in this kind of thing than you do. If something goes wrong, we'll be sitting in matching electric chairs. We don't need to take risks like that.Let it go. Just forget about Robert James Austin."

## 71

A S CLOSE A FACSIMILE OF the Garden of Eden as anyone was likely to find on planet Earth, the island of Bulakala rose from the Koro Sea in the Fijian archipelago like a gift from God. Approximately fifteen square miles in size, its volcanic mountains were covered with lush tropical rainforests that gradually thinned at lower elevations to coconut groves and mangroves framing an azure lagoon that was speckled with coral reefs teeming with colorful marine life.

Bulakala was one of the largest uninhabited islands in Fiji and was a cherished property in Huo Jin Gao's extensive portfolio of real estate holdings, both for its rarity and utility. Shortly after acquiring Bulakala, Gao had proceeded to build an exclusive luxury resort offering unparalleled levels of opulence and privacy, with only thirty guest accommodations, the least expensive of which cost its occupants twelve thousand dollars per night. As the world's rich got progressively richer over the years, and the newly rich displayed an unquenchable appetite for extravagance, Bulakala had become a profitable enterprise which was never Gao's intention. The public aspect of the resort was just a front. The real purpose of Bulakala was to serve as a secluded playground, far from prying eyes, in which Gao could entertain governmental officials and others with whom he was currying favor and building guanxi. During these times, the resort was closed to the public. As Bulakala had its own airstrip that was able to accommodate personal and corporate jets, invitees could land on Bulakala without anyone from the outside world knowing their destination. Of course, Gao also offered transportation to and from Bulakala on his Gulfstream G650ER.

When Gao was hosting an official together with his or her family, the resort offered a full panoply of activities, including golfing, horseback riding, boating, game fishing, snorkeling and scuba diving. More frequently, however, Gao's guests consisted of just one or a few highly prominent persons and on those occasions, a more intimate entertainment was provided. Each of the twelve beach-front villas would be staffed and outfitted by Gao to feature a different opportunity for his guests' dissipation. For this purpose, Gao imported a gaggle of female and male courtesans of uncommon beauty and skill who would interact with the guests in whatever combinations were desired. Gao spared no expense to ensure that his guests enjoyed an adult entertainment experience at Bulakala like no other, with no fear of being observed. One of the villas was even decorated as a historically accurate recreation of a sumptuous late-nineteenth-century opium den, with all of the luxurious trappings, including female attendants attired in period costumes, pipes, oil lamps and an unlimited supply of drugs. By keeping careful records of the predilections of his guests, Gao ensured that they were never disappointed when they partook of his hospitality at Bulakala. Of course, the goings on in each villa were recorded on hidden video equipment, in case the day should come when Gao needed to remind an invitee of what a good time he or she had on Bulakala.

Because of the seclusion that it offered, Bulakala was selected by Gunther Ramirez for a meeting at which only he, Gao and Viktor Bazhenov would be present. The purpose of the meeting, as dictated by Colum McAlister, was to discuss the further implementation of financial strategy.

It was a blustery early morning in March, the rainiest month of the year in Fiji, when three private jets arrived within an hour of each other, fighting the crosswinds to land on the wet tarmac of Bulakala's airfield. The first plane to land was Gao's Gulfstream, followed by Ramirez' Dassault Falcon 7X and Bazhenov's Bombardier Global 8000. A late-model silver Range Rover traversed the winding muddy roads to deliver its occupants to Gao's personal residence, a massive structure perched atop the highest mountain on Bulakala. The rambling house was designed in the style of a *bure*, the traditional Fijian wood-and-straw hut, but to ensure that it could withstand the cyclones that frequently pummel the area, Gao's architects had utilized steel beams and reinforced concrete construction, cleverly disguising these industrial materials by sheathing them with masterfully applied local doga timber, sago palm leaves, coconut husks and bala bala fern stems to create the appearance of an authentic island residence.

"Quite an impressive hideaway you have here, Mr. Gao," said Bazhenov as he flashed his famous smile and moved towards Gao to engulf the diminutive man in a bear hug.

Taking two steps back to avoid the embrace, Gao extended his hand to Bazhenov. "You can rent it for half a million a week when I'm not here."

"You're joking right?" replied Bazhenov.

"Please follow me gentlemen," said Gao as he led Ramirez and Bazhenov through an atrium whose forty-foot pitched ceiling was supported by elaborately carved wooden beams. At the end of the atrium, Gao ushered his guests into an octagonal room whose walls, ceiling, and most notably floor, were made almost entirely of glass. The room projected forward from the main body of the house and was cantilevered over the lush valley three-quarters of a mile below. Even in the inclement weather, the view over the rain forests to the South Pacific Ocean was breathtaking. Bazhenov looked beneath his feet and grasped on to the arm of a nearby chair.

A sumptuous buffet had been set on a long dining table and three servers, a bartender and a sommelier stood at the ready. "Gentlemen, please let me indulge you with some hospitality. I think we all could use some refreshment after our journey here," said Gao.

The odd thing was how little Gao and Bazhenov had to say to each other. While they knew each other by reputation, they had never previously met and appeared to have little interest in establishing even the modicum of a rapport. Partners in perhaps the largest financial manipulation in history, neither of them was inclined to expend any effort in making polite conversation. The meal was brief and none of the men drank any wine or liquor. When Gao signaled, his servants vacated the room and closed the heavy doors.

"Gunther, why don't you start?" said Gao.

"Thank you, Huo Jin. Firstly, let me convey warm wishes to both of you from Colum McAlister, the wizard who conceived of our adventure together. I am sure you share my admiration for him. As you know, our enterprise is up ninety-two billion dollars since we began. You were able to liquidate your holdings at a high and then sell the markets short with leveraged trading to spectacular advantage. The financial markets never recovered from Rakut and now, with each new city that Ansar Jamaat destroys, the markets decline further. They are now thirty-six percent below pre-Rakut levels. No doubt, this has been the most profitable venture that either of you have ever engaged in."

Bazhenov leaned back in his chair, his long legs extended, his hands resting in his lap. "Gunther, I'm sure I can speak for Mr. Gao when I say that we and our investors are enjoying this party."

Gao nodded. "But you don't judge a party until it's over. In my experience, the most important thing to know about a party is when to leave."

"That's why Colum and I asked you to come to this meeting," said Ramirez. "Something is going to happen soon and that will create our next opportunity."

Bazhenov wagged his forefinger. "Things are going to get worse. It's just a matter of time until the disease spreads from the Mideast. Then we'll see real panic. There'll be a complete financial collapse when the West gets hit. We should keep shorting the markets. The only problem is to find anyone to take the other side of the trading positions. This is what's limiting us now."

Ramirez didn't acknowledge Bazhenov's comments. Instead, he stood up, walked to the far side of the room, tilted his head back to look through the glass ceiling and then gazed out the glass walls and the glass floor beneath him. "Damn, I feel like I'm a bird. Huo Jin, this room is spectacular. You should have gotten a design award for it."

Annoyed by Ramirez' diversion, Bazhenov snapped, "Gunther, do you agree the disease will spread?"

"Yes Viktor, but the markets will go up," replied Ramirez.

Gao frowned. "That makes no sense."

"It does if a cure is announced," said Ramirez.

Gao stared unblinking. Bazhenov's left brow raised. Almost in unison they asked, "A cure?"

"That's right. There is a cure and it will be announced in a few weeks. That's why we're having this meeting. You need to prep your trades to go long. The markets will turn to the upside, and there's another fortune to made on the ride back to the top."

"How does McAlister know this?" asked Bazhenov.

Gao cut in. "Is he or Bushings Pharmaceuticals involved with the cure?"

Ramirez's face told nothing. "All you need to know is that McAlister knows. Everything has gone according to plan and everything that was promised you is happening. As I told you when we first discussed this project, McAlister and I aren't taking you to the casino, we're taking you to the bank."

# 72

FOUR WEEKS AFTER RAMIREZ' MEETING with Gao and Bazhenov in Bulakala, media reports were filled with the grim news that Ansar Jamaat had annihilated its eighth city, Kabideen in Syria. The death toll was reported to be over fifty-six thousand people. Apparently, Colonel Fahd had determined that there were enough Alawites, Shia, Ismaili, Christians and Druzes to satisfy the "sixty-eight percent rule." Perhaps Kabideen's important strategic location had influenced Fahd's numerical count. The extermination of Kabideen's population brought the combined death toll caused by the Sword of the Mahdi to more than three hundred twelve thousand souls.

Two months earlier, in preparation for this day, Colum McAlister had finished drafting the press release that he would require Schlumberger Foch to issue as soon as it received the go ahead from McAlister's Geneva law firm which, in turn, was awaiting an authorization text from Ramirez with the predetermined one-word message, "Go." The press release that McAlister drafted read as follows:

Schlumberger Foch, the Swiss pharmaceutical company which has been serving the health needs of the public for one hundred and twenty-three years, takes pride in today announcing that it is in possession of what it believes is a cure for the disease that has caused the deaths of hundreds of thousands of victims of the Ansar Jamaat terrorist group. The Schlumberger Foch formulation has undergone extensive laboratory testing according to the most rigorous standards and has evidenced the capability to definitively destroy the biological agents of this disease.

Schlumberger Foch is optimistic that field tests on infected human beings will bear out the effectiveness of the treatment. Schlumberger Foch will coordinate with international health authorities and relevant governments so that field testing can take place on an expedited basis. In anticipation of the success of those field tests, Schlumberger Foch will begin to negotiate manufacturing licenses with other pharmaceutical companies to ensure that the public demand for this treatment can be met in a timely fashion.

Within twenty-four hours of Schlumberger's press release, the leaders of no fewer than thirty-two countries, including those in which the Sword of the Mahdi had been unleashed, made public statements lauding the drug company's accomplishment and offering their assistance to facilitate testing of the cure in the field.

# 73

A S SAEED WATCHED THE PRESIDENT of the United States on CNN, his gaunt body was rigid and his unblinking obsidian eyes fixated on the television screen as if he were under a spell. Without losing focus on the president, he grabbed the dagger that hung from his waist and slammed the point of its blade into the top of his wooden desk with such ferocity that the blade's tempered steel groaned audibly. As he listened to the president's words, Saeed dug the blade deeper and deeper into the wood. With a magnitude of strength that one wouldn't think a thin man would have, Saeed pulled the sunken blade back and forth across the length of the ornate desk until its top looked like a piece of scrap wood. The president's message was unequivocal:

> "Today is a day on which all decent people feel profound hope and gratitude. For too long, the nations of the world have been held hostage by a genocidal maniac, Yusuf al-Saeed, under threat that if they acted to oppose him, he would infect their lands with the dreaded biological weapon that

his terrorist organization, Ansar Jamaat, has used to murder hundreds of thousands of innocents.

The announcement by the pharmaceutical company, Schlumberger Foch, that they believe they have invented a cure for this horrific disease, now referred to as "HRFS" (Hemorrhagic Respiratory Failure Syndrome) is the news that we all have been waiting for. We applaud Schlumberger Foch's extraordinary efforts. The United States will work tirelessly in coordination with an alliance of nations to expedite the field testing of this drug.

This will be the first step in a chain of events that will lead to the eradication of Yusuf al-Saeed, Ansar Jamaat and the immoral caliphate that they have sought to build on the corpses of their victims. The terrorist scourge of these mass murderers will be wiped from this planet. Let us pray that the results of our efforts are successful and speedily accomplished."

As soon as he heard the president's speech, Colonel Fahd rushed to Saeed's headquarters, stopping only to get Mahmoud. When the contingent of guards outside Saeed's office permitted Fahd and Mahmoud to enter, they found the room empty. Neither man sat down.

"What happened to his desk?" asked Mahmoud softly.

Fahd grimaced. "Are you stupid?"

The hallway was filled with the commotion and clatter of six heavily armed Ansar Jamaat troops moving quickly, Saeed in their midst. When Saeed entered the office and slammed the door, Mahmoud felt as if he had been punched in the stomach.

"You! Mahmoud! Look at me," commanded Saeed as he walked over to Mahmoud and stood inches away from him. Mahmoud raised his head slightly, his jaw muscles squeezed tight. "Look at me, I said." Mahmoud allowed his eyes to meet Saeed's, but it was hard for him to maintain eye contact because Saeed's gaze was so full of rage and contempt. Saeed grabbed Mahmoud's chest with both hands, his fingernails digging into Mahmoud's skin through his shirt. Saeed moved so rapidly that it seemed like he was running as he propelled Mahmoud backwards with such force that when Mahmoud slammed into the wall, the air was knocked out of his lungs and his legs gave way. Saeed pulled Mahmoud up, his fingernails embedded in his chest like hooks. "You told me there was no cure for the Sword of the Mahdi. You promised me that. You knew that all of my plans were based on there being no cure. If I wanted a disease that had a cure, I could have bought twenty of them. I didn't need you for that." Saeed's face was so close to Mahmoud's that as Saeed spoke, his spittle pummeled Mahmoud's eyes and nose. Saeed's left hand tightly grasped the hilt of his knife and his right hand was now cupped against Mahmoud's chin, pushing it upwards.

Colonel Fahd coughed several times in an effort to get Saeed's attention. Saeed didn't appear to notice. Fahd then cleared his throat loudly. "Caliph, may I please say something?" Gambling that Saeed's silence constituted permission to speak, Fahd said, "Caliph, this just means that we need to accelerate our plans. It will take them months to do comprehensive field tests on this so-called cure. And there's a good chance their cure won't work. I'll bet there's a fifty percent chance it won't work well enough or the side effects will be lethal. In the meantime, we should accelerate. They won't resist us until they know they have a viable cure."

Saeed seemed frozen, his right hand still positioned on Mahmoud's throat. After a few moments, his body began to lose its rigidity as he slowly rotated his head from side to side. Saeed released Mahmoud from his grip and walked to the windows of his office. Turning to Fahd, he said, "The president of the United States declared war on our caliphate. He called it immoral. This is a man whose country was built on the extermination of the American Indian and on the backs of millions of slaves. It is a country of hypocrites that never lifted a finger to stop the genocides in Cambodia, Uganda, Rwanda or the Sudan. It is a country that never cared about the deaths of people whose skin wasn't white. But now they self-righteously declare war on us and feign concern for the people who have been sacrificed to create a caliphate that will bring peace and unity to the world. The United States is not concerned about them. The United States is afraid for itself—afraid that the Sword of the Mahdi will strike them down for their corruption and degeneracy."

"Caliph, our prophet commands us to action. *Allahu Akbar,*" shouted Fahd.

The corners of Saeed's mouth raised almost imperceptibly.

# 74

S PREADING THE DISEASE WAS EASY; containing it was difficult. Saeed no longer wanted to contain it. To the contrary, his desire was to expand his Mideast caliphate as quickly as possible while Ansar Jamaat still had immunity from military interference because it possessed a biological weapon for which there was no field-tested cure. Saeed needed to act while the Sword of the Mahdi retained the ability to cause armies to abandon their weapons, cities to surrender and the nations of the world to stand down.

Saeed's immediate targets were highly populated cities in countries in which Shia Muslims, whom Saeed regarded as infidels, constituted more than a majority of the population; those countries were Azerbaijan, Bahrain, Iran and Southern Iraq. Also on the list were Yemen and Lebanon, where Shias were just shy of a majority.

Colonel Fahd realized that infecting numerous population centers in many countries simultaneously could not be accomplished by the use of artillery shells equipped with weaponized aerosol devices, which had been Ansar Jamaat's previously preferred method. Ansar Jamaat did not have the physical resources to effectuate an artillery attack of such scale; nor did Ansar Jamaat have the equipment or technology for long-range missile delivery of an aerosol warhead. Similarly, Ansar Jamaat did not have the capability to drop bombs, as it had no air force and even if it did, planes would be subject to interception by the ground- and air-defense systems of target nations.

Fahd decided that his best option for delivering the disease on a mass scale was to have operatives on the ground in each city deploy aerosol devices in strategic locations. Any place that was populated by large numbers of people would be an appropriate target, including movie theatres, schools, places of worship, shopping malls, the ventilation systems of office and residential buildings, bus and railroad terminals, airports and planes. Fahd was particularly interested in the placement of the devices in transportation hubs and on transportation conveyances because those who became infected would then spread the malady well beyond a city's borders through person-to-person transmission of the highly contagious disease, the first symptoms of which were barely noticeable. Geometric progression would ensure a pandemic.

For the first time in human history, a multinational war would be conducted clandestinely and in silence. There would be no fire, no smoke, no flashes of blinding light, no mushroom clouds, no shockwaves and no deafening sounds. There would be no warnings. Death would come quietly and there would be no escape.

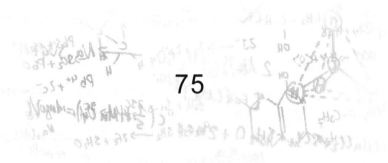

# 75

"**D**AMN, YOU'RE LOOKING GOOD, COLUM. That hair, that physique. Did you meet somebody in this joint?" Ramirez chaffed.

McAlister ignored the crack. "It's time to price the cure and inform Schlumberger Foch of my decision. They already know that all of the sublicense deals they do with other drug companies have to be structured as profit-sharing, with seventy percent of the profits going back to Schlumberger. There's no way I was going to let those fools accept some piddling license royalty."

"How much does Schlumberger pay to your offshore company?" asked Ramirez.

"Seventy-five percent of the profits from batches of the cure that SF manufactures itself, and eighty-eight percent of the profits from the sublicensing deals that they do with other companies."

"Impressive. How did you get them to agree that?"

McAlister smiled. "Step number one in negotiating is to know the strength of your hand. I delivered the cure to Schlumberger. It had no research-and-development costs. And it won't have any marketing costs. I'm putting that moribund company back on the map. It will be lauded as a savior. You can't put a price on that. Those SOBs are lucky I'm letting them keep anything."

Ramirez nodded. "You handed those guys the winning lottery ticket."

"I did, but they'll serve their purpose. People always trust Swiss drug makers. There's something about that fastidious little country with its fancy wristwatches, chocolates and snow-covered peaks that instills confidence."

Ramirez laughed. "Yeah, if it's Swiss, I'll put it in my mouth. So, tell me, how quick does the cure work? How many doses does a person have to take?"

"To cure the disease takes one hundred forty pills. Five per day for four weeks. But the treatment has to begin before pustules appear on a person's face. Once that happens, it's too late."

Ramirez appeared to be deep in thought. After a few moments, he said, "Let's charge one hundred thousand dollars per person. That's a fraction of what other companies charge for drugs that do a lot less. You know that from the stuff Bushings used to sell. Our drug is a God-send."

During his long tenure at Bushings, McAlister had been the architect of price gouging. Taking full advantage of the absence of drug-price regulation in the United States, he led the pharmaceutical industry in charging punishing amounts for medicines that the public desperately needed. Wagging his head, McAlister said, "Unfortunately, that kind of pricing won't work here. We can't charge more than six thousand dollars per patient."

Ramirez' face went pale. "Why so cheap? That's crazy."

"If the cure is too expensive, it will become a drug of privilege. That will limit our sales and reduce our profits in the long run. If we keep the cure affordable for governments and insurance companies, we could be looking at tens of millions of customers, maybe hundreds of millions. At my price point, the governments and insurers can find a way to pass most of the cost on to the user."

Ramirez grinned. "It could be billions of patients if things get crazy."

"But if we get greedy, governments will gang up and take the cure away from us. They'll appropriate the drug patents. They'll nationalize the business under some kind of emergency legislation or executive order. We can't risk that. It will finish us."

Lighting a cigarette, Ramirez asked, "What's the profit margin on the cure?"

"On six thousand dollars, the profit is five thousand four hundred thirty-three dollars."

"Sweet God on high," muttered Ramirez as he took a long drag on his cigarette and tried to calculate the quantum of fortune to be made. After a few moments, he noticed McAlister's teeth gleaming in the sunlight. "Geez, Colum, what did you do to your teeth? They look so white."

"Do they really?" asked McAlister as he made a clown smile while he patted his well-coiffed silver hair. "I asked the prison dentist what he could do and gave him a roll of hundreds. Next thing I knew, he brought in a bleaching machine and did as good a job as my Park Avenue guy used to do."

Before Ramirez could respond, perhaps with a sarcastic comment, a coughing fit overtook him, causing a huge billow of smoke to be expelled from his lungs in McAlister's direction. "Keep that goddamn smoke away from me," hissed McAlister as he waved the air around him. "You should quit that filthy habit or you'll never live long enough to spend the money you'll be making."

Ramirez dropped the cigarette on the ground.

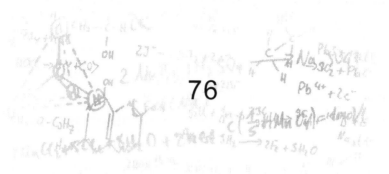

# 76

CHRISTINA, BOBBY AND MIRIELLE SAT second row center in the auditorium of the Plum Cove Elementary School on Hickory Street in Annisquam. They were surrounded by the parents and siblings of the other students who would be performing in the school's annual talent show that evening. No one in the audience knew that the man sitting in the second row was the greatest scientist in human history. And that was exactly the way Bobby and Christina wanted it to be. They cherished their anonymity under the WITSEC program.

When Pete walked on to the small stage, he faced the audience and smiled at his parents and sister. Dressed in gray slacks, shiny black shoes, a light blue shirt, red bow tie and dark blue blazer, he looked clean and polished, an unusual state for a nine-year old boy. "I'd like to play a composition I wrote which was inspired by Schumann, one of my favorite composers," Pete said to the audience.

Sitting down at the piano, he closed his eyes, lowered his head, and for almost a full minute did nothing at all. The silence in the room became awkward and the crowd began to shift in their seats and murmurs could be heard. And then he began to play.

His young hands took command of the massive instrument as his body movements punctuated the melodic beauty and rhythmic complexity of the original piece of music that he had created. When the crescendo parts of the composition required the hand and arm strength of an adult, Pete stood up as he played to give his small body added leverage. No one had ever heard that auditorium piano thunder as it did under his touch. It became an extension of the boy and it didn't seem possible that the majestic music that tumbled from it was made by a child. Even those in the audience who didn't like classical music were stunned by Pete's technical and emotive powers. When he finished performing and turned to face the audience, many for the first time noticed the intensity of his Austin eyes which sparkled in the stage lights like translucent sapphires. It was evident to everyone that they were in the presence of a musical genius.

After the talent show was over, the audience filed into the school's gymnasium for refreshments. Pete went off to play with his friends and joined them in pulling down the multicolored streamers and balloons that decorated the room. Mirielle stood in front of the cookie tray consuming brownies as quickly as she possibly could. As Christina and Bobby sipped fruit punch, they were greeted by Pete's teacher, Faye Toth. "You must be so proud of Pete. He was wonderful. How does a child write music like that? I have no doubt that one day he'll be famous."

"We're very proud of him," said Bobby.

Faye's eyes twinkled. "I always marvel at the different aptitudes that children have. No two are alike. Some of my pupils are so gifted in English that poetry and stories just spill out of them. Others are whizzes in math and science. Pete, on the other hand, is an extraordinary musician, composer and a wonderful visual artist.

What he lacks in the academic disciplines, he more than makes up for in the arts." Faye took a sip of her punch before turning her attention to Mirielle whose mouth and chin were covered in chocolate. "Now, who is this lovely girl? I don't believe we've met before." A little embarrassed, Christina wiped Mirielle's face with a napkin.

"My name is Mirielle. I'm Pete's sister," said the diminutive six-year-old.

Faye gently stroked the top of Mirielle's head and then bent down to eye level. "You're a very lucky young lady. You've inherited your mother's beauty. You should be thankful for that."

Mirielle took a few steps back so that she was out of Faye's reach. "My parents taught me that what's important is the beauty that you have in here," said Mirielle as she patted her heart.

Nodding in agreement, Faye asked Christina, "How come Mirielle isn't enrolled here at the school? Is she attending private?"

Bobby answered. "Actually, we're homeschooling Mirielle for the time being."

"Really. Do you have the time?"

Christina took the ball. "Mirielle's an incredibly quick learner, a self-starter in many respects. She's been that way ever since she was a baby. I'm teaching her reading and writing, and Sean supplements that with math and science." Bobby's head jerked in Christina's direction and she read the alarm in his eyes.

Christina's comment wasn't lost on Faye. "I know that you're a mathematician, Deborah, but I didn't know that Sean was involved in the sciences, too."

Bobby laughed. "Well, I'm not in Deborah's league, that's for sure." He cast a playful glance at Christina. "I'm really just a student of sorts. Curious about everything. You don't have to be Einstein to teach a six-year-old and spark her interest."

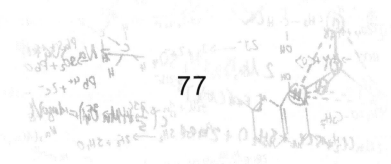

# 77

T HE DECREPIT BUILDINGS THAT SERVED as Saeed's headquarters in Syria surrounded a vast courtyard. The buildings blocked any breeze and the sun relentlessly reflected off the structures' concrete walls so that the yard became an oven.

Saeed and Fahd lay their prayer mats down on the hard-packed sand of the courtyard. Prostrating themselves on their mats in the stifling heat, their foreheads touched the ground as they recited the seven verses of *Surat al-Fatihah.* Behind them, sixteen hundred black-clad Ansar Jamaat troops did the same thing as the sun beat down on them.

When the prayer session ended, the troops stood at attention in ten long rows so that Saeed and Fahd could walk among their ranks and inspect them. Saeed and Fahd then stood in front of them on a two-foot tall platform. A makeshift public-address system had been set up. Saeed spoke first:

"You are here today because you have been chosen for a mission of the greatest importance to the caliphate. Your selection is the highest honor that can be bestowed upon an

Ansar Jamaat soldier. You have distinguished yourselves as being the most dependable and resourceful. And you have demonstrated unfailing loyalty and a willingness to subsume your own well-being to our blessed cause."

Saeed then raised his hands to mid-chest level, his palms facing outwards towards his troops. Closing his eyes, he recited the following *du'a*, his sonorous voice filling the courtyard:

"O, Allah, You are our strength and you are our support. For Your sake, these warriors go forth. Restrain our enemies and give us refuge in you from their evil. O, Allah, bless those that serve You selflessly. Glory is to Allah. Praise is to Allah. Allah is great."

Fahd then stepped forward. He raised his right hand high over his head and waved it back and forth ten times. Those closest to him could see that he was holding a small canister that was no larger than a two-ounce can of shaving cream.

"Here in my hand I hold the Sword of the Mahdi." Fahd then clamped his hand closed. "Look, I close my hand and you can't even see it. But the Sword does not have to be long or broad or heavy to be the most powerful weapon on Earth. This tiny aerosol device contains enough toxin to kill one hundred thousand infidels. And every infidel who is infected will then infect countless more. In your pockets or in your backpacks, you will hold enough to take down millions who stand in opposition to the caliphate. No warriors have ever had such power."

The sea of black erupted into a collective roar. Pounding their right arms into the air, they chanted in unison, *"Allahu Akbar, Allahu Akbar, Allahu Akbar."*

After a moment, Colonel Fahd signaled for quiet.

"You will position each of these devices in an undetectable place in each target area. I will instruct you how to identify these targets. These devices have been designed so that they can be remotely detonated by you after you have reached a safe distance from it, thereby ensuring that you do not become infected and—"

Saeed interrupted Fahd in midsentence as he stepped in front of him. His deep voice was heavy with gravitas and his dark eyes focused intensely on his troops.

"Let me make something clear: You have been selected because we trust in your ability to assess each situation. If it would be more effective for you to manually release the spray at the target location instead of doing so remotely, then you must do that. Even though you will become infected you will have at least eighteen days of mobility within which to use all of the devices that have been given to you. And in so doing, you will serve the caliphate in a way which will bestow the greatest glory upon you. Once the Sword of the Mahdi has touched you, you become the Sword. All that you then need to do in order to wield its blade is to mingle with as many infidels as possible."

# 78

WHEN THE PRESIDENT OF THE United States gave his speech promising to implement immediate field-testing of the cure, he neglected to mention that there weren't any living infected victims on which the drug could be tested, as all those who had been infected with the disease had died. The world wouldn't have long to wait however.

Within three weeks after the president spoke, Ansar Jamaat simultaneously attacked eighteen cities in Iraq, Iran, Libya, Lebanon and Syria. The United States and many other countries imposed a travel ban against anyone seeking to enter from the Mideast. With foresight, Saeed had already dispatched twelve hundred Ansar Jamaat operatives to the United States, the United Kingdom, France, Germany, Spain, Italy, Japan, China, Russia, Brazil, South Africa and Australia. Many of them were Caucasians with Anglo names who carried EU passports. They also carried the poison with them in inconspicuous cosmetic containers that comported with regulations. International shipments of the toxin to locations throughout the world had also been prearranged and awaited pickup by them. All they needed was Saeed's command to attack.

As countless people became infected in the Mideast cities that were targeted by Saeed and the death toll mounted, over three thousand hazmat-suited doctors and epidemiologists converged in those areas to begin testing the cure and trying to determine the proper dosage and the most effective stage of the disease in which to administer the drug. Schlumberger Foch didn't know the answers to those questions because their tests had only been done on human blood samples, not on living infected human beings. Colum McAlister knew the answers, because they were in Mahmoud's journal, which had been delivered to him in Geneva. McAlister never divulged the information to Schlumberger, because he couldn't. The drug formula that he had delivered to Schlumberger was designated as a pharmaceutical with an unknown application since, at that time, Mahmoud's disease had not yet been unleashed. McAlister's silence ensured the secrecy of his insidious relationship with Mahmoud.

The drug was first administered by the testers to the people whose suffering was in the most advanced state, their faces covered with pustules, their skin bluish in tint, the sclera of their eyes yellowed and a black mucus-like substance caked on or leaking from their noses and ears. When the drug did nothing to help them, it was declared to be a failure. Worldwide panic ensued. Saeed rejoiced at the news.

"What the fuck is going on, Gunther? The cure doesn't work. Our long positions are going to collapse. We'll lose everything," bellowed Bazhenov. "Gao and I better liquidate before we're wiped out."

"Don't panic. The cure does work. Don't sell anything. Use this downturn to buy more long positions. They'll be cheaper than ever. Hang tough and have faith," replied Ramirez.

At the urging of Schlumberger Foch, the testers persevered. Finally, they reversed course and began to try the drug on those victims who were in the early stages of the disease. Four months later, it was announced that the cure was, in fact, effective and that the necessary dosage was five pills per day for four weeks and that the drug regimen had to begin prior to the appearance of pustules on the face.

More than two million people died while the testers fumbled around for months trying to figure out what McAlister already knew. But he remained resolute in his belief that there was no blood on his hands. As he told Ramirez, "I didn't create the disease and I didn't unleash it. Because of me, there's a cure. You think I wanted those people to die? I would have preferred them to be customers. There's nothing I could do."

When the announcement of the cure's efficacy was made, those closest to Saeed noticed a change come over him. He began to spend most of his time in seclusion, isolated from everyone other than Colonel Fahd, whom he would summon to his living quarters. These meetings were frequently very brief, but sometimes went on for the better part of the day or night, Saeed's voice growing hoarse as he boomed an unrelenting diatribe.

At the end of one such meeting, Fahd said, "Caliph, permit me to say something for your benefit. Your doctors are worried. You need to eat more. They say your consumption has dwindled to a subsistence diet. Food will give you strength. We feed our prisoners more than you are eating."

Saeed glared at Fahd. "I don't need to be told what to eat."

"In times of crisis, the body needs to be fed well, not starved."

Saeed's right eye began to twitch. "I am not in crisis. Ansar Jamaat is not in crisis. The caliphate is not in crisis. Are you in crisis, Fahd?"

"No, of course not, Caliph. I'm just concerned for your well-being, as are your troops."

"What about my troops?" asked Saeed.

"You don't communicate with them anymore. You have me do it."

Saeed's eyes seared into Fahd. "And they don't like that? Why is that, Colonel? Are you not doing a good job? Are you a bad communicator?"

Fahd didn't answer, hoping that there would be no more salvos.

"Is there anything else I should know about my troops?" asked Saeed.

Fahd trained his eyes on the ground as he said, "They are concerned that you have changed your routine."

"What routine?" asked Saeed.

"Your nightly regimen."

Saeed's eyes searched Fahd. "What are you talking about? You're speaking in riddles."

Fahd didn't look up when he said, "You no longer have young female prisoners brought to you every night. This worries the troops. They viewed that as proof of your strength and virility."

Saeed was silent. Fahd immediately regretted what he said. Given the mood that Saeed was in, a physical assault was not out of the question. Suddenly, Saeed began to laugh. It started as a chuckle but quickly escalated. Fahd had never seen Saeed laugh. In fact, he hardly had ever seen the man smile. Fahd was unsure if he should join in the laughter since he had no idea what precipitated it. Wary about what might come after, he decided that remaining stoic was the prudent course.

When Saeed finally caught his breath, he said, "If my troops think that my strength lies in fornicating with slaves, then we are all wasting our time. The infidels will wipe us out."

# 79

MOST WESTERNERS THOUGHT THAT YUSUF al-Saeed was a radical Islamic terrorist, and he was frequently characterized by politicians and the media as such. Perhaps that might have been an accurate description of him at one time, but as his bloodlust grew along with his territorial ambitions, he began to believe that he had been divinely selected to lead a struggle of biblical proportions. The prospect of his caliphate being destroyed by international forces that were now empowered by the existence of a cure became the catalyst to his final metamorphosis. Calling him a radical Islamist at this point was wishful thinking. He now fully subscribed to the theological doctrine of apocalyptic Islam, a genocidal eschatology or End Times theology.

Saeed had no doubt that he was living in the End of Days as predicted by ancient prophecies and that the return to Earth of the Muslim messiah, the Mahdi, was imminent. The Mahdi would reveal himself for the purpose of establishing a global Islamic kingdom under Sharia law, and he would come only when the entire world was awash in blood, pandemonium and slaughter. Saeed now intended to do everything in his power to hasten the

Mahdi's return. Saeed's service to the Mahdi would be discharged by annihilating all manner of *kuffar* and *zindiq*, wherever they could be found. Those on Saeed's extermination list included everyone whose religious practices did not comport with Saeed's standards for true Islam, and for those who did comport, but were unfortunate enough to live in countries which Saeed deemed to have degenerate cultures, they too would perish. Saeed was in a race against time to foment worldwide chaos and carnage before the cure could be manufactured and distributed in sufficient quantities to save those whom he had targeted. Now dressing completely in black, his face had become inscrutable and his eyes had no more life in them than the cloth from which his tunic was made.

Saeed was confident that he would have help. As relayed in the ancient Islamic texts, the Mahdi and his followers would be assisted by the Mahdi's deputy, Isa ibn Maryam (Jesus, son of Mary), the second-most revered prophet in Islam. According to these writings, Jesus would return to Earth to declare himself to be a Muslim, abolish Christianity, correct the Christian misrepresentation that he is the Son of God or a savior, enforce Sharia law worldwide, kill the false messiah (known in Muslim apocalyptic literature as Al-Masih ad-Dajjal), and force non-Muslims to convert to Islam under penalty of death.

Saeed was not the first leader of apocalyptic Islam. But he was the first leader of apocalyptic Islam to acquire a genocidal weapon. Saeed articulated his objectives in the following speech that he delivered to rally his troops the day after the cure's effectiveness was announced in the world media:

"We will vanquish the apostates. They cannot hide from us. We will break their crosses, destroy their Rome, enslave their women and exterminate their children. The descendants of the Crusaders and all other infidels will find no mercy. From the time of creation, the caravan of humanity has been advancing toward the final climax which is now upon us. The Mahdi is coming soon and we, the true sons of Islam, are prepared. We will be the glorious fighters in history's final hour. We will purify the world and the Mahdi will reward us on the Day of Judgment."

Two days later, Saeed sent word to his overseas operatives that it was time for them to attack.

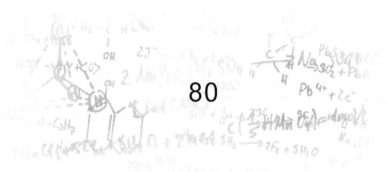

# 80

WHILE THE CURE WAS IN the process of being tested, Schlumberger Foch finalized sublicense agreements with the fifty largest pharmaceutical companies in the world, each of which would mobilize its subsidiary companies in local markets in order to maximize the production and distribution of the cure. Each license agreement was on a "most favored nations basis," meaning that all of the licensees were treated the same. This allowed the agreements to get done quickly. Schlumberger held the cards in the negotiations, because no company wanted to be left out of the cornucopia of riches that a worldwide pandemic could bestow. Everyone wanted their place at the feeding trough. Colum McAlister had succeeded in creating the largest bonanza for the pharmaceuticals industry that had ever existed, and he would be the biggest beneficiary of the bounty to come.

As soon as the cure's effectiveness was confirmed, manufacture of the drug began. Never before had so many pharmaceutical companies been marshaled to produce and distribute one drug. Schlumberger Foch was the clearing center for the placement of orders. In the first week alone, it received orders directly from government health agencies for forty million patient treatment packages; this equated to a purchase price of two hundred forty billion dollars. Because the disease needed to be treated in its earliest stages, no one wanted to risk being short on treatments. One days' delay in the administration of the drug could be the difference between life and death. It soon became evident to Schlumberger and its licensees that the demand for the cure would be so great that they each would have to commit entire manufacturing facilities to produce this one pharmaceutical.

The testers of the cure were enthralled when they discovered that a person could not be re-infected by HRFS once he or she had been cured using the drug. Of course, Mahmoud knew this and he considered that feature of the cure he invented to be one of its most important, given that those who had been cured were likely be exposed to the contagion repeatedly.

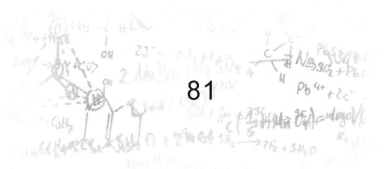

# 81

I T WAS 4 P.M. EASTERN time on Tuesday, September 24, when all television broadcast and cable networks throughout the United States interrupted their programing for a special announcement by the president of the United States. This announcement was streamed on the internet by all news outlets:

"My fellow Americans, several hours ago, I was advised by the Centers for Disease Control and Prevention that the first case of the disease known as HRFS, Hemorrhagic Respiratory Failure Syndrome, was diagnosed in the United States. Since then, I have been informed that an additional sixty-one cases have now been diagnosed here. The sixty-two infected persons are disbursed among thirty-one different states. We expect the number of afflicted individuals to increase daily and rapidly.

This is not a time for panic. Our federal health agencies including the CDC, NIH and the U.S. Army Medical Research Institute of Infectious Diseases, working in conjunction with state and local health authorities are well prepared for this. We were expecting it after what happened in the Mideast. Here in the United States, we have in stock and on hand, ready for distribution, over seventy million treatment packages of the cure and we will be monitoring the situation hourly so that we can order additional treatment packages in anticipation of demand. We have been assured by the inventor of the cure, Schlumberger Foch, that supply of the drug will be timely met as need dictates. The cure has been proven effective and is being manufactured twenty-four hours a day by fifty leading pharmaceutical companies and their subsidiaries throughout the world.

I repeat: This situation is under control, but to keep it under control, all of you must do your part. You must be vigilant and diligent. There is no room for carelessness. The following is what I need everyone to do.

First, the initial symptoms of HRFS are similar to a common cold. The next stage manifests itself with respiratory flu type symptoms. Do not wait. As soon as you experience any of these symptoms, immediately report to the nearest quarantine centers for diagnostic blood tests. The sooner that you are diagnosed, the quicker the cure can be administered and the quicker your recovery will begin. Medics from the National Guard and all other branches of the armed forces are being dispatched to assist in every city in the diagnosis and treatment of the disease.

I cannot overemphasize the importance of quick detection of the disease. If you wait too long, then you will become incurable, and you will be a danger to others.

Once you are diagnosed as having the disease, you will need to be isolated in accordance with procedures that will be made clear to you when you commence treatment, so as to ensure that you don't infect anyone else. HRFS is highly contagious. We do not yet know how long the risk of contagion persists after medication begins. No doubt, this will become clear as time goes on.

Protective breathing masks will be distributed at no charge to everyone by police and fire departments and EMT workers; the masks will also be available at no charge in all schools, supermarkets, drug stores and gas stations. These must be worn at all times when you are outside of your homes. Failure to do so will subject you to arrest.

The terrorists who are seeking to spread this disease are doing so using aerosol containers from which the toxin is discharged. If you see anyone with an aerosol or similar container or otherwise engaged in suspicious activity, report it immediately and if possible, take a photograph of the person in question to accompany your report. We have arranged for a report hotline to be available nationwide by dialing HRFS* or 4737*. Reports can be filed verbally or by text.

Today, I am issuing a presidential order imposing an immediate ban on all civilian travel into the United States from any nation, and on all civilian travel from the United States to any nation. Many other countries will be doing the same, as all have joined forces to contain the spread of this pandemic, which has already infected people on every continent.

I understand the fears that you all are experiencing at this time. But let me emphasize to you that the only thing that can stymie our ability to overcome the challenge we are facing is panic. We can and will prevail, but to do so we must all remain calm, rational and vigilant.

God bless you, and God bless the United States of America."

———————

By the Thanksgiving holiday in late November, only two months after the first cases in the United States had been diagnosed, four hundred fifty-six thousand people had been infected with HRFS in the United States. Throughout the rest of the world, there were twelve million diagnosed cases.

By Christmas, the number of diagnosed cases in the United States had risen to over three million two hundred fifty thousand, and in the rest of the world, over sixty-three million.

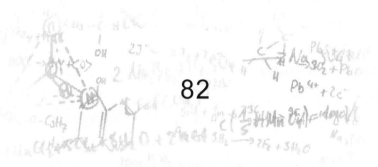

# 82

MAHMOUD WAS BARELY RECOGNIZABLE. AT five feet nine inches tall, he now weighted one hundred eighteen pounds. He ate only one meal a day and had trouble keeping down the little that he consumed. Unable to sleep for more than two hours per night, his dark eyes had receded deep into their sockets as if the gravity of his sadness had pulled them closer to his heart. The lines and wrinkles on his face had become so pronounced that they obscured the definition of his features, which was unusual for a man of only fifty-one years of age. Stooped and listing when he walked, his left foot dragged behind him. He had never fully recovered from the stroke that he suffered shortly after Saeed began his expanded attack.

Sitting at his office desk, Mahmoud buried his face in his hands. *It wasn't supposed to be like this. It's all gone so wrong.…* His mind reeled as he pondered the same questions yet again. *Why did McAlister wait so long to announce the cure? Why didn't he tell anyone about the correct doses and when the treatment must start? I provided exact instructions in the journal I gave Nizar Khouri.*

As Mahmoud hunched over the trash basket, puking up the

little that remained in his stomach, the bony spine of his emaciated body pressed against his shirt making him look like a scavenging reptile. *Millions died while they were trying to figure out what I already knew.*

Mahmoud had hoped that the cure would cripple the disease so that his sins would be partially mitigated. But no matter how many lives his cure was saving, millions had died and would continue to die. A cure can only work if it is available to everyone who needs it. But as had been the case with other lifesaving drugs in the past, the poorer nations that were reliant on international aid to pay for the cure were the last to have access to it, while the wealthier nations hoarded more than they needed.

Volunteer doctors and nurses who usually would have been available to work in third-world countries were already overwhelmed in their own nations diagnosing and treating the infected. And in certain strife-torn countries in the Mideast, Asia and Africa, there were reports that the cure was purposely being withheld by those in power from areas occupied by political dissidents; those rulers knew that the disease would be more efficient in cleansing the areas of opposition than their troops could be.

———————

"Come on, get in line and keep moving. Everyone into the truck," said the Ansar Jamaat soldier as he poked the slowest of Rakut's survivors in their backs with the barrel of his automatic rifle. Facing Mahmoud, he scowled, "I don't know why we haven't killed these dogs yet. All we do is feed them and drive them around. They're worthless."

"That's for me to decide, not you," said Mahmoud. The soldier joined the prisoners in the back of the truck. Mahmoud looked at his map and then, with difficulty, pulled himself into the seat next to the driver. Pointing to a city which he had circled, he nodded to the driver to proceed. A large panel-truck followed behind them.

When they were ten miles from the target city, the vehicles stopped and everyone other than the prisoners disembarked. The driver of the panel truck flung open its back doors to reveal several dozen hazmat suits hanging on racks. The driver removed four, kept one for himself and distributed one each to Mahmoud, his driver and the soldier, all of whom put them on. The men then re-entered the vehicles and drove on to the city center. It had now been thirty-six days since the toxin had been released there.

"Get out. You know the drill," said the soldier to the Rakut survivors, who exited the truck without hazmat protection.

The drivers remained with the vehicles while Mahmoud led the way and the soldier walked behind the prisoners with his weapon at the ready. Of the original twenty survivors that had been found in Rakut, only seventeen remained alive, as three had been shot by Ansar Jamaat soldiers as they tried to escape during an expedition similar to this one.

After walking for a few minutes, Mahmoud raised his right hand and the line of hapless souls from Rakut stopped in front of the entrance to a hospital emergency room. "This will be a good place to start," he said. Entering the large chamber, Mahmoud surveyed the surreal canvas of human devastation in front of him. No artist had ever painted a picture more grotesque than the fetid landscape of death that confronted him. Breaking out in a cold sweat, Mahmoud stood motionless, taking it all in. His eyes filled with tears. His breathing became labored. His legs began to wobble. He staggered to the side and grabbed onto a chair as he tried to steady himself, but the chair tipped over and Mahmoud stumbled forward dragging the chair behind him. His groans could be heard through the microphone of his headgear as a crippling pain rippled through his chest, torso and neck. Dropping to his knees, Mahmoud fell backwards, his head hitting the floor. The goggles of his hazmat suit fogged and his body convulsed.

As the prisoners reacted to Mahmoud's collapse, the soldier waved his gun at them and shouted, "Stay in line or I'll shoot you all."

Faris Khalili, the handsome young man who was the only member of his family to survive the annihilation of Rakut's population, rushed forward. "He needs help. I think he's had a heart attack."

"Are you a doctor?" asked the soldier.

"No."

The guard sneered. "A nurse? You're pretty enough."

Faris had gotten used to comments like that long ago. "My mother had a heart condition. Her doctor taught me what to do. Let me help him."

The soldier shook his head denying permission. "Why do you want to help him? He takes you to these cities of death and makes you do disgusting things. You should want to see him die."

"He needs help or it will be too late. He'll stop breathing and suffer brain damage."

"How many trips like this as he taken you on?"

"Twenty-three," replied Faris.

"Then why would you want to help him? The soldier spat a huge wad onto the ground and gruffly wiped his bearded face. "I was wrong to call you dogs. You and the others are less than that. You're just guinea pigs for Dr. Frankenstein to experiment on."

Faris took a few steps closer to Mahmoud. "Doctor Mahmoud saved us. Saeed was going to shoot us all in Rakut. Mahmoud stopped him. Whatever he's doing, we're still alive. He hasn't hurt us. But if he dies, you will kill us. You will kill us today, right here."

The soldier laughed. "Damn right I will. No reason to keep you alive if Mahmoud is dead. I shouldn't let you help him. I hate these trips." Seeing some of the prisoners beginning to put distance between themselves and him, the soldier moved aggressively towards them. "On the ground, now, all of you! Lie on your bellies or I'll shoot."

"Please. We're running out of time," implored Faris.

The soldier stared at Mahmoud's lifeless body. *If the Caliph finds out I didn't let this kid help Mahmoud, he'll slit my throat.* Pointing his rifle at Faris, he said, "Go, do what you want."

Faris knelt beside Mahmoud and placed the heel of one hand on the center of Mahmoud's chest. He then placed the heel of his other hand on top of the first hand and interlaced his fingers. Keeping his arms straight, he pushed down hard, using his body weight to add force to the compressions, which he pumped out at the rate of almost two per second. After four minutes, Faris was exhausted but not giving up.

"Okay, you've had your chance. Get on over there with the others, facedown," said the soldier.

Faris ignored the command and kept pumping. The soldier kicked Faris hard in the ribs, grabbed him by his long hair and dragged him ten feet away from Mahmoud. Faris crawled back and resumed his frantic pumping of Mahmoud's chest. Just as the butt of the soldier's rifle was about to meet the back of Faris' head, Mahmoud's eyes opened. A gob of spit landed on Faris' leg as the soldier muttered, "Fuck…"

"I think I had a heart attack," stammered Mahmoud in a voice that was no more than a whisper.

"You did. I gave you a heart massage. You're lucky to be alive."

"Lucky to be alive," echoed Mahmoud mournfully. The only thing Mahmoud was thankful for was that his breathing apparatus spared him the stench of the decaying corpses that surrounded him. *The boy thinks he saved me. He didn't. Allah won't let me die. He will not release me. I am where I deserve to be.*

After a few moments, Mahmoud motioned to the soldier from his reclining position. "I'm going to just rest here. This one will stay with me. Walk the others through the town and have them do everything that I always have them do. Don't rush it. They need to have as much exposure to the disease as possible."

When they returned approximately two hours later, the soldier called for the trucks to meet them. As usual, each prisoner was then given a hazmat suit so that he or she would not infect any *Ansar Jamaat* personnel at the base camp that they might come into contact with prior to their being returned to the sealed observation cells in which they lived.

After each of these descents into hell, Mahmoud followed the same procedure. He would wait for five days, at which point he would conduct his first physical examination on the Rakut survivors. Successive physical examinations would follow at five-day intervals over the course of the next four weeks.

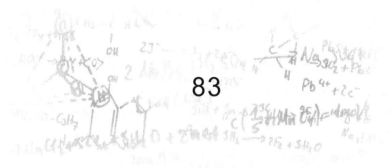

# 83

"**L**ET'S ONLY USE FIRST NAMES on this call. Who's on?" asked Ramirez.

"Huo Jin here."

"Viktor present."

"Thank you, gentlemen. While it would have been preferable to have an in-person meeting, given the current circumstances, I'm sure we're all happy to remain in our safe havens free from the possibility of infection. Where are each of you now?" asked Ramirez.

"In that glass room you admired so much," replied Gao cautiously.

"I'm on my yacht in the middle of nowhere," said Bazhenov. "What about you, Gunther?"

"A small island off the coast of Sweden. I bet neither of you know that there are over ten thousand Swedish islands."

"Difficult for anyone to find you," said Gao. "I'm impressed."

"Gunther, what is this call about?" asked Bazhenov impatiently.

"I wanted to see how our investments are doing," said Ramirez.

Bazhenov spoke up. "I was anxious for a while, but you were right. Your partner is a wizard. He knows the future. Or maybe he creates the future. Who cares. It works. We took your advice, and when the cure looked like a failure and the markets bottomed, we maxed out our leverage and went long on every good asset class we could find. Now that the cure has been successfully deployed and optimism is returning to the markets, we're making more money than I ever thought possible."

Gao took the floor. "And because you told us the cure would be viable when everyone thought it wouldn't, we went long not only on Schlumberger stock but also on the entire pharmaceutical sector. So far, over nine hundred million treatment packages have been sold and it's only going to increase. We are profiting mightily in this pharmacological feeding frenzy." While the participants in the call couldn't see it, the corners of Gao's mouth turned upwards.

Ramirez replied, "Sales of the drug could be even bigger. Too many people who need it aren't getting it."

"Huo Jin has some dark theories about that," said Bazhenov.

"I wish they were only theories but they are not. I come from a country where human life is the most plentiful and least valuable resource. But China isn't the only country where there are far too many people. India, Indonesia, Bangladesh, Brazil, Pakistan, Nigeria, Ethiopia—the list goes on. Too many people to feed, too many to educate, too many to employ, too many to control. The people who matter will get the cure and the people who don't, won't. Those who will perish are those who are a burden to their nations. The powerful want the herd to be culled. It will make things easier for them."

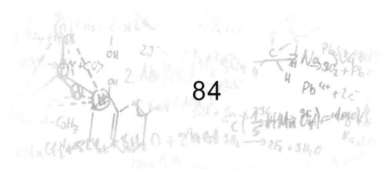

# 84

" **P**RINT OUT THOSE EQUATIONS THAT you wrote and let me see them," said Bobby. He waited by the printer in his office as thirty pages of small print streamed out of the machine. Bobby picked up the papers and sat down at his desk, his eyes intently focused on every line. No one could read and analyze mathematical notations quicker than Bobby, but it took him more than fifteen minutes, as these were particularly complicated.

"What do you think, Daddy? Did I get it right?" asked Mirielle, impatient to receive her father's approval.

"Almost. You have to be careful not to get caught up in the old math. That will fence you in. Use the new language I've taught you. It has no boundaries to limit your imagination, and as your mathematical vocabulary increases, so will your reach." Bobby kissed his seven-year-old daughter on the top of her head. "You're getting there, hon. A little further every day."

Bobby had been teaching Mirielle ever since she was five months old, which was when he first began to think that she had unusual intellectual gifts. There was something about the way she returned his gaze even at that young age, an uneasiness that he felt when she locked eyes with him. She didn't look at anyone else the way she looked at her father. Or was that just his imagination? He was sure it was not. He sensed a subliminal connection between them. A cognitive energy radiated from her that was entirely incongruous with her age. At that time, Christina didn't see it at all. Mirielle was her adorable baby girl, plain and simple. But Bobby knew that there was something happening inside his daughter's head that was all too familiar to him.

At six months old, he taught her the alphabet in two days. By the end of her ninth month, she was reading books written for five-year-olds. He thought that he would be able to teach her addition and subtraction in two weeks. It took four days. Multiplication and division were mastered in a month, before she was eleven months old. By the time she was eighteen months of age, she was able to look things up on the internet, which allowed her to learn at her own accelerated pace and to make progress when Bobby was unavailable to teach her, due to his work schedule.

At that time, Bobby and Christina decided Mirielle would be homeschooled. Christina would teach Mirielle reading and writing, and Bobby would teach her math and science. This would allow Mirielle to be educated away from prying eyes, and she would be spared the social ostracism and narrow scientific curriculum that Bobby had endured when he was a student at the Institute for Advanced Intelligence Studies—the school run by the Office of Special Strategic Intelligence Services (OSSIS), which was then under the auspices of Orin Varneys prior to his elevation to CIA Director.

As Mirielle sat on a stool at Bobby's desk reviewing the corrections that he had made on her equations, Bobby thought back to the discussions he had with Christina almost five years earlier.

"I don't want her to be like me," said Bobby. "To live the life that I've lived, and have the problems and pressures I've had... I want her to be a normal happy kid with friends her own age. She shouldn't be treated like an oddity, cloistered away and exploited. I want her to own her life."

"It will be okay," replied Christina. "Remember, she has us. And so far, she's not suffering from nightmares and she doesn't fall into trances. Maybe she'll only get the good stuff from you and none of the bad."

"Well, if that happens, it will be because your genes smoothed out the rough edges of mine."

"That doesn't sound particularly scientific," quipped Christina.

"I just hope she gets more of you than she gets of me, that's all."

"How great are her intellectual abilities? Can you tell at this point?"

"It's way too early. She's started out fast as lightning, but this is a long game. She's very young. Often prodigies burn out as time goes by. It's a question of whether or not she continues to develop, and at what pace and for how long before she stops. Only time will tell that."

# 85

H UMAN BEINGS HAVE A UNIQUE capacity to adapt. After eighteen months of the cure being widely distributed throughout the Western nations, there was no remnant of panic as a result of HRFS. Getting infected and taking the cure as soon as symptoms first appeared had become part of an accepted routine. While more and more people were becoming infected due to the highly contagious nature of the disease, there was a prevalent feeling that matters were under control since a person could not contract the disease again after being cured.

Gao had been prescient in his ability to discern that the judicious deprivation of the cure would become a way of dealing with intractable problems. Among the fortunate, the disease had created an obsession with self that depleted the small reservoir of concern which had previously existed for those who had no voice. Little media coverage was given to the fact that millions of refugees fleeing war, persecution, hunger and the ravages of climate change had not received the cure, nor would they. Similarly absent from first-world consciousness was a recognition that the governments of many nations had tacitly used the untreated disease as a tool of social engineering to rid them of portions of their populations that they viewed as burdens with no upside.

The investor groups led by Gao and Bazhenov had profited beyond their wildest expectations, as did Colum McAlister and Gunther Ramirez. Although their names would never show up on the *Forbes* list, because their wealth was hidden in a maze of offshore corporations, McAlister and Ramirez were now among the richest people in the world, having received their thirty-percent cut of the Gao/Bazhenov investor groups' profits, in addition to the lion's share of profits from the drug.

---

Orin Varneys was among the first to be informed by the U.S. Army Medical Research Institute of Infectious Diseases (USAMRIID) that there was a problem. Dr. Stephen Marcantel explained the circumstances in a meeting which he had with Varneys and Clive Stone, Director of Homeland Security, at Varneys' office in Langley, Virginia.

Varneys wasn't sure if Marcantel had a physiological problem, or if years of working with infectious diseases had caused a behavioral tick. In any event, Varneys found it annoying that every forty seconds, with metronome-like regularity, Marcantel scrunched-up his nose and sniffed in loudly.

"We and the CDC began to notice after the first eleven months of the drug's distribution, that progressively larger doses of the HRFS cure began to be needed," said Marcantel between sniffs. "Our observations have been confirmed by the ECDC and WHO. We were hoping that this trend might level off but it hasn't. That's why I wanted to see you both today."

"Is the disease getting stronger, more virulent?" asked Varneys.

"That's one way to look at it, but that's really not what's happening."

"Doctor, no riddles please. Exactly what is going on?" Varneys asked.

"The cure is becoming less effective in its ability to fight HRFS. It's taking larger and larger amounts of the drug to do the same job."

"Have you checked the pills? I bet those scumbags at the pharmaceutical companies are diluting the formula so they can sell more pills and make more money. I knew we should have nationalized that drug," said Varneys.

Marcantel sniffed in deeply before responding. "We did check that. Repeatedly. It's not that. It's because the disease is gradually developing an immunity to the cure."

"How?" asked Clive Stone.

"Diseases aren't static. They're living things. Their goal, like that of all living things, is to survive and propagate. As long as they can continue to find and infect hosts, then they evolve to survive where their previous incarnations could not."

"But we've had cures for certain diseases that have continued to work for decades. What's different here?" asked Varneys.

Marcantel pressed the tragus of his left ear repeatedly as if he were a diver who had just gotten out of a swimming pool. "Two things. Diseases whose replication is DNA-based are less prone to mutation than those that are RNA-based—like HRFS, so if a cure is found for a DNA-based disease, then it is likely to remain potent for a much longer period of time. The other factor is the newness of the disease. When a disease is suddenly introduced into the human population as was the case with HRFS, it manifests accelerated rates of evolution. HRFS is particularly resilient and aggressive."

Varneys drummed his fingers on his desk. "Where are you going with this, Doctor?"

"It's now taking twice the original dosage of the drug to cure the disease," replied Marcantel.

Varneys shrugged. "Who cares? Just give people bigger and bigger doses. We'll negotiate with the drug companies not to raise the prices."

Marcantel was silent for a moment and then replied, "I'm afraid it's not that simple. The drug is going to stop working completely. It will just cease to be effective."

"How can you be certain of that?" asked Stone.

"We are. There's no doubt about it. It's just a question of 'when'."

As Varneys' blood pressure began to rise, his face took on a blotchy appearance. "I assume you have something in the pipeline to replace it. You guys must have been working on alternatives."

"We've tried, but HRFS is very different from anything we've previously encountered."

His voice hardening, Varneys asked, "When was the last time you guys dealt with a man-made disease?"

Marcantel's sniffing intensified. "Never. Our analysis shows that HRFS probably started as a hybrid of at least four known diseases. That witches' brew was then combined with other biotoxins and bioengineered viruses and accelerators to heighten HRFS' resistance and increase its virulence. The mixture of all of these elements then evolved into something new. The disease took on a life of its own. Frankly, we can't figure out how Schlumberger Foch ever came up with a cure in the first place."

"So, let me understand this," said Varneys, contemptuously. "Essentially, you're here today to tell me and Director Stone that everyone is fucked. The whole world is going to be plunged headfirst into the crapper, and you guys don't know what in God's name to do about it. Am I missing something?" Expressionless, Marcantel stared at the floor.

Varneys walked over to his wall of windows that framed the CIA campus. At first, he gazed blankly out the windows, his arms folded across his chest. Then he slid his hands into his pockets and he began to slowly pace the length of his office. After a few moments, he broke the funeral parlor silence that had settled into the room. His voice was uncharacteristically soft. "How long will it take for the cure to be worthless?"

"We can't tell yet. It all depends on the rate of mutation. Based on the average rate of mutation of HRFS to date, we could be looking at nine months before the cure does nothing. But it could be sooner if the rate of mutation accelerates."

Stone interrupted. "What's the likelihood of that?"

"There's no way of telling."

Varneys' eyes skewered Marcantel. "You're so full of answers, Doctor."

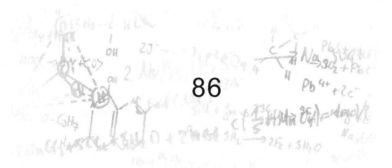

# 86

I T WAS A TUESDAY MORNING and Susan sat at her desk sifting through the mail. There were the usual invitations to decline on Bobby's behalf, letters enclosing donations to the Edith and Peter Austin Foundation for Medical Research, requests from scientists asking Bobby to review and comment on their treatises, and letters pertaining to Uniserve business.

At 11:30 a.m., the lab's receptionist buzzed Susan. "There's a call for you from a Mr. Orin Varneys. Should I take a message?"

Susan paused before responding. She had never liked Varneys, but after his attempt to blackmail Bobby with the videos, she particularly disliked him. Her inclination was not to accept the call. Nevertheless, she wasn't contacted by the director of the CIA every day. "Put him through."

"Hello, Susan. Orin Varneys here."

"To what do I owe the pleasure of this call, director?"

"The last time I visited Robert at the lab, he wasn't expecting me. We didn't have a productive meeting. I need to speak to him about an extremely urgent matter. I'd like to arrange a time in advance, so he's not taken by surprise."

"I understand. Let me check his schedule." Susan slowly and

noisily flicked through the pages of a novel she was reading. "Geez, he is so tied up. One appointment after another. But I can squeeze you in on Thursday, the eleventh at four. That's three weeks from now. But that assumes you don't need more than twenty minutes."

Varney's voice hardened. "Susan, don't play footsie with me. I don't need your permission to see Robert. I'm trying to be nice."

"Really. So I should give you an appointment for you to blackmail him again, or threaten him or make him work on your spy stuff—"

Varneys cut her off. "What did you just say? Did Robert tell you everything he and I discussed in my office? That was secret, highly classified information. I warned him about that."

"Director, you just don't get it, do you? Bobby, Christina and I are family. The last time you told Christina and me to keep your bullshit a secret, look what happened. We did—and it was terribly damaging to all of us. So, don't tell him or us anything that's a secret, because it won't be kept. Secrets are your world, not ours."

Varneys remained silent for a moment so he didn't lose his composure. Susan couldn't see the broken pencil that was intertwined between the fingers of his left hand. "Let's not argue. Get me in there in the next two days."

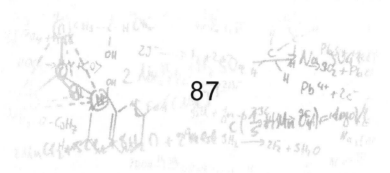

# 87

B OBBY DIDN'T WANT TO MEET Varneys in his laboratory office, as that was his personal inner sanctum, so Susan led Varneys into the conference room that Bobby used for staff meetings.

"Hello, Robert. How are your beautiful wife and wonderful children doing?"

Bobby groaned audibly. "Can we please dispose of the perfunctory niceties and get down to what you want, Orin?"

Varneys inhaled deeply. "There's a problem—and your help is needed."

"Cyber again?"

"No. Something that's right in your bailiwick." Bobby cocked his head.

"HRFS," said Varneys.

"From what I understand, the cure is working out very well."

"Let's put a past tense on that."

"What do you mean?"

"It used to work very well. Its efficacy is decreasing quickly. I just met with Dr. Stephen Marcantel of AMRIID. He told me that HRFS is quickly building immunity. Larger and larger doses are needed for the cure to be effective. They estimate that in nine months or less, the cure won't work at all. This is a pandemic, Robert. It's capable of killing everyone on this planet."

Bobby' face paled. "When did they find out that the cure was diminishing in effectiveness?"

"About five months ago."

"Why did they wait so long to tell anyone?" asked Bobby.

"They were hoping it would fix itself."

"That never happens. They never should have waited. They've lost valuable time."

"What do you make of this?" said Varneys.

"Their estimate of nine months is probably too optimistic. As diseases mutate, they usually become more inventive in their ability to build immunity to static drugs. With so many millions of people infected at one time, the disease has had countless hosts to use as guinea pigs to develop immunity. And with no changes having been made to the cure, the disease has been able to modify its genetic code without resistance or diversion. This is exactly what a disease hopes for."

"Hopes for? Are you kidding? This is a fucking disease. Bacteria or a virus or whatever. It doesn't hope. It's a primitive thing."

"Nothing that can annihilate the human population is primitive, Orin."

"I don't want to get into a debate with you about your cockamamie theory that diseases are empowered by some supreme force of evil. The bottom line is that we need a new cure and it needs to be ready before Schlumberger's becomes useless. Marcantel told me neither AMRIID, the CDC, ECDC, WHO or anyone else has a clue. Your help is desperately needed."

Bobby threw up his hands. "I don't know anything about this disease."

"I'll get you everything you want. Blood samples, chemical analyses of the disease, the formula for Schlumberger's cure. I can have all of that to you in twenty-four hours. And needless to say, the full resources of every disease agency and the federal government will be at your disposal."

Bobby' brow furrowed. "This disease was invented by a terrorist group's scientists. It's not a naturally occurring disease. Correct?"

Varneys nodded. "Yes, that's correct. We still can't figure out how a bunch of desert rats concocted this. I never thought it was so easy."

"It's not. It must have taken them years."

"Can we count on you, Robert?"

Bobby stood up and walked to a corner of the room, his back towards Varneys. After a few moments, he sat down next to him. "I'll do everything in my power to help, but, first, we need to take care of some personal business between us."

Varneys looked at Bobby quizzically. "What's that?"

Bobby's voice became resolute. "I want all copies of that phony video, and I want a written and a recorded statement from you attesting that the video was a fake that the CIA put together for the purpose of controlling me, and that I didn't do any of the things shown in the video. Susan will write up the text for your statement, and I want her and Christina to witness it and to be in the video with you for authentication purposes."

The veins in Varneys' right temple began to pulsate as he glared at Bobby. "I can't believe you're imposing conditions on helping humanity. I'll give you my word that no one will ever see that video."

Bobby shook his head. "I'm not imposing conditions. But

something may happen when you're not around or you lose control and that video leaks out. I don't want to have to deal with that. What you did was despicable, and it needs to end now."

Varneys exhaled loudly. He then looked away momentarily. When he faced Bobby, his thin lips had all but disappeared into his mouth. "I don't want to waste any time. Have Susan write up the statement now and I'll sign it and let's make the recording. I'll have the videos delivered to you tomorrow."

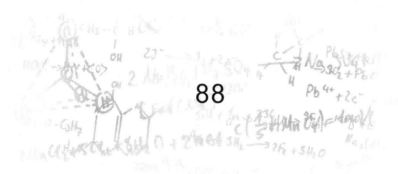

**88**

"COLUM, ONE OF THESE DAYS, you *have* to get out of here. You're too rich to be locked up. You need to be free so you can spend some of your hard-earned money."

A faint smile crossed McAlister's lips. "I'm already working on it. I've been making some large well-placed political donations through my D.C. law firm. They know what to do. I always told you that when I want to be out of here I could make it happen."

"What's the time frame?"

"I'd say within four months. Now, how are we doing financially?"

"Better than ever. Gao and Bazhenov have maxed all their long bets. They're going to ride it to the top and then sell."

"Tell them not to sell too soon. They'll leave a lot of money on the table. They should hold on and stay invested until I say otherwise."

"They know better than to second-guess you. They think you're a genius."

McAlister chuckled, allowing his perfect veneers to come into view. "I'm beginning to think so, too. If my ex-wife had shared that opinion, she'd be one of the richest women in the world now."

"Unfortunately for her, she ran for the exit door when the feds came calling. Not one of the brightest moves. Everything in life is timing, even with divorce," said Ramirez.

It didn't take much to satisfy McAlister's appetite for casual conversation, and he was now sated. "How are sales of the cure doing?" he asked.

"Better than ever."

"More people getting treated?"

"A lot more, but it's not just that. Your lawyers told me Schlumberger increased the dosage so it raised the price-per-treatment package proportionately. Revenues are soaring. It's the gift that won't stop giving."

"What did you just say?"

"I said that revenues are soaring."

"No, before that."

"I said that Schlumberger increased the dosage, so the price of each treatment package has gone up proportionately."

"I don't know if I like the sound of that," said McAlister.

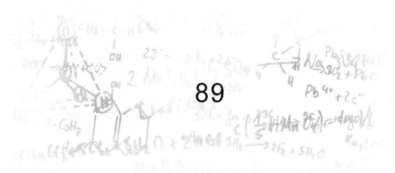

# 89

MAHMOUD PEERED OVER THE FRAMES of his eyeglasses as he pressed six numbers into the electric combination lock on a metal interior door in his laboratory. His left foot dragging behind him, he clutched the railing tightly with both hands as he slowly navigated down a steep staircase. At the foot of the staircase was another door that Mahmoud unlocked. He then walked into a long corridor which was lined on both sides by floor to ceiling glass panels which formed the outside walls of a series of sealed containment rooms, each of which was ten feet long by eight feet wide. It was these rooms that housed the Rakut survivors. The glass walls allowed Mahmoud to visually observe his prisoners without having to wear a hazmat suit.

It had been three months since Mahmoud had suffered a second heart attack. During that time, Ansar Jamaat had continued its assaults on cities throughout the Mideast, while Saeed's overseas operatives attended to the rest of the world. Mahmoud had conducted a further fourteen expeditions into newly infected areas with his Rakut survivors in tow during that three-month period. The last expedition had taken place ten days earlier.

Stepping close to the glass wall, Mahmoud looked into Faris

Khalili's cell. Faris had his back to the glass. Mahmoud knocked hard several times to get his attention. When Faris turned around, Mahmoud inhaled sharply. Faris' eyes were red and watery and he was perspiring heavily. Mahmoud pressed on the intercom button, "Faris, are you alright? What are you feeling?" Faris began to answer when his words were cut off by a coughing bout. He held up his hand to signal Mahmoud to wait, but the coughing wouldn't stop and Mahmoud noticed that Faris' hand was spotted with small red pimples. Unable to catch his breath, Faris squatted on the ground gasping for air. "No, no…" exclaimed Mahmoud as he pressed himself against the glass wall.

Mahmoud moved to the next cell, one occupied by Laela Bishara, a nineteen-year-old who had been the only one in her family to survive the attack at Rakut. She was in bed lying on her side, the blankets pulled up to her chin. Mahmoud pressed the intercom. "Laela, what are you feeling? Tell me." Laela's shivering was so intense that Mahmoud could see her body shaking under the blankets, and he could hear her teeth chattering. Her face was flushed, but he could still discern that it was dotted with red pimples. Laela's eyes had an unfocused, vacant look that indicated to Mahmoud the likelihood of a very high fever. As Mahmoud stared at her, she began to cough so vociferously that her body heaved. A thick yellow phlegm was expelled from her mouth onto the floor.

Mahmoud quickly went from one cell to the other. All the prisoners had the same severe respiratory flu symptoms, even though they had been healthy when Mahmoud conducted the five-day examinations. Their immunity had protected them from the first stage of the infection, but not the second stage that typically showed at the tenth or eleventh day.

His hands trembling as he grasped the staircase railing, Mahmoud pulled himself back up to his office as fast as his lame leg would allow. Once there, he collapsed into his desk chair and covered his face with his hands.

Mahmoud's Rakut survivors had been the barometer he used to determine if the disease was mutating. He had dragged them to thirty-seven cities that Ansar Jamaat had attacked, subjecting them to the most virulent contagion. He had made them crawl among corpses and smear their skin with secretions dripping from the pustules of the dying as they breathed air rife with the toxin. Through all of this they had remained safe, shielded by their natural immunity. But something had changed. During the last expedition, they had become infected.

Mahmoud pressed his hands on his desk to give himself support as he labored to stand up. Within seconds of being on his feet, he sagged back into his chair. The wet heat of panic surged through his body and his vision blurred as apocalyptic images collided in his mind. His head began to pound as his blood pressure rose, and he was certain he could see his heart beating beneath his shirt. Mahmoud massaged the left side of his chest to try to alleviate a blistering pain.

Like the disease itself, Mahmoud's nightmares had undergone a metamorphosis. No longer confined to his subconscious, they had become his reality. Mahmoud knew that if the prisoners' immunity failed because the disease had mutated, then his cure would also fail.

Burying his head in the waste basket like an animal searching for food, Mahmoud tried to vomit to relieve his intense nausea, but he couldn't even manage to do that. *I have done the work of Shaitan. I am Shaitan.*

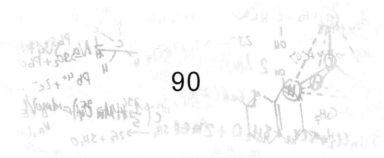

# 90

CHRISTINA HAD GONE TO SPECIAL pains to set the dinner table. She placed china that was a wedding gift from Susan on top of a beige floral jacquard table cloth that had belonged to her grandmother. In the center of the table were two antique silver candlesticks that Alan Gottschalk gave them on *Dreamweaver* after they had exchanged wedding vows aboard the yacht. In between the candlesticks, was a Lalique Bacchantes vase filled with yellow long-stemmed roses, Bobby's favorite flower. A crystal ice bucket stood on the side of the table, chilling a bottle of champagne. The bucket and the matching champagne flutes were a gift from Dean Walterberg of Tufts University on the occasion of Bobby's winning his first two Nobel prizes when he was twenty-five years old.

"Christina, this is such a beautiful table. You've outdone yourself," said Bobby.

Christina smiled, but Bobby noticed that her eyes were watery. "Well, this is a very special occasion. I wanted to surround us with gifts from people who are precious, who have changed our lives."

Bobby slowly ran his fingers over the carved female figures on the Lalique vase. "This was Joe's favorite piece. He had it next to his bed when he was sick. I was nineteen years old then, and every day I put fresh flowers in it. I never wanted him to see anything deteriorate or die." Bobby lowered his head and then covered his eyes with his left hand. When he looked up, he seemed far away. Christina's gaze met his, and she could feel the sense of loss that he was feeling at that moment. She understood the intensity with which Bobby experienced emotions, a vestige of the so-called "overexcitability factors" that Dr. Uhlman had diagnosed when Bobby was four years old. While these "OEs", which are directly proportional in intensity to a person's intelligence, no longer dominated him as they did when he was a child, they still played a significant role in his personality, despite his efforts to contain them.

Christina knew that there were very few people who saw the real Bobby. Most only had a professional association with him, and thought he was cold and detached—that his intellect was his ruler. But she fell in love with a different Bobby, a man of acute sensitivities who felt the suffering of others more deeply than his own pain; a man of limitless kindness and generosity. And a man whose passion for her was incendiary.

Christina raised her champagne glass. "A toast to Joe Manzini, a wonderful man."

"And a toast to Alan Gottshalk, without whom my first day of life would have been my last," said Bobby.

Susan tapped her glass with her fork. "And a toast to Dean Walterberg, without whom I never would have become part of this wonderful family."

Bobby got up from the table and stood behind Susan's chair. Bending down, he wrapped his arms around her and kissed her. He then reached for his glass and raised it, "And a toast to the second most wonderful lady in my life."

Susan turned around to face Bobby and gave him an exaggerated pinch on his right cheek. Chuckling she said, "I liked you from the first moment I met you."

Bobby was surprised by the dinner celebration as he wasn't aware it was going to happen, but clearly Christina had put in a great deal of effort. As roast beef, haricot vert, baked Brussels sprouts wrapped in bacon, and potatoes au gratin found their place on the table, Bobby said, "This is an amazing feast. It's like Thanksgiving."

"It is a thanksgiving," said Christina. We have finally closed the book on Varneys' lies and subterfuge. He'll never manipulate and divide this family again. Susan told me that one of his agents delivered the videos."

Susan nodded. "Yes, the videos and Varneys' confessional are tucked away in the vault, safe and sound. How did you get him to do it, Bobby?"

Bobby took a sip of his champagne. "Let's say I appealed to his better nature."

Susan laughed. "Try again. He doesn't have any."

"How about, that I made him see the error of his ways?"

"Varneys? I don't think so," said Christina as she brought a champagne flute to her lips. "Really, what did you do?"

One corner of Bobby's mouth raised. "Now's not the best time to talk about it. Let's just enjoy this delicious meal."

Christina frowned. "I hope you didn't agree to do anything military-related."

"Or espionage," said Susan.

Bobby waved a hand. "I would never agree to those things, you know that. He requested my help on something that I would have done anyway. I just took advantage of the moment and, frankly, I think in a peculiar way he was glad I did."

"So, what are you doing for him?" asked Christina.

"It's not for him. It's a problem with a disease."

"Which disease?" asked Christina.

"HRFS," replied Bobby.

"What's the problem? There's a cure. Millions of people are taking it. There's a supply here at Wheatleigh in case it's needed for the lab staff or us. The cure's been a phenomenal success," said Christina.

"It was," said Bobby.

"It is," replied Christina.

"It was."

"Wait a minute. I feel like I'm back in French class conjugating verbs. What's going on?" asked Susan.

Bobby took a deep breath before responding. "The cure is going to stop working. The disease is building up an immunity to it."

Stunned, Christina said, "Oh my God."

"But this thing is so contagious. Without a cure…" Susan didn't need to finish the sentence.

# 91

A S SOON AS BOBBY HAD received all of the data on HRFS from the CDC, he increased his lab staff to one hundred ten people in preparation for round-the-clock research and analysis. At his request, Dean Walterberg committed forty-five technicians at Tufts Medical School to be on standby alert, awaiting their marching orders from Bobby. Also crammed into the Wheatleigh lab were more than twenty scientists from the CDC, WHO and AMRIID who had invited themselves to be on site. All in all, the main floor of Wheatleigh was as crowded as a beehive and buzzing with an equal mix of anxiety and expectation.

Bobby created a computer program to analyze the rate of mutation interrelated with the declining effectiveness of the HRFS cure. According to his calculations, AMRIID, the CDC and WHO were wrong in their estimation that it would take nine months for the cure to become completely ineffective. The disease's rate of accelerating mutation was so high that Bobby calculated seven months for complete failure, and that within four months it would take eight times the original dosage to be effective.

What alarmed Susan at the end of Bobby's first month of

working on HRFS was that she saw something in his eyes she had never seen before. In all the years that she had known him as he labored on one malady after another, she had seen frustration, anxiety, obsession, exhaustion, anger and despair. But until now, she had never seen panic.

"I brought you a café Americano, just the way you like it. Hot milk on the side, two sugars," Susan said as she placed a small tray on Bobby's desk next to his computer. "How's it going?"

Bobby said nothing as he continued to stare at his computer screen. Susan put her hand on his right shoulder. "You'll get it. Sooner or later."

"Later is the problem, Susan. There is no later. The current cure will be no more effective than aspirin in a few months. Bobby ran his hands through his hair and then began to simultaneously scratch both of his arms.

Susan pulled over a chair and sat close. Leaning into him, she said. "Slow down and look at me." Bobby diverted his eyes from his computer and focused on Susan. "Bobby, you've been to this rodeo many times. You know how to crack these things. Just stay calm. Don't let the pressure overtake you."

Bobby nodded. "I hear you, but the way I've cured diseases in the past takes time, usually at least a few years. HRFS is so easily transmitted and it kills quickly. It's everywhere." Bobby scratched his left hand as he spoke, "There just isn't enough time. Half the world's population will be dead before my old techniques even have a chance to bear fruit." Susan noticed that Bobby had developed a rash, not only on his hands and arms but also on his forehead. "I have to think of something different, otherwise we're totally..."

Bobby gave his head an abrupt shake as if to reset himself. "I'm sorry, Susan, but I have to get back to work."

Susan rested her hand on Bobby's shoulder before walking to the door. Pausing in the doorway, she looked back at him. Bobby sat motionless as he stared at the computer screen.

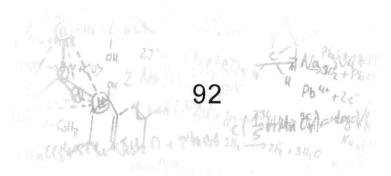

## 92

B Y THE END OF THE sixth week of his working on HRFS, Bobby stopped assigning work to his lab staff and reduced its size by eighty percent. He asked Susan to advise Walterberg that the Tufts' technicians were no longer needed. Susan requested that the personnel from the CDC, WHO and AMRIID vacate Wheatleigh.

"It's all a waste of time, Susan. We're getting nowhere. Every angle we're pursuing will take too long," said Bobby.

Bobby stopped coming to the lab. He divided his time between long solitary walks around the grounds, sitting on a lawn chair at the farthest point of the peninsula reading treatises on astrophysics, and camping out in the cabin atop the old stone tower.

Walking over to Bobby's lawn chair, Christina noticed that it was positioned dangerously close to the edge of the cliff. The chair was surrounded by dozens of periodicals on theoretical physics that were strewn on the ground. Oblivious to her presence, Bobby sat with his eyes closed, his back straight and his hands resting on his knees. "Bobby, what's going on?" The annoyance in Christina's voice was discernible. Bobby didn't reply. "Bobby, it's me. The kids and I are back from visiting my mom. We need to talk." Christina crouched down directly in front of him. Having not seen Bobby for twelve days, she was alarmed by his appearance. Bobby's forehead and neck were covered with rashes, as were his hands. He had never suffered from eczema, psoriasis or any other skin ailment until he began to work on HRFS. There were prominent dark circles under his eyes which accentuated bags that had become increasingly pronounced, and his eyelids were red and swollen. His lips were cracked, probably from dehydration caused by excessive alcohol consumption, his hair was greasy, and it was obvious that he hadn't shaved in at least a week.

Christina placed her hands on the sides of Bobby's face, leaned into him and rested her forehead against his, her silken hair engulfing them. As she remained in this position, her mind traveled back to a less troubled time and her physical closeness to Bobby ignited memories that resonated deeply within her. "Come back to me," she whispered.

When Bobby gradually opened his eyes, he looked dazed—as if he was still in the process of returning from some place very far away. "You're here," said Bobby softly. "I'm sorry. I know I've been acting weird."

Christina smiled. "More than usual, you think?" Stroking his hair, she said, "So are you ever going to wash this? And what's up with these rashes?"

"Everything's topsy-turvy now."

"What's going on? You stopped going to your lab. You're spending your time reading astrophysics articles when you've never been interested in pure science. You're drinking too much. And it sure looks like you've given up on trying to find a cure for HRFS."

Bobby pressed his face into his hands, which Christina noticed were trembling. When he looked up, his voice was strained and his words left his mouth in a torrent. "Please don't put more pressure on me. I have enough. I've never felt like this. I had to get out of the lab. I couldn't think there. I know what my responsibilities are. It may not look like it to you, but I'm working. I haven't given up. I will never give up. I will never *ever* give up. You should know that. Now please, leave me alone so I can do what I have to do. Time is running out."

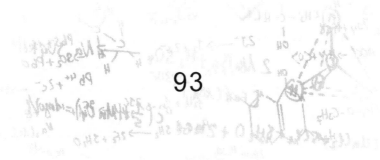

# 93

" **F**AKE NEWS" WAS A POTENT force, particularly when the overwhelming majority of people around the world obtain their news from social media platforms. The story that garnered over one billion views was fictitious, but those who read it didn't know that. The headline was all that mattered: "Woman Dies from HRFS While Taking Cure."

Perhaps in response to that, legitimate news sources began to shine a light on what many already knew, i.e., that the prescribed number of pills in the treatment regimen was now four times what it had originally been. While drug industry representatives and government spokespeople were careful to say nothing that would raise alarm, journalists and bloggers began to express serious concerns. One didn't have to be a scientist to realize that if four times the original dosage was now required to cure a disease, then something had fundamentally changed regarding the efficacy of the drug in question and its long-term prospects. As an increasing number of media outlets directed their attention to the subject, the pharmaceutical industry and governmental agencies lost their ability to control the narrative. The following excerpts from an interview conducted by The *London Times* with Dr. Lucas Krister, an eminent virologist, gained international traction:

*The Times:* Why is the original dosage of the cure no longer sufficient?

**Krister:** It can mean one of two things. Either that the disease is mutating specifically for the purpose of developing an immunity to the cure, or it can mean that the fundamental genetic structure of the disease is changing as it evolves.

*The Times:* Does it make a difference which of these is happening?

**Krister:** Practically speaking, no. In either case, the medication is losing efficacy.

*The Times:* But it will always be effective, it's just a question of the dosage needed. Correct?

**Krister:** Actually, no. There reaches a point where the medication will have no ameliorative effect.

*The Times:* But it must continue to do some good. To help in some way, surely?

**Krister:** No.

*The Times:* And when would that complete inefficacy of the drug occur. How long from now?

**Krister:** I don't have the necessary data to venture an opinion on that.

The *London Times* article spawned a public demand for more information from authoritative sources as to exactly what was going on. Schlumberger Foch issued the following media statement:

"Schlumberger Foch, the inventor of the cure for HRFS, is aware that there has been public speculation as to why the recommended dosage of the cure has increased over time. In fact, this is in keeping with Schlumberger's original forecasts and is not a matter for concern. Rest assured that the cure is and will remain effective, even as Schlumberger actively works to further refine the drug in the normal course of its research and development regimens."

In fact, the Schlumberger statement was patently false. Schlumberger had played no role in developing the cure, nor did it even understand how it worked. The cure had been licensed to them as a finished product by McAlister's offshore entity. Schlumberger had kept this bit of information to itself so that it could claim credit for the invention as it reaped huge profits and saw the value of its stock quintuple in the course of a year. Neither it nor any of the fifty pharmaceutical companies that held sublicenses from Schlumberger to manufacture and distribute the drug had any idea as to how the cure could be modified to become more potent in fighting the rapidly mutating disease.

As is often the case, the financial markets were a bellwether. The controversial news about the cure's efficacy caused the world's stock markets to begin a steady slide, along with the currency, commodity and real estate markets. Nothing was holding its value, not even gold or the United States dollar. Bazhenov and Gao faced daily margin calls on their investments which were now leveraged at an average of thirty-five times. They demanded an emergency meeting with Ramirez.

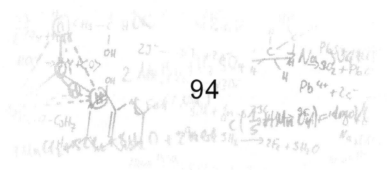

# 94

F EW HOMES IN THE HAMPTONS have their own helipads, but when a residence is purchased for one hundred forty-seven million dollars, some amenities can be expected. Old Cedars, the eighteen-acre oceanfront estate on Further Lane in East Hampton, that Bazhenov had purchased four years earlier had not one, but two helipads. The property's size afforded Bazhenov the privacy that he coveted and would also ensure that when his twenty-year-old daughter, Milika, used the house as her crash pad during the peak summer party season, her libidinous indiscretions would be well out of view.

Bazhenov had purchased Old Cedars in the same year that he purchased Maison Fleur de Lys, a sixty-five thousand square foot mansion in Palm Beach, Florida, for ninety-eight million dollars, and a twelve thousand square foot penthouse at 15 Central Park West in New York City for one hundred five million dollars. He always paid the asking price for the properties he wanted, and if there were any other bona-fide prospective purchasers, he would make a preemptive offer well in excess of the asking price to close the sale down. While many thought that Bazhenov overpaid for the real estate he purchased, he didn't care. Any property that he owned outside of Russia was a bargain to him. If the *Ruka* couldn't confiscate it, because it was located in a Western country, and its ownership was held through a labyrinth of offshore companies that were managed by major international law firms, then the price of the property was of secondary importance to him. Bazhenov was confident that he could sell his extraordinary residences for at least what he paid for them because there would always be someone like him who needed to wash his money in a safe haven that would also provide a pleasant place to hang one's hat.

It was winter, so Further Lane in East Hampton was deserted. Despite the fact that the houses on Further Lane were among the most expensive in the world, they were summer homes, not full-time residences. Bazhenov's helicopter arrived first, followed within minutes by Gao's. Ramirez was the last to arrive. As his helicopter hovered over the property, Ramirez gazed woefully at the gray ocean and the barren formal gardens whose trees and shrubs were wrapped in burlap like mummies to protect them from the winter's saltwater winds.

Each of the helicopters' occupants was separately transported to the main residence on the Old Cedars property by a navy blue Range Rover which was driven by a Bazhenov employee who looked more like a professional wrestler than a chauffeur. The house was a sprawling structure built in the French chateau style that would have been better suited to the Loire Valley than the beaches of Long Island.

When Ramirez entered the mansion's library, Bazhenov and Gao were already seated at the head of an enormous gilded Louis XVI wood table. Bazhenov nodded to Ramirez and pointed to a chair at the other end of the table. Bazhenov's bloated face was florid. Gao's expression was stoic.

"Gunther, we are very concerned," said Bazhenov.

"Very," echoed Gao.

"It was only a few months ago that you told us that Colum McAlister wanted us to go long on our investments. We followed that advice," said Bazhenov.

"We went to maximum leverage on that advice," said Gao.

"We didn't take profits that we could have taken. We stayed invested," said Bazhenov.

"Now we're getting daily margin calls for great amounts of money," said Gao. "Our investment partners are upset, and they are not the kind of people that you want to upset."

"And we can't liquidate the investments because there are no buyers for our positions," said Bazhenov.

"There's a serious market contraction taking place—and it looks like it will get worse," said Gao.

Bazhenov glared at Ramirez and said nothing further for a full minute. The silence in the room became ominous and Ramirez stiffened in his chair. When Bazhenov finally spoke, he enunciated every word with deliberation, "It was Colum McAlister's job to know that the cure was faltering. He is supposed to know these things and advise us on the basis of that knowledge. He failed to do that."

A small smile appeared on Gao's face. "You know what you told us, Gunther. You said that you and McAlister were worth thirty percent because you weren't taking us to the casino, you were taking us to the bank. Do you remember that?" Ramirez nodded. "The way it is looking now, we weren't taken to the bank or to the casino. We were taken to the cleaners," said Gao.

Ramirez spoke up. "That's ridiculous, that's not..."

Bazhenov cut him off. "We're beginning to think that you and McAlister are playing us. That you and he are shorting the markets on the inside information that he always seems to have. We think that you both decided that thirty percent isn't enough when you can have one hundred percent by fucking us." Bazhenov stood up and walked to the end of the table where Ramirez was seated. He put his face so close to Ramirez that Ramirez found himself examining the pores of Bazhenov's skin. Slamming his massive fist on the table, Bazhenov growled, "What the hell is going on, Gunther?"

Ramirez pushed his chair away from the table so that he could get some distance from Bazhenov. "Do you mind if I smoke?" he asked Bazhenov.

Bazhenov waved his hand signaling that he didn't care. Ramirez slowly removed his gold cigarette case from his inside jacket pocket, opened it and took out a Davidoff cigarette. As he walked towards the library's ocean-facing windows, he reached into an exterior jacket pocket and removed a gold cigarette lighter. Looking out the windows, he lit his cigarette and inhaled deeply and then turned to face Bazhenov and Gao.

"Gentlemen, firstly let me say that I am deeply offended that you would think even for a minute that Colum McAlister and I would act in a manner contrary to your best interests. You and we are partners. Plain and simple. We have no side bets going in the financial markets. I say that to you unequivocally, and I would stake my life on it."

"You already have," said Gao softly.

"As to the subject of the cure faltering—if McAlister knew that was the case, then he would have advised you of that. We are your partners. When you make money, we make money. We want you to make money. That's the whole point."

"But you have no money at risk. We and our investors do," said Gao.

"That's right. That's why we're only getting thirty percent. Up until now, you've had no complaints. You were making money hand over fist. You couldn't believe how good it was," replied Ramirez.

"That may be. But if things don't turn around, we and our investors will get wiped out. That's unacceptable," said Bazhenov.

Ramirez held up his hands. "Look. Schlumberger Foch says everything is fine. All the fear is just conjecture. Millions of people are still being cured right now. And if there's a problem, all these drug companies and the governments will fix it. As people calm down and all this news coverage blows over, the markets will rebound. Then you can get out if you want and we'll all just take the profits, even if they are a bit less than they ideally would be."

Before either Gao or Bazhenov could say anything in response, Ramirez continued, "And by the way, McAlister has another thing up his sleeve. I shouldn't tell you this but he has a little secret weapon to be sure the world doesn't end and our investments stay safe."

"What's that?" asked Gao.

"Dr. Robert James Austin."

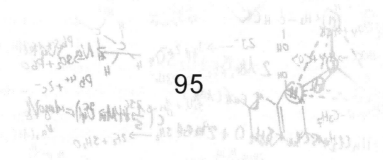

# 95

I T WAS A SUNNY, HUMID day in early July, and at eight-thirty in the morning the temperature was already eighty-two degrees. Fourteen girls ages nine through eleven were talking to each other animatedly, their bodies almost vibrating with excitement. Some even jumped up and down as they stood on line, an unconscious response to the anticipation that had been building for weeks. They all wore their Girl Scout uniforms and, to the extent that they were permitted, many of them had added individual flourishes to personalize their dress. What differentiated their appearance from the generations of Girl Scouts that had preceded them were their government-issued face masks that hid all but their eyes and foreheads from view.

"Okay, scouts. Form two rows, tallest girls in the back and shortest in the front. You know where to stand!" yelled the scout leader as she raised her camera and took a group photograph, being sure to capture the large wooden sign above them, carved in the shape of an alligator, that read: Miami Everglades Adventure Park.

The Girl Scout troop was the first to arrive at the park that morning, and a full day of activities awaited them. A fleet of airboats was lined up at the floating docks and the scout leader had booked a ride for her troop that was much longer than the ride usually offered to customers. The three-hour journey was billed as an "eco-safari" which would take them deep into the Everglades, thereby ensuring that they would see more alligators, crocodiles, sea turtles, water snakes and pelicans than most tourists. And after that, there was the wildlife show featuring alligator wrestling, the alligator and crocodile farm, and the scenic hiking trails surrounded by Everglades vegetation.

As the girls piled into an airboat large enough to accommodate them all, the scout leader shouted out, "Okay, girls. Put on your sunscreen now and get your cameras ready. We're heading off."

By the time five in the afternoon arrived, the scouts looked exhausted but very satisfied. The leader marched them into the parking lot to board the bus and each child carried a souvenir bag emblazoned with a bright green alligator. "Was that a great day or what?" shouted the leader as the bus pulled out of the lot.

Eight days later, Manfred Korman, the Director of the CDC received the following email, which was marked "Extremely Urgent":

> Dear Director Korman:
>
> I am Dr. Robert Shoro, Chief of the Infectious Disease Department at Jackson Memorial Hospital in Miami.
>
> I want to report that in the last 24 hours, fourteen girls ages 9 to 11 were admitted to my hospital through the emergency room, all showing definite symptoms of HRFS. Additionally, a woman aged 42 and a man aged 56 were also admitted during this time period with the same symptoms. What is peculiar about this is that all of the girls

are members of the same Girl Scout troop that went on a boating expedition deep into the Everglades outside of Miami seven days ago; the 42-year-old woman is the scout leader and the 56-year-old man was the driver of the boat. All of the patients were wearing face masks and none of them had any contact with people known to be infected with HRFS.

Korman read the email three times. "What the fuck is this all about?" he muttered as he pressed the intercom button and called in his assistant. "Get Andy Taylor to put together an emergency team. At least ten investigators. They need to leave for Miami today. Give Taylor a copy of this email."

The next morning at 8:00 a.m., a dozen CDC agents led by Andy Taylor, clothed in hazmat suits, arrived at Miami Everglades Adventure Park, closed it to the public and began to perform onsite testing of all the park's employees.

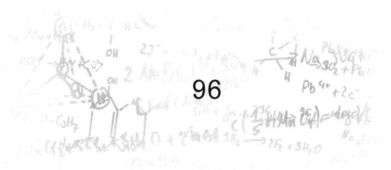

## 96

THE CDC INVESTIGATORS WERE AS thorough as they could possibly be. They conducted contamination tests on the park's kitchen and bathroom facilities, and food and water supplies. They swabbed doorknobs, countertops, and the seats and railings in the boat and bus that transported the scouts. They administered blood tests to the employees and the bus driver. Everything came up negative. The investigators were baffled.

Taylor and two of the investigators then met with Dr. Shoro at Jackson Memorial. "We haven't found anything at the park," said Taylor.

"That's very strange," said Shoro.

"We must be missing something. Have you examined the girls thoroughly?" asked Taylor.

"Of course, we have," replied Shoro with a trace of annoyance in his voice.

"I mean is there anything out of the ordinary, Doctor?"

"Other than HRFS?" replied Shoro.

"You know what I mean."

"Nothing that wouldn't be expected," said Shoro.

"What does that mean?" asked Taylor.

"The usual. What you'd expect if people are out in a boat in the Everglades for a whole day in the hot sun," replied Shoro.

"Sunburn?" asked Taylor.

"Yes, that and…" Shoro was interrupted by a nurse who came running over to him. "What's wrong?" he asked.

"One of the Girl Scouts. She's taken a turn for the worse. She doesn't seem to be responding to the medicine," replied the nurse.

"I'm sorry, Mr. Taylor, but I have to get back to my patients," said Shoro as he began to hurry off.

Taylor ran after him. "Wait. You didn't finish your sentence. You said there was nothing unusual, only what one would expect when people are out in a boat in the Everglades for a whole day. You mentioned sunburn."

"Right. Sunburn and some mosquito bites."

Taylor cocked his head. "Mosquito bites?"

"Yes. There's nothing unusual about that. It's hard not to get a few bites anywhere in Florida, let alone in the Everglades."

"How many of the Girl Scouts have bites?" asked Taylor.

"I'd have to check again. But probably all of them."

"The scout master and the boat driver, too?"

"I'll have to check again and get back to you," said Shoro as he took off down the hall to check on the scout who wasn't responding to the Schlumberger cure.

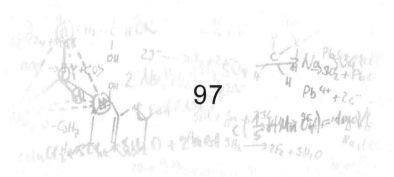

# 97

TAYLOR DIDN'T WAIT TO HEAR from Dr. Shoro. He and his team of investigators rushed back to the park, clothed in protective gear. They were hunting for mosquitoes. Their van was filled with dozens of vacuum-equipped collection bottles that would allow them to suck mosquitoes out of the air without killing them.

First, they gathered mosquitoes in the entrance and concession area of the park and labeled the collection bottles accordingly. Next, they gathered mosquitoes in the area of the wildlife show and labeled those bottles. Then, they gathered mosquitoes on the hiking trails, separately bottling mosquitoes every quarter mile. The scout leader had told Shoro that the scouts had walked about two and a half miles into the trail before turning around, but Taylor and his team hiked the entire trail length.

When that was completed, the investigators boarded an airboat and drove to the farthest point that the boat driver had taken the scout troop. Mosquito collections were made there, and then at every quarter mile on the way back to the park. Suffice it to say, that at least two thousand mosquitoes were collected in discrete batches in labeled bottles by the end of the day.

Taylor called CDC Director Korman from the van on the way to the airport for the flight back to CDC headquarters in Atlanta on a government jet.

"What's going on down there?" asked Korman.

"We're flying back today with lots of samples."

"What kind of samples?"

"Live mosquitoes."

"Why?"

"The scouts and probably the troop leader and boat driver all had mosquito bites."

"Big deal. Everyone in Florida has mosquito bites. Schlumberger Foch's tests confirmed that no animals, birds or insects are vectors for HRFS. That's the only good thing about this disease."

"I know that. But this is all we have to go on for now. We have to test these insects."

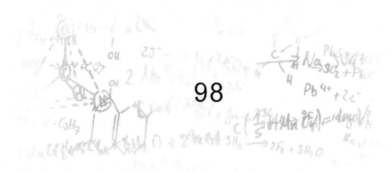

# 98

I T TOOK NINE DAYS TO complete the tests on the mosquitoes, captured in fifty-four separate collection bottles. Of that fifty-four, the mosquitoes in fifty-one of the bottles were negative. They were not carrying HRFS, but the mosquitoes in the remaining three bottles were. Those three bottles contained mosquitoes that had been gathered at the farthest distances from the park's entrance. Andy Taylor realized that this is why the scouts were infected when the park employees and other guests were not. The scouts had ventured to much more remote areas as part of their all-day deluxe adventure. It also was possible that if some other people had traveled far enough to encounter the infected mosquitoes, they may have done so at a time of the day when the mosquitoes were dormant, or the wind was strong or they may have been wearing strong mosquito repellent.

While Schlumberger's tests to see if mosquitoes could transmit HRFS indicated that they could not, those tests were conducted in the early days when HRFS was the disease that Mahmoud had created. But since that date, HRFS had mutated and that mutation was not only giving the disease immunity to the cure, but it also had altered HRFS' genetic structure in such as manner as to allow HRFS to be transmitted to humans by the most ubiquitous and efficient disease-spreading vector on Earth.

The mosquito has long been regarded by scientists as the most dangerous animal on the planet, responsible for more human deaths every year than any other creature. More than seven hundred million people annually contract mosquito-borne illnesses such as West Nile virus, chikungunya, yellow fever, malaria, hepatitis, encephalitis and Zika. More than one million people are killed every year by mosquitoes.

Taylor knocked once on Director Korman's door before entering. Korman looked up from his computer. "What's wrong?" Taylor didn't answer. He just nodded his head affirming the worst.

"Oh God," said Korman. Taylor remained silent. "I'll have to tell the president. How long do you think we have?"

"Maybe a few weeks," replied Taylor. "But I doubt that long. Once this gets going, it will move very fast. Mosquitoes that carry HRFS will infect people, and then other mosquitoes that aren't carriers will bite people who have been infected, and then those mosquitoes, in turn, will become carriers and they will bite and infect other people, and on and on it will go in a never-ending geometric progression. Every mosquito everywhere will be a disease spreader. It's going to be particularly devastating in Latin America and Africa. They've never been able to effectively control mosquitoes."

Korman wiped the perspiration off his forehead with a crumpled tissue that he found in his pants pocket. His eyes slowly closed in what looked like an involuntary action. Leaning forward, he planted his elbows on his desk and covered his face with his hands. When he looked up, Taylor could sense that the self-confidence that Korman was known for had drained out of him in a matter of minutes. "Just when you think it can't get any worse. First, the Schlumberger cure goes into the crapper, then we hear Austin's given up, and now this," said Korman. We are totally fucked."

---

In his wildest apocalyptic reveries, Saeed could not have hoped for more. The Sword of the Mahdi would now be wielded by a two-hundred-million-year-old pest whose legions number in the trillions and span the globe.

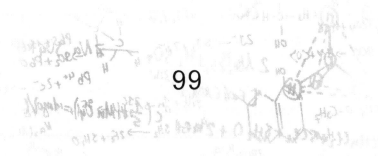

# 99

ONLY THIRTEEN DAYS AFTER TAYLOR'S meeting with Korman, the reports started coming in; not just for countless mosquito transmissions of HRFS in Florida, but for much of the United States as well, and Europe, Latin America, Africa and Asia. The public responded with the panic that one would expect, and the media only inflamed the situation.

As people sequestered themselves in their homes rather than risk exposure, and the financial markets tanked, the President of the United States commandeered television and radio transmissions to relay the following message:

"As many of you have already heard, it has recently come to the attention of medical authorities here in the United States and elsewhere that HRFS can be transmitted to human beings by mosquitoes. I would be less than candid with you if I did not admit that this is reason for concern. But it is only reason for concern. It is not reason for panic.

I have been in touch with the governors of every state in this great nation, and I can tell you that at this very moment, aggressive measures are being taken to eradicate mosquitoes throughout this country. Killing mosquitoes is not complicated. We have the expertise and the wherewithal to do this with tremendous efficacy. We will eliminate this method of spreading the contagion. I commend our investigators at the CDC for their quick discovery that HRFS' mutation has empowered HRFS to be spread by mosquitoes. That was not the case originally, and the CDC was on top of this development.

My fellow Americans, I say to you now what I said to you when HRFS first appeared on our shores. We are fully capable of defeating this disease and we have been resoundingly successful in doing so, to date. There is nothing that is going to change that. Some of you may have read articles that purport to indicate that the cure is ceasing to be effective. This is misleading information. Protecting Americans from this pandemic is the highest priority of my administration, and every resource that our federal, state and local governments have is dedicated to this. We have been successful in defeating this disease, and we will continue to be successful. Of course, bumps in the road will occur and they must be expected, whether it be mosquitoes or something else that arises in the future. But, rest assured that this road leads in only one direction, and that is the survival of humanity. Please join my family in prayer for the salvation of those who live far from our borders as they face their challenges.

God bless you and God bless the United States of America."

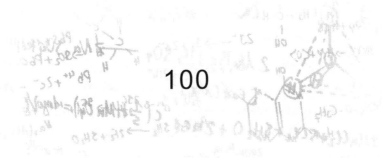

# 100

F OUR MONTHS AFTER BOBBY STARTED working on HRFS, the complete failure of Schlumberger's cure first manifested itself—not in the general population where the cure still was effective, albeit requiring eight times the original dosage—but in those individuals with undeveloped or compromised immune systems. Children under age five began to die, as did the elderly, those with leukemia and those who were undergoing chemotherapy or radiation treatments. The CDC, AMRIID, WHO and the drug companies knew what this meant. The cure would soon fail for everyone.

Two black Chevrolet Suburbans approached Wheatleigh's gates. The guards at the gatehouse knew better than to argue with the CIA agents. The vehicles were waved through and within two minutes, Orin Varneys blustered his way into the lab and headed straight for Bobby's office. Without knocking, Varneys entered the room and bellowed, "Robert."

One of the laboratory staff ran into Susan's office to inform her of the intrusion and Susan hurried into Bobby's office to confront Varneys. "Looks like you left your manners in your car," said Susan to Varneys.

Varneys glowered. "I don't have time to play games with you, where is he?"

"He's not here and he's not seeing anybody."

"What the hell does that mean? He should be working on HRFS. This is no joke. We're down to the wire."

"He stopped coming to the lab months ago."

"Where are all the technicians? It's almost empty out in the main room," said Varneys.

"We sent them home. There's nothing for them to do."

"So it's true. Austin gave up. He's not even trying. It's just like I heard."

"That's not the case. He's been in isolation. He's not seeing anyone, not me, not even Christina or his kids."

"What's he doing? Making his peace with God?"

Susan frowned. "Maybe."

"Where's Christina? Is she here?"

"Why?"

"Because she's his wife and I want to talk to her, that's why."

Susan walked over to the intercom to call Christina, but that wasn't necessary. Christina appeared in the doorway to Bobby's office. "Hello, Director. I heard you were here. Uninvited, as usual."

Varneys walked over to Christina and held out his right hand. She cocked her head, confused as to the gesture. "Christina, I am not your enemy, nor am I Robert's. As weird as the circumstances might have been, you know that I brought you two together. So let's be truthful and candid today because we may not have many more days left." Varneys turned to Susan, "Would you please give Christina and me some private time?" While he phrased it as a question, it was clear that it wasn't. Susan left the room.

"Christina, we—no I mean—the world...is in a very serious

situation. The CDC estimates that the HRFS cure will be worthless within twelve weeks. When that happens, this planet will experience a death toll that is incomprehensible. Frankly, it may be the end of the human race or human civilization as we know it. Our only hope is Robert. Yes, it is pathetic that he is the only one, but that is the reality. So why has he given up?"

"He hasn't given up. He's been working constantly. I don't even know if he sleeps at all because of his nightmares. But he told me a while ago that something new and drastic is the only hope. I don't know what it is, but he's been working on it tirelessly. He never stops."

"Where is he now? I have to see him."

"He won't see anybody. He can't be disturbed."

"Can you get a message to him?"

"What's the message?"

"That we have very little time left," said Varneys.

"He knows that better than you, Director."

Varneys didn't respond. He just stood there awkwardly, as if there was something he needed to say but couldn't. As Christina's eyes probed his, she felt that the mask was falling away and she was getting a glimpse into the person who lived behind it. "Goodbye, Christina," said Varneys with a finality that made her shudder. When he reached the doorway, he turned around and faced her. "Robert isn't the only one who has nightmares. I have them, too. All the time."

"And why is that, Director?"

"Because I took a fragile kid with the most tragic life history and I threw him to the dogs when he wouldn't do what I wanted him to do. He wanted to save lives and that wasn't good enough for me. So I took everything away from him. His teachers, his friends, his schools, his home, his entire life. And now, I stand here, almost thirty years later, hoping that the person I tried to destroy can save the human race."

Varneys exited the office.

# 101

" **Y**OUR BIG DAY HAS ARRIVED, McAlister. I don't know how you did it, but the warden said you're being released today. You must have some powerful friends." The guard handed McAlister a large plastic bag that contained the clothing he had worn when he first arrived at Butner.

McAlister shot back, "Here's a piece of free advice, officer. The people who help you the most are rarely your friends."

Through his Washington D.C. lawyers, McAlister had made periodic payments totaling seven million dollars to various super PACs serving the president's political party. This largesse was rewarded with a presidential commutation of his sentence. When the president was criticized by the media, the White House press secretary responded as follows:

> "This is not a pardon, it is a commutation of sentence. Mr. McAlister intends to devote himself to community service using his substantial executive abilities to help small business startups in our inner cities. The prison term that he has already served has set a sufficient example to others."

Standing outside Butner's gates, McAlister took a deep breath and looked around. A white Jaguar F-Type coupe approached much faster than the posted twenty miles-per-hour speed restriction. Stopping directly in front of McAlister, the driver rolled the passenger window down.

"Need a lift?" Ramirez said with a smile. McAlister got in the car. "This is a very good day for me," said Ramirez.

"That's kind of you," replied McAlister.

"I don't mean because you got out. Today's the last day on which I'll have to impersonate that fucking lawyer of yours and wear this goddamn face mask. I'm wearing it today because this parking lot is full of surveillance cameras."

"Attention to detail, Gunther. Always your strong point."

"As you requested, we'll go directly to the airport and fly to New York. I assume we'll go to your apartment in Tribeca, or did Barbara get that in the divorce also?"

McAlister scowled. She got the townhouse on East Seventy-Second Street. I got to keep the apartment. Of course, the townhouse is worth five times as much."

Ramirez laughed. "You can't put a price on love, Colum. She tolerated you for how many years?"

McAlister's attention was focused on the passing scenery as they drove along the streets on the way to the highway. "It's good to see something other than that prison. Even the ugly stuff looks better than I remember it," said McAlister.

"Well, the pen wasn't much to look at, but you sure did some good work in there. You're about two hundred times richer now than when you went in."

"That's true. And for a while, I was a savior of the world."

"What are we going to do about that?" asked Ramirez. "We have some very nervous business associates."

"As soon as we get to New York, we're going to a storage locker I have in Brooklyn under an assumed name. The feds never found it. I paid nineteen years of storage fees in advance to be sure that my stuff would be there when I got out even if I served the full sentence."

"What's in there?"

"The only hope we have to keep Gao and Bazhenov from killing us."

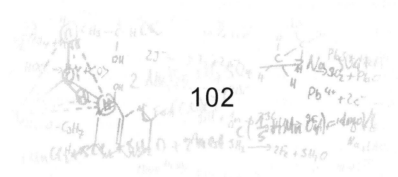

# 102

TYPICAL OF HUNDREDS OF SIMILAR establishments throughout the five boroughs of New York City, Bushwick Self-Storage existed because New York apartments had a miniscule amount of closet space. So residents had only two choices: they could rent or buy larger dwellings with more closets at prohibitive cost, or they could rent storage units for much less. As apartment rents and purchase prices skyrocketed in New York City, because even the youngest of Wall Street "bankers" were paid astronomical amounts of money for contributing nothing to society, and the tsunami of overseas wealth consumed Manhattan, ordinary New Yorkers, often sharing apartments with others because they couldn't afford their own, became increasingly dependent on storage units. Savvy real estate entrepreneurs answered the call and converted abandoned factories and warehouses into self-storage units. It was a lucrative business because a building that housed a thousand cheaply-built storage units only needed five minimum-wage employees to run it. Bushwick Self-Storage had once been a shoe factory employing over four hundred people at union wages, but that was before its parent company moved manufacturing to Indonesia, where its workers were paid forty-eight cents per hour.

Aside from their utilitarian function, storage facilities provided a degree of anonymity that could not be obtained at one's personal residence or office. While most people used the units for legitimate purposes, it was no secret that more than a few storage lockers were used to house contraband of one type or another, be it stolen goods, illegal drugs, firearms or stashes of cash garnered from illicit pursuits.

To the casual observer, the contents of Colum McAlister's unit were prosaic, but they were not. There were several tall file cabinets crammed with documents, but these were no mere office files. They were McAlister's dossiers on scores of politicians, regulatory agency and law enforcement officials, executives and business moguls, containing incriminating evidence he had collected over the years that had been instrumental in his rise to the top of Bushings Pharmaceuticals and the furtherance of his agenda there. There were scores of DVDS, but these weren't Hollywood films or home movies. They were copies of sexually explicit videos in which government officials were the unwitting actors, having been entrapped by McAlister as they engaged in career-killing lascivious activities. McAlister had used these videos to good advantage throughout his career, and the originals were among the items that the FBI had confiscated from his Lands End estate, leading to his conviction. And then there were four cartons filled with currency: U.S. dollars, pounds sterling, Swiss francs and Japanese yen, totaling the monetary equivalent of approximately one million eight hundred thousand dollars. McAlister kept this cash for unforeseen emergencies, together with passports from six different countries which bore his photograph under various assumed names.

But none of these items was the reason why McAlister and Ramirez rushed to Bushwick Self-Storage in Brooklyn immediately after McAlister's release from prison.

"Help me move this stuff," said McAlister to Ramirez. "I need the bottom box." Ramirez frowned as he looked at a stack of boxes almost seven feet high.

"Damn, these are heavy. What's in them?" asked Ramirez as he lifted one down after the other.

"Books and magazines," replied McAlister.

"Are you planning to open a coffee shop?" McAlister ignored the comment.

Ramirez grabbed an empty duffle bag into which he threw McAlister's passports and wads of cash. "We may need these."

When only the bottom box remained, McAlister pushed it to a clear area in the room. "Do you have a knife to cut the tape?"

"Really? We weren't flying private," replied Ramirez.

"Then give me the car keys."

McAlister ripped through the packing tape with the edge of a key, and emptied the contents of the box, scattering dozens of books and magazines on the ground. When he got close to the bottom, he pulled out a thick tome whose gray cover was faded and worn. "Here we go. This is it," he said.

Ramirez craned his neck so he could read the book's title: *Being and Nothingness* by Jean-Paul Sartre. Grinning, Ramirez said, "I never thought you were an existentialist, Colum. Most existentialists aren't as greedy as you. And if you think giving Gao and Bazhenov that book is going to change their attitude, I think you are dead wrong. And I emphasize the word *dead*."

Oblivious to Ramirez' banter, McAlister opened the book to reveal that it had no pages. It was a faux book that functioned as a box from which McAlister removed a thick black notebook. Flipping through it, he muttered, "This is it. Exactly the way it looked in Geneva."

Ramirez smiled. "I guess that's why you paid for climate control in this unit. So, what is it?"

"It's the journal of Aamir Mahmoud, the scientist who invented HRFS for Ansar Jamaat, and then invented the cure for me. It contains the formulas for both, and his accompanying notes. This journal made us billionaires."

Ramirez raised his eyebrows. "That was yesterday. What do you need it for today?"

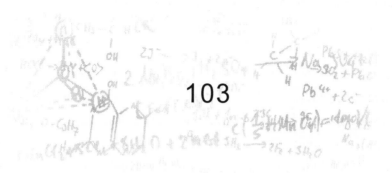

# 103

A FED EX TRUCK PULLED UP to the Wheatleigh gates with a package addressed to Dr. Robert James Austin. The package was marked: URGENT/FOR AUSTIN'S EYES ONLY.

"What the hell is this?" said one guard to the other. "He never gets any mail or deliveries. No one is supposed to know he's here. Who sent this?"

After researching the sender's name and address for more than an hour, and cross-checking with the Manchester Police Department which, in turn, was able to tap into the FBI database, it was clear that the identity and address of the sender were fictitious. The guards then ran the package through an X-ray machine to be sure that it didn't contain any explosives or incendiaries. After that, one of the guards brought the package to Susan.

Susan cautiously opened it up and found a black notebook with the following unsigned letter clipped to it:

Dr. Austin:

The journal that accompanies this letter was written by Aamir Mahmoud, a biochemist who at one time worked for Tyer Drun Pharmaceuticals in Philadelphia, and then was recruited by Ansar Jamaat to create an incurable new disease. Dr. Mahmoud's invention is HRFS. For reasons that you don't need to know, he simultaneously formulated the cure for that disease, and it is that cure which eventually was manufactured and distributed by Schlumberger Foch. While Dr. Mahmoud's cure saved many millions of lives, it is rapidly losing efficacy, as you know.

I am sending this journal to you in the hope that it might assist you in finding a new cure for HRFS. As you will see, Dr. Mahmoud goes into great detail regarding his exact formulation of HRFS. I don't believe that the CDC or anyone else knows his formula for the disease. Perhaps knowing how he created this disease will lead you to discovering a cure.

You may be wondering who I am and how I came to possess this journal, and how I found your address. The answers to all of these questions are irrelevant.

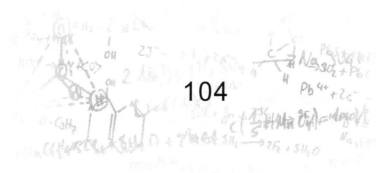

# 104

B OBBY HAD BEEN MESMERIZED BY the stars ever since he first viewed them through the telescope his foster father had purchased for him when he was three years old. At the Institute for Advanced Intelligence Studies, he had spent countless hours as a young student experimenting on astrophysics problems by programming the Institute's planetarium to interface with its mainframe computer for real- world-type testing of formulas and theories. But when Bobby's attention turned to discovering cures for diseases, he abandoned what he called "pure science," and instead focused on biochemistry, biophysics and genetics, which he supercharged with the unique mathematical language that he invented.

With HRFS only a few months away from devouring humanity, Bobby knew that he needed a revolutionary idea to defeat HRFS before the current cure became completely ineffective. Whatever he devised had to overcome HRFS' ability to quickly mutate to protect itself. Bobby turned his eyes to the heavens for an answer.

While Susan and Christina thought that Bobby's immersion in astrophysics after he left his lab was a sign that he had given up on devising a cure for HRFS, they were wrong. Bobby was spending endless hours in the cabin atop the stone watchtower working on how he could translate the astrophysical concept of antimatter into medical science. The adaptation into human biochemistry of abstract theoretical concepts rooted in quantum physics, special relativity and atomic-particle analysis seemed not only implausible but impossible. For Bobby, it posed the greatest intellectual challenge that he had ever faced.

According to the theories of particle physics, antimatter is almost identical to its counterpart, ordinary matter, except that antimatter and ordinary matter carry opposite electrical charges and spins. When matter and antimatter meet, they instantly annihilate each other. The positron, with its positive electrical charge, is the anti-particle to the negatively charged electron. Upon contact with each other, the positive and negative cancel each other out, and there is nothing left of either one. In astrophysics, the result of this annihilation is the release of energy, sometimes in great quantities, but that would not be relevant to what Bobby was doing, as he was adopting the theoretical concept, not applying it to the interaction of particles on the atomic level.

Bobby wanted to find a way to apply this concept of "matter meets antimatter" to genetics. His goal was to create a reverse or "negative" genetic mirror-image of the HRFS genome that would have the ability to negate or nullify the original "positive" genome of the disease when the two genetic structures came into contact with each other. If this could be done, then the disease would be eradicated at its genetic roots, and it would not have the ability to mutate or evolve. Bobby called this process "genetic cellular nullification" or "GCN". In order to accomplish this, Bobby marshalled his massive knowledge of genetics, physics, biochemistry, molecular electronics and his unique creative abilities to synthesize solutions that transcended the boundaries of any one scientific discipline. His mathematical language allowed him to generate formulas and equations that were processed by computer in virtually infinite permutations and combinations. As Bobby worked on this, he found that even if the original genome would try to defensively mutate when it came into contact with its reciprocal opposite, its opposite would simultaneously mutate in lock-step reverse until the original genome was destroyed through genetic negation. There would be no escape from the genetic death spiral.

Once Bobby's calculations confirmed that he had formulated the reverse mirror-image of the HRFS genome, he worked with a team of geneticists and chemists at Tufts Medical School to encapsulate the artificially created genome in a form that would be ingestible by human beings who were infected with HRFS. He ran test upon test on the formulation, vetting it from every angle, and being sure that it worked with every human blood type. But as he got closer to the final answer, he became increasingly uneasy. Something was wrong.

# 105

WHEN MAHMOUD ARRIVED AT SAEED'S headquarters, he was escorted into his office by two of Saeed's guards. Colonel Fahd was already there. "You wanted to see us?" said Fahd.

Mahmoud nodded. "Yes, to bring you and the Caliph up to date on my experiments. It's been quite a while since our last meeting."

As Saeed approached him, Mahmoud instinctively took two steps backwards. Following protocol, he lowered his head to avoid eye contact, but he could still see Saeed's flowing clerical garments moving in his direction. Mahmoud noticed that Saeed was dressed completely in white, rather than in the black shrouds that he began to clothe himself in after the cure was announced. When Saeed's cold hand reached under his chin and tilted his head back, Mahmoud shuddered. The last time this happened Saeed was about to slit his throat.

"Look at me, Mahmoud," said Saeed, almost in a whisper. When Mahmoud reluctantly complied, he saw that Saeed was smiling at him. Saeed placed his hands on Mahmoud's shoulders, gave him a playful shake and pulled his rigid body closer. "When the infidels announced a cure, I thought you had failed me. Had it not been for Fahd, I would have killed you. But your genius was greater than I imagined. The disease that you invented had the ability to get stronger, to evolve so that it could defeat the cure. I have read that the cure is now virtually worthless. Is that true?"

Mahmoud nodded. "Yes Caliph. It is true. This is why I wanted to come here today. So I could tell you that."

Saeed kissed Mahmoud on each cheek. "*Allahu Akbar*," Saeed proclaimed loudly.

Fahd rushed over to join them. Wrapping his arms around Mahmoud and Saeed, he began to chant, "*Allahu Akbar, Allahu Akbar, Allahu Akbar*," and didn't stop until Saeed held up his right hand.

His face only inches away from Mahmoud's, Saeed said, "Look how far have we have come, Aamir Mahmoud. It was not that many years ago that I selected you for the most holy of missions, and now you and I, with Colonel Fahd's help, have changed the course of human history. Allah has blessed your creation. He has now enlisted his most abundant and humble creature, the mosquito, to join our mujahideen and carry the Sword of the Mahdi to the far ends of the Earth. There will be no escape for the infidels."

"No escape," echoed Fahd.

"Yes, Caliph, no escape," said Mahmoud softly, closing his eyes as if in prayer. Removing a small atomizer from his pants pocket, he pumped it three times. One spray into Saeed's face, one into Fahd's, and the last into his own.

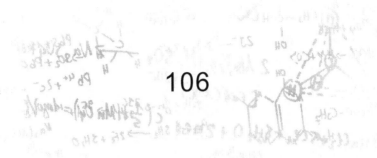

# 106

CHRISTINA TRAMPED OUT OF THE Wheatleigh main house and headed for the stone watchtower. It was one o'clock in the morning and she couldn't stand it anymore. She hadn't seen Bobby in weeks. He was sequestered in the cabin on top of the tower, and he kept his phone turned off.

Using her cell phone flashlight, she climbed the stairs to the top of the tower and turned the door knob, only to find that the door was locked. She began to bang on the door. "Enough is enough, Bobby. I have to speak to you." No answer from him. She kept banging. No response. She started to kick the door. "I don't even know if you're alive." No response.

Christina slammed her hand repeatedly against the door and kicked it even harder. Worried and infuriated at the same time, she began to cry as she yelled, "If you don't respond, I'll have the guards break the door down. Let me in. I'm your wife, goddamn it." After a few minutes, she slumped against the door.

"Christina, please stop crying," said Bobby in a hoarse voice as he leaned against the other side of the door.

"Let me in, Bobby."

"I can't."

"Let me in." Bobby didn't reply.

"Why are you doing this?" she asked.

"You need to go away now."

"I can help you."

"Not this time, Christina."

Bobby shuffled away from the door and went into the cabin's small bathroom. He looked in the mirror. Festering pustules marked his face, hands and arms. A black mucus-like substance was caked in the corner of his yellowed eyes and leaked from his nose and ears. Whatever portion of his skin that wasn't covered with pustules had a bluish tint. He was finding it increasingly difficult to breathe and could barely stand. His brief interchange with Christina exhausted him. He ran his pocked hands through his hair and clumps fell into the sink.

## 107

"**N**ow I become death, the destroyer of worlds." These words haunted Bobby. They had been uttered by Robert Oppenheimer when he witnessed the first detonation of an atomic bomb at Alamogordo, New Mexico on July 16, 1945. Oppenheimer was the theoretical physicist who led the Manhattan Project that developed nuclear weapons for the United States during World War II. He understood that he had unleashed on humanity a force of destruction never before known to mankind.

*The destroyer of worlds.* Bobby couldn't get that phrase out of his mind. He kept saying it over and over as he milled around the small cabin. Two weeks prior, on the night Christina came to the door of the cabin, Bobby was in the midst of conducting the fifth test on himself. The four prior tests that he did were at earlier stages of HRFS. Those tests were successful. For the fifth, he wanted to let the disease ravage him for two more days before taking his pill. He needed to know if the cure would work on advanced cases. Hundreds of millions of lives would depend on it.

He felt sick to his stomach. While the technology he had invented to cure HRFS was effective at all of the disease's stages, and he was in the process of recovering, he realized that his invention was capable of being weaponized. He had carefully formulated the HRFS reverse genome to nullify only the genetic structure of HRFS, but its application did not have to be so limited. He began to think that the cure he had invented was even more dangerous than the dreaded disease it was designed to defeat. And there was something else that was bothering him. Throughout the period during which he was working on genetic cellular nullification (GCN), he had no nightmares. For decades prior, whenever he worked on cures, he was plagued by night terrors that were so severe that they imperiled not only the progress of his research, but his physical and mental health. *So why didn't I have any this time?* he wondered.

# 108

B OBBY CHECKED THE LAST OF the blood tests that conclusively confirmed that he was no longer contagious. For the first time in over seven weeks, he walked into the main house of Wheatleigh. Pale, gaunt and perilously skinny from the abuse that he had heaped on his body by repeatedly infecting himself with HRFS, Susan was the first person that he encountered.

"Oh my God, you look like death warmed over," she said as she wrapped her arms around him, pressing her face against his emaciated chest. Bobby hugged her as he rested his cheek against the top of her head, the first physical contact he had had with another person in almost two months.

"Are you okay?" asked Susan. Not waiting for an answer, she said, "You look like shit. I've never seen you look so bad—and I've seen you look pretty damn bad."

Bobby forced a smile. "I'm alive. And that's saying quite a bit under the circumstances. Is Christina here?"

"She's at work. She should be home in around an hour."

"Where are the kids?"

"Oh, you remember you have kids?" replied Susan. The

expression on Bobby's face made Susan instantly sorry she had said that. "Christina sent them to her mom's for a while. She's been very upset. I've never seen her this way."

Bobby nodded in recognition. "She must be very mad at me. I don't blame her."

"It's not just that, Bobby. She's been extremely worried about you. You never isolated yourself like that, been so distant and uncommunicative. And all of us are petrified about HRFS. Varneys was here a while ago and told us that we're just weeks away from…" Susan didn't finish the sentence. "She's terribly afraid for Pete and Mirielle. People are dying all over the world. The cure is almost worthless."

His voice, a tired monotone, Bobby said, "I'll just wait for her in the sunroom." He dragged himself into the glass-enclosed porch that faced the winter's browned-out grass and gray ocean. Plopping down into a plaid cushioned chair, he stared out at the dull sea. Exhausted from the ordeal he had put himself through, he fell asleep in a few minutes.

When Christina walked through the front door of the house, Susan directed her to the porch. As Christina approached the room, she saw a frail-looking figure slumped in the chair. It took her a moment to realize that it was Bobby. He had lost more than forty pounds since she had last seen him. His beautiful auburn hair had thinned and there were bald spots where clumps had fallen out. His face was cadaverous and haggard. The veins in his hands protruded like those of an old man. Christina bent down and kissed him on the head and then crouched in front of him. As she stroked his face, her eyes filled with tears. "What happened to you?" she whispered. Taking his hands in hers, she kissed his fingers and then held them to her lips. When Bobby awoke and his eyes opened, the infinite pools of blue that had mesmerized her the first time she met him looked at her, but now his eyes were sunken in their sockets and his sclera was still partially yellow.

"I never wanted to hurt you," he said softly.

Christina began to cry. "I was so worried. I didn't know what to think."

Bobby ran his craggy hand over Christina's cheek. "Please get Susan. I have to talk to you both."

Christina and Susan sat down opposite Bobby. Christina's hands began to tremble as she took in the full measure of Bobby's decrepit physical condition. "Don't worry, Christina," said Susan. "A few weeks of home cooking will put some meat back on his bones and some color in his cheeks. The hair, I'll leave that to you."

Before Bobby could say anything, Christina's eyes met his and she said sternly, "I need you to promise me that you will never isolate yourself from me like that again. That's not what we're about. I could have helped you. I should have been there with you. I can see that the night terrors tore you apart."

Bobby looked down at the floor. "I didn't have any," he replied somberly. "That's part of the problem."

Christina looked at Bobby quizzically. "Problem? What do you mean?"

Bobby paused before responding, and Susan and Christina could see that it was a physical effort for him to have a prolonged conversation. "I devised a technology to cure HRFS."

Stunned, Susan and Christina asked in unison, "What did you say?"

"I devised a technology to cure HRFS, but there's a problem with it."

"Did the journal that was sent to you help?" asked Susan.

Bobby shook his head. "HRFS had mutated so much that knowing its original formula was of no use. Whoever sent it obviously didn't understand that."

"Does your cure work?" asked Christina.

"Yes," replied Bobby.

"Are you sure your cure works?" asked Susan.

"The Tufts medical team and I did extensive tests on human blood and tissue samples."

"Is that enough? Won't it have to be field-tested on infected people in the same way as your prior cures?" asked Susan.

"There's no time for that. People need it right away. That's why I tested it on myself."

"You did *what*?" asked Christina.

"I tested it on myself."

"I— I don't understand," said Christina, as she leaned forward in her seat.

"I infected myself with HRFS five times. Each time, I let the disease progress to an increasingly advanced stage so I could be sure the cure was effective at all phases."

Susan's eyes widened. "Jeez…. Now I understand why you look so terrible," she muttered.

Christina's face was ashen as she asked a question she knew was rhetorical. "But what if your cure didn't work?"

"I couldn't ask anyone to take the risk if I didn't take it first."

"So that's what you were doing in the cabin," said Christina softly.

"The night you came up the stairs, I was in the final stage of the disease."

Christina's body began to rock back and forth involuntarily as she sat on the edge of the sofa, her arms wrapped across her chest and her eyes staring blankly at the floor. Susan buried her face in her hands. For several moments, all three were engulfed by silence as the gravity of what Bobby said hung in the air. Finally, Susan wiped her eyes with the backs of her hands and quietly asked, "Are you sure it will work on other people?"

"After the tests on myself were satisfactory, the Tufts medical team volunteered. It had one hundred percent efficacy."

Susan sprung up. "We have to call the CDC."

Bobby held up his hand. "It's not that simple."

"Why not?" asked Susan.

"This cure isn't a medicine. It isn't a drug. It's something very different."

"What is it?" asked Christina.

"It's a genetically engineered compound that causes the destruction of the HRFS genome by means of a process I call genetic cellular nullification."

Susan nodded. "Right...so, like all cures, it kills the virus or bacteria or whatever causes the disease," said Susan.

"No. It doesn't kill anything. It eradicates the HRFS and the HRFS eradicates it. Mutual, simultaneous annihilation."

"This is going over my head, Bobby. Can you put it in layman's terms?" asked Christina.

"I got the idea from astrophysics. What I did was adapt antimatter theories to biochemistry and virology. I created a genome that is the reverse or "negative" genetic "mirror-image" of the HRFS genome. In the reaction that takes place, my genome targets the "positive" HRFS genome. When these two "mirror-image" genetic structures come in contact, they negate each other. I programmed my genome so that it will self-replicate in the human body only to the extent necessary to exactly counter the HRFS genome that is present in the body. So when the process is complete, no HRFS remains and none of my reverse genome remains. This is why I call it genetic cellular nullification. And because this technology eradicates HRFS at its genetic roots, there is no way for HRFS to mutate or evolve to defeat the process. I can show you on the computer what it looks like."

Christina waved her hand. "Show me later. You mentioned there was a problem. What's the problem? If it works, it works," said Christina.

"The problem is that the technology to create a reverse genome can be weaponized. If the same technique is applied to human hematopoietic stem cells, the human race will be wiped out. The body will be unable to replenish the two hundred billion red blood cells, ten billion white cells, and four hundred billion platelets that die every day in the human body. Genetic cellular nullification can be used to eradicate human DNA. There is no way to stop the GCN chain reaction once it starts and it works very fast."

"How fast? How long is the treatment process for HRFS?" asked Susan.

"It just takes one pill."

"One pill. How can that be?" asked Christina.

"Because this isn't a medication. It's a physio-genetic reaction. When HRFS is in an advanced state in a patient, it will be eradicated within four hours. It will be much quicker for earlier stages of the disease. Physical recuperation takes the normal amount of time, but the HRFS is gone, as if it never existed."

Susan stood up and began to walk in circles. "But how could something like that be weaponized? You can't make whole populations take a pill," said Susan.

Bobby took a deep breath and settled further back in his chair. His voice became hoarse and it seemed harder for him to muster the lung power to explain, but he knew he had to. "The HRFS cure will have to be manufactured by dozens of drug companies in order for everyone who needs it to get it in time. I won't have control of it. Sooner or later, some of those companies will figure out the technology behind it, as will the military. They'll reverse-engineer, decompile or disassemble it. History has demonstrated that all scientific discoveries are capable of weaponization. And who is to say that nature won't inadvertently play a role? Perhaps vermin or mosquitoes will carry it—just like HRFS. Anything is possible. It's the atom bomb all over again, but worse."

"Why worse?" asked Christina.

Bobby leaned forward as he began to push himself up to a standing position, but when he was halfway up, he fell back into his chair. Rubbing his gnarled hands together, he said, "Nuclear weapons require vast resources, rare materials and complex facilities to produce and launch. Each one that is deployed is the result of a specific decision. That provides a measure of control. Genetic cellular nullification is not controllable. Once it gets started, it can't be stopped. GCN is its own end game."

Christina was focused on the here and now, and she knew she had to get Bobby onto the same wavelength, as he was easily capable of becoming dominated by abstract potentialities. "You don't know how, when, by whom, or if your discovery will be weaponized. That's all speculation. But what you do know is that people need your cure desperately right now."

"I realize that. But the fact is that I'm laying the foundation for the total annihilation of the human race: the doomsday weapon."

"The doomsday weapon is already here. It's called HRFS," said Susan.

"GCN is more powerful than any disease. That's the reason I didn't have night terrors when I was working on it."

"What are you saying, Bobby?" asked Christina. "You think that some supernatural evil, some universal force of destruction helped you?"

"It didn't help me, but it didn't try to stop me or slow me down, like it did with all the other cures I worked on over the years. This is the first time I had no interference. It didn't care that I was eliminating HRFS, because that disease is just another arrow in its quiver. It knew that the technology I was developing was more important to it. I gave it what it always wanted. A solution. A final solution. An unstoppable way for humanity to destroy itself."

Susan's face turned chalk-white. "That's crazy. Please don't tell anyone that, or they'll put you away, Nobel prizes and all."

# 109

F OR THE FIRST TIME IN several months, Bobby lay in bed with Christina. He was too weak to even think about any romantic activity, and he knew that he looked like a scarecrow, but he was just so grateful to be lying in a large comfortable bed next to the woman he loved. Feeling the warmth of her embrace and the sensual closeness of her body against his, he pressed his face against her shoulder as he breathed in the scent of her skin. It was an elixir that he was in desperate need of, but his comfort would be short-lived. After Christina fell asleep, Bobby moved to the edge of the bed. Lying motionless, he stared at the ceiling, consumed by doubt and moral confusion.

His physical deterioration was not a concern to him. He knew that time would mend his body, but he was in a state of spiritual meltdown, mired in an ethical dilemma that had shaken him to his core. In all the years of his research to find cures, he never had any ethical concerns. He was doing the right thing. There was no question of that. But now, for the first time, he doubted the morality of his efforts. While he knew that his HRFS cure would save millions of lives, he realized that its release would open a door to a technology that might only close when the human race was destroyed. In response to time pressures created by the impending inefficacy of Schlumberger Foch's drug, he had harnessed his unique genius to create a revolutionary technique that had destructive powers of a magnitude greater than any that had ever been contemplated, even by the most insane despot. While Susan and Christina had never subscribed to his belief in a universal force of mayhem and destruction that was the antithesis of God, he believed that he had delivered to that force a tangible form of negativity that was profound in its capacity to devastate humanity.

Bobby was aware that he wasn't the first scientist who had grappled with the morality of his discovery. There was Nobel laureate Hans Bethe, a senior member of the Manhattan Project, who called on all scientists to "cease and desist from work creating, developing, improving and manufacturing nuclear weapons and other weapons of potential mass destruction." There was Lewis Fry Richardson, a mathematician and meteorologist who abandoned his work and destroyed his unpublished research, because the military wanted to use it to model the best ways of deploying poison gas. There was Arthur Galston, a botanist, whose inventions were subverted by the military into the development of Agent Orange, a chemical weapon which was used in the Vietnam War and killed or maimed over four hundred thousand people. He subsequently became an activist against chemical weapons and convinced Richard Nixon to ban Agent Orange in 1971. There was Paul Berg, a pioneer in the technique of recombinant DNA, who halted experiments he was conducting when he realized that new strains of viruses he was developing could create a cancer pandemic if they escaped the confines of his laboratory; abandoning his research, he campaigned for guidelines to control recombinant DNA. In the fields of artificial intelligence and information technology, the legendary software pioneer Bill Joy, said, "The twenty-first century technologies of genetics, nanotechnology and robotics are so powerful that they can spawn whole new classes of accidents and abuses. Most dangerously, for the first time, these accidents and abuses are widely within the reach of individuals or small groups. They will not require large facilities or rare raw materials. Knowledge alone will enable the use of them. We are on the cusp of the further perfection of extreme evil, an evil whose possibility spreads well beyond that which weapons of mass destruction bequeathed to the nation-states, on to a terrible empowerment of extreme individuals."

Bobby got out of bed and walked into the bathroom. A grim figure confronted him from the mirror and offered no solace. He stared at his reflection as if he didn't recognize his own face. The eyes that looked back at him were not the eyes that he knew. They were dull and defeated. "After all these years of refusing to work on military applications, what have I become? Who am I now?" he muttered. Bobby entered the shower and turned the faucet to maximum cold. As the water rained down on him, he began to shiver. He wanted more of it. He wanted to freeze. He pointed the showerhead to the far corner of the stall where he squatted on his haunches like an animal hiding from a predator. Raising his face to meet the frigid stream that pummeled him, he asked the questions again: "What have I become? Who am I now?"

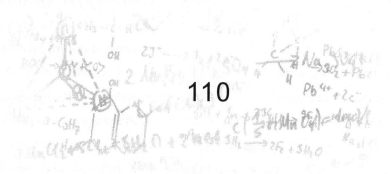

# 110

WHILE BOBBY REALIZED THAT HE had no choice but to release his cure, despite the dark power that lay within it, his fear of the future consequences of his discovery plunged him into profound despondency. His propensity for self-loathing surfaced and manifested itself in an acute sense of personal failure. *There had to be another way. Another solution. I should have found it. I should have done better. Now it's too late.*

When Christina awoke, Bobby wasn't in the bedroom. As she rushed out of the house on her way to work, she said to Susan, "Be sure he eats a good breakfast. I don't want the kids to see him until he looks a little better, or it will scare them to death."

Susan looked for Bobby in his lab. He wasn't' there. Nor was he on the sun porch. She doubted that he would be in the tower's cabin, but she checked there, too. Surveying the property from the cabin's windows, she looked down towards the sea cliffs. There was Bobby, standing motionless at the cliff's edge.

Susan hurried down the tower's steps and walked over to him.

"What are you doing out here so early? It's cold. Come into

the house. We'll have some hot coffee and a good breakfast," said Susan. Bobby didn't respond. "How long have you been out here? Christina got up at six-thirty and you were already gone."

"I wanted to see the sun rise," he said, avoiding eye contact as he continued to stare at the ocean.

"Was it beautiful?" He didn't answer. "What's wrong, Bobby? What's going on?"

When Bobby looked at Susan, she saw that his eyes were bloodshot. "I don't know who I am anymore," he said.

"Why are you saying that?"

"Because of what I've done. The technology I invented."

"You've done what you always have done. Help people."

Bobby's eyes hardened. "I failed. I lost my direction." Bobby shook his head. "My whole life, I tried so hard to do the right thing. What would Joe say now?"

"He'd say your HRFS cure is the best piece of work you've ever done."

"Today it's a panacea and tomorrow it's a scourge," said Bobby.

"We don't know that. You don't know that. You have to have some faith."

"Faith in what Susan?"

Susan stepped in front of Bobby blocking his view of the sea and slammed his shoulders, pushing him backwards. "Faith in what? I can't believe you're saying that to me. You, a person who is here only because of one thing. Have you forgotten who you are? What you are? Where you came from? Who am I talking to?"

"Calm down, Susan."

"No. Tell me who I am talking to."

Bobby scrunched up his face. "You're talking to me. What do you mean?"

"And who are you?"

"What the fuck, Susan. You know who I am."

"No, I want to hear you say it. Who are you?"

"I'm Robert Austin. Robert James Austin."

"Oh, you think so? Well, you're not. I'll tell you who you are. You're "Dumpster Baby", "Garbage Bag Boy", "Johnny Doe", #2764. You're a newborn in a garbage bag who was thrown into a dumpster and left to die. And you did die. Amidst the stink and the vermin. You were never saved. You never did anything other than rot in that bag like the rest of the trash. You died on the first day of your life." Susan slammed Bobby's shoulders again, pushing him back further. "Does that sound right to you?"

Bobby's face was red and he wagged his head, confused. "But—"

Susan cut him off. "There's only one reason your story has a different ending. There's only one reason why you didn't die in that dumpster. And there's only one reason why you're such a goddamn genius. One reason, Bobby. One explanation. Do I have to spell it out for you again? Like I did thirty years ago? You think about that."

# 111

T HE TEXT THAT RAMIREZ RECEIVED was short. GBRM515 10APH. Ramirez showed it to McAlister.

"Who's that from?" asked McAlister.

"Gao."

"A man of few words. Actually, a man of no words," said McAlister.

Ramirez grinned. "He always sends texts that are unintelligible unless you know how to read them."

"Well, we knew we'd be hearing from those guys, particularly since they must have read all the hoopla about me getting out of prison. So, what does it mean?"

"It says: Gao, Bazhenov, Ramirez, McAlister: meet on May fifteenth at ten a.m. at Air Pegasus Heliport."

McAlister chuckled. "Amazing. You guys make Twitter look verbose."

"I've been texting with Gao for years. There's a methodology to this."

Frowning, McAlister said, "Maybe we shouldn't meet with them. A phone call may be better."

"That won't work. And, besides, you have some good news for them. And remember, we haven't done anything wrong."

When McAlister and Ramirez arrived at Air Pegasus Heliport on Thirtieth Street and Twelfth Avenue in New York City, adjacent to the Hudson River, there were six helicopters on the tarmac.

"I hate helicopters," said McAlister as he pressed his hands against his head in an effort to shield his perfectly coiffed hair from the wind. "Which one is it? Do you see Gao or Bazhenov?"

Ramirez surveyed the area and then pointed to a large cobalt blue Airbus H225. "It's that one. I remember seeing it at Bazhenov's house in East Hampton."

"Impressive toy," said McAlister.

"State-of-the art," replied Ramirez. "Fast, and long-range."

As they began to walk towards the copter, a giant of a man wearing a black suit that looked three sizes too small for him approached them. Ramirez recognized him as the chauffeur from Bazhenov's East Hampton estate. "Mr. Ramirez. I am Sergey. I drove you at Mr. Bazhenov's house in Long Island." He then extended his massive hand to McAlister. "And you must be Mr. McAlister." Pointing to the H225, he waited for Ramirez and McAlister to take the lead as he followed behind them, speaking into his cell phone. When they arrived at the helicopter, two flight attendants greeted them, one male and one female, and it was difficult to discern which one was a more beautiful representation of their gender. The female, five-foot-ten, long black hair, gray eyes and high cheekbones, spoke first, "Hello, gentlemen. On behalf of Mr. Viktor Bazhenov, welcome aboard. My name is Karina and I will do everything I can to make your trip enjoyable and—"

McAlister cut her off. "Where are Bazhenov and Gao. Aren't they meeting us here? That was our understanding."

The male attendant, who probably could make more money as a *GQ* model, stepped forward. "They will be meeting you at the destination which is only a short flight from here. My name is Anton. We have a wonderful selection of beverages and hors d'oeuvres for you onboard."

Sergey moved to the fore. "For security reasons, we have a few rules on all of Mr. Bazhenov's air and sea vessels. Please give me your cell phones, your wristwatches, any other electronic devices that you have, cigarette lighters and any firearms. Of course, they will be returned."

Once Ramirez and McAlister complied, Anton stepped forward, holding a wand. Ramirez recognized that the model that Anton was using could detect not only weapons and plastic explosives but also GPS and implanted subdermal chips. "Please stand with your feet apart and arms spread wide. I apologize for the intrusion."

The helicopter ride was much longer than Ramirez and McAlister expected, and almost all of it took place over the Atlantic Ocean. Ramirez knew that the H225 had a cruising speed of two hundred miles per hour. He estimated that they were traveling for at least seventy-five minutes so they had covered a distance of approximately two hundred fifty miles. As the helicopter began to descend, an oil supertanker came into view. Now only five hundred feet away from the ship, McAlister saw its name on the stern: *Volshebnik.*

"*Volshebnik*, what language is that?" he asked Ramirez.

"Russian. It means 'magician.' This tanker definitely belongs to Bazhenov."

"Why do you say that?" asked McAlister.

"Because *Volshebnik* is his nickname."

"He does magic tricks in his spare time?"

"No. He got the name because he makes his enemies disappear."

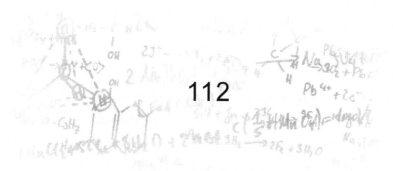

# 112

THE SUPERTANKER, *VOLSHEBNIK*, WAS THE largest ship that Ramirez and McAlister had ever seen, let alone been aboard.

"You could land fighter jets on this thing," said McAlister. "It's bigger than an aircraft carrier."

"It's a floating money machine. Bazhenov has at least six of these," said Ramirez.

"How do you know?"

"I helped him get his money out of Russia and buy assets. He likes ships because he can keep them in international waters and then move them to areas that are safest for him, politically."

As Ramirez, McAlister and Sergey exited the helicopter, a short stocky man wearing a dark blue windbreaker and what appeared to be a captain's hat walked quickly towards them. Sergey stepped forward and had a brief interchange with him in Russian. The captain then addressed Ramirez and McAlister in heavily accented English.

"Gentlemen. Welcome aboard *Volshebnik*. I am Captain Orlov. Unless you need to use the lavatory first, I will escort you to the conference room for your meeting with Mr. Bazhenov and Mr. Gao. They are eager to begin." As they all began to walk in the direction of the bridge, the sound of the helicopter taking off caused Ramirez to spin around.

"Where are they going?" asked Ramirez.

"We didn't get our phones back," said McAlister.

Captain Orlov smiled. "Do not be concerned, gentlemen. The helicopter will return shortly. All of your belongings will be held for you until you are back in New York City. We have the same security precautions on *Volshebnik* as exist on the helicopter. Sergey should have told you that."

Ramirez and McAlister trailed behind Orlov as he took them on what felt like an endless trek. *Volshebnik* was as long as four football fields, and almost as wide as two, and once they were inside the gargantuan vessel, a labyrinth of metal corridors stretched in all directions. "I apologize that my ship doesn't have a conference room with luxurious appointments," said Orlov as he opened a door, "but this room is the quietest. The sound of the engines won't disturb you here." The three men entered a bare gray room which housed only a metal conference table and six folding chairs. "Mr. Bazhenov and Mr. Gao will join you momentarily. Please make yourselves comfortable," Orlov said as he left the room.

"I'm not getting a warm fuzzy feeling about this, are you?" asked Ramirez. Before McAlister could say anything, the room was filled with a crackling sound. It was only then that the two men noticed that there was a speakerphone on the table and that hanging on one of the walls opposite the table was a large television screen.

"We hope your journey wasn't too arduous," said Gao, whose image appeared on the right-hand side of the monitor.

"You've sampled my fleet by both sea and air today," said Bazhenov with a hearty laugh. His image appeared on the left-hand side of the television screen.

"We can see you both, of course," said Gao.

Ramirez' eyes were wild. McAlister stretched his neck from side to side as if he had just been punched in his face. "If you wanted to do a video call, we could have done it in New York. We didn't have to come all this way," said Ramirez, the strain in his voice revealing his anger.

Ignoring Ramirez' comment, Gao smiled coyly. "What a pleasure it is for Viktor and me to finally meet the famous Colum McAlister. Our partner."

"The pleasure is all mine, but I have to say that I am disappointed we're not meeting in person. Gunther and I certainly thought that was the plan."

"It really is fine. We are all here thanks to the miracle of technology," said Gao.

Bazhenov spoke up. "I have to ask you, Colum. How did you get the President of the United States to commute your sentence? He took a lot of shit over that in the press."

"Oh, come on, Viktor, you know the answer," said Gao. "Colum is a wizard. Gunther taught us that."

McAlister waved his right hand dismissively. "I paid a lot of money to the right people, the right way, at the right time. Nothing magical about that."

Gao's smile was as inscrutable as ever. "Well, gentlemen, let's get down to business. Is there anything either of you would like to tell us before we raise a few items?"

"I do have something important, but I'll hold it for the moment," said McAlister.

Gao massaged his nose before speaking. His words then were released with deliberation. "Colum, we know that you own the

Schlumberger cure and you licensed it to Schlumberger. You've made a colossal amount of money."

McAlister did a double-take. "Where did you get that from?"

"An unimpeachable source," replied Gao. McAlister turned and glared at Ramirez.

Bazhenov cleared his throat. "No, it wasn't Gunther. We, too, know how to pay money to the right people to get things done. A helpful person in the accounting department at Schlumberger told us that Schlumberger pays a very large licensing fee to an offshore company that was represented by a Swiss lawyer named Luca Muller at the Geneva law firm, Muller, Schmid, Graf & Frei. Mr. Muller is now deceased. You'll be gratified to know that he took his confidentiality obligations to you very seriously. Eventually, however, he identified you as the beneficial owner of the offshore company, and even said that you determined when the cure would be released to the public and what the drug would cost."

"Your point to all of this?" McAlister said calmly.

"The point is that you would have been one of the first people to know that the cure was starting to fail," said Gao.

"And you would have known this long before anything appeared in the media," said Bazhenov.

Gao's voice took on an edge as its volume increased. "You should have told us to liquidate our investments as soon as you knew the cure was failing, so we wouldn't get caught in the market panic."

Bazhenov's huge hand wrapped around the edge of the table at which he was seated. "But that didn't happen. And we know why," he said.

Gao's facial muscles tightened visibly. "Someone began to short Schlumberger stock and that of the five biggest manufacturers of the cure three weeks before the first negative media announcement.

That put huge pressure on our long positions and resulted in devastating margin calls. Those drug stocks were very strong before the media coverage, so only someone with inside information and huge financial resources would place that trade. You knew your licensing fees from Schlumberger would soon dry up and you found a way to capitalize on your drug's impending obsolescence."

Ramirez cocked his head and looked at McAlister skeptically.

McAlister smirked as he slowly clapped his hands. "My compliments to the writer. That's an interesting story, very creative. But it's not my story. I never had any direct communication with Schlumberger—even before I was in prison. I only dealt through my lawyer and once I was incarcerated, I didn't even deal with him. Gunther did all the communicating regarding the drug. I relied on him. He's my equal partner on everything." McAlister looked at Ramirez. Gao and Bazhenov did the same.

"Hey, hey, don't look at me," said Ramirez, holding up his right hand. "Maybe I should have paid more attention to what was happening with the drug itself, but I was only looking at revenues and they were soaring. That was my only concern. And I certainly never sold any stocks short. As I told you both at Viktor's house in Easthampton, we are your partners. We want you to do well. When you do well, we do well."

"But we haven't and you have," replied Gao.

"Now, wait a minute," said Ramirez, his voice rising. "I told you from day one that Colum and I had our own action and you were not a part of it. We discussed that in detail. You do remember that, don't you?"

"Yes, very clearly," replied Gao. "And you said that your side venture would benefit us. That isn't what happened is it?"

"It worked great for a long time. You and your investors were making more money than you could imagine. Don't blame us if you didn't take enough winnings off the table when you could have. You're the investment gurus. You're supposed to know how to protect yourselves and hedge your bets, not us."

Gao folded his hands. "But Colum was the sage, the oracle. The master of timing. You told us to rely on his counsel."

Bazhenov sprang up from behind his desk and because he was such a large man, his head and torso disappeared from the camera's view. His voice, now gruff and menacing, could still be heard coming from somewhere above his belt buckle. "You didn't have any skin in the game. We and our investors took all of the risk. The arrangement was flawed from the beginning."

McAlister paused before responding, and then in the honey smooth voice he had always used in delicate negotiations, he said, "Viktor, Huo Jin, please. Recriminations are not productive. I have some good news I want to share with you."

Ramirez chimed in, "I hinted about it when I met with you both at Viktor's house in the Hamptons."

McAlister inhaled deeply, puffing out his chest. Speaking slowly, he imbued his words with as much gravitas as he could muster. "I have enlisted Dr. Robert James Austin to find a cure to replace the Schlumberger one." McAlister smiled triumphantly.

Gao's lips pursed and he tipped his head almost imperceptibly. "It hardly seems possible that Dr. Austin would help the man who was convicted on thirty-one counts, all aimed at harming him."

McAlister's voice exuded confidence as he responded, "My enlistment of Dr. Austin was conducted anonymously, of course. I came into possession of the journal written by the scientist who created HRFS for Ansar Jamaat. That journal contained the exact formula for HRFS, complete with accompanying notes. I recently furnished this journal to Dr. Austin."

Bazhenov had sat back down so his face was visible again. "How the hell did you get your hands on that?" asked Bazhenov. A raised eyebrow was McAlister's only reply.

"Didn't Schlumberger or the CDC figure out the formula for HRFS already?" asked Gao.

"No, they didn't. They weren't able to. What I gave Austin is unique. I have no doubt that armed with this information he will be able to create a cure quickly."

"And how exactly does this help us?" asked Bazhenov.

"First, when the word gets out that Austin is working on a cure, that alone will calm people down. Nobody has credibility like him. And when he does find the cure, the markets will skyrocket because the HRFS nightmare will finally be over. You and your investors will be able to liquidate the investments profitably and our partnership will be over," said McAlister.

Ramirez and McAlister could see that Gao and Bazhenov were eyeing each other. Gao spoke up, "Give us a few minutes to confer." The screen went dead and the speakerphone emitted a thumping sound indicating that the microphones were off.

Ramirez pulled his chair close to McAlister. "Thanks for throwing me under the bus. That was great, partner."

"It was the smart thing to do. They aren't suspicious of you, but they are of me. Remember, they have no history with me. They've dealt with you for many years."

"What do you think they're talking about?" asked Ramirez.

"They're trying to decide if they should stick to their original plan, which was to dump us into the Atlantic Ocean today," said McAlister.

The speakerphone crackled once again and the television screen came back on. Bazhenov had now positioned himself too close to the camera so his face was distorted in a manner reminiscent of a fun house mirror. "Earlier in today's discussions I complained that you two had no skin in the game, and that was a fault in the arrangements between us from day one. Huo Jin and I have a plan to change that. Huo Jin will explain."

The beatific smile that appeared on Gao's face irritated McAlister. *This guy thinks he's so fucking superior to us. Condescending little shit. Ramirez should have disposed of him and Mr.* Volshebnik *as soon as they started to complain.*

Gao folded his hands and began to speak. "We are in agreement that if Dr. Austin cures HRFS, that would help us mightily. We applaud Colum's efforts to make this happen. *Volshebnik* is on its way to Lagos to pick up a shipment of crude oil. You will remain guests onboard for this trip. *Volshebnik* will arrive in Lagos in approximately twenty-eight days. Hopefully, by the time the ship arrives, there will be an announcement of a cure. If so, you will immediately be flown back to New York on Viktor's plane. If not—"

Ramirez interrupted, "If not, you'll have us killed, which was, no doubt, why you arranged today's meeting in the first place."

"Gunther, don't jump to conclusions. Viktor and I are not that simplistic. You and Colum may be aware that HRFS is rampant in Nigeria. For political reasons, those in power there have withheld the Schlumberger drug from large parts of the population ever since it became available. If Dr. Austin has not announced a cure by the time you arrive in Lagos, then we will make arrangements for you both to be infected with the most recent strain of HRFS. At that point, from my understanding, you will have approximately thirty more days to live while the world awaits a cure from Austin. We will ensure that you are among the first to get that cure, if there is one. All told, you will have almost two months from now for this to play out."

Bazhenov's fat face came into focus on the screen. "*Now* you have skin in the game."

# 113

MANUFACTURING AND DISTRIBUTION ARRANGEMENTS FOR Bobby's cure needed to be made quickly, because delays would cost lives. Bobby gave detailed instructions to Susan and she, in turn, requested Orin Varneys' help. Despite her and Bobby's feelings about Varneys, they knew that no one had the ability to make things happen like he did. A meeting was to be arranged within five days' time at which the following people would need to be present; no substitutes were permissible:

1. The CEOs of the fifty largest pharmaceutical manufacturers in the world
2. The heads of the twenty-four major disease control agencies in the world
3. Jonathan Bick, Attorney General of the United States
4. Clive Stone, the Director of United States Homeland Security
5. Hoon Kim, the Secretary General of the United Nations
6. United Nations Security Council representatives for the five permanent and ten non-permanent members

7.   Orin Varneys

8.   Robert Walterberg, Dean of Tufts University

The gathering would take place at a location in Boston that would be identified on the day of the meeting. While the attendees were not advised of the agenda, they were told that the meeting was of the greatest urgency and pertained to the HRFS crisis. To ensure that certain recalcitrant invitees would attend, Varneys asked the president to make some calls, which he did. For security reasons, Varneys insisted that the only attendees who would know that Bobby would be in attendance would be Bick and Walterberg. No media would be present or alerted to the fact that the meeting was taking place.

———————

On the day of the meeting, Bobby awoke at seven in the morning and sat on the edge of the bed staring at the floor. When Christina's alarm clock rang thirty minutes later, he was still sitting there. Christina moved across the bed and began to knead the stressed muscles in his shoulders. "What's wrong?" she asked.

"There's no turning back after today. Pandora's box will be open."

Christina brushed her lips against Bobby's right ear into which she whispered, "You have it wrong. Today's the day that you save the world."

Bobby turned his head and looked directly into Christina's eyes. She had never seen him appear as vulnerable as he did at that moment. "I hope so. I'm going to pray for that," he said as he squeezed her hand.

"What did you say?"

"I'm going to pray for that," replied Bobby.

"I never heard you say those words before."

## 114

A CARAVAN OF LIMOUSINES AND SUVs lined up on Sudbury Street, which was closed off to traffic so that it could serve as a high-security parking area for the JFK Federal Building, which was the venue for the meeting. After the attendees' credentials were checked and their cell phones and PDAs were handed over, they entered the building through a restricted-access back entrance, and were brought to the eighth floor via a service elevator operated by federal marshals. From there, more marshals ushered them into a cavernous room in which eight conference tables had been arranged so that one table was perpendicular to seven others, which were placed end-to-end. These eight tables would be sufficient to accommodate all of the attendees. The table that was perpendicular to the others was the head table at which Bobby would sit in the center, flanked by Dean Walterberg, Jonathan Bick and Susan.

Four marshals with seating charts directed each attendee to the correct seat, which was identified by a large place card so that everyone's identity would be readily visible. In front of each attendee was a sealed gray envelope, eleven by thirteen inches in size, on which the words, DO NOT OPEN UNTIL INSTRUCTED were stamped.

Susan walked into the anteroom in which Bobby was waiting with Christina. "Everyone's present and accounted for," she said. Bobby nodded. "Should I wait for you?" Susan asked.

"No, I'll be there in a minute," he replied.

Christina gave Bobby a hug and then brushed his jacket collar with her hand. "You look very handsome."

"Is it growing back? How are the bald spots?" he asked.

"Your hair is coming in nicely. You'll be as good as new soon. At least on the outside," she said as she playfully punched his arm.

Bobby shook his head. "I can't believe I have to go in there and see all those scumbags from the drug companies."

Christina took hold of his hands. "Remember, keep your cool. You invited them. You need their help to get the cure out quickly. If any of those Big Pharma guys say something that bothers you, let it go. Don't let them set you off."

Bobby walked to the door leading to the meeting room and opened it partially. Recalling what Christina had said to him that morning as they sat in bed, Bobby turned to her. "So, why don't I feel like I'm about to save the world?"

As Bobby made his way to his chair, some of the attendees in the audience took notice of the strikingly handsome, tall, thin man with high cheekbones, aquiline nose, piercing blue eyes and long auburn hair who was taking his place at the table. Sitting down between Johnathan Bick and Dean Walterberg, Bobby planted his left elbow on the table and rested his chin on his hand as he looked out at the audience pensively. After a few moments, Bick leaned in towards him. "Are you okay, Robert? You seem so somber. Today is a great day." Bobby massaged his temples and then took a deep breath. He tapped several times on the microphone that was sitting in front of him, and the loud thumps got peoples' attention. "Hello. I see that I don't have a place card. My name is Robert James Austin. Thank you for coming here on such short notice."

There was a rumbling commotion caused by the attendees' shock at Bobby's presence, but the room quickly quieted due to the solemnity of the occasion. Bobby felt the sting of one hundred hostile eyes boring into him. He knew that the fifty Big Pharma CEOs in attendance loathed him. The cures that he had invented over the years had rendered many of their companies' most profitable cash-cow treatment drugs obsolete and gutted countless billions of dollars of annual revenues from their coffers. While Colum McAlister's criminal trial and conviction had made him a symbol to the public of Big Pharma greed, many of the CEOs in attendance viewed him as a crusader for their industry who just went too far and made the mistake of getting caught. Bobby knew that what was going to happen today would not increase his popularity with them.

Bobby cleared his throat. "We have a lot to cover at this meeting, so please forgive me for getting straight into it. As you all know, the Schlumberger Foch treatment for HRFS is no longer viable. This disease is capable of decimating the world's population. We are here today to talk about next steps."

Bobby paused and bit his lower lip. He then pressed his right hand hard against the back of his neck in an effort to ease a muscle cramp that was worsening. "Sitting to my right is Dean Robert Walterberg of Tufts University. I want to thank him for the role that his medical school played in formulating and testing a new cure for HRFS, which is effective at all stages of the disease, and cannot be defeated by HRFS' propensity to mutate." Gasps could be heard in the audience. "If everyone in this room pulls together, there is no reason why this cure can't be ready for worldwide distribution within the next several weeks."

The room erupted into chaos, but people acted out in different ways. Some sprung up out of their seats. Others just sat in their chairs and looked dazed. Several began to cry in relief. As Bobby tried to bring the room to order, he was interrupted in his efforts by Dean Walterberg, who rapped the table repeatedly with his hand until the crowd settled down so he could be heard.

"I must interject before we continue. Dr. Austin is far too generous. The extraordinary achievement that we are here to discuss today occurred only because of him. It is solely the result of his unique genius, his tireless work and the personal risks that he took in devising this cure. I want that to be clear. Yes, my university played a role, but it was a highly subordinate one that was directed at every step by Dr. Austin."

Manfred Korman, the Director of the CDC, stood up and said, "This is remarkable news for which we all are incredibly thankful, but are you sure this drug works? What was the testing regime?"

Walterberg responded. "The regimen was thorough, both in the laboratory and on human subjects, the first of whom was Dr. Austin. He infected himself with HRFS on five separate occasions to test the cure at progressively advanced stages of the disease. It was only after his repeated success in treating himself that he permitted other human testing to take place. Hundreds of Tufts volunteers then infected themselves, and the efficacy rate was one hundred percent."

Silence engulfed the room as all eyes focused on Bobby. The Head of the World Health Organization was the first to stand, quickly followed by the Heads of AMRIID, CDC Europe, all of the other health agencies, the United Nations' Secretary General, and the fifteen Security Council members. As their applause reached a crescendo, decorum gave way and many in the distinguished group shouted accolades. After a few minutes, those standing turned their attention to the fifty drug czars who remained glued to their seats, until they too finally stood.

Jonathan Bick leaned closer to his microphone. "Ladies and gentlemen. There is an envelope in front of each of you which contains certain documents that I have prepared at Dr. Austin's specific request. Putting aside the legalese, I will summarize the documents. First, you will find an agreement for each CEO to sign, and for the heads of each disease agency to sign, which confirms that none of the pharmaceutical companies or agencies will seek, directly or indirectly, to reverse engineer, decompile, disassemble, or otherwise attempt to figure out the underlying technology of Dr. Austin's cure; additionally, the agreement provides that each manufacturer will produce and distribute the cure as its top priority on a completely gratis basis. There also is a robust confidentiality clause. The other document in the envelope is to be signed by the members of the U.N. Security Council, in which they agree to a resolution that mandates that all U.N. member nations distribute the cure free of charge to all persons living within their borders without exception, discrimination or delay. As you are aware, the Schlumberger cure was withheld from many in various countries for political reasons. This resolution is designed to ensure that this doesn't happen with Dr. Austin's cure."

Charles Farner, CEO of Kenderson Cooper Pharmaceuticals, shifted his obese body forward in his chair as he raised his hand. His voice was constrained by his heavy breathing. "I don't understand why we aren't free to delve into the underlying methodology of this cure. With all of Dr. Austin's prior cures, he published full analyses of his methods with the hope that those could be used by others to find further cures. Why is this different?"

Bobby leaned into his microphone. "This cure is not a drug or a medicine. Its underlying technology has the potential to be used in a destructive manner with devastating ramifications. There is nothing to be learned from what I invented. It needs to be left alone."

"Can you at least tell us something about the science behind the cure so that we understand how it works. It sounds revolutionary," said Farner.

"No, I can't. I'm sorry."

Anthony Bello, the CEO of Myer Bessel Laboratories, pushed his chair back abruptly as he stood. His greased black hair was combed straight back from his forehead, which only served to draw attention to his rodent-like eyes and the prominent mole on his particularly pointy nose. "Dr. Austin, your animosity to the pharmaceutical industry is well-known. While I applaud your accomplishment with this cure, I take exception to your trying to make our companies eat the cost of manufacturing and distributing it. Why should we be out of pocket? There likely will be tens of billions of pills that we will have to manufacture, maybe even hundreds of billions."

"Not true," said Bobby. "The entire treatment for each patient consists of only one pill. I think that the fifty drug companies in this room can handle that cost."

"Really. One pill? How can that be?" said Bello sarcastically. "Are you saying that even for an advanced case of HRFS, only one pill is required to cure the patient?"

"That's correct," replied Bobby. "Where the disease is in an advanced state in a patient, HRFS will be eradicated within four hours. It will be quicker for earlier stages of the disease. Of course, physical recuperation will take the normal amount of time, but the HRFS will be gone. It will be gone, as if it never existed." The clamor of excited voices became tumultuous as the words "one pill" and "four hours" reverberated through the room as they were repeated by the attendees.

Not finished, Bello stood up again. "Nevertheless, Doctor. We don't know what the cost of manufacture is for your miracle drug and with all due respect, it's not appropriate for you to put your hand in our pockets. Cost is a matter for governments and insurance companies to deal with."

Bobby's face reddened and his voice rose as he replied. "Your industry already made a fortune from HRFS. Millions of people who should have received the previous treatment didn't, in many cases because of what was charged by the companies represented in this room. I think the time has come for your industry to make a contribution, instead of a profit." Bick held up his hand, signaling Bobby to give him the floor.

Training his eyes on the cabal of CEOs, Bick said, "Tomorrow, an official press statement will be issued about Dr. Austin's cure, and the procedures which will be followed to guarantee its free and rapid distribution throughout the world. Those drug companies who do not agree to what is being proposed here today will be cited in that press release. At this historic moment, I trust that everyone in this room wants to be on the good side of the ledger."

Varneys nodded to Susan from the back of the room where he was standing with Christina. Susan then pulled her microphone close to her. "Ladies and gentlemen. Let's take a short break. We'll reconvene in twenty minutes."

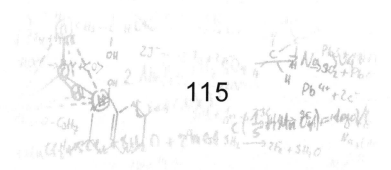

# 115

T HE INTERMISSION HAD BEEN PLANNED in advance by Varneys and Bick. It was "showtime" for them. Together they walked over to the several clusters of pharmaceutical company CEOs that had formed. Like predators who had identified their prey, Bick and Varneys moved in.

Bick maneuvered his six-foot-four-inch svelte frame among the CEOs. Some of them knew him personally and some didn't, but all were aware of his reputation as the unrelenting prosecutor who had sent Colum McAlister to prison for nineteen years, and now had the power to determine where the Justice Department aimed its guns. Addressing each CEO by name in his patrician Boston drawl, Bick shook hands and patted backs like a consummate politician. His message left nothing to conjecture. "I know I can count on you today. We're all on the same team, aren't we?"

Orin Varneys was known by all of the CEOs, whose multinational companies had the occasional interaction with the CIA, whether desired or not. As he navigated among them, his delivery was not as polished as Bick's and certainly less subtle, but equally effective. "We're not going to have any problems today, correct?"

Susan tapped her microphone several times. "Ladies and gentlemen. Please take your seats so that we can continue our meeting. In your envelopes, you will find the agreements that are pertinent to each of you. Please take a few minutes to read them."

Varneys slowly walked toward the head table as he scanned the crowd with his dark dead eyes. Now standing next to Susan, he whispered into her ear. A moment later, she said, "The original plan was for me to do a roll call of each attendee and ask if he or she is ready to sign the relevant documents. In order to avoid that laborious process, I ask that any attendee who is not willing to sign should please stand now, identify himself or herself, and articulate the problem so that the members of the organizing panel can address those concerns."

Susan waited for a full minute but nobody stood. The room was filled with the sound of papers being shuffled and stuffed into envelopes. Before the meeting was adjourned, the marshals confirmed that they had collected signed agreements from all attendees.

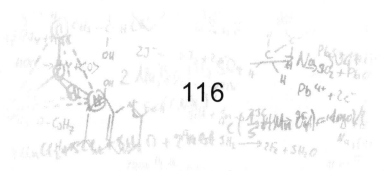

# 116

FIVE DAYS AFTER THE MEETING at the JFK Federal Building, a black Chevrolet Suburban pulled up to the gates of Wheatleigh. The driver showed his identification card and was waved through. Arriving at the front of the house, he and two other agents exited the vehicle, opened the back doors and the tailgate and proceeded to unload eighteen large boxes. The lead agent entered the reception area and asked for Susan.

"Hello, Ms. Ryder. I have a delivery for Dr. Austin from Director Varneys. My orders are to deliver it directly to him."

"What is it?" she asked.

"I don't know, but it fills eighteen heavy boxes."

"Give me a minute," she said.

Susan knocked on the door of Bobby's office and then entered. Bobby had pulled his desk chair up to the windows that faced the ocean and was sitting staring out at the sea. "There's a delivery for you from Varneys. I have no idea what it is, but his guys are under strict orders to give it to you personally. Can I have them bring it in?" asked Susan. When Bobby didn't answer, Susan walked over to him and tapped him on his shoulder. When she still was not acknowledged, she leaned over Bobby and saw that his eyes were half-closed and unfocused. He wasn't present. Susan gave his right shoulder a gentle shake, and then did it again, harder. Abruptly dislodged from one of his trances, Bobby almost jumped out of his seat. "Are you okay?" Susan asked.

"Yes. I was just thinking. What's up?"

"There's a delivery for you from Varneys. I don't know what it is, but his people are under orders to give it to you personally. Can they bring it in?" Bobby nodded.

It took the agents fifteen minutes and a lot of huffing and puffing to bring all of the boxes into Bobby's office. Varneys had instructed them not to stack the boxes but to lay them down individually so that they could be easily opened. Just before leaving, the head agent handed Susan a sealed envelope and said, "Please give this to Dr. Austin after all of the boxes have been opened."

When the agents departed, Susan and Bobby looked at the lines of boxes. "Well, I don't hear any ticking," she said.

"Any chance this is a liquor delivery? I *am* running low," said Bobby.

Susan proceeded to cut the tape on one of the boxes. It was filled with newspapers. She opened another box. More newspapers. She opened them all. Every box was filled to the brim with newspapers. She began to pull the stacks of papers out of the boxes and scatter them on the floor. Newspapers from all over the world, in dozens of languages. By looking at the ones from the United States, France, Spain, England, Italy and Brazil, it became apparent that the front-page headlines of all of the world's newspapers were almost identical, as they proclaimed in the biggest and boldest letters that their formats would accommodate:

**WE ARE SAVED**

**AUSTIN'S ONE-PILL MIRACLE**

**RJA'S CURE FREE FOR EVERYONE**

**HRFS NIGHTMARE OVER**

**AUSTIN INFECTED HIMSELF**

**OUR PRAYERS ANSWERED**

**MIRACLE FROM MIRACLE MAN**

Standing in the midst of more than one thousand newspapers, Susan handed Bobby the envelope the agent had given her. He opened it to find a handwritten note from Orin Varneys which read:

*Robert—*

*The world's newspapers never hailed the inventor of the atom bomb as a savior. You are not Oppenheimer.*

*—Orin Varneys*

## 117

THE WAITING PERIOD FOR PEOPLE already infected with HRFS was excruciating. They had to try to stay alive until Bobby's cure became available. The Schlumberger drug had become almost completely ineffectual, and it was now administered in staggeringly large dosages in a last ditch effort to have it do *something*. The idea was to try to slow down the progression of the disease until Bobby's pill was on hand. In the final days, the dose of the Schlumberger treatment was increased to twenty-six times what the original had been.

Never before had the full force of governments, disease agencies, the United Nations and pharmaceutical companies worked so effectively together. This was a race against time to keep as many people from dying as possible. When the drug companies began to manufacture Bobby's cure, there were more than nine hundred million, six hundred twenty thousand people throughout the world known to have been infected with HRFS, and millions of new cases were reported every day. Without Bobby's pill, every one of those people would die. HRFS was an extraordinarily effective killer, and with each mutation, it became that much better at annihilating human beings.

Bobby was intent on ensuring that his cure would be immediately available to everyone, including the most underprivileged and underserved. He had a standing call every day at noon with the United Nations Secretary General to review the availability of his pill throughout those areas where he suspected there would be foul play: parts of Latin America, Asia and Africa. But that wasn't enough for him. He arranged a meeting with Orin Varneys at Wheatleigh.

"Orin, we've had our differences, to say the least, but I have to acknowledge that you have great talents in certain areas."

"As do you, Robert."

"I know it's not in your job description, and you have a lot on your plate, but I would personally appreciate if you would help me with one thing."

"And what is that?"

"It's very important to me to know that my cure will be distributed quickly at no charge, and with no exclusions or corruption, everywhere. While I have some confidence that this will happen in many countries, I'm very concerned about certain others. I know what happened with the Schlumberger treatment, and I can't have that happen again."

"We pushed through the U.N. resolution. What you want is mandatory throughout the world. The secretary is on the case."

"But you can ascertain what's really going on at the street level. I'm asking you to not only be my eyes and ears—but to make this happen. I know that you have your ways, more so than the secretary or, for that matter, the president. I have enough reservations about the technology I created, but at least I need to know that my cure is there for everyone, the way it's supposed to be."

Varneys nodded his agreement. "Unlike you, I can't perform miracles, but I do know how to twist a few arms. I'll do my best."

Varneys rose from his chair to leave, but then he sank back down. For a few moments he was silent, drumming the fingers of his right hand on his knee. Finally, he said, "I don't know when we'll next see each other." Varneys paused and glanced down at the floor. He then looked up and locked eyes with Bobby. "Robert, there's something I need you to understand, no matter how difficult it may be for you. I did not create those videos. They're real. As you decide how you are going to deal with the problem of your GCN technology—you need to accept that there is a side of you that is very dark. A side of you that you do not control. A side of you that serves a force, whether internal or external, that is antithetical to everything you have devoted your life to. If you don't come to grips with this, then how are you going to slay the dragon you created?"

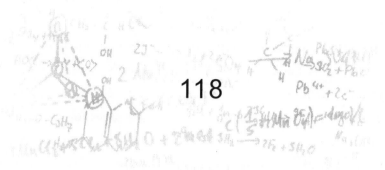

## 118

A S THE ROLLOUT OF BOBBY'S cure got underway, the results were immediately astounding. Just as Bobby had promised, within hours of patients taking the pill, blood samples showed no signs of HRFS, not even remnants. It was gone—as if by magic. It didn't matter if the patients had contracted HRFS one day ago, or if they were in the most advanced stage of the disease. It was gone.

Articles in medical journals expressed disbelief that any cure could work so completely and so quickly. How could a dosage of just one pill cure a complex ever-evolving disease that had been well on its way to obliterating human life on planet Earth? What everyone wanted to know was why Bobby had kept the methodology to this cure a secret. The explanation that he gave fell on deaf ears. Even the Nobel Prize Committee, upon awarding him the prize for medicine, expressed disappointment that he had not elucidated the scientific underpinnings of the cure. The committee, in uncharacteristically critical language, indicated that had Bobby done so, he likely would have been awarded several additional Nobel Prizes in other scientific disciplines for the breakthrough discoveries that he had no doubt made in connection with the HRFS cure.

For the first time in a career during which he had won fourteen previous Nobel Prizes (including the three that he had recently been awarded for his AIDS cure and related scientific breakthroughs), Bobby declined to accept a Nobel for inventing the HRFS cure. While he didn't give a reason to the committee, Susan and Christina knew that it was because of his apprehensions about the genetic technology that he had invented.

An urgent mandate rippled through the worldwide scientific community to figure out exactly how the cure worked. There was a rush to unlock its miracle technology, despite the warnings that Bobby had issued. Some of this was just academic curiosity, but many expressed the view that if the methodology could be adapted to other diseases, medical science would be immeasurably advanced. The dawn of a new age was predicted.

Of course, this was exactly what Bobby had feared all along. He wasn't so naïve as to believe that the agreements the drug companies and the disease agencies signed at the JFK Federal Building would be honored indefinitely. He also was certain that his work would be hacked by militarists and that this would eventually lead to it being weaponized. Pandora's box was open.

As the worldwide scientific community mobilized its resources to deconstruct Bobby's invention, he fell into a deep depression. Convinced that he had become an instrument of darkness, unwittingly laying the foundation for the destruction of humanity, Bobby spent his days sitting on a lawn chair at the edge of the peninsula's furthermost cliff, staring vacantly at the water.

---

"You mind if I join you?" asked Orin Varneys, who didn't wait for a response as he pulled a chair over and sat next to Bobby. "I was in Boston and I thought I'd stop by and see how you're doing."

Bobby was unresponsive.

"I just want to tell you that you did the right thing, Robert. You saved a huge number of lives. This is your greatest accomplishment."

Bobby continued to stare at the ocean, his eyes squinting, running his tongue over his dry lips, like an old man.

"Look, I know what you're afraid of," said Varneys. "You think you created the doomsday weapon. But that's what the scientists who created the A-bomb thought. Now how long has that been around? We're still here, aren't we? What I'm saying is—don't assume the worst will happen."

Bobby looked at Varneys with dull eyes. "It takes a lot of bombs to destroy humanity. But with weaponized GCN, all it will take is one lunatic and one dispersion—and there's no turning back. GCN is the recipe for an extinction event. The negation of human DNA. The erasure of the human species. And as you've seen in the news, there's a race going on in the scientific community to discover how GCN works. They're ignoring my admonitions. Like kids playing with a loaded gun."

Varneys stood up, faced Bobby and put a hand on Bobby's shoulder. He winced when he felt how thin Bobby had gotten. "Robert, I have faith in you. You will find a way to control what you created. At this moment, that may seem impossible, but it won't always be. But right now, you need to clear your mind and build up your health."

---

Fearing that Bobby's withdrawal from the present would accelerate, Christina knew that a change in environment was desperately needed.

As Bobby pushed his food around his plate at dinner, she said,

"You, me and the kids are leaving for Islamorada the day after tomorrow. It's all been arranged. We're staying with Alan at his house."

Bobby did a double take as a smile lit up his face, the first smile Christina had seen on him in many weeks. "Really? Is Alan okay with that? Are you sure? I don't think he's used to having an entire family as house guests."

Holding up her hands to accentuate her enthusiasm, she said, "Are you kidding? He's ecstatic. He's buying twenty pounds of charcoal for the grill, and filling his freezer with hot dogs, ribs and shrimp. He said he can't wait to take the kids fishing."

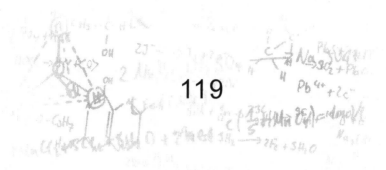

# 119

"**W**HY ARE YOU OPENING THE shades? The sun is killing my eyes."

"Stop complaining," said Ramirez as he looked out the windows of McAlister's Tribeca apartment. "Ever since we got back from Nigeria, it's been one complaint after another. Be happy. We could be dead."

The sclera of his eyes still yellow, Colum McAlister scowled as he examined his pocked skin in a mirror and turned from side to side to assess how much hair remained on his head. "That was too damned close for my taste."

Ramirez' eyebrows arched upwards. "But Gao and Bazhenov kept their promise. I don't think anyone got Austin's cure before us. They must have had the first two pills plucked off the conveyer belt. That's what I call *well connected*."

"Of course, they're well connected. They're fucking billionaires who own millions of shares of drug companies' stock." McAlister raised his chin as he examined his neck. "Even my neck is marked from those pustules. I look ten years older than when we boarded that goddamn tanker." McAlister fell silent for a few moments and then took a deep breath. "If you think this is over between them and us, you're wrong."

"Let it go, Colum. We made a lot of money, and so did they. Mission accomplished."

"Maybe that's your view of the world, but it's not mine. There's no way I'm going to let them get away with what they did to us. It was a miracle that Austin came up with the cure in time. As far as Gao and Bazhenov were concerned, they condemned us to a gruesome death. That doesn't go unpunished in my book."

Ramirez walked to the window and stared pensively at the traffic below. "In my experience, vindictiveness is counterproductive. Look at your life. You were vindictive against Austin when you were CEO of Bushings, and it cost you your job, your reputation, your marriage, a lot of money—and it landed you in prison with a nineteen-year sentence. Then not long ago, you wanted to relaunch your efforts to kill him. If I hadn't stopped you and you succeeded, Austin wouldn't have been alive to invent the cure that saved us in Nigeria." Ramirez' eyes burned into McAlister. "Do you get my point?"

McAlister broke eye contact with Ramirez and then took a deep breath before he said, "Let's put a pin in that subject for the moment. What's more interesting is that a tremendous opportunity has just been laid at our feet, funnily enough by Austin, so maybe you're right."

"What opportunity?"

"The genetic technology that he created. It's the biggest invention since the internet. It will revolutionize the pharmaceutical industry, but that's just the tip of the iceberg. Whoever cracks Austin's code first and figures out how to manipulate it, holds all the cards. Austin knows this. That's why he wants to keep it a secret. There's no better place for us to put our resources to work."

Ramirez smiled. "You don't miss a beat, do you?"

"We're going to have to spend a lot of money. Are you in?"

"I'm surprised you thought you had to ask," replied Ramirez.

# 120

A LOOK OF CONCERN CAME OVER Pete's face. "Dad, how do we get from the plane to the beach," he asked as the pontoon plane which took the Austin family from Miami to the Florida Keys landed in shallow water thirty feet off shore from Alan's Islamorada cottage.

"We're going to walk," replied Bobby.

"Are there sharks?"

"No, Pete."

"Jellyfish?" Bobby shook his head.

"Crabs?"

Bobby tussled his son's sandy-blonde hair. "We are two fearless men. You and me. Do I look worried?" Bobby asked as he disembarked the plane, jumping into the warm ocean water, which only came up to his knees.

As they all waded ashore, greetings were shouted to Alan Gottshalk who stood on the beach, his long, tan, bony legs extending from faded plaid cargo shorts. Alan was now eighty-two years old. Spry as ever, he still manned the Conch Shack as cook, order taker and fisherman six days a week. He lived alone in his small beach house on Islamorada, and never forgot how his life had been transformed five decades earlier when he walked down a deserted rainy street in Chicago searching for food in dumpsters, and found a newborn in a garbage bag among the refuse.

"Bobby, why do you look older every time I see you, but Christina just gets more beautiful?" asked Alan.

"She has better genes than me," quipped Bobby as he hugged Alan and patted his back. "It's so good to see you. I can't tell you how good it feels."

"Look at these kids of yours," said Alan. "Damn, they've grown. They're getting older, but thank God I'm not." Alan spread his arms and motioned to Pete who came in for a hug. "How old is my favorite pianist?"

"Twelve," said Pete.

"I still remember the first time you played Bach for me when you were three."

"Let me help you with that," Alan said as he walked over to Mirielle who had a heavy-looking duffel bag slung over her shoulder. "And you look more and more like your mother every time I see you, except for that gorgeous auburn hair of yours that reminds me of—"

Mirielle stood on her toes and planted a kiss on Alan's cheek. "I know. You say it every time. My hair reminds you of my dad. It's great to see you, Uncle Alan."

Alan hugged Mirielle and kissed her on the top of her head. "You're nine now, right? I better not have missed a birthday."

Alan's face was weathered, more from years of too much sun than age, but his eyes sparkled with vigor and reflected the love that he felt for the family that stood in front of him. As they walked toward the house, Alan said to Bobby, "From what I've seen on TV, it looks like you've been pretty darn busy."

Bobby stopped walking and held his face up to the sun until the golden rays forced his eyes shut. Inhaling deeply, the warm breeze filled his nostrils with the fragrance of warm sea air and bougainvillea. "I forgot how peaceful it is here. A different world from what I'm used to."

"We'll talk about your lifestyle later. Maybe this time you'll listen to me," said Alan.

As they continued toward the house, Alan's mind flashed back to a newborn that he had cradled in his arms when he was living in a rambling homeless community that the media cynically dubbed Riverview Estates. Through all the decades during which he and Bobby had been separated, his memory of the stunning blue eyes of the infant he called "Little Fella" had never faded. Today, Alan saw a sadness in those eyes that he had never seen before.

"Thank you for letting us come here, Alan. Once again, you are a lifesaver," said Bobby.

The next few days couldn't have been more perfect. Pete and Mirielle romped in the ocean with Christina, while Bobby basked in the sun, so happy to have a respite from worry. Alan kept up a steady stream of ice-cold freshly squeezed lemonade and his special rum, vodka, Cointreau and pineapple juice concoction that he called the "Got Shock" cocktail, which tasted harmless, but was so strong its effect was almost hallucinogenic. After a few drinks, Bobby would lie on the sand, his head resting on a folded arm, his eyes focused on the grains directly in front of him, tiny kernels of glossy quartz intermixed with broken shell fragments and the occasional long strand of dried black seaweed. At this angle of vision, the sand and the ocean formed a continuum, with virtually no break between them, and the muffled sound of the waves lulled him to sleep.

"Hey, lazy bones, get up and come into the water. It's warm!" yelled Christina.

"Yeah. Come on in, Dad," said Mirielle.

Sitting up, Bobby watched his family frolic in the surf. "I am such a lucky man," he said to Alan, who was nestled in a lounge chair next to him, beer in hand. "I shouldn't even be alive. Three times I almost died—and that's just the three I know about. Look at my kids. Look at my brilliant, gorgeous wife. I am blessed."

"You are blessed, Bobby. Now get in that water with your family while I get lunch going."

The grill was the instrument that Alan played and he was a virtuoso. Something delectable was always in process: lobsters, shrimp, oyster fritters, ribs, hot dogs and corn on the cob that dripped with melted butter. Everyone stuffed themselves and made no apologies for it. Bobby loved the rustic simplicity in which Alan lived. The house was small and sparsely decorated, but the sun filled its rooms throughout the day. Alan rarely used the air-conditioners, and instead kept the windows open for the sea breeze. A profusion of fragrant flowers imbued the air was a soft sensuousness, and a large vegetable garden served up a fresh supply of carrots, tomatoes, broccoli, beets and squash.

One morning at breakfast, Alan gave Pete and Mirielle aprons emblazoned with the Conch Shack logo and plopped logo baseball caps on their heads. "You guys are coming with me today to the Conch Shack to help in the kitchen and take food orders from the customers. The kids beamed. As the three walked out the door, Alan said to Bobby and Christina, "Now you two can have some alone time."

# 121

"**L**ET'S TAKE A SWIM," SAID Bobby.

"You think you can keep up with me?" asked Christina.

"Of course not," he replied.

They swam about a hundred yards from shore and then flipped over on their backs and floated next to each other. "This is so incredibly beautiful," said Bobby.

"Remind you of something?" asked Christina.

"Bolongo Beach in St. Thomas. Our first date," said Bobby.

"I wouldn't call it a date. You were stalking me and tracked me down at my hotel. You lied to me about who you were."

"That makes it sound so unromantic. I like my version better," said Bobby.

"Well, you certainly were persistent. I have to give you that."

"I didn't have a choice. I knew I couldn't lose you."

"Oh, did you, Dr. Austin?" said Christina, chuckling as she righted herself and began to swim closer to shore. Bobby caught up to her in water that was too deep for her to stand, but fine for him. He placed his hands under her hips and pulled her close. Christina's arms encircled Bobby's back as she wrapped her legs around his waist and leaned into him, resting her head on his shoulder. Bobby pressed his face against her neck and breathed in deeply. He loved the smell of Christina's skin as the saltwater evaporated on it, intermixing with the coconut oil in her suntan lotion. Even through the water, he could feel the heat of her body as her breasts pushed against his chest. Holding her in this position, Bobby began to slowly walk through the surf parallel to the beach, the buoyant sea adding a soft bounce to his steps. For the first time in a very long time, he was fully present in the moment. His mind was quiet. There were no distractions and no worries. The only thing he felt was grateful. As the warm ocean currents massaged their bodies, and the sun bathed their faces in its radiance, there was nothing that needed to be said.

Once back on shore, they spread several beach towels on the sand and lay next to each other, face to face. "I'm sorry I put you through so much all the time. I'm a lousy husband."

Christina moved closer to him. "When you love someone, you take the person as they are in their entirety." She gently rubbed her lips against his and bit his lower lip playfully. "I don't think I'm going to trade you in quite yet."

Bobby pulled back slightly. "There's something we have to talk about," he said.

Christina placed her forefinger across his mouth. "Not now." Without breaking eye contact, Christina maneuvered her body over his and pulled a large beach blanket over them. "Just go with me," she whispered as her lips brushed his right ear.

## 122

"OKAY, BOBBY, TODAY IT'S YOUR turn to help. You and me are going crabbin'. The Conch Shack needs a fresh supply, and the kids aren't keen on catching things with claws."

Bobby laughed. "We don't have to do that sober, right?"

"If sobriety were a prerequisite for crabbin', I would have sold the Shack twenty years ago. All we got to do is get in my boat, empty the traps and lay new bait."

"I think even *I* can do that," said Bobby.

As Alan filled up a cooler with ice and a twelve pack of beer, he said, "With a little bit of luck, I'll get you home with all your fingers intact."

———— •••• ————

Alan's twenty-foot boat, *The Foundling,* had seen better days, and with a weathered fiberglass hull, now yellowed with age, it was an eyesore in comparison to the sleek yachts and state of the art sports fishing boats that plied Islamorada's waters. As *The Foundling* rode the wake of a boat three times its size, Alan pointed to the luxurious vessels around them and said, "I've been fishing here before these guys even knew Islamorada existed. When I settled here, Islamorada was a pit stop on the way to Key West. There was one gas station, one motel that rented rooms by the half-hour, and one decrepit marina, with a handful of slips. That was it. That's how I bought my house and the Conch Shack land so cheap. Who knew that it would become 'The Sport Fishing Capital of the World'?"

Bobby laughed. "So now you're a real estate visionary."

"Believe me. A day doesn't go by that I don't thank God for what I have. You know what my life was once like," said Alan. Bobby nodded as he opened the ice chest and pulled out two beers and handed one to Alan. "Let me cut the engines so we can sit down and enjoy these before we get to the serious business of crabbin'," said Alan as a smile crossed his face. "You know, I read an article that said that if prohibition had continued in the United States, the recreational boat industry would have been dead in the water. No pun intended." Beer in hand, Alan took a seat on the back lounge and motioned for Bobby to join him. After a long pull on his beer, he said, "So, how are you doing, Bobby? I didn't like the look in your eyes when you arrived the other day."

Bobby turned his head and focused on the ripples in the water which caught the sunlight in a particularly beautiful way. Taking a swig of his beer, he replied, "Actually, not that great."

"You must be exhausted. You went straight from the AIDS cure into HRFS, and you infected yourself like a guinea pig."

"It's not just that. I recently found out something about myself that's disturbing," said Bobby.

"So? Big deal? You like to drink. You're under a lot of pressure. It obviously doesn't interfere."

"It's not that. I wish it was," replied Bobby.

"Okay. So you're on the computer eighteen hours a day and you need some distraction from your work, so you look at porn. Big deal. The whole world does it. That doesn't mean you don't love your wife. It's just human nature."

Bobby shook his head. "I'm actually not into porn."

"Well, whatever. It can't be that bad. How bad can it be?" asked Alan.

"I blew up my own lab."

"Holy shit."

"Well, I'm not absolutely positive about it. But it appears that there may be an alternate side to my personality that I wasn't aware of. It's a dark, destructive side. I have no control over it. No awareness of when it takes over. It might be lurking all the time. I don't know."

Alan smirked. "Who put that cockamamie idea in your head? Dark side? What a load of horse shit. You're a saint. There's never been anyone like you. If everyone had a dark side like yours, this world would be unrecognizable. So where did this crazy idea come from?"

"The director of the CIA. A guy named Orin Varneys."

Alan began laughing so hard that he choked on his beer. "Are you kidding me? Those CIA guys are the biggest liars and manipulators in the world. If they gave me a buck, I'd assume it's counterfeit. Anything he told you, forget it. It's bullshit. You know who you are."

"That's exactly what I thought. Varneys showed me videos of me building bombs and destroying my computer records. I told him they were fake, but now I'm not so sure."

Alan got up and walked to the cooler, took another beer, and then sat down close to Bobby. "Let me tell you something. This guy Varneys could use those abracadabra high-tech digital effects to create a video that makes it look like I'm having sex with the president's wife. They can do anything. I'm telling you, it's all crap. Forget it."

Bobby nodded and downed the rest of his beer. "You don't happen to have any scotch that I can use as a chaser for this stuff, do you?" he asked. Alan shook his head as Bobby continued. "I never trusted Varneys, but there's something about the way he told me that the videos were real, that got me thinking."

A vein on Alan's temple swelled up as his voice began to rise. "I'll tell you what you should be thinking about. It's what I've been saying for years. It's time to retire. You've been under too much pressure for too long. Too much weight on your shoulders. Too much responsibility. Too many hours working. Nobody can take that. It's a wonder that you're not totally nuts. Move down here with Christina and the kids. Get off the treadmill. You've done a thousand times your share. I'll find you a house nearby. Stop while you can, Bobby."

Bobby inhaled deeply and then bit his lip. "It's not that simple. The way I cured HRFS was with a new genetic technology that I invented. It's extremely dangerous. No one except me knows how it works, but eventually they'll figure it out. When they do, that will be the first step to it being weaponized. I have to find a way to neutralize the technology, neutralize the genetic reaction. If I don't, I'll leave the world worse than I found it."

"Then do it. And that will be the last thing you do," said Alan.

"I've been trying, but I don't see any way."

"If anyone can do it, you can."

Bobby turned away and stared at the sea for a moment. When he faced Alan again, his eyes were watery. "I don't know if I can be trusted to do it."

"What do you mean?" asked Alan.

"The other in me. The other may not let me."

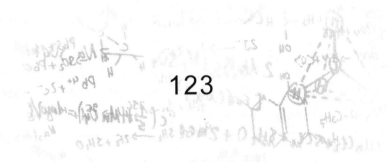

# 123

P ETE, ALAN, CHRISTINA AND BOBBY were planted in front of the television in Alan's living room watching *A Shot in the Dark*, the classic Peter Sellers comedy. As they all were enjoying Inspector Clouseau's crazy antics, Mirielle called out from the far side of the living room, "Guys, can you please lower the volume, I'm trying to concentrate." Every night after dinner, Mirielle would sit down at a small desk that was tucked into a corner of the living room, and she would spend several hours engrossed in the materials she had brought with her.

"What are you reading, Mirielle?" asked Christina.

"*The New England Journal of Medicine.* What Dad wrote about the Sentry Virus."

"You mean, the four volumes?" asked Christina. "Each one is over three hundred pages."

"Yes. I'm in volume three now."

Christina got up from the sofa, walked over to Mirielle and looked at the stack of thick tomes. They contained the mathematical formulas, scientific equations and lab proofs that established the veracity of Bobby's groundbreaking work in curing malaria and numerous other vector transmitted diseases that preyed upon the most economically disadvantaged people in the world. "I haven't seen these in years. So that's what you had in your duffel. Where did you get them?"

"Dad gave them to me."

"When?"

"Right before we came down here."

"And you're in volume three already?"

"Yup. Almost done."

# 124

O N ONE OF THE LAST nights of their Islamorada vacation, Christina and Bobby planned a dinner for two at Pierre's on Morada Bay. Set amidst a palm-lined beach, the white two-story plantation house was exotic in its architectural eclecticism, as were many buildings in the Florida Keys, combining Victorian and Queen Anne elements with West African colonial features.

As the maître d' showed them to their table on the expansive veranda, the flickering gaslight from numerous hanging Moroccan lamps created ever-changing geometrical patterns on the ceiling that cast seductive shadows on the diners. Votive candles on each table lightly perfumed the air with the scent of rose petals, peonies and oud. Christina and Bobby took their seats, side by side, on a pillow strewn banquette facing the water. As Bobby put his arm around Christina's waist, they looked out at the thousands of glimmering lights that hung like fallen stars from the riggings of boats anchored in the bay.

"Can I get you some drinks to start?" asked the waiter.

"A bourbon on the rocks with a Coke back. Blanton's if you have it," replied Christina.

"A Bombay Sapphire martini, very dry, straight up, olives, please," said Bobby.

When the drinks arrived, Bobby consumed half of his quickly. He motioned for another. As Christina sipped her cocktail, she leaned in towards him provocatively. It took only seconds for Bobby's focus to lower from her eyes to her décolletage. "Got ya," she said laughing. "So much for your famous powers of concentration."

Bobby smiled. "A man has to have his priorities. You smell amazing, by the way."

Christina whispered, "I'm not wearing any perfume. That's just me."

"Really?"

"Of course not," said Christina as she ran her forefinger along his lips. Her voice took on a sultry tone. "The other day on the beach couldn't have been more perfect."

"I wish we had more days like that. We never seem to have the time." Bobby rested his hand on Christina's thigh and gave a gentle squeeze. "I don't say it often enough. I hope you know how much I love you."

"I know," said Christina as her glimmering emerald eyes met Bobby's. Just as Bobby was about to kiss her, the waiter appeared with Bobby's second drink.

"So, what did you want to tell me? A few times now, you mentioned there was something on your mind," said Christina.

Quickly downing the rest of his first martini, Bobby said, "Do you remember when I told you that I asked Varneys to help ensure that the HRFS cure got distributed everywhere, free of charge?"

"Yes, and you said that he agreed."

"Yeah. And he did a really good job," replied Bobby.

"No one ever said he wasn't efficient."

"Well, at that meeting, just before he left, he said something to me that I've been thinking a lot about." Christina looked at Bobby quizzically. "He told me that the videos weren't fake, that he didn't create them, and that I should keep that in mind as I try to find a way to neutralize the GCN technology."

Christina looked down at her drink and slowly stirred its ice with her swizzle stick for several rotations before raising her head. "But you were adamant that Varneys created the videos."

"I know. But I just don't see why he would bring them up again. He doesn't have the videos anymore, I have them. So he has nothing to protect. His effort to use them to blackmail me failed. So why would he raise the subject when he knows it's a huge sore point between us?"

"Maybe he doesn't want you to think he's a treacherous scoundrel—so you'll trust him in the future?"

Bobby shook his head. "There was something about the way he said it to me. The look in his eyes when he said it. Almost like he wished the videos *were* fake."

"So... What are you thinking?"

Bobby leaned in towards Christina. When he spoke, his voice was soft, almost conspiratorial in tone. "I was talking to Alan about this when we were on his boat. I think I have to consider the possibility that something destructive, something negative that I have no control of, has wormed its way into me. I'm not buying Uhlman's psychology 101 theories, but for my whole life, the force has tried to stop me. Maybe it found a way to get into me, like an infection. An infection that lies dormant until it flairs up when the force wants it to. And when it does, I have no awareness that it has taken over."

"And when would that be?" asked Christina.

"When I get too close to doing something that it doesn't want me to do. Like when I got too close to finding the AIDS cure, it wanted my lab destroyed."

Christina's eyes lost their light. Taking a long swig of her drink, her body posture became rigid. "I was hoping we were going to have a romantic dinner tonight. I guess that's out the window."

"I'm sorry. I shouldn't have said anything."

"What are you driving at, Bobby?"

Bobby lowered his voice to almost a whisper. "It didn't try to stop me from curing HRFS because it wanted me to invent GCN. That was more valuable to it. Now It's going to do everything it can to prevent me from finding a way to neutralize the GCN technology."

Christina's face was deadpan. "You're saying it will try to kill you?"

"It doesn't have to. If it has embedded itself in me, that could be all it needs to keep me from being effective."

"What do you mean?"

"I always blamed myself for not finding an HRFS cure that didn't involve a radical technology. I told myself that I couldn't come up with anything else in the time frame I had to work in. But maybe it's not that simple. Maybe other ideas were stymied within me, sabotaged internally by something that I couldn't control—that I wasn't even aware was there. Something evil that was put in me."

"Put in you? Something that was put in you? Really?" Christina stared down at her empty cocktail glass.

The muscles in Bobby's face tightened. "Why does that sound strange to you? Where do you think my intellect came from? There's no rational or logical explanation. It was God-given, Christina. What I am saying now is just the flip-side of that, the reciprocal."

Christina took a deep breath. "Bobby, I'm not following what all this means and where it's going."

Bobby's eyes focused in on Christina with an intensity that she found unsettling. His words were annunciated with slow deliberation. "It means that there is something dangerous, something evil in me that I can't control. It may not let me do what needs to be done."

When Christina heard this, she physically recoiled. She didn't realize that her eyes had closed until she had to make a herculean effort to open them. She then looked down at her dinner napkin, slowly lifted it and patted her lips robotically. "Excuse me," she said as she pushed the table to the side so she could leave.

The other women in the restroom had no reason to suspect that the smartly-dressed lady bent over the sink hyperventilating was dealing with a personal crisis that could have ramifications for billions of people. Her hands trembling, Christina pulled a thick wad of paper towels from the restroom dispenser and soaked them with cold water. Leaning over the sink, she pressed the compresses against her eyes as she inhaled deeply, held her breath for ten seconds and then slowly exhaled. She did this repeatedly for several minutes, and then placed one of the cold compresses on the back of her neck and one on her mouth.

Christina heard a soft voice. "Are you okay, sweetie?" A gentle hand rested on the back of her shoulder. "You seem to be having a hard time." Her face still at sink level, Christina turned to see who it was: a blonde-haired woman, mid-thirties, with warm brown eyes was looking at her with concern. "Are you okay?" the woman repeated. Christina felt unable to engage verbally. She just waved her hand to signal that she wanted to be left alone and listened as the woman's heels clicked across the bathroom tiles, followed by the sound of the door closing.

When Christina finally straightened up, her eyes were smudged with mascara. Staring at herself in the mirror, she knew that everything in her family's life was about to change.

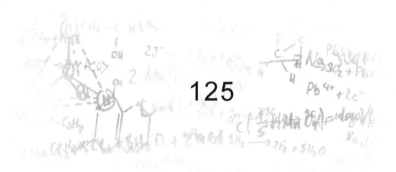

# 125

AFTER REGAINING HER COMPOSURE AND adjusting her makeup, Christina returned to the dinner table. Bobby was busy scribbling equations in a small notebook. Immersed in what he was doing, she had to squeeze his shoulder a few times to get his attention.

"Oh, I'm sorry. Something just came to me and I had to write it down," he said.

Christina grasped Bobby's hands as she said, "You created something very powerful, but no one else understands how it works. For the first time ever, you didn't publish your formulas, equations and methodology and you refused to answer any questions about it and—"

Bobby interrupted. "I had to. I had to keep it secret."

Christina nodded. "I know that. But if anything happens to you, physically or mentally, then the technology you created—which you used for wonderful healing—will be lost forever. Think of all the good that GCN can be used for if it is available to other researchers once the proper safeguards are in place. And if, as you fear, GCN can be weaponized and for whatever reason, you are not capable of inventing something to neutralize the technology so it can be controlled, then we all will be lost. All of us. Do you understand that Bobby? Do you understand the dangers inherent in the current situation?"

"I know, but there is nothing I can do about it."

"Yes, there is."

"What?"

"You can't work alone anymore. You need someone to help you. Someone you can train. Someone you can trust implicitly. Someone who can work alongside you. Someone who has the mental capacity to pick up the pieces and continue on."

Bobby shook his head adamantly. "No. I don't want to thrust her into this maelstrom. I don't want her to live like me and have the pressures I've had."

"There's no choice anymore, Bobby. The stakes are too high."

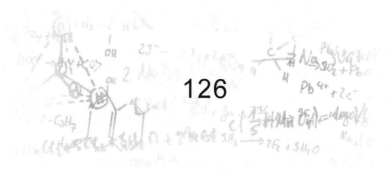

# 126

THE NEXT MORNING, ALAN TOOK Mirielle and Pete fishing for a few hours. Bobby and Christina placed two large mugs of coffee, toast, butter, jam and several tangerines on a tray and carried it outdoors to the small patio table which was adjacent to the kitchen. After they sat down and had a few sips of coffee, Christina's gaze became fixed on the ocean which shimmered in the morning's brilliant sunlight. "I was just thinking about when I got pregnant with Mirielle. The doctors said I wouldn't be able to carry her."

Bobby nodded. "We almost lost her three times during the pregnancy. And by the sixth month, you were in very bad shape. I was petrified something awful was going to happen to you. Every day was touch and go. It was rough."

"But we made it through. She was our miracle baby."

"She certainly was," said Bobby as he placed his hand on Christina's. "And from the first day, we knew there was something unusual about her, we tried to do everything right."

"We made sure she didn't grow up in the pressure cooker that you did."

Peeling his tangerine, Bobby said, "Can you imagine if Varneys knew how special Mirielle is? He'd be all over us, like flies on sh—"

"Bobby, we're eating."

"You know what I mean," said Bobby as he smeared butter on his toast and dabbed it with marmalade.

Christina smiled. "It is ironic. Varneys' crazy scheme to make sure you had kids to inherit your intelligence maybe wasn't so crazy after all. What did Perrone say was the name of that CIA project when he tried to recruit me to be your high-IQ bitch?"

Bobby shook his head. "I've repressed the entire episode."

"Oh, yeah, 'Project World Save,' that was it, said Christina.

"Varneys is old-school through and through. When Pete was born, he kept sniffing around to find out if Pete had inherited some of my abilities. But with Mirielle, it never even occurred to him."

Christina laughed. "And do you remember how crestfallen he was when he realized that Pete was a prodigy, but in music and not science? He looked like he was going to cry."

Downing the rest of his coffee, Bobby said, "Yup. We definitely made the right decision about homeschooling for Mirielle."

Christina began to peel a tangerine. "One thing is for sure. No one could teach her math and science the way you did."

Bobby took another piece of toast and painted it with butter. "And you've done a fantastic job with her on the humanities, but sometimes I wonder if she gets enough exposure to other kids."

"Oh, you mean like you did at the Institute?"

Shrugging Bobby said, "Yeah, that didn't work out so well. I was ostracized there, and at MIT, and Harvard. *The little kid from outer space.* And that was the nicest thing they called me."

Christina brushed a lock of hair from Bobby's eyes. "You were so young. You just didn't fit in. And, let's face it, you've never operated in the realm of normalcy, and people do notice that. Mirielle is much more socially adept than you ever were."

454

"Ouch, Christina. I need to have at least three cups of coffee before enduring criticism."

Christina picked up a piece of the tangerine with her long, graceful fingers, and Bobby watched her as she deftly placed it in her mouth. "Mirielle has a nice group of friends. She's a happy, well-adjusted kid," said Christina.

Bobby stood up and headed to the kitchen to get the coffee pot as he said, "And I want her to stay that way."

When he sat back down, Christina asked, "So you really think she's got it?"

Before answering, Bobby plopped two sugars in his coffee, stirred it, and took a sip. "A few weeks ago, after Mirielle read the formulas and equations on my autoimmune cures, she told me that I missed some shortcuts. She showed me. Because she has fully absorbed the improvements I made in my integrative math language years after I published those cures, she was able to use that to create alternative ways to accomplish the same result more elegantly."

"Oh my God," said Christina.

Bobby nodded. "She's very creative and she doesn't let herself get boxed in with preconceptions. She's a free thinker and she can focus for hours without a break. Her powers of abstraction, conceptualization and synthesis are very unusual."

"Like you."

"Not there yet, but she's still very young. If her abilities keep on developing at their current rate for the next seven or eight years…"

"She'll be as good as you?"

"No."

Christina patted her mouth with her napkin.

"She'll surpass me," said Bobby.

# 127

MIRIELLE LOOKED MUCH MORE LIKE her mother than her father. While she was only nine years old, her facial structure was already taking on the sculpted appearance that would one day make her a beautiful woman. Her high forehead was punctuated by large almond-shaped green eyes which stood out like jewels against her olive skin and silky dark hair. But despite the physical resemblance between mother and daughter, there were differences. While Christina's eyes reflected warmth and sensitivity, Mirielle's were cold analytic instruments. When she looked at someone she didn't know, her eyes bore into them like a forensic tool, which made people uneasy. Orin Varneys was the first to feel this sting when Mirielle stared at him through her playpen at only four months old, and her intensity increased with each passing year. Despite the innocent smile and long pigtails, there was something about Mirielle, something intangible and inchoate, that imbued the girl with a gravitas that was inapposite to her age.

Mirielle, Pete and Bobby were playing paddle ball on the beach and Bobby was getting clobbered by them. When Bobby was huffing and puffing too much to continue, he held up his hands. "I give up.

You kids are too good. And you're too young for me. My lungs can't compete." Pete laughed as he picked up his skimboard and headed to the shoreline.

"Mirielle, let's take a walk. There's something I want to talk to you about," said Bobby.

"Sure, Dad."

"So now that you've gotten to know the ins and outs of my math language, what do you think of it?"

Mirielle smiled. "It's incredible. It opens the door to everything. I don't know why everyone doesn't use it."

"Unfortunately, it seems to be too complicated."

"But It's not complicated, it's perfectly logical," said Mirielle.

"Well, it works for you and me, and that's what I want to talk to you about."

Mirielle bent down and picked up a small flat rock whose surface had been polished by the sea. She threw it onto the water so that it bounced repeatedly. "There, I did it. Five bounces. That's as many as you did the other day," she said gleefully.

Bobby took hold of her hand. "I want you to work with me on a few things."

Mirielle looked up at him. "You mean you're giving me more homework?"

"No. Some real projects for you and me to work on together."

Mirielle's young brow creased. "Me? Are you kidding?"

"Yes you," said Bobby as he playfully pulled on one of her pigtails. "I want to teach you how I cured HRFS using the GCN technology. It's very complicated, so I don't expect you to understand it quickly. It's going to take a long time, and I don't want you to get discouraged."

Mirielle nodded. "Is it similar to how you cured other diseases?"

"No. Completely different."

Mirielle stopped walking and bent down. "Look. Sea glass. Can you put these in your pocket?" Bobby held the tiny fragments of glass up to the sun. "These are great," he said.

As they began walking again, Mirielle asked, "Why haven't you written about GCN like you wrote about all your other discoveries?"

"Because GCN could be used by bad people to create a terrible weapon, so I don't want anyone to know how it works."

"Except me?"

"That's right, except you."

"Will the bad guys ever be able to figure it out on their own?"

"I hope not, but I know they're going to try. Every time a scientist invents something that helps people, there always are those who want to find a way to use it to hurt people."

"What happens once I understand GCN? Then what?"

"Then I'm going to need you to work with me to find a way to stop the chain reaction that the technology creates. If we can do that then we can neutralize any weapon that is based on it."

Mirielle fell silent for a few moments. Scrunching up her nose, she asked, "Why do you need me? Why don't you just do it yourself?"

"Two heads are better than one, aren't they? Finding a way to neutralize GCN is going to be very difficult. I can use your fresh perspective."

Mirielle stopped walking and looked up at her father. "This sounds very weird to me, Dad. You're in a whole different league from me. You can out-think me in a second. Is there something you're not telling me?"

Bobby pointed to a nearby grove of sea grape trees. "Let's get some shade up there," he said. Walking towards the grove, they passed teens who were basking in the sun as they lay close to each other on overlapping beach towels, families whose kids were busy digging holes, and a blonde woman with oversized sunglasses and earbuds sitting under an umbrella trying to keep the wind from blowing her large floppy straw hat into the ocean.

Sitting down on the powdery sand under the trees, Mirielle and Bobby looked out at the sea, which at this time of the day was a kaleidoscope of undulating colors. "Finding a way to neutralize GCN is extremely important to protect people. For a lot of reasons, I may not be able to do it. So, I need to know that at some point in the future you will be able to finish this work, with or without me."

In an instant, Mirielle's eyes flooded with tears. "Are you okay, Dad? Is there something wrong with you? Are you sick?"

Bobby gently caressed Mirielle's cheek. He then bent over and kissed the top of her head. "There's nothing for you to worry about. I'm fine."

She moved close to Bobby. Leaning into him, she rested her head against his shoulder. Mirielle picked up a twig from the sea grape tree that was lying on the sand and she began to twirl it in her fingers. "Will I be like you one day?" Mirielle asked as she looked up at him.

"Do you want to be? Is that what you want, Mirielle?"

Bobby stared at the ocean, focusing on the horizon, his left hand balled in a fist. For the first time in almost three decades, he had no idea what the future would hold and what place he would have in it.

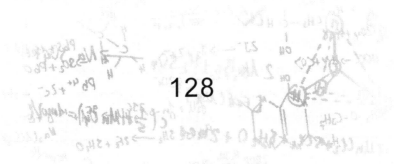

# 128

O RIN VARNEYS WAS SITTING BEHIND his desk. A thick file lay open in front of him. He pointed to a guest chair. Calvin Perrone sat down.

"Good job on supervising the surveillance, Agent Perrone. I wanted you to be involved, since you were in charge of this matter at its inception."

"Thank you, sir. It certainly has been a long haul."

The faintest of smiles appeared on Varneys' face. "The lesson for you to take away from this is that you have to be prepared for the long game. The long game always wins."

Perrone tipped his head. "You certainly knew how to play him, sir."

Leaning back in his chair, Varneys said, "He took the bait on the videos, believed what I said. And that ultimately led us to—"

"The girl," said Perrone.

"Exactly right. When I first saw her as a baby, I had my suspicions. The way she looked at me. It was weird. Not normal. You know I have a sixth sense."

"And the homeschooling," said Perrone.

"That factor was not dispositive given Austin's paranoia, but I figured why would the daughter be homeschooled and not the son?"

"Did you listen to all of the tapes, sir?"

Varneys nodded. "The ones from Gottshalk's house, his boat, Pierre's restaurant and the last tape, of course."

Perrone shook his head approvingly. "Agent Raynor. She's the best at electronic surveillance. The restaurant was easy for her, she was sitting just a few tables away, but beaches are always difficult. She didn't miss a word."

Varneys smiled. "Yes, I particularly enjoyed Austin's beach chat with his daughter. It was the last piece of the puzzle."

Perrone had learned not to overstay his welcome. As he stood up, he said, "Congratulations, sir. Project World Save is a success. We have an heir to Austin's genius, just as you planned."

Varneys' oversized leather chair tilted back as he relaxed into its cushions. Folding his arms, he said, "It's even more than that. The girl is being trained by Austin to work on what is simultaneously the single greatest threat and the single greatest opportunity for this country. If anyone can figure out how to control the weaponization of GCN, it will be the two of them. Once the United States has that, it will be untouchable."

As he headed for the door, Perrone said, "Do you think Mirielle will be even more incredible than her father one day?"

"I don't know. But there is one thing I do know. She has a giant's shoes to fill."

## THE END

William R. Leibowitz practices law internationally and prefers not spending too much time in any one place. Fortunately, his wife, Alexandria, and his dog, George, share his wanderlust.

Dear Reader: I hope you enjoyed *The Austin Paradox*, which is the sequel to *Miracle Man.*

If you haven't read *Miracle Man*, perhaps *The Austin Paradox* will interest you in doing so. It covers Bobby's life from birth through the laboratory explosion and it will give you invaluable insight into the evolution of his character, his intellectual and emotional development, and many of the interpersonal relationships which continue into the second novel. Additionally, you will get an in-depth understanding of certain pivotal characters in Bobby's life such as Joe Manzini, Alan Gottschalk, Susan Ryder, Christina Moore, Dr. John Uhlman and Orin Varneys.

Please email me at wrlauthor@gmail.com and it will be my pleasure to send you a personalized gift to welcome you to the Miracle Man family. The saga of Robert James Austin *will* continue, and I'd be delighted to hear your thoughts and answer your questions. Please also visit miraclemanbook.com where you can hear/read my media interviews and access other content.

---- And if *The Austin Paradox* was special for you, then please tell your friends about it and please post a review on Amazon.

Many thanks—WRL

# THE
# AUSTIN
# PARADOX

## WILLIAM R. LEIBOWITZ

A READERS CLUB GUIDE

# ABOUT THIS GUIDE

The suggested questions are intended to help your reading club find interesting and provocative topics for the discussion of William R. Leibowitz' *The Austin Paradox*. We hope that these ideas will enhance your conversation and increase your enjoyment of the book.

# QUESTIONS AND TOPICS
# FOR DISCUSSION

1. In the first novel, *Miracle Man*, Orin Varneys launched Project World Save which ultimately resulted in Bobby meeting Christina. In *The Austin Paradox*, we see that both Mirielle and Pete are extraordinarily gifted children. Does this vindicate Varneys or did his actions constitute inexcusable governmental interference?

2. Did Orin Varneys really need "insurance" against Bobby?

3. Do you believe the reasons Orin Varneys gave Bobby for why he searched through the surveillance videos from Bobby's lab?

4. How and why did Bobby lose his intellectual powers?

5. How and why did Bobby regain his intellectual powers?

6. Why didn't Bobby's intellectual powers return in full force? Why did he have to work so hard to regain them in their entirety?

7. In a conversation which Bobby had with Susan Ryder,

he speculates that his mind shut down his intellect as a "self-protection" mechanism. Do you think there was any truth in that?

8. Bobby believes that his intellectual powers were given to him by a benign force. Do you agree with Bobby or is there another plausible explanation?

9. When Bobby lost his powers – did he also lose his belief in God?

10. Is Colum McAlister evil or is he a savior?

11. Are Viktor Bazhenov and Hou Jin Gao any worse than other financial market speculators?

12. Do you believe what Gao said regarding who would receive the Schlumberger Foch cure and who would be deprived of it?

13. When Susan confronted Bobby as he stood on the cliffs of Wheatleigh after inventing the HRFS cure – it appeared that he had lost all "faith". Do you believe he did—and if so –why did that happen?

14. Was Bobby being paranoid about his ethical dilemma concerning his GCN technology or was he being realistic?

15. Christina expressed her view that there was no choice other than for Bobby to recruit Mirielle to assist him in finding a way to neutralize GCN. Do you agree with her?

16. Do you think that Bobby will pressure Mirielle to follow in his footsteps?

17. Is Bobby being realistic when he says that he "can't trust himself" to find a way to neutralize the GCN technology?

18. There are many paradoxes in *The Austin Paradox*. Which paradoxes can you identify?

19. What do you think is the central paradox in the novel?

20. Will Mirielle develop into a genius of Bobby's level?

21. Will Mirielle's abilities eventually exceed Bobby's?

22. Do you think that Mirielle will want to devote her life as selflessly to helping people as Bobby did?

23. Do you think Mirielle will develop night terrors or any of the other problems that have plagued Bobby?

24. Why did Christina and Bobby name their daughter, Mirielle?

If you haven't read, *Miracle Man*, the first
book in the Robert James Austin saga,
Turn the page for the prologue of...

# MIRACLE
# MAN

# PROLOGUE

A TALL FIGURE WEARING A BLACK hooded slicker walked quickly through the night carrying a large garbage bag. His pale face was wet with rain. He had picked a deserted part of town. Old warehouse buildings were being gutted so they could be converted into apartments for nonexistent buyers. There were no stores, no restaurants and no people.

"Who'd wanna live in this shit place?" he muttered to himself. Even the nice neighborhoods of this dismal city had more "For Sale" signs than you could count.

He was disgusted with himself and disgusted with her, but they were too young to be burdened. Life was already hard enough. He shook his head incredulously. *She had been so damn sexy, funny, full of life. Why the hell couldn't she leave well enough alone? She should have had some control.*

He wanted to scream out down the ugly street, "It's her fucking fault that I'm in the rain in this crap neighborhood trying to evade the police."

But he knew he hadn't tried to slow her down either. He kept giving her the drugs and she kept getting kinkier and kinkier and more dependent on him and that's how he liked it. She was adventurous and creative beyond her years. Freaky and bizarre. He had been enthralled, amazed. The higher she got, the wilder she was. Nothing was out of bounds. Everything was in the game.

And so, they went farther and farther out there. Together. With the help of the chemicals. They were co-conspirators, cosponsors of their mutual dissipation. How far they had traveled without ever leaving their cruddy little city. They were so far ahead of all the other kids.

He squinted, and his mind reeled. He tried to remember in what month of their senior year in high school the drugs became more important to her than he was. And in what month did her face start looking so tired, her complexion prefacing the ravages to follow, her breath becoming foul as her teeth and gums deteriorated. And in what month did her need for the drugs outstrip his and her cash resources.

He stopped walking and raised his hooded head to the sky so that the rain would pelt him full-on in the face. He was hoping that somehow this would make him feel absolved. It didn't. He shuddered as he clutched the shiny black bag, the increasingly cold wet wind blowing hard against him. He didn't even want to try to figure out how many guys she had sex with for the drugs.

The puddle ridden deserted street had three large dumpsters on it. One was almost empty. It seemed huge and metallic and didn't appeal to him. The second was two-thirds full. He peered into it, but was repulsed by the odor, and he was pretty sure he saw the quick moving figures of rodents foraging in the mess. The third was piled above the brim with construction debris.

Holding the plastic bag, he climbed up on the rusty lip of the third dumpster. Stretching forward, he placed the bag on top of some large garbage bags which were just a few feet inside of the dumpster's rim. As he climbed down, his body looked bent and crooked and his face was ashen. Tears streamed down his cheeks and bounced off his hands. He barely could annunciate, "Please forgive me," as he shuffled away, head bowed and snot dripping from his nose.

Made in the USA
Monee, IL
05 April 2024

56457340R00277